The Tucker Girls

Allen Notlem

The Tucker Girls

Paperback Version
ISBN 979-8-218-08243-7

E-Book Version
ISBN 978-0-578-99938-8

Table of Contents

The Tucker Girls

The Tucker Girls

CHAPTER ONE
Hunter

The sounds of the drumming bass of the party and the crowd chanting my name envelop me, drowning out everything except for Lexi, my best friend, who is silently pleading with me to climb down from this roof. She's known me long enough to realize I wouldn't have come up here if I hadn't already made up my mind. You'd think it's the pressure of letting down the entire senior class of Ulla Meyer, my high school here in Amberly, Texas, that's compelling me to perform this dangerous stunt, however, I could care less what they think about me. I'm already a god in their minds.

No, I'm not up here for glory. I've earned plenty of their empty praise starring on Ulla Meyer's football team the last three years. Football is life in Texas. We live and breathe it. Ulla Meyer won three straight district titles, and I quickly became a household name in Amberly.

None of it matters, though. I hate this town with immense passion. Its suffocating noose has been around my neck since a young age, and I can't wait to escape its death grip and never return. For this reason, I'm going to jump; for those few seconds I'm falling, I will be free of every trouble that threatens to break me.

Lunging from the ledge, I tuck my knees into my chest and seamlessly pull off a backflip as I fall from Clint Dieker's roof. Sure enough, in those blissful seconds I hang in the air, I am thousands of miles from my troubles. My mind shuts off and the thrill fills my soul completely. I can truly breathe, and it rejuvenates me.

The Tucker Girls

It's a fleeting freedom, though. Seconds later, the pool water slam's into my back like I've been hit with a baseball bat, sending pain shooting throughout my body. Pain is an old friend and I gladly welcome it back. It demands attention, picking up where the thrill ends and providing a distraction from the terrible memories that beg to creep back into my thoughts and suffocate me.

When I finally pop my head above the surface of the water, I hear the excitement of the crowd, which is still pleased by the show. Their worship falls on deaf ears as they crowd around, fist-bumping me and slapping me on the back in congratulations for the brief entertainment I offered. They all wish they could stop caring and be free, but they have no idea the price I've had to pay to get to be this way. My classmates don't understand what it's like to be pushed to a breaking point where things that should matter become insignificant.

I wouldn't expect them to understand, though. Only three people in this world genuinely know me: Lexi, Brady and Elijah. They are the only redeeming things about Amberly and are closer to family than friends. We've known each other since elementary school and have been inseparable since. The four of us live by our own rules, and maybe that's the reason for our popularity - other than Elijah, Brady and I starring on the football team.

Ulla Meyer refers to us as *The Untouchables* due to our unquestionably cliquish nature and their inability to lock any one of us down since Mick Pearson, a pathetic excuse of a human being, broke up with Lexi and devastated her heart freshman year. I proceeded to break some of his bones, and since then, no one has had the guts to pursue her.

Needless to say, I have trust issues to a fault. Elijah, Brady and Lexi may not be as extreme as me, but we all grew up with shit parents, so they understand my insistence to keep our circle tight. We're the only family I will ever need.

"You're an idiot," Lexi grumbles as she shoves a towel against my chest the second I emerge from the pool.

"Call me that again and I'm dragging you into the pool with me," I playfully threaten, considering she's one of the few people here not in swimwear. "Besides, this is far from the stupidest stunt I've pulled. You should stop being surprised by now."

"It's not you that I'm worried about," Lexi retorts, jerking her head toward the roof.

I spy Brady lining up the same jump I just took, and I immediately understand Lexi's frustration. Always the follower, Brady plans to imitate my stunt because, unlike me, he craves the attention and the worship of his fellow classmates. He eats it up like candy.

"Brady!" I yell, drawing his attention away from his peers. I wave for him to come down to me, though he silently refuses my request with a shake of his head.

He's going to force me to drag him off the roof. Brady can make the jump, but it's risky, and I value his safety too much to allow it. If he misjudges the angle even slightly, he'll hit concrete. But, unlike me, he has a future worth living for, and I won't let him throw it away attempting to impress the mindless sheep around us.

"I'll go drag his ass down," Lexi replies when I start to move towards the house. "You're dripping wet. Clint will be pissed if you get his parent's hardwood floors soaked."

"Alright. Just be careful."

Lexi responds with an eye roll, though I know beneath her tough exterior she appreciates my words. Her frigid mother never bothers to care about her wellbeing, so she needs someone to tell her that she matters - which she absolutely does. Lexi's the closest thing I have to a sister.

I ponder where I can get my next thrill from as I wipe myself dry. There's a poker game in Clint's den that I may be

The Tucker Girls

able to still get in on. It's only a few minutes after ten o'clock, so I need to kill a few more hours before I consider going home.

"Nice jump," a voice calls out as I dry off my face.

I pull down the towel, expecting to see the praise coming from one of my classmates. The blonde girl I find standing there doesn't look familiar, though. I'm at a loss for words as I stare at the flawless beauty in front of me. She's one of the few girls at the party tonight not in a bikini - besides Lexi. Her bright blue eyes, that mirror the color of the pool, take me in as I try to place her, but eventually concede that she's a complete stranger to me.

"Do I know you?"

"Nope. I'm new to Ulla Meyer. My name is Serena Tucker," she replies, flashing a warm smile.

"Nice to meet you, Serena," I reply as I continue studying her for a single blemish but come up empty. *Damn.* She's perfect and easily the most attractive girl at our school.

Ulla Meyer is one of Texas's most privileged private schools, dripping wealth from the most affluent families in our area. We have our fair share of hot girls, but Serena puts them all to shame.

Serena's cheeks blush when she notices me eyeing her head-to-toe, particularly appreciating her legs that go for miles. Her eyes dazzle as she intently meets my gaze, communicating an interest I've seen countless times from my peers. She likes what she sees as well.

"You're Hunter, right?"

"Yeah, that's right," I reply, surprised that she already knows my name. Someone has done her homework. "Where are you transferring from?"

Just before Serena can respond, Brady crashes into the pool sending the crowd around us wild. Water sprays everywhere, including onto Serena, who squeals as she's rained down on. She slides in closer to use me as a shield, but it's too late. She's already soaked but also beaming with excitement.

The Tucker Girls

Most girls would have freaked out at getting doused, but Serena surprised me by laughing at the whole experience. Her easy-going demeanor is easy to like, as well as her smile that she flashes up at me when she's finally clear of Brady's aftermath. She's radiant, and I immediately feel drawn to her. I'm desperate for anything that will brighten the darkness that hovers over me every day, and I'm tempted to latch onto her for that very reason.

"You alright?"

"Yes! That was a bit unexpected," she replies, attempting to assess her damp clothing. "Y'all do things differently here in Texas."

"Are you not from around here?"

"I'm transferring in from Georgia. Someone from the student council gave me a heads up about this party tonight, so I wanted to come and meet my future classmates."

"Transferring your senior year? That sounds brutal. What did you do to make your parents do that to you?"

"My dad had a great opportunity in Dallas that he couldn't pass up," Serena answers with a shrug, though it feels like she might be holding back.

"Well, what do you think so far?" I ask, waving around at the party that is bustling around us.

"I like what I'm seeing," she says as she sweeps her eyes over my bare chest before meeting my gaze once more. Yep, she's very interested, and that's going to be a big problem.

Brady pushes out of the pool with a cocky smile, interrupting our conversation. His emergence causes Serena to edge closer to me, and I cannot help but notice her hand slipping onto my forearm.

"I told you not to jump, you ass," I grumble at my friend.

"No, you waved at me to come to you. Well, here I am," Brady boasts with a big grin, spreading his arms wide. "Besides, I needed to prove to everyone that I can one-up you."

The Tucker Girls

I pinch the bridge of my nose at his idiocy. A part of me feels guilty, as I gave him the terrible idea to begin with. I pass him my damp towel, which he proceeds to wipe his face with.

"Brady, have you met Serena? She's new to our school."

"Yes, we've already met," Brady chimes in, flashing his famous smile that makes girls swoon. "Have you changed your mind about going off with me tomorrow night?"

"As tempting as that sounds, I'm still going to have to pass."

Serena's eyes are fixed on me, and I get the sense I'm the reason she's passing up Brady's offer, although I'm not entirely sure why. She just met me. She has no idea how big of a deal it is that Brady's snobbish ass is asking her out. Ulla Meyer isn't good enough for him, as he tends to only pursue girls from Monteppe Prep Academy - our rival school in Amberly.

"Suit yourself," Brady replies with a shrug, not the least bit disappointed. "Let me know if you change your mind. You'll soon realize that I'm the best thing this town has to offer."

Brady saunters off, walking straight into a group of girls eager to praise him for his recent performance, though he barely pays any attention to them.

"He's kind of full of himself, huh?" Serena asks when Brady is out of earshot.

"Yeah, you can say that. Just wait till you meet Elijah. His ego is the size of the state of Texas."

"He's the football star, right?"

"Yeah," I mumble in agreement, feeling a pit in my stomach thinking about the football team. I was a star, too, until I broke my forearm last spring and decided against playing my senior year when it didn't heal quite right. Football was my ticket to a scholarship to Ulla Meyer - which, thankfully, they will still honor for my last year - and my best opportunity out of this town. I was talking to several college scouts before the injury disrupted everything.

The Tucker Girls

"So what do you say we get out of here and you show me around town?" Serena asks, giving me a light tug on my arm.

Serena would be a fantastic distraction from all of my troubles. Forget the poker game. I can tell from our limited interactions that she'd be fun to spend time with, and she's drop-dead gorgeous.

The only problem is I can't afford any mistakes now that football is out of the picture. I'd spent the last couple of years having fun with girls and ignoring my problems, but this year I need to graduate and save all the money I can to get out of this hellish town. Allowing Serena to divert my attention would threaten all of my plans.

"Serena, you seem like a nice girl, and to be completely honest, I'm not a nice guy," I start sincerely, attempting to squash whatever this is before it starts.

"Oh, believe me, I've heard," Serena interjects before I can finish. "You're a hot topic with your classmates. Half of them adore you, and the other half despise you. The problem is I have a hard time believing you're a bad boy who drinks too much, constantly fights and sleeps with a different girl every night."

I have to blink a few times to comprehend her disbelief.

"And why is that exactly?" I ask in confusion. She absolutely should believe it, considering it's all true - at least it was until this summer.

"I've been here two hours and I haven't seen you touch alcohol, fight, or flirt with a girl the entire time," Serena states confidently.

"Two hours doesn't really tell you much …."

"I'm willing to take my chances," Serena interjects again, throwing caution to the wind with a smirk. "It may sound crazy, but I have a good feeling about you."

"Serena, I'm complicated," I respond, stunned by her confidence in my character. She has way more faith in me than I do, but she's definitely picking up on my attempts to be a better person. I realized earlier this summer that I was becoming my father and that scared the shit out of me. I haven't touched a lick of alcohol or messed around with any girls since that revelation.

Serena inspects me closer, searching my face for the meaning behind my words as if she can somehow read my mind. My vague answer is going to have to suffice, though. I'm not going to divulge all my problems to a stranger, even when she does look like a goddess.

"Hunter!" I hear Chaz, one of the guys on the soccer team with curly auburn hair, call out over the chaos from the other side of the pool.

"Yeah?"

"Clean up on aisle Devon," he yells, jerking his thumb towards the house.

Great. Devon, Elijah's friend and football teammate, is plastered and likely making a fool of himself. This is the second time in the last two weeks. Somehow it's always my responsibility to clean up these messes, and luckily I have plenty of experience managing drunks.

"Be right there!"

"Is there a problem?" Serena asks when I turn to face her again.

"Yeah, someone at the party has had too much to drink. So, I'm going to make sure that he gets driven home."

"Alright, we'll figure out what night works for you and we can hang out then," Serena states, picking right back up where we left off.

"Look, I'm sure you are a lot of fun ...."

"I am fun," Serena interjects before I can finish. "Just tell me this: are you interested in me or not?"

"I am interested .... *very* interested. It's just ...."

"Good! Then it's settled. We are hanging out, and we are going to have fun. Let me know when you want to take me out. Anyways, I have more classmates I need to meet. See you around, future husband."

Future husband? What the hell? Serena's confidence leaves me speechless as she saunters off into the crowd. What just happened here? I attempted to do the honorable thing, and she completely shut me down. I guess this is Amberly torturing me a little more before I can escape her grasp.

Our conversation continues to swim through my head even after I shove Devon into an Uber. The only thing I'm sure of is that Serena's persistence will be a major problem. She's an enticing distraction that would make it easy to fall back into my old habits, and I can't allow that to happen. At least, I *hope* I don't let that happen.

CHAPTER TWO
Serena

Staring at my reflection in the bathroom mirror, I try to collect myself after that embarrassing exchange with Hunter. What possessed me to call him my future husband? If he didn't think I was a stalker yet, he clearly does now. This isn't me at all. I'm not the one that chases down boys, harassing them until they agree to take me on a date. *What the heck, Serena?* It's a monumental mistake on what had been a successful social outing up to that point.

Having moved to Amberly only a week ago, this party is critical to making friends at Ulla Meyer. Moving to a new school for my senior year sucks, but I have managed to meet several future classmates and am feeling pretty good about the upcoming school year.

I even spotted a smoking hot boy who was clearly interested in me as well. I waited for him to notice me and introduce himself, but I finally caved and made my move. We *are* in the twenty-first century now, so there's no reason Hunter had to be the one to make the first move. It wasn't until we started talking that I let my nerves get the best of me. The words coming out of my mouth weren't me at all. I never believed in falling in love at first sight, but Hunter has me reconsidering everything.

Pulling my cell phone out of my clutch, I text my younger sister for help. She's my best friend. I need to vent to someone before stepping out of this bathroom.

Serena: SOS. Need help. Met boy of my dreams and then made a complete fool of myself.

Lindsey: Nope.

Serena: What do you mean nope??

Lindsey: You don't need another boy. Dain is still calling you every night. You're moving on too quick. Slow down.

Dain was my boyfriend in Savannah, but we agreed that neither of us wanted a long-distance relationship.

Serena: Ok Mom.

Real mature response, Serena. It figures Lindsey wouldn't understand. She's entirely unlike me, but I was hoping she would at least try to empathize with my embarrassment. Lindsey is a walking social misstep, never quite fitting in at school, mostly because she's never been willing to put herself out there. She's an introvert through and through. Surely there's a sympathetic bone in her body that she can tap into for me.

Lindsey: Whatever. It's called tough love. Someone has to be straight with you.

Serena: Please. I'm hiding in a bathroom because I'm so embarrassed. Ugh. I've never said such cringeworthy things in my life.

Lindsey: Who texts "cringeworthy"? *Nerd.*

Serena: *Loser.*

The Tucker Girls

Lindsey: Call me.

Serena: No it's okay. I'm just going to get back out there.

Lindsey: You're gorgeous, smart and all-around amazing. The complete package. Boy of your dreams would have to be a moron not to see all that.

Serena: I told him he's going to marry me.

Lindsey: Bahahahaha

Serena: Ok. Bye.

Lindsey: I love you.

Serena: Next party I need you to come. I need backup.

Lindsey: Don't love you that much. You know I hate high school parties.

A knock on the door cues me to tuck away my phone. Though Lindsey wasn't particularly encouraging, I always feel better talking to her even though she's the reason I'm even in this situation. Lindsey's predicament forced Dad to look for other work opportunities in order for her to have a fresh start. I tried to put on a good face because I knew it was the best for my sister, but moving before my senior year really, *really* sucks.

I consider having another drink before returning to the party to calm my nerves, but instead, I work my way through the crowded house until I get outside, only to discover the deck is more congested than when I left it. Most of the pool crowd has migrated closer to the house, and I scan my peers, looking for someone I should introduce myself to, but my eyes quickly find Hunter.

Of course that's where my eyes drift. My cheeks flush with embarrassment once more, and thankfully he doesn't spot me.

Hunter is occupied with a girl, with barely any clothes on, who is practically standing in his shoes. For a split second, I consider continuing Operation Future Husband, but somehow I hold firm and choose not pursue him further - at least for tonight. Closing my eyes, I take a deep breath and give myself a brief pep talk. I need to stay on task and meet as many new classmates as possible rather than focus solely on Hunter.

When I open my eyes, a pretty girl with wavy, chestnut-colored hair smiles my way and pats a chair next to her, inviting me to sit down. I do a quick check around me to see if she's motioning to someone else, but she waves me over in a reassuring way. I recall seeing this girl near the pool earlier in the night, but that doesn't explain why she's extending this invitation.

"Hey, I'm Serena," I state as I drop down in the chair.

"Lexi," she replies, still sporting a warm smile.

Holy crap. This is *the Lexi* - Hunter's Lexi. She's the girl my classmates have described as cliquish, yet somehow I just received an invite to sit with her. I feel immediately on edge, given my recent social miscues with Hunter. I can't afford any other faux pas, especially with the most elite clique in school.

"You looked like you were having a moment over there," Lexi states.

"It was that obvious, huh?" I respond with a chuckle. "Yeah, I was giving myself a little pep talk to avoid your friend."

"Which one?" Lexi asks with a sigh. I'm sure I'm not the first girl to lose her cool around one of *The Untouchables.*

"*Hunter.*"

Lexi lets out a laugh before cutting her eyes in his direction.

"Good for you. If I were you, I'd keep avoiding him."

"Wait, I thought you were friends?"

"We are. He's one of my best friends, but his track record with girls isn't great, so if you want to keep your heart intact, I'd stay clear. One day, he'll decide to grow up."

"Well, thank you for rescuing me. I'm new here. I just transferred from Georgia."

"Serena Tucker, right?"

"Yeah ... uh ..."

She laughs at my confusion.

"Sorry. Janna, a friend of mine on the student council, mentioned we had a transfer this year who was going to be valedictorian at her prior school."

"Oh ... yeah. That's me," I reply, still shocked by Lexi having the scoop on me. It's true that I was a lock to be valedictorian at my high school in Georgia, but thanks to some unfortunate transfer rules, I will have to pass several students if I want to graduate with that honor at Ulla Meyer. "I'm the girl trying to get her bearings at a new school her senior year."

Lexi gives me a sympathetic look.

"No, it's fine. Really." I say as I wave off her pity. "I'm going to make the most of this experience. There's got to be a reason the universe would do this to me, right?"

"Yes! There's definitely going to be good coming from this. If nothing else, you've met a new friend tonight," she replies, pointing inwardly.

Friend. The word lingers in my head as I try to truly grasp what she said. Her offer sounds sincere, and it's undoubtedly welcomed; it was just entirely unexpected. Based on everything I've heard tonight, Lexi tends to be standoffish and wouldn't extend her friendship flippantly. But, before I can express my appreciation for her kindness, an attractive guy slides in behind Lexi and slings an arm across her, pulling her into his chest.

"What's this about you making a new friend?" the guy asks with his nose affectionately nuzzled in her hair, but Lexi simply rolls her eyes in response.

"I was just saying it's nice to make a new friend. My *old* friends are too clingy."

"Ha! Don't play," he responds with a chuckle. "You'd be lost without us. What would you do with all your spare time when you're not taking care of us?"

I finally put two-and-two together, realizing that this mystery guy is Elijah. His smooth talking voice, swagger and athletic build seem to fit his reputation.

"You must be Elijah," I comment when his eyes cut to me.

"Hello, beautiful. Who might you be?"

"Serena Tucker."

"I'm going to need your number, Serena Tucker."

Lexi slaps Elijah's arm in response, which garners a brilliant smile from Elijah.

"Back off, Elijah. I saw her first," Brady chimes in, having just stepped up so that his knees almost brush mine. He lowers his gaze at me, but I refuse to meet it. It's my turn to roll my eyes. Don't get me wrong, the boy is drop-dead gorgeous, but I have my sights set elsewhere.

"This ain't a Monteppe party, Brady," Elijah counters. "You must be confused."

Brady and Elijah slip into back-and-forth banter, and I notice Lexi simmering with frustration at the two for their antics. I can't help but see how much their bickering feels like siblings rather than friends. Their group is tight, and it makes me long for my friends back in Georgia. We'd never had *this*, but they were still great friendships that I miss dearly.

The Tucker Girls

My thoughts are interrupted when my gaze gravitates to Hunter, and I can't help but wonder how he fits into this dynamic. Brady is the carefree, laid-back personality, while Elijah is clearly the smooth-talking flirt. Lexi is more reserved and harder to read, more like Hunter. I was expecting the guy who jumped off the roof like he had a death wish to be wilder, but all I discovered was a very guarded boy. He has walls behind walls, and if things go my way, I will work my way through each and every one of them.

I feel a foot nudging my leg, and it snaps my attention back to the group in front of me. Lexi looks at me expectantly, knowing I've missed some vital detail.

"Huh?"

Lexi follows the path where my eyes were just fixed and turns back to face me. *Yep.* I was caught red-handed checking out her best friend.

"Hunter!" Lexi calls out, commanding his attention.

"Lexi! No!" I protest, but she waves me off with a smirk.

As Hunter and Lexi make eye contact, he dismisses the girl and wanders through the crowded deck to where we stand. My heart starts rapidly beating, reminding me of how I acted the last time I was around him. I've been around my share of hot guys before, but something about Hunter makes me get all my wires crossed.

"I see you have met Lex," Hunter states in his raspy voice that makes my stomach flutter. I can't help but notice that he keeps his leg pressed against mine as he sits next to me.

"Yep!" I respond, keeping it short and sweet. I will not have another mishap with words again tonight.

"And Elijah," I add nervously. *Come on, Serena, get your stuff together.*

"That's unfortunate," Hunter replies with a smirk, causing Elijah to let loose a deep laugh.

21

"Hunter doesn't like competition," Elijah explains to me. "That's why he quit football."

"Stop it!" Lexi interjects, glaring at Elijah and attempting to get up from his lap, but he manages to keep her in place.

"I quit because your ego barely fits in the locker room," Hunter retorts.

"A star gotta shine, baby."

"Some of us make plays without running our mouths," Brady interjects.

"Maybe that's why your name never makes any news headlines," Elijah shoots back playfully. "You lack swagger."

"Or it's the fact that linebackers get no love."

"Good ones do."

"Okay, I've had my fill of you all bickering for the night," Lexi chimes in while successfully breaking free from Elijah's lap. "Serena, do you want to come get a drink with me?"

"Wait!" Hunter reaches in front of Lexi, impeding her escape. "Have you … uh … have you seen Janna tonight?"

"Uh, oh. Is Hunter considering a repeat?" Brady enthuses. "What? Jocelyn wasn't good enough for you?"

Hunter responds with a scowl before turning an inquisitive glance at Lexi.

"No. Even if she was, you're going to stay away from her."

"It's not what you think."

"I mean it, Hunter. Leave Janna alone," Lexi replies sternly, then turns back to face me. "I need some alcohol. You in?"

"Sure! That sounds good to me," I reply, deciding that I should regroup before I make another attempt with Hunter. Besides, throwing myself at him would just put me in the same category as countless other girls he routinely runs through. So I need to separate myself from the pack, which means playing the long game.

Spying Hunter gazing at me intensely as I stand to leave, I feel heat trickling down my neck. It feels incredible when I have his attention zeroed in on me. It's an intoxicating feeling that leaves me reconsidering staying, but I fight back that urge and continue walking away.

After grabbing our drinks inside the house, Lexi and I stroll around the pool and chat. It's the longest conversation I have had the entire night, and Lexi makes it easy to just be myself. Our conversation flows naturally, leaving me feeling like it's the highlight of a very successful outing.

Hunter's crew is fun hanging out with, and I hope I get to do it again. I'm not the only one. The entire school wants to break into their clique. Now that I've been given a glimpse into their dynamic, my hopes will be crushed if I show up to school Monday and they blow me off. Having their friendship would be the one thing that could totally redeem this transition year.

CHAPTER THREE
Hunter

The first day of the school year is upon us, and this year Lexi and I stick with our tradition of riding in together. Elijah and Brady are both in the midst of their football season and were required to show up before dawn for conditioning. Their season officially kicks off this Friday. Based on Elijah's subdued mood, I'm not expecting much from the team this year.

"Who are you texting so much?" I inquire as Lexi and I walk through the cafeteria entrance. Her phone has been buzzing with notifications for the last twenty minutes.

"Serena," she states without looking up from her phone.

Surprised by her revelation, I come to a complete stop. Lexi just met Serena less than a week ago. Now they are texting non-stop like the best of friends.

"I didn't realize you two were texting?"

"We hung out Saturday. I like her," Lexi offers with a shrug.

"That's it?" I scoff, particularly perturbed by her vague answer. "You share my business with Elijah, but can't give me any more details than 'We hung out'?"

I confessed to Lexi that I'm not sleeping around any longer - after my realization that I was becoming more and more like my father - and she thought it would be a great idea to share that secret with Elijah. Of course, the guy can't keep a secret, and she just gave him ammunition for thousands of jokes I will suffer through for the next few weeks. To say I'm pissed is a massive understatement.

Lexi finally looks up from her phone and scowls.

The Tucker Girls

"Serena and I traded phone numbers at the party. She sent me a text asking if I wanted to hang out Saturday, so we went shopping and got dinner. I really enjoyed hanging out with her. There's not much more to say."

"Did I just hear you say Serena?" Elijah asks as he walks up to us sporting a cocky smile. "I need the latest update. I have a lot of money riding on Hunter's vow of celibacy."

"What are you talking about, Elijah?" I question, irritation still seeping through my voice.

"There's a bet on when you will ditch this crazy vow, and Serena's my top prospect," Elijah replies smugly. "You're not going to last the week the way you were eying her up at the party. The entire football team has bets placed."

"Did you know about this?" I ask Lexi.

"Of course! Everyone knows about it," Lexi retorts with her eyes still glued to the phone. "I put money on Homecoming being your breaking point."

"*Are you kidding me?* What is happening right now? My family is turning on me."

Lexi nudges me with her elbow, but I simply scowl back.

"Tell me this. How many times did Serena ask about me Saturday?" I inquire, figuring Serena took the opportunity to gain intel.

"Actually, you never came up. Shocking, right?"

Elijah lets loose a boisterous laugh that echoes throughout the cafeteria.

"Didn't see that one coming, did ya Hunter? Guess that game of yours isn't so impressive," Elijah teases. "Speaking of the devil, here she comes. Wonder if she even remembers your name, lover boy."

Serena appears extra bubbly as she approaches our group, bouncing with each step she takes. Unlike her, mornings are my worst time of day. I am typically groggy until after lunch and don't reach peak awareness until the evening hours.

"Hey Lexi," Serena says excitedly. "Took you long enough to get here."

"Sorry, I had to wait for this bum to get up," Lexi replies, motioning to me.

"Good morning, Elijah," Serena greets him with a warm smile.

"It certainly is," Elijah replies, pulling Serena into an embrace while raising his eyebrows in my direction. "Every morning is good when I get to see your lovely face."

"Oh lord. I think I'm getting a cavity from your lame-ass sweet talking," Lexi complains.

I expect some acknowledgment from Serena, but she keeps her back to me. I'm not sure what bothers me more: the fact that Serena effortlessly fits in with my friends or her purposely ignoring me. I've seen tactics like these before, and it's definitely a role reversal from the girl who approached me at the pool party last Friday night.

Serena turns towards me as if preparing to finally greet me but yells Brady's name instead. She slides past me to meet him before he reaches our group, and Elijah's glee has now reached unbearable limits. He's savoring each move Serena makes. I'm not in the mood to deal with his instigation, so I start walking toward my locker so I can erase the memory of his ridiculous grin.

"See you all at lunch," I mutter as I walk away.

"Hunter, wait up," Lexi calls as she speeds up to catch me.

"Here," she pulls out a plastic tub and a sheaf of paper from her backpack and offers them to me.

"Lex, you don't need to give me supplies like I'm a kid."

"Did you pick up any supplies for classes?"

No, of course, I didn't. I would have just bummed supplies from my classmates.

"I have a lock."

"Great!" Lexi snaps back sarcastically. "Any pens or pencils? No, I didn't think so. Just take mine. I always buy extra for you."

I lean in and kiss her forehead.

"Thank you."

"Someone has to take care of you boys," she mutters as she walks away. "See you at lunch."

Though Elijah and Brady are both excellent students, neither would be accused of being responsible. Lexi has always been the most dependable among us. Elijah and Brady are held accountable for their grades to play sports, so their coach holds their hand when it comes to school. Since I dropped off the team for medical reasons, I no longer have any adults looking out for me. My mother bailed on us years ago. Pete, my father, keeps the lights on at home. That's the full extent of what he's capable of offering me.

Stuck in my head, dwelling on what I lack while I shuffle items into my locker, a familiar perfume snaps my attention back to the present. Turning towards the smell, I find Serena leaning against the nearby lockers adorning a playful smile that immediately brightens my lingering darkness. Every bitter feeling I held on to after she ignored me dissipates at her unexpected arrival, but I keep my excitement concealed. I am not going to fall for this girl. I can't allow any distractions in my life, especially ones that dig my roots deeper in Amberly.

"Hey," Serena states softly.

"Good morning, Serena," I answer, masking any enthusiasm that tries to sneak out. "Is there something I can do for you? Do you need help finding your classes?"

"No, thank you. I arrived early this morning to ensure I knew where I was going."

"Always good to be prepared," I comment, having never concerned myself with such things. If I am tardy, the world still spins. I refuse to fret about the small stuff. I have enough shit to worry about.

"Absolutely. I even dropped in on a few of my teachers. They all seem great."

I shake my head at her overachieving inclinations. Lexi mentioned that Serena was on pace to be valedictorian at her prior school, and it makes more sense now. She takes her studies very seriously - unlike me.

"What?" she asks with a perplexed look.

"Nothing. Just admiring your go-getter mindset."

"Was that admiration? Looked more like disappointment," she teases and gently pushes my shoulder. "Afraid you are going to have competition?"

"Ha! No, I'm what they call academically challenged."

"Like you have a learning disability?"

"No, like I lack the motivation to do well. I'd rather leave the hard work to you overachievers."

It's Serena's turn to shake her head in disappointment. Maybe my lack of achievement in academics will squelch her interest.

"Shoot. I was hoping we would have some of the same classes."

"I'm not in any of the advanced courses. You will likely see Lex and Elijah, though. They are in the top fifth percentile of our class."

"Yeah. Lexi and I have nearly identical schedules. It's nice to have one familiar face in class," Serena replies, her eyes falling to the floor. "Well, if you need someone to help you stay motivated, then I'm your girl. I'm a great tutor as well."

"Thank you. I may take you up on that offer if I get behind."

The Tucker Girls

"Really? Good! Okay ... well, now you put me in the awkward position of rooting for you to struggle."

"It's pretty much a guarantee," I state, giving her hope that I shouldn't.

Serena's eager eyes meet mine once more. First bell is quickly approaching, but it appears as if she has more she wants to say. After giving her a moment to compose her thoughts, she finally gets it out.

"We don't have to wait for a study session to hang out. Do you want to go off sometime? I mean .... it can be totally low-key. Just as friends," Serena says with an unexpected timidity in her voice.

"Just you and me?"

"Yeah," she responds quickly, eying me carefully. Serena is trying to get a read on me and notices how I shift my weight from foot to foot. I know I should decline, but a part of me wants to see where this would go. I want to believe that it wouldn't end just like all of my flings - with me stealing every bit of light that sparkles in her eyes. Regardless of whether she thinks it would be platonic or not, I don't hang out with girls one-on-one unless we are going to end up naked. Lexi is the sole exception, but she is more like a sister to me.

"Or with your group," Serena counters as she interprets my facial expressions.

"We will all be at Chaz's party Friday night after the game. You should hang with us."

Serena cringes at the notion, biting at her bottom lip.

"What's wrong?"

The bell rings, warning us we have two minutes to be in class.

"I'm supposed to be watching my sister Friday night. My parents will be out of town."

"We'll figure something out. You'd better get going to class," I encourage Serena, assuming it would traumatize her to receive a tardy on the first day. "We'll catch up at lunch."

"You're okay with me sitting with you and Lexi?"

"Sure," I smile reassuringly. "Sounds like you are already closer to Lex than I am now. I should be asking to sit with you two."

"Okay! Cool."

Serena flashes her wonderful smile as she waves goodbye, scurrying off to class. As much as I don't want to, I really like Serena. I genuinely enjoy talking to her.

Rubbing my hands down my face, I exhale loudly. If I hang out with her, I need to be careful not to let my guard down. I can't break her heart like the others. My father's legacy needs to end.

Lunch is after the fourth period, which ends just after noon. When I arrive at our table in the bustling cafeteria, Serena is already flanked by Elijah and Brady. Lexi is sitting across from Serena, with Janna sitting next to her.

Janna's face goes two shades paler when she sees me sit down. Her eyes drop to her food to avoid my gaze. I really messed her up last year, and I know I need to apologize to her, but I haven't seen her since July. Janna and I hooked up one night at a party in May, and then I gave her the cold shoulder for three weeks when she thought it was leading to something more.

I'm distracted from my thoughts when I overhear Elijah and Brady bickering over Rebecca Knight, a redhead in the senior class.

"Back me up here, Hunter," Elijah pleads.

"I'm team Brady until you end your stupid bet," I retort.

"You can't still be upset about that?" Elijah protests.

"What bet?" Serena interjects.

"How long Hunter's vow of celibacy will last," Brady explains. "Winner gets two thousand dollars."

Janna snorts to herself.

I glare at Lexi, still regretting having ever mentioned such a personal detail to her. She's typically so careful with my secrets.

"I'm sorry, Hunter! It just slipped out," Lexi says.

"Elijah? Really? You might as well have broadcast it over the school intercom," I growl back.

"Is there still time to place bets?" Janna asks while still avoiding looking in my direction.

"Yeah, I will text you the website," Brady replies.

"*There's a website?*" I exclaim, throwing my hands in the air.

"You've gone big time, Hunter," Brady states with a slap on my shoulder.

Locking eyes with Serena, I notice her inspecting me closely. I'd love to know what she's thinking at this moment. Is it possible that my promiscuous prior life finally gives her pause? If the rumors were not enough, now I have a flipping website tracking my next hookup.

"Chaz put fifty dollars in the pot that he won't get through the rest of the school day," Elijah informs Janna with a chuckle.

"Ew," Janna replies, clearly disturbed by the implications of what that means. Chaz must have heard about what Alexis and I did in the band room sophomore year. "I would put twenty dollars that he won't make it past Friday night."

"Can we change the subject?" I demand. "Speaking of Friday night, Lexi, can one of your friends babysit? Serena needs someone to watch her little sister so she can come to Chaz's party."

"No, it's not like that," Serena rapidly interjects. "Lindsey is only a year younger than me. She doesn't need a babysitter."

"Oh," I reply, having clearly misinterpreted our conversation earlier in the morning. I could have sworn Serena said she needed to watch her. Now I'm wondering why Serena is required to look after her sister if she is sixteen years old.

"Well, just bring her with you," I suggest, not understanding the hang-up.

Serena fidgets in her seat while she silently weighs the decision, and the thought of bringing her sister to the party seems to bother her.

"Yeah, you should totally bring Lindsey," Lexi chimes in. "I'd like to meet her. We will look after her and make sure none of the senior boys bother her."

"She's not really into the party scene, but I will ask," Serena sighs with a less than hopeful look.

For the remainder of lunch, Serena simply picks at her food without taking another bite. Whatever her hang-up is around bringing her sister, I can see it weighing heavy on her mind. I can empathize with family drama. If hers is anything like mine, the last thing you want is people prying into your business. I make sure no one brings the subject up again.

Before going to my fifth-period class, I follow Janna to her locker to attempt to reconcile with her. Considering she's avoiding me like the plague, I can't imagine she will be thrilled to talk to me, but I need to start atoning for my past - something my father never has done.

"Hey, Janna."

Janna jumps at the sound of my voice before continuing to twirl her combination lock.

"What do you want?" she asks flatly, pulling a book out and slipping it into her backpack.

The Tucker Girls

"Look, I'm trying to …. uh …. turn the page on who I used to be … if you can believe that. I know that I treated you poorly this summer. I hurt you and feel terrible about what I did."

"Whatever," she snaps as she slams her locker shut. "Just leave me alone."

Janna brushes past me and walks quickly towards the main hall before I can fully articulate my apology. Scurrying after her, I touch her arm to get her attention once more. Janna jerks around as soon as she feels the contact.

"I'm sorry. That's all. I just wanted to say …."

Before I can finish my apology, the palm of her hand connects with my cheek, making a smacking noise that echoes throughout the main hall. The busy hallway suddenly freezes. All eyes are drawn to our conversation as I lean back in pain. My cheek burns from Janna's fury.

Janna's eyes widen in shock, and her cheeks flare bright red. It's immediately apparent that her slap was not premeditated. I don't fault her for it, though. I deserved much more than a slap for how terrible I had been to her.

"Don't ever touch me again," she blurts out once she regains her composure. Janna scurries away, leaving all eyes still glued to me. It takes me another minute longer to shake off the shock of her violent reaction.

"You all enjoying the show?" I grumble at the bystanders still gawking, causing them to avert their eyes and disperse quickly.

"Guess you're going to have to find some other girl to break your vow with," Devon chuckles as he casually walks by, looking much better than he did Friday night when I had to carry him to his Uber.

"Shut your mouth, Devon," I snap.

So much for a drama-free school year.

CHAPTER FOUR
Hunter

"*Mr. Bowden*," a familiar voice calls out.

I recognize the voice but can't place it. I'm not just asleep. I am entirely numb to reality. There is nothing other than the darkness of the back of my eyelids. This might be the best sleep I've gotten in over a week, but a nagging sound keeps trying to break through my peace.

"Mr. Bowden!" Mrs. Seldon calls out again; this time, her shrill voice aggravates my ears and successfully pulls me out of my slumber.

"Yes, Mrs. Seldon," I mumble as I snap to attention, scanning my surroundings quickly to gain my bearings.

Several expletives fly out of my mouth, but they were muttered in such a low tone that they escape Mrs. Seldon's ears.

"Were you just sleeping in my class?"

"No, ma'am. I would *never* do that," I lie.

"Really? What was I just talking about?"

"Trigonometry, ma'am."

The class roars with laughter at my vague answer. Clearly, everyone is aware that I'm treading water trying to avoid detention. The classroom's glee seems to fuel her anger. She knows she caught me sleeping and is determined to prove it.

"Obviously! *Congratulations*. You know what class you are in. I'm asking what I was specifically teaching before I called your name?"

My mind begins frantically attempting to recall anything I remember hearing, but it all comes up blank. I have no idea how long I have been asleep. The last thing I remember was

The Tucker Girls

Mrs. Seldon introducing a new lesson at the start of class. It's already Friday. The entire first week has been filled with informational packets, classroom rules, and other pointless topics that I've successfully tuned out. Today is the first day of new material. I should know it by heart, considering I've already taken and failed this course once.

A blonde-haired girl with oversized, round glasses, sitting diagonally from me, casually taps her notebook with her pen. I spy the word 'Angles' written in large letters at the top of her paper and decide to roll with it.

"You were introducing angles, ma'am."

Mrs. Seldon lets out an exasperated sigh. It's unclear if I was correct or not, as she turns towards the board and continues teaching. I hope I somehow managed to satisfy her suspicions.

I mouth the words 'Thank you' to the blonde girl that saved me. She smiles back, blushing at my gratitude. I can't recall her name as I honestly haven't paid any attention to my class peers up until now. This girl is now my heroine, and I make a mental note to learn her name after she rescued me from Mrs. Seldon's wrath.

I would have never fallen asleep had Drake not needed my assistance late last night. Drake is the owner of Stirred Up, a swaggy bar and grill restaurant that is a local favorite in Amberly. The live music is a big draw, leaving standing room only most nights, and the tips are really good for a high school job. I'd worked there for the last two years.

Drake has taken me under his wing like I was his younger brother, training me to run a restaurant one day, which means slowly teaching me all the inner workings of the restaurant business. One of these responsibilities is the monthly accounting for the restaurant's inventory. We didn't finish until three in the morning, but Drake paid me time and a half. I need the money, so I didn't pass up the opportunity.

The Tucker Girls

"Mr. Bowden," Mrs. Seldon calls out after the bell rings, indicating class is over. "Please stay after class."

I patiently wait as the other students file out before approaching her desk.

"Yes, ma'am. Is something wrong?"

"If you fall asleep in my class again, I will send you straight to the principal's office. Do you understand?"

"But ...." I start to counter before she interjects again.

"I don't tolerate disrespectful behavior in my class. You already failed this course once. I highly recommend you try harder this time. Do you understand?"

"Yes, ma'am," I reply. "Is that all?"

"Yes, that's all. You may leave now."

My day doesn't get any better following Trigonometry. Janna had been eating lunch elsewhere following my attempted apology, but I arrive at the cafeteria to find her sitting next to Lexi again. Leave it to Brady to not have any tact regarding the issue.

"So we have to hear it," Brady says shortly after I take a seat.

"What's that?" I ask, unsure of what Brady is referring to.

"I'd like to hear about the slap heard round the world. Everyone's talking about it. I need details. Janna, hold nothing back." Brady requests with an impish grin.

Janna stiffens at the mention of our brief encounter Monday. The entire school got word of the altercation before school let out that day. The gossip has died down as the week progressed, though. I refused to discuss the topic with anyone. I figured it wasn't appropriate to share since it involved Janna too.

The Tucker Girls

If the administration gets wind of her hitting another student, Janna could end up suspended for the altercation.

Of course, Brady wouldn't pass up the opportunity to screw with me. Janna hesitates, looking like she may throw up if forced to recount the whole story.

"Janna gave me a well-deserved slap to the face. There's nothing more to the story," I state flippantly.

Brady opens his mouth as if he wants to request additional details, but his enthusiasm wanes when he spies my burning glare. He reconsiders whatever he was planning on saying and takes another bite of his sandwich with a look of disappointment.

"Next time, knock his ass out," Lexi directs Janna with a smirk. It's hard to tell if she actually means it, but a second later, Lexi winks at me playfully.

"Don't tempt me, girl," Janna replies with a smile.

"So are y'all good now?" Elijah asks as his eyes dance between Janna and me.

"Yeah, we're good," Janna replies as she picks at her food.

A weight lifts off my shoulders at the sound of those words. I don't know if I genuinely have her forgiveness, but she sounds like she's willing to bury the past and move on. I want nothing more. I'm not going to approach her again, though.

I decide to interpret her sentiment as sincere, and it's an immense relief to have some closure. This gives me the motivation to continue the process of making amends with other girls that I've wronged.

"Next topic," I declare, desiring to move on from discussing the slap.

"I heard a rumor you fell asleep in Trig," Serena states from across the table.

"I hate this school," I mutter, dropping my fork and tossing my head back. The gossip is out of control. Nothing can be kept private in Ulla Meyer. Does everyone have nothing better to do than to discuss every mistake I make?

"This is news because …. ?" Elijah inquires with a chuckle. "He's been sleeping in class since we have known him."

A cold chunk of carrot bounces off my cheek, causing me to jerk my head forward. Lexi, who tossed the vegetable, is giving me a death glare.

"Are you serious? Are you trying not to graduate?" she fumes.

"It's all good. I have a back-up plan. Serena is going to tutor me."

Serena gives me one of her wonderful smiles, reassuring me that the deal is still on even if I manage to sabotage my grades.

"There's nothing funny about this," Lexi continues to rant.

"Can we talk about someone else's drama for a bit?" I plead with an agitated tone.

"No. If I hear you're sleeping in another class, I'm going to Janna you so hard you won't remember your own name," Lexi growls.

"Did you just use Janna's name as a verb?" Brady clarifies.

"Sure did. And I meant it too," Lexi replies, finally releasing me from her stare and returning to her food.

Brady gives me wide eyes while Elijah jiggles as he tries to contain his laughter. It had been a while since I'd seen Lexi this fired up.

Serena smiles as she picks up another sliced cucumber from her Tupperware container.

"You all are something else," Serena mutters, which I think she means in a good way.

The Tucker Girls

"Were your friends in Georgia as dysfunctional as us?" Lexi asks.

"Correction - as amazing as us?" Elijah chimes in.

"No. Not at all," Serena replies.

"How'd you even hear about what happened in Trig anyways? That was just last period," I ask.

"Oh, I have spies everywhere," she teases, her eyes sparkling with satisfaction.

"Fine. Keep your secrets for now, but I will find out soon enough."

I push away from the table, deciding that a walk before fifth period would do me good. All this drama is exactly what I've sworn to avoid. Was my life always a hot topic within the school? Or is this year different? There must be more exciting topics than me sleeping in a math class.

"Hey, Hunter," Elijah calls out before I can take three steps.

I look in his direction and raise my eyebrows.

"You need me to come with you? I'd hate for you to get jumped by another chick in the halls."

"Go to hell, Elijah," I mutter back.

Brady and Elijah roar with laughter. I have a love/hate relationship with my family, but today it's leaning more towards hate.

Chaz's party kicked off earlier than expected because our football team got plastered. We were losing by four touchdowns at halftime, combined with the uncomfortably humid weather, so students started filing out before the second half kicked off.

Lexi, Serena and I hung around until the very end, cheering on Elijah and Brady despite the unfortunate outcome. The team's morale appears at an all-time low, with most of our sideline's body language dripping with disappointment. I hope this mood won't carry into the party.

Once the final horn sounds, Lexi and I continue on to the party, which is already hopping. We are required to park almost half a mile away due to the number of cars that line the neighborhood streets. It's as if the entire school has shown up this evening.

The heat has me sweating by the time Lexi and I reach the house, leaving me grateful that the party is indoors. Pushing through the thick crowd of people congregated in the foyer, I spot another one of my prior casualties in the corner of the dining room, conversing with a small group of people. With Janna's success still in mind, I part ways with Lexi to continue my apology tour.

"Hey Emilia," I call out over the drumming music, immediately drawing her attention away from her friends.

Emilia cuts her eyes at me and sighs heavily. She's clearly not thrilled by my sudden appearance. Seeing her up close again reminds me of our hookup this time last year. Before we finally slept together, there'd been some heavy flirting between us. But, unlike Janna, Emilia never shed any tears over me. I'm pretty sure she was happy to settle for the bragging rights, but that fact doesn't alleviate my guilt.

"Whitney. Joan," I state, acknowledging her friends - both seniors at Ulla Meyer - who smile politely in return.

"What do you want?" Emilia inquires with a frosty tone in her voice.

Looking between Emilia and her friends, I consider asking to speak with her privately only to remember what school we attend. This conversation will be public knowledge by the end of the evening.

"I just wanted to say I'm sorry for how things ended between us last year. I shouldn't have blown you off the way I did after ... you know ... everything went down."

"Okay," she replies flatly.

Emilia's response fires back instantly as if she hadn't even processed what I said. I wait for something else to come out of her mouth or a slap to the face. Neither occurs. Emilia averts her eyes across the room, purposely avoiding eye contact.

"Well, that's all I had to say. You girls enjoy the party," I say as I bow out of the conversation.

As I step away from their group, I wrestle with how I delivered the apology. Did I adequately express the genuine regret I feel? It sure didn't feel like my message was received, but it didn't feel that way with Janna either.

I navigate to the kitchen and grab a beer, ignoring two girls who try to get my attention. I haven't drank all summer, but I need something to silence my thoughts. I'm still replaying the conversation with Emilia in my head when my phone vibrates with a text.

Serena: Send me Chaz's address.

Serena is likely lost trying to navigate the web of roads that weave through Chaz's neighborhood. Lexi and I should have just given her a ride here. I remember getting lost leaving Chaz's party last year. This neighborhood is a confusing maze.

I text her the address but get distracted when the football team begins arriving. I give Elijah and Brady a sympathetic look when they pass by, and I can tell they both desperately need some fun.

When ten more minutes slip by, and Serena still hasn't shown up, I decide to check in with her. Setting down my empty beer, I slip out the front door to call Serena and bump into a brunette girl hanging out on the porch. Wearing a baggy sweatshirt, at least two sizes too big, with the hood pulled up and a backpack strapped across both shoulders, the girl looks sketchy waiting alone. Her attire alone doesn't set off any alarms; rather,

her nervous demeanor and how she wrings her hands remind me of a friend who used to behave the same way when searching for his next drug fix. This girl is clearly on edge, jumping in surprise the second I open the door.

"Look, if you are one of Marcel's girls, you can get lost," I bark, pointing back towards the street.

Marcel Thomas is a junior at Ulla Meyer and the only drug dealer in school. He is tied up with a gang, so no one else risks their neck to try and cut in on his market. I despise the kid with a passion. If Marcel thinks he can send a girl to strike up business at Chaz's party, he's completely mistaken.

"Huh?" the brunette grunts out, barely glancing in my direction.

"If you are dealing, get lost! We don't need that shit here."

"Leave me alone," she growls, still refusing to look my way. She's acting shady as hell.

I guess I'm going to have to drag her ass to the curb. Before I can do that, she turns towards the front door as if she wants to escape into the house, but I slide over to block her path. If she manages to sneak into the house, I will lose her in the chaos.

I'm pretty confident this girl doesn't go to Ulla Meyer. I would have remembered a face like hers. Her gray eyes are something you don't see every day.

The girl's trembling hands ball up into tight fists, her knuckles white with rage leaving me wondering what her next move will be. She looks ready to lash out at me.

"Hunter!" Serena calls out as she scurries up Chaz's driveway. "What's going on?"

Seeing Serena reminds me of why I stepped outside in the first place. I meant to call her but got distracted when I stumbled upon this high-strung girl.

The Tucker Girls

"He won't let me inside," the girl protests, looking to Serena for help.

"Hunter, seriously? Let Lindsey in!"

The sudden realization that the girl is Serena's sister hits me like a sucker punch. My eyes dart between the two siblings, barely able to notice any familiarity in the girls' appearances. It isn't often that I'm left speechless, but this moment rises to the occasion. I feel a wave of humiliation flood over me. I'd entirely misread the situation.

"I ... uh ... sorry," I mutter weakly as I step away from the front door. "You're Serena's sister?"

Even standing next to each other on the porch, the two sisters don't favor each other in the slightest. Lindsey's straight caramel-colored hair, peeking out of her hood, and gray eyes are entirely different from Serena's wavy blonde hair and blue eyes. I would have never guessed these two were related.

"Yes, moron," Lindsey replies, purposely hitting me with her shoulder as she pushes past.

Lindsey opens the front door and slams it shut. Serena's face looks utterly mortified as she folds her arms across her chest.

"I begged Lindsey to come here tonight, despite her hating these types of parties because you said you all would look out for her. Not terrorize her! *What the hell?*"

"I messed up," I confess, running my hands over my face. "I'm sorry, Serena. Lindsey was jumpy, like she was hyped up on something. Then I saw her with the backpack, and I thought she was dealing drugs."

"Lindsey's jumpy because she doesn't want to be here. She's not like us. She doesn't like loud parties or social events. So now I have to go talk her down off the cliff. I'll be lucky if she agrees to stay."

"I really screwed up. I will go apologize."

"Good! Make it a good one because I owe her big time," Serena states as she lets out an audible exhale.

I watch the anger dissipate from her face. It's obvious Serena cares a lot for her sister, and I touched a nerve by upsetting Lindsey.

"Your sister's a real charmer, huh?"

Serena lets out a loud laugh.

"Lindsey's an acquired taste. You have to get to know her. She has a heart of gold, and she's my best friend. So you better play nice."

"I will. Now go join the party. I need a few minutes to prepare for the massive apology I'm going to deliver."

CHAPTER FIVE
Hunter

I throw down a shot of whiskey, enjoying the burning sensation, before parting ways with Serena and beginning my search for Lindsey. It's not lost on me that my sobriety pledge is out the window. Too bad no one bet on when I'd start drinking again.

Lindsey disappeared in the masses. The large crowd forced the party to expand outside, so I am forced to cover quite a bit of territory to hunt her down. Chaz's backyard spans several acres and backs into an expansive lake. It's where the whole party would be tonight if not for the scorching heat.

After making an unsuccessful pass out back, I am working room by room when I finally discover Lindsey lying on a couch, reading a book, in a sitting room towards the rear of the house.

"Hey, Lindsey. May I have a word?"

Lindsey thumbs another page of her book, taking her sweet time to turn it without bothering to lift her eyes up to me. The commotion of the party is loud, but I am standing close enough that I know she heard me. Everyone else in the room stops to stare, yet she seems content to ignore me.

"Hey, Lindsey."

Still nothing. She doesn't even flinch at the sound of her name. Reaching down, I tap her book with a finger. Lindsey turns another page and continues reading her copy of Pride and Prejudice as if it's completely consuming her. Finally losing patience with this annoying girl, I snatch the book out of her hand.

The Tucker Girls

"Do you mind?" Lindsey growls in irritation.

"*Hey Lindsey*," I repeat for the third time, plastering on as close to an authentic smile as I can manage. I try to take the edge off my voice, but some of my annoyance manages to seep through. "My name is Hunter."

"I know who you are, *jerk*. Now give me back my book."

"I will. I just want to say sorry for how I treated you outside."

"No, you're not. You're a self-absorbed prick who is only apologizing because you have a thing for my sister. I'm sure she told you to apologize, so consider your obligation fulfilled. Now give me back my book and leave me alone."

I grit my teeth in frustration. Serena was wrong. This girl isn't an acquired taste. Lindsey could possibly be the most infuriating person I've ever met. It's impossible to build up a tolerance to her brand of poison.

"Like you know anything about me," I shoot back.

"I know enough. Between what I've seen and heard, I've decided I don't want to know anymore. In fact, stay away from my sister. She doesn't need people like you in her life."

"What exactly have you seen that has you so concerned? You've been at our school for a whopping week."

"I sit right in front of you in Trig. I guess you've been too busy sleeping to notice."

I must admit, I didn't see that one coming. It makes more sense now how Serena knew about my sleeping incident. Lindsey is her spy.

"Ah, okay. You caught me sleeping. So now you know everything about me."

"Pretty much."

"I see. So, I'm a self-absorbed prick that thinks he's better than everyone else? I look down on those around me because they are inferior?"

The Tucker Girls

"Exactly," Lindsey replies with a phony smile.

"That's ironic."

"How so?"

"Sounds like you're projecting Mr. Darcy's qualities on me," I retort, tossing the book back in her lap.

"Oh, very clever. You must have watched the movie. I can't imagine you're the reading type."

Exasperated, I lift my gaze to the ceiling. I pause to take a deep breath and exhale. Normally I would have walked away from this conversation minutes ago, but it is important to Serena that I make amends.

Looking around the room, no one is trying to hide their gawking, even as I stare a few of them down. Once I regain my composure, I give it one more shot.

"I'm sorry I was abrasive outside. I misinterpreted your nervousness for you being strung out. Please forgive me."

Lindsey opens her book again, thumbing through the pages until she finds where she left off. I wait silently for her to acknowledge my apology, but she's not going to oblige. I hear snickers from the kids in the room, likely wondering why I'm still bothering with this impossible person.

Storming off in frustration, I think about how much better my life was before meeting this obnoxious girl. Unfortunately, Lindsey's going to be difficult to avoid if I'm going to have any kind of relationship with Serena. Lindsey and I will have to learn to coexist - if that is even possible. I'd been treated more civilly by people that hated me. Sure, I had blocked her entry into the house, but that didn't deserve the level of contempt that she was putting off when I said I was sorry.

My agitation continues brewing as I fight through the swarm of partygoers on my way to the kitchen. When a hand reaches out and grabs hold of my shoulder, I lurch, ready to attack whoever that hand belongs to.

"Woah there," Chaz backs up with his hands raised. "What's gotten into you?"

"Nothing. What's up?"

"Hey, we're getting ready to take the boat out. You in?"

"Definitely. Meet you down at the dock in five," I reply, thinking that the change of scenery would be welcomed. I'd love to get as far away from Serena's sister as possible.

"Sounds good. Let me go grab the keys," Chaz states, weaving his way towards the stairs.

Snaking my way through the crowd, Jocelyn slides into my path before I can escape the kitchen.

"Hey, Hunter," she says sweetly, giving me the same look she gave me last Friday night at the pool party. I entertained her playful flirting then, but I'm not in the mood tonight despite how hot she looks.

"It's not happening, Jocelyn."

"You haven't heard what I'm offering."

She slides in close to me, pressing herself up against my body.

"I've heard about your vow and the bets the football team has been conducting. I just want you to know that I can be *very* discreet."

"As tempting as that sounds, it's a *'No'* for me."

Jocelyn lets out a huff in frustration.

"You've changed, Hunter. You used to be more fun. You haven't been yourself since the new girl showed up."

"Serena doesn't have anything to do with it."

"So you aren't *with* her?"

"No."

"I mean, she's hanging out with you at lunch and then at the football game tonight. Is she part of your crew now?"

"What does that have to do with anything?"

"I'm just saying that people have taken notice that she's everywhere *The Untouchables* are. That's why no one is messing with her. But if she's not with you, she should be warned. Eventually, people are going to challenge her."

Closing my eyes, I try to digest Jocelyn's words. She's not wrong. Ulla Meyer can be brutal. Thankfully my family is at the top of the food chain, and no one dares challenge us anymore. The few that came after us were dealt with, and I'm not proud of what I was required to do. I will always protect my family, though.

"Thanks for the helpful tip, Jocelyn. I'll see you around."

I don't bother answering her question because Serena will continue to have some protection if people assume that she's with us. It's better not to set the record straight.

I step by Jocelyn and proceed to the dock for a much-needed escape from this drama.

Chaz drove us out to the middle of the lake and then cut the engine. The boat slowly rocks from its own wake, and I immediately feel calmer getting some distance from the party. The music still hums in the background, but it's more muted this far away.

Taking a sip of my beer, I wave my hand in rejection of Brady offering me a cigar. Chaz broke out several of his father's Cuban cigars for our enjoyment, but it's not something I'm in the mood for tonight. Smoking has always irritated my lungs, and right now, I just want peace - or what little peace Amberly will ever offer me. The buzz that's kicking in is helping calm the storm that Serena's sister stirred up in me.

"You shouldn't be smoking if you're going pro one day," I suggest to Elijah as he lights his cigar.

"My lungs are golden," he replies with a cocky smile. "Smoking every now and then won't hurt anything, Mom."

The Tucker Girls

I roll my eyes. Lexi would lecture me later about why he shouldn't be smoking, but I won't continue to nag him.

Elijah has the most potential out of all of us. Every major college in the country is sending him letters weekly. He could be doing a lot more devastating activities than smoking an occasional cigar.

"This is it fellas," Chaz states as he leans back in his cushioned seat. "Our last ride. Senior year is upon us. It all went by so fast."

"That it did," Elijah agrees. "Have you decided where you are headed next?"

"Texas State," Chaz replies. "You?"

"It's not official yet, but I'm going to commit to UCLA."

"Nice!"

"That must be why Lexi has pamphlets in her bedroom for UCLA then," I chime in, observing Elijah's reaction.

"Huh, didn't know," Elijah shrugs. "All are welcome to join me in sunny California."

His deflection tips me off that I'm right. The bastard will end up wreaking havoc on Lexi's heart, though she'd never admit she has feelings for him.

"What about you?" Brady asks, likely trying to decide who he should follow. "Where are you going, Hunter?"

"Penitentiary U." Elijah mutters with a grin.

"If I'm going there, it'll be because I beat your ass," I counter.

"What for?"

I eye Elijah sternly. Although he looks perplexed, he knows I'm talking about Lexi. We've been friends too long for him not to get the message.

"I'm getting as far away from this town as possible," I finally offer, answering Brady's question.

"You should come to LA too," Elijah states.

The Tucker Girls

I nod silently but know that Los Angeles is way too expensive. I don't have the money, like Lexi or Brady, to follow Elijah to California. I will be lucky if I find a steady job a couple of hours away. Whatever it will take to get a fresh start.

"The new girl is hot," Chaz comments.

"Got that right," Brady agrees.

I don't need to ask who they were talking about. I already know they are referring to Serena.

"Are you going to make a move already? Cause if not, I'm calling dibs," Brady chimes in, his gaze locking in on me.

Brady is referring to a system that Elijah, Brady and myself have adhered to since middle school to prevent us from competing for the same girl. If one of us calls dibs, the others have always backed off. We've never broken our code.

"I got a lot going on right now," I mutter indecisively.

My brain is trying to convince me that it's a bad idea to let anything happen, but every other part of me is urging me on. The weight I carry with me feels lighter when I'm with her, making me want to keep her close.

"Hunter, If you are going to get back in the game, she's the one," Elijah interjects, taking a more serious tone than I have been accustomed to hearing lately. "Serena is all about Hunter Bowden. She ain't looking at anyone else. You're stupid if you blow her off."

"Thanks for the advice. I'll take it into consideration."

"So, to be clear, you're not interested?" Brady clarified.

"I didn't say that. I am interested, but I need to figure out my shit first. Anyone would be crazy not to be interested in Serena."

"Exactly. I'm calling dibs. You are obviously not making a move any time soon, so I'm moving in," Brady declares, triggering Elijah and me to sit upright.

I stare at Brady in complete disbelief. I wasn't prepared for him to make such a hasty move.

"Wait. Brady's pursuing a girl, and she doesn't even attend Monteppe?" Elijah sings out. "Hell has frozen over! It's the end of times."

"Shut up, Elijah," Brady retorts, color spreading across his cheeks. I hadn't been paying close attention to Brady recently, but it's clear he has feelings for Serena deeper than mere attraction.

"Elijah's just jealous. His stone heart isn't capable of love," I counter when I am not sure what else I can say. I'm not breaking our code, which means I need to back off. Honestly, this may be for the best. I don't want to drag Serena into my mess.

"Better a broken heart than a broken brain. You're the one passing on the finest girl you will ever meet," Elijah shoots back with a tilt of his head.

"I didn't pass up on Serena," I bark back.

"Will you two girls stop bickering?" Chaz growls as he blows out a smoke ring.

"Nice," Elijah compliments as he admires the ring floating above us.

"I guess it's settled then. I will back off Serena. Now you all hurry up and smoke those cigars, or I will have to jump into the lake. This heat is unbearable," I direct, suddenly ready to put some distance between Brady and me.

By the time the boat pulls up to the dock, my shirt is drenched in sweat. I strip it off and sling it over my shoulder, allowing me to enjoy the faint breeze. September hasn't been able to shake the summer weather. Hopefully October will have more success.

Claire Lamanory, head cheerleader and queen bee of Ulla Meyer, and her minions are congregating by the dock when we arrive. Overdressed as usual, Claire frantically waves me down. I try to avoid lengthy conversations with her. Our talks always seem to dovetail into gossip that I honestly have no interest in.

"Hunter!" Claire calls out, falling in step with me. Her legs are working hard to keep up with my long strides, which is impressive considering she is in heels. I don't have to look back to know her minions are trailing behind us.

"What can I do for you, Claire?"

"I have an issue that you should be aware of," she declares, her face appearing distressed.

"If this is about the bet, I'm not in the mood to discuss it."

"The bet? Oh, your hookup bet. No, I have no interest in discussing that either. We have a more important issue. There's a homeless girl in Chaz's sitting room, and it has everyone worried. It's quite disturbing, and someone needs to tell her we are not a charity event. She can go to a shelter if she wants free food."

A boisterous laugh ripples out of my body when I realize she is referring to Serena's sister. It is equally Claire's absurdity, thinking Lindsey is homeless because she is wearing a hoodie to this party, and the thought of Lindsey's reaction if she had overheard the accusation. Miss 'acquired taste' would likely punch Claire in the face for her comment.

"What is so funny?" Claire demands with a dumbfounded look on her face. "I don't see anything funny about a homeless person at our party."

"I know you don't have much experience being around homeless …." I start before she interjects.

"Duh. Why would I?"

"But the girl is not homeless. She's not bothering anyone. Just leave her be, okay?"

"You know her?" Claire asks, mortified. "We used to have standards at parties like this. When we were freshmen, the seniors didn't allow people like that to attend. We've gone soft. This girl would have been publicly shamed for showing up."

"Claire," I state with as much patience as I can.

"Yes?"

"Leave the girl alone. I mean it."

"But," she begins to counter.

"No buts. Leave her alone. She's Serena's sister."

"*No!*" she howls out in disbelief.

"*Yes.* So, leave her be. This is likely the last time she will attend a school party, so just bear with her another hour or so. Okay? If you torture her, I will take it personally."

Claire halts at my threat. She's not malicious like other catty girls in our school but isn't above pestering Serena's sister.

"*Fine!*" she replies with a pout. "Speaking of Serena, she's plastered. She's a drink away from embarrassing herself. She can barely walk straight. You should do something before a video ends up all over social media."

Claire is actually looking out for Serena. I stare at her, likely longer than I reasonably should, in disbelief as once again I'm struck by the unexpected tonight. I've never seen her look out for anyone but herself and her devoted followers. Maybe I'm not the only one turning a new leaf this year.

Claire nods in the direction of a group playing cornhole. I spot a pair of slender arms rising up in celebration, immediately recognizing the blonde Claire was trying to point out. Serena loses her balance, thankfully catching herself before she falls by grabbing hold of a boy's arm nearby. Sure enough, there's a crowd gathered nearby, and any one of them could take this opportunity to ruin Serena's reputation.

"Thanks, Claire. I'll take care of it."

"Anytime," she replies with a phony sweetness to her voice.

Hustling over to the cornhole game, I observe Serena wobble unsteadily as she tosses a bean bag. I brush off the nearby guy, who's eyeing her opportunistically, and slide in beside her.

"Hey, Hunter!" Serena exclaims loudly, her eyes appearing unfocused and glazed over.

"May I talk to you …. privately," I whisper, leaning in close to her ear, attempting to show discretion amidst the crowd surrounding us. I doubt this is the first time she's had this much to drink, but based on the beads of sweat on her forehead, I'm guessing she may also be dehydrated. I try not to assume the worst; that something was slipped into her drink.

"Suuurre. Anything for you, babe," she replies, tapping my nose with her finger and smiling.

Yep, she's beyond drunk. Seeing her sway with her first step, I reach around her waist and pull her to my side. Not only does Serena not protest, but she willingly leans her whole weight on me. Despite her impaired state, I now have her full attention. Serena takes the opportunity to run her hand down my bare chest.

"Serena, you have me worried. Can we go back inside? I don't want you to get dehydrated."

"But I'm in the middle of a game," she whines.

I let out a sigh. If she's not coming with me, I need a backup plan. There aren't many options that would be subtle, not that there is an individual who is oblivious to her drunken state. I'm willing to throw her over my shoulder and carry her if I have to because her impaired condition is preventing her from making good decisions right now.

It's not lost on me that I feel an odd responsibility for her wellbeing, even more so than I would handling Devon or some other drunk friend from school.

"I do feel a little dizzy," she finally confesses, giving me the opening I needed.

"Okay. Let's go inside for a bit, and we can finish the game later. Does that sound good to you?"

"I'll go anywhere with you," Serena replies, laying her head on my shoulder.

Before we start walking back to the house, I feel her unintentionally shift her weight away from me. I tighten my grip on her waist to secure her because I'm the only thing preventing her from collapsing.

"Do you mind if I pick you up?" I ask with the most charming voice I can muster. I'm not above using my persuasive powers at this moment. Serena needs to lie down.

"I'm all yours."

Serena lets out a whoop as I sweep her off her feet, but that excitement quickly fades as she lays her head against my chest. I don't waste time carrying her across the thirty yards to Chaz's backdoor.

"Chaz!" I holler, stealing his attention away from a conversation. "I need a path to a bed."

My voice must convey an appropriate amount of urgency because Chaz hustles over and helps me fight through the crowd, leading me towards the nearest staircase. Serena's eyes are closed, and her head is firmly planted on my bare shoulder, likely trying to combat the dizziness plaguing her.

Chaz opens a bedroom door on the second floor, immediately setting off protests from a couple having a private moment. Chaz gives an apologetic wave, slowly starting to close the door when I kick it violently open with my foot.

"Get out!" I roar, scaring the two individuals into a quick exit from the room. They both rush out before they are completely dressed.

When it comes to caring for my family, I can be a little over dramatic. It dawns on me, at that moment, that I consider Serena a part of my inner circle. I guess this answers Jocelyn's question. Having known her for two weeks, it seems rushed. I usually find it difficult to trust people, but she's somehow maneuvered her way around all the walls I have built up.

"Chaz, can you grab Lexi? And I need some water bottles and a trash can. Can you get those too?"

"Sure thing. I got you."

"And Chaz."

"Yeah?"

"Thank you."

Chaz smiles and nods in my direction before heading toward the stairs. Serena's eyes are still closed as I lay her on the bed. I gently brushed loose hairs out of her face, affectionately running my fingers down her cheek.

"Don't worry, I've got you," I whisper. "I am going to need you to drink some water, though."

"Mmmhmmm," Serena replies as she wiggles into a more comfortable position on the bed.

Seeing a few people walk by with prying eyes, I make my way to the bedroom door to close it. I want to give Serena privacy from the rest of our school. The gossip chain will already tell stories from seeing me carry her up the stairs while shirtless. I don't want them seeing her throw up if it comes to that.

"What are you doing to my sister?"

The high-pitched scream startles me, accompanied by swinging fists that violently slam into my chest. Surprised by the unexpected onslaught, I manage to grab hold of both of Lindsey's arms, but not before she catches me in the side of the face with a left hook.

"Calm down," I bark out, yanking the girl towards me until her chest collides with mine.

My cheek hurts like hell from where she clocked me. Her knuckles are lucky they didn't break from the impact.

"No! Leave her alone!"

Lindsey flails her arms, trying to break free from my grip, but to no avail. She attempts to knee my crotch, which I avoid at the last second with a turn of my hip.

"Lindsey, calm down! I'm not doing anything to your sister. She's drunk."

"Let me go!"

"No."

"What did you give to her?"

"Lindsey, stop," Serena whimpers, finally opening her eyes.

Lexi bursts into the room holding two water bottles, beelining straight to the bed and dropping down next to Serena.

"Serena, here, drink this," Lexi instructs her, offering the water bottle.

"Satisfied?" I ask Lindsey, hesitantly releasing both of her hands. I eye her carefully, preparing myself in case she is planning to unleash another barrage of attacks. She hurries to the other side of the bed, quietly talking to Serena.

"Lex, can you hang out here? I need to step out just for a second."

"Yep, I'm not going anywhere," she replies.

Moving out into the hallway, I meet Chaz, who hands me a bucket. He shows me their family's linen closet, where I grab a few washcloths. Chaz even offers for us to use the room for the night. His parents are out of town all weekend. By the time I dampen the washcloths and return to the room, Serena lurches up and begins vomiting.

Serena is in for a long night.

"She needs to keep pushing water," I direct, only for Lexi to give me an incredulous look.

"I got it. Thanks."

"*Now* you do."

"What's that supposed to mean?" Lexi shoots back.

"Where were you while Serena was getting plastered?"

"I haven't seen her since the game. How about you turn some of that guilt around on yourself."

The Tucker Girls

Lexi and I glare at each other until I finally break eye contact. She's right in that it's really my fault. Before running off to smoke with the guys, I should have checked in with Serena. I can't expect her to always be the responsible one. It's too much pressure for her to reasonably bear.

"I'm sorry. You're right. This is on me," I confess.

I whip out my phone and text Elijah and Brady. I am going to need their assistance.

"This is so embarrassing," Serena whimpers as Lexi offers her water once more.

"Don't worry about it. If it would make you feel better, I can tell you some stories of Hunter throwing up," Lexi replies with a wicked smile. "In fact, I think I took a couple videos in case I needed to blackmail him."

Serena's lips turn up ever so slightly.

"Did you let anyone make you a drink tonight?" I ask Serena, finally trying to answer the burning question that has been bothering me since I found her in this state.

"Simon brought me one a while ago," Serena responds.

Just then, Elijah and Brady both pop into the room.

"She okay?" Elijah inquires with a look of concern.

"No. Simon got her drink tonight. Go find out if it was clean," I demand.

Elijah nods and takes off towards the stairs.

"Go get Lexi something to sleep on. See if Chaz has an inflatable mattress," I bark at Brady.

He hesitates at the door, eyeing Serena on the bed, then proceeds to hunt down Chaz.

"Does he always order people around?" Lindsey asks Lexi with an annoyed tone.

"Nope. He's just worried about your sister," Lexi replies reassuringly. "Are we hunkering down here tonight?"

"Serena's in no shape to go anywhere right now. Chaz offered to let us use the room since his parents are out of town. I figure if we can get you something comfortable to sleep on, Lindsey and Serena can have the bed," I answer, my head spinning from adrenaline. Thankfully I'd gone easy on alcohol this evening - if you call two beers and a shot *'going easy'*. The buzz I felt on the boat is already receding.

"Serena would be more comfortable in her own bed," Lindsey counters, likely looking for a reason to disagree with me. "We would all sleep better."

"Do you want to explain to your parents why your car smells like vomit for a week?" I shoot back.

Lindsey refuses to look at me, and when she doesn't have any reply, I assume that means she consents to my plan.

"If you are lucky enough to get her home without incident, how do you plan to get her in bed? Are you carrying her?"

Lindsey is smaller than Serena. There's no way she's pulling that off without someone to help her. My point must have been made because Lindsey doesn't offer any counter arguments.

Unfortunately, the rest of the evening is eventful, with Serena's last spell of vomiting ending around three in the morning. Lexi sleeps on an inflated mattress while the guys try to rest while leaning against the wall. I remember drifting off to the serene sound of Lindsey singing Serena to sleep, with the guilt of this entire incident weighing heavy on my conscience.

CHAPTER SIX
Hunter

"Morning, Sweats," I declare as I plop down in my Trigonometry desk.

Sweats is my new nickname for Lindsey, seeing as she insists on wearing unflattering sweatshirts every day regardless of whether the weather calls for it.

My routine, for the last few weeks, has been to use the nickname as much as humanly possible. I can tell, by the way she shifts her weight, that it bothers her, but she refuses to give me the dignity of a response. In fact, she has been pretending I don't exist since the night Serena got sick. I'm confident, deep down, that she still blames me for that night, and frankly, I do too.

I'm finding too much enjoyment in ruffling her feathers. It's also turned into a full-blown sociological experiment in seeing how far I can push things before she snaps. If I walk by, I'll *accidentally* nudge her backpack with my foot so it will topple over. I'll tap my foot on the leg of her desk to some random beat. I even sat in her desk yesterday hoping she'd confront me, but instead, she asked Mrs. Seldon to make me move. It's all juvenile behavior, but it passes the time.

She's going to combust soon. I'm going to get the version of Lindsey that was throwing haymakers the night she thought I was about to take advantage of her sister. I picture Lindsey trying to contain her rage by throwing darts at a poster of me in her bedroom at night.

I know she's been scrolling my social media account because she accidentally liked a selfie I posted last school year.

61

The Tucker Girls

By the time I received the notification, she'd already removed her like, but her secret is out. She's stalking my account, and that has piqued my interest.

What's going on in that head of yours, Lindsey Tucker?

"Morning, Hannah," I call out.

Hannah is the name of the blonde girl with glasses who'd saved me from Mrs. Seldon's inquisition a few weeks back. I've made a concerted effort to be friendly to her since then. She blushed the first few times I greeted her but seems more accustomed to the attention now.

"Hey," she replies meekly, casting a nervous glance over at Lindsey in the process.

I'd since learned that the two were friends, which likely puts Hannah in an awkward situation when I speak to her, considering Lindsey despises me. The two eat lunch together every day.

The classroom is still relatively empty since I arrived early today. It isn't a habit of mine, but I made it my mission to begin getting to know the other students in this class. I am determined to prove Lindsey's assumption that I am a self-absorbed prick wrong. Yesterday I made a point to talk to Patrick, the kid who sits directly behind me, about Call of Duty for five minutes. I'd never played myself, but he is very passionate about gaming and carried the conversation once we landed on a topic he loves.

Reaching into my binder to pull out my completed homework, I overhear Lindsey saying something indiscernible to Hannah. Though I am sitting directly behind her, it was barely a whisper, so I couldn't make it out. Hannah's face falls in response.

"No, he just wanted to talk about our Chemistry project," Hannah replies sullenly. "Has Stephen asked you yet?"

Lindsey's head nods.

Hannah squeals with ear-piercing excitement, her shoulders bobbing up and down.

"That's awesome! I wish Rich would just ask me. He keeps bringing up the dance but then never gets around to it. I think he's on the verge of asking every time we talk. It's so frustrating."

"Are you all talking Homecoming?" I chime in.

Lindsey's body goes rigid at the sound of my voice. Hannah's eyes dance between us, looking unsure if she should answer. I don't really need her to confirm my suspicion, though. The Homecoming dance is weeks away, and I doubt there is any other dance they could be referring to.

"Hannah, could I give you some advice?" I ask, leaning across my desk in her direction.

Lindsey grips the edge of her desk, the white of her knuckles reflecting the fluorescent light. I wish I could see the look on her face. It requires her full restraint to not engage with me, which makes me entirely too happy. I'm an awful person, I know.

"I mean ... sure," Hannah replies with uncertainty.

"I don't know Rich, but it sounds like he has cold feet. From my perspective, I think you have two options. You could ditch the old-fashioned notion that the boy needs to ask the girl and invite him to the dance."

"No, no, no. I couldn't do that," Hannah fervently shakes her head. "What's option two?"

"Give him a push. Wait until Rich is within earshot and tell someone that you've been asked to the dance but that you are waiting for a special someone to ask before you give them a response. Hell, you could say I offered to take you. That'll give him some motivation."

Hannah gawks back. She's clearly not accustomed to this sort of plotting. Lindsey doesn't budge, though. Her hands still grip the desk as if she were riding a rollercoaster on the verge of a dramatic drop.

"And uh .... what do I do if he still doesn't ask me?" Hannah inquires.

"Then I'll take you to the dance," I answer with a shrug. "That is, as long as you are okay with that. Or you can just use my name. I'm good either way."

"Oh," Hannah's cheeks are blushing intensely.

"Hannah, don't," Lindsey mumbles in a low voice.

"No hard feelings if you don't want to go through with it, but I think it may be the push Rich needs," I continue, ignoring Lindsey's comment. "Trust me. I know how guys think."

"Okay. Let's do it," Hannah states as she peers down at her hands.

"Great!" I exclaim. "Let me know how it goes."

Leaning back in my seat, I am satisfied with my plan to help Hannah. The fact that Lindsey disapproves is icing on the cake. I can't be that big of a self-indulgent prick if I'm helping her friend.

If Rich does have a crush on Hannah, hopefully he will have enough sense to realize she is waiting on him. It will be inconvenient to take Hannah if he still can't bring himself to ask her, but I didn't have plans on inviting anyone else to the dance.

My cheerful demeanor persists through the remainder of class, despite having a pop quiz that I likely bombed. It isn't until the bell rings and I notice someone hovering over my desk that my demeanor wavers.

"Can I help you?" I ask, looking up at Lindsey as she glares down at me.

"Stop screwing with my friends," she growls in a low voice.

I finally did it. I pushed the girl to her breaking point. I look around to see the rest of the class filing out of the room entirely unaware of the impending drama. Typically, our student body is eager to eavesdrop, but maybe Lindsey's not yet on their radar.

"I honestly have no idea what you are talking about," I counter with a smirk, attempting to stand up when Lindsey shoves me back in my seat.

"You aren't taking Hannah to Homecoming," she snaps, still keeping her voice low. Mrs. Seldon hasn't noticed us lingering around yet. "I know your reputation. There's no way I'm trusting you to take her anywhere. Hannah is a sweet girl. You are trying to get in her pants just to screw with me. On top of that, Serena is expecting you to take her. Did you even consider that?"

Standing up once more, I catch her hand before it can shove me again. Lindsey's constant pushing and punching are getting old quickly.

"I'm not after Hannah. I don't do that type of stuff anymore, even if it's to mess with you. Contrary to what you think, I just want to help her out. I'm not entirely self-absorbed. I hope Rich mans up and invites her. That would be great," I retort in a stern yet hushed voice. "Serena …. My situation with Serena is complicated."

I don't feel the need to explain that Serena is off-limits now. After Brady called dibs, I will do my best to put some distance between us. I won't be inviting her to the dance. It would betray our code. I don't even know if I would have asked had Brady not called dibs.

"What's so complicated? She likes you. I think you like her. Are you purposely messing with her head? Playing games with her?"

"No, that's not it. I wouldn't …. Just forget it. I don't have to defend my actions to you."

"You're a liar."

"And you want a *liar* to take your sister to the dance?"

"Die in a fire," she grumbles, attempting to flee, but I still have a hold of her hand, preventing her from escaping.

"You make no sense at all. You realize that, right? Have you considered - for a second - that I'm trying to help your friend?"

"I don't think you do anything that doesn't benefit you."

"News flash! I'm not the villain here."

"Everyone is the hero of their own story. Now, let go of my hand," she demands, ripping it from my grasp.

My heart is pounding from this frustrating conversation. Granted, I've been trying to get Lindsey to confront me, but she finally decides to attack the moment I intended to help someone she cares about. She's absolutely impossible.

Lindsey grabs her backpack and storms towards the classroom door. I shrug at Mrs. Seldon, who has been spying on the conclusion of our conversation.

Hustling after Lindsey, I am determined to catch up to her and finish our discussion. The last thing I need is for Serena to catch wind that I'm arguing with her sister again. I consider owning up to Brady's claim to Serena, but that would surely infuriate Lindsey further. I need her to understand that I have zero interest in hooking up with Hannah.

My eyes divert from Lindsey to a heated argument in the hallway. I instantly recognize Marcel and his thugs staring menacingly at three other students who aren't backing down. I sense something terrible is about to go down. Marcel's gang is on the verge of brawling. I've seen enough fights to recognize that this will get ugly.

With her eyes on her feet, Lindsey is caught up in her own head and distracted as she walks right into the tense situation. She has no idea she's about to stumble into a chaotic scrum.

Seeing the gleam of a knife blade held by one of the guys sends me into a panic. This isn't going to be a fight settled with just fists. Marcel begins hurling curses at the other group's leader, wagging his finger in the other guy's face. The tension is dialing up to a climax.

Managing to get ahold of Lindsey's arm, I yank her towards me just before the first punch is thrown. She yelps to protest how hard I pull her, but that doesn't give me any pause. I wrap my arms around Lindsey in a hug and sandwich her between me and the lockers.

Bedlam breaks out behind me. Screams of bystanders fill the space as the brawl starts. I am unnerved by my inability to see what is happening, but I refuse to let go of Lindsey and turn around.

A body slams into my back, pressing me uncomfortably close to the girl that hates my guts. The guy collapses to the floor but quickly returns to his feet to rejoin the fight. Ear-piercing shouts continue to fill the hallways, making it impossible to understand what exactly is happening. I can barely think clearly in this chaos.

Teachers file into the hallway attempting unsuccessfully to break up the altercation. Noticing a path to a nearby classroom is clear and hearing the scuffle moving to the other side of the hall, I attempt to move Lindsey to safety. Her body won't budge, though. She is rigid as a stone.

"Come on," I plead to no avail. Go figure that she doesn't listen to me even when I try to keep her safe. I'm sure she'll do more mental gymnastics to blame this fight on me as well.

Lindsey isn't going to willingly move from this spot. Despite that realization, I decide, for both of us, that it's not safe to linger around in this hallway. Reaching under her thighs, I lift Lindsey off the ground and carry her into the classroom. Lindsey, with two fist fulls of my shirt, refuses to budge. Her face is hidden from me, buried in my chest even after I release her. I can feel her trembling body rattle against mine as she struggles to catch her breath.

The panicked screams can still be heard from the hall, which certainly isn't helping Lindsey gain her composure. Stretching out my foot, I kick at the classroom door. When it slams shut, Lindsey lets out a fearful yelp that manages to wreck all the walls I have built against this girl. She's on the verge of a panic attack - that is, if she's not experiencing one already.

"You are safe," I whisper, wishing there was more I could do to help bring her down from the height of her attack.

I continue reminding her of that fact while remaining as still as possible. I'm entirely ill-equipped to handle this situation. I consider reaching for my cell phone and texting Serena. Lindsey and I aren't even friends. Maybe her sister would know how to help her.

It occurs to me that Lindsey likely doesn't appreciate being this close to me, let alone the fact that I carried her. I attempt to pull back, hoping that giving her space will help her calm down, but Lindsey responds by tightening her grip on my shirt. Of course, I would make the wrong assumption.

I lift my hands to touch her but then freeze when uncertainty creeps into my mind. If this was Lexi, it wouldn't even be a question, but I have no idea what will help soothe Lindsey. Finally, I give in to my instincts and gently rub her back. A shiver runs through her body when my chin accidentally touches her cheek, and I'm pretty sure it has nothing to do with her shocked state.

"Lindsey, I got you. You are safe. I'm not going to let anything happen to you."

Lindsey's trembling stops, and she begins to release her death grip on me. My t-shirt continues jutting out from where her clenched hands had taken hold. Stepping back from my chest, her gaze remains locked on the floor.

"Hey," I state softly, attempting to get her attention.

The Tucker Girls

Lindsey refuses to look up at me. Is she embarrassed by her reaction?

"Lindsey. Are you okay?"

"I'm fine," she replies flatly.

"It's okay if you aren't."

"I said I'm fine! I just had a moment. That's all."

Watching her closely, I look for any sign that would indicate she is still struggling. When her gray eyes finally meet mine, I can see in her eyes that she is herself once more. There's contempt in her gaze that's all too familiar. I finally allow myself to sigh in relief.

"Hunter, you're bleeding!" Lindsey exclaims, causing me to jump at the unexpected shout.

Looking at the floor, I see a puddle of blood by my right sneaker. Inspecting myself, I discover a six-inch rip on my rear shoulder that must have been cut during the skirmish. The fabric is soaked in blood near the tear, so I've been bleeding for a while.

"Great," I mutter, pulling my t-shirt over my head to get a better look at the wound.

"You need to go see the nurse."

I ignore Lindsey's order, dabbing the trickling blood with my t-shirt before tossing it in the trash. Opening several cabinets underneath the blackboard, I discover a first aid kit and set it on the counter.

"Why aren't you listening to me? You may need stitches."

"It's just a scratch," I counter.

"*That* is not a scratch!"

"I will survive. I have experience patching myself up."

"Do I even want to know why?"

"I'm clumsy," I lie as I tear open an antiseptic wipe.

Lindsey lets out a growl as she walks toward me.

"You are the most infuriating person I know. Hand it over! I will do it."

"I don't need your help," I retort, only for her to snatch the wipe and push on me, so my shoulder faces her. Lindsey doesn't hesitate when wiping my arm.

"Easy," I bark out as the pain from the alcohol burns.

"The nurse would do a better job. Want me to get her?"

"No."

"Okay then. Suck it up."

Thankfully, despite her words, she is more gentle in applying the gauze and tape. Moving my arm around, pain radiates through my shoulder. It's unpleasant but tolerable. I've lived through much worse.

"How's that?" Lindsey asks.

"Perfect. Thank you."

Placing the first aid kit back where I found it, I grab a roll of paper towels and wipe up the mess on the floor. I am thankful that the teacher to whose classroom this belongs has still not returned. The sight of blood would undoubtedly have led to an incident report, and incident reports lead to parent phone calls. I don't want any drama, and an administrator getting in touch with Pete will surely cause drama.

I notice Lindsey closely examining me from the corner of my eye. She quickly averts her gaze when I turn in her direction. I wonder what Lindsey has gleaned from my reluctance to go to the nurse's office. Was she able to interpret the meaning behind my comment about having experience patching myself up?

Why does it matter what she thought of my remark? It shouldn't matter, but for some infuriating reason, it does.

Forcing my racing mind to stop dwelling on possibilities, I move towards the door and crack it open. The remnants of the fight are still visible, with one kid lying on the floor injured and the others lined up against the far lockers.

The Tucker Girls

Security officers and teachers finally have a handle on the situation, meaning Lindsey and I are free to go to lunch.

Both our backpacks are still lying in the hallway, so I retrieve them before returning to the room. Handing over her backpack, I can't help but notice that she's still intently watching me. I refuse to meet her stare, though. I don't want to answer any of the questions that may be running through her head right now.

We both wordlessly exit the classroom in lockstep. I purposely carry my backpack over my injured shoulder to hide the bandage. Despite it painfully rubbing against my wound, I can't have anyone notice that I was bleeding. My gym shirt, stuffed away in my locker, will have to suffice for the rest of the school day.

"How do you walk around shirtless like it's no big deal? Don't you feel a little awkward?" Lindsey asks, breaking the silence.

Though a scattering of people is lingering in the halls, no one seems to notice my lack of attire.

"Do you feel awkward dressed like an Eskimo?"

Lindsey glares at me, clenching her fists in anger.

"Why are you so annoying?"

Sighing, I figure I can have the decency to respond without being sarcastic, considering the traumatic experience she just went through.

"No. It doesn't bother me. Most of the school has seen me without a shirt on. Besides, it's their problem if they don't like what they see. Definitely not mine."

"I wish I possessed that ability - to not care what people think."

"You sure put off the vibe that you couldn't care less."

Lindsey's gaze meets mine with a puzzling look. She intently stares at me again, her gray eyes searching for some

71

undisclosed answer. I am suddenly unsettled by the intensity of her evaluation, but I can't force myself to break free of her hold.

"Do you promise you're okay?" I ask out of genuine concern.

Before she can answer, Serena's frantic voice calls out her sister's name from the main hall ahead. Serena hustles towards us, her heels clacking against the floor the entire way. By her expression, I assume Serena assumed the worst when Lindsey didn't show up for lunch on time.

"There you are! You gave me a scare! I heard about a fight, and then you weren't at your table," Serena continues.

"Everything's fine," Lindsey replies in a calming voice, likely attempting to downplay the incident. While she's definitely calm now, there were moments Lindsey was ready to come undone from the chaotic situation.

"And Hunter, where is your shirt?" Serena asks in a bewildered voice.

"It got torn, so I decided to toss it," I respond with a nonchalant shrug.

Serena's eyes dart back and forth between Lindsey and me as a curious look develops across her face.

"What are you all not telling me?"

Lindsey and I look at each other, and in that momentary glance, we inexplicably come to a silent agreement that we shouldn't discuss the fight.

"Plenty," I say, purposely staying vague and short. "I'm hungry. Let's go eat."

Serena gives an exasperated sigh but doesn't ask any other questions. She falls into step with Lindsey and me as we head towards the main hall; silence falls over us once more. I welcome the quiet, hoping it will give me time to process everything that just occurred.

The Tucker Girls

"Oh, Hunter," Serena stops walking and grabs hold of my arm. "Before I forget, some junior girl is telling people you are taking her to Homecoming."

"Hannah Miles? Yeah, that's because I am."

"What?" Serena exclaims in surprise.

"No, you're not!" Lindsey chimes in, her cheeks flaring up with color once more.

"I don't understand. Why would you do that?" Serena responds.

"He's trying to hook up with my friend," Lindsey cries out. "Hunter, listen to me. You are not taking Hannah to Homecoming!"

"Lindsey, *I am not* interested in your friend. Stop saying that. I'm simply doing her a favor," I shoot back. "Serena, I was going to tell you later. I didn't think it would get around school this quick. It's got to be an all-time record."

"Why her?" Serena inquires, a hurt look crossing her face.

Reading into her hurt, Lindsey was right that Serena was expecting me to ask her.

"Serena, I can't take you to the dance. Brady called dibs on you. He wants to take you to the dance."

"Dibs? What the hell is dibs?" Serena exclaims.

"It's our way of making sure we aren't competing for girls. Dibs is a system we've been using since middle school so we don't end up fighting."

"What is my sister? A piece of meat. You're all a bunch of chauvinistic Neanderthals," Lindsey rants.

"Seriously? Brady called dibs on me? Is this why you've been distant since I got sick at Chaz's party?" Serena rages.

"Yeah."

"I thought it was because I grossed you out from all the vomit," Serena confesses, putting both hands on her head. "Why couldn't you call dibs on me?"

"I .... uh …. you see …. It's complicated. I'm working through some stuff ...."

"So you decided to ask Hannah?" Lindsey jumps in.

This Tucker tag team deal isn't enjoyable at all.

"Serena, I told you that I'm ...."

"Complicated. I don't even know what that means," Serena mutters, averting her eyes in irritation.

"Complicated as in he's trying to get in my friend's pants," Lindsey chimes in. "You need to go tell Hannah you aren't taking her."

"Yeah, that's not going to go over well," I retort. "Imagine the shame Hannah will face if she's forced to recant the story. She will be ruthlessly ridiculed."

The lightbulb goes off in Lindsey's head as she realizes the implications of me backing out on my commitment. The only thing that would save Hannah from utter embarrassment will be if Rich steps up to the plate.

"Fine! Take her, but you answer to me if you hurt her," Lindsey threatens.

"Just so you know," Serena chimes in. "I'm telling Brady he doesn't get to have dibs on me. I'm calling dibs on myself. So he will have to back off or break the code."

Serena raises her eyebrows at me in defiance, and I can't help but smile back at her. I would love to be the fly on the wall when she has that conversation with Brady.

"Well, now that we have all that settled. Anything else we need to air out?" I ask, hoping that there is nothing else to discuss.

"Yes. You are coming over to meet my parents," Serena declares out of the blue. "They want to meet the new friends I have been hanging out with."

The Tucker Girls

"Sure. I'm free Saturday night."

"That will work. You better not stand us up," Serena adamantly warns. I'd never seen her worked up like this. For the first time, I notice the fire in Serena's eyes that I have grown accustomed to seeing from her sister.

I slowly back away while still being assaulted by their fiery glares. I want to wave the white flag and surrender, which means making sacrifices I'm unwilling to make. I won't allow Hannah to suffer at the hands of her peers or betray Brady's trust and pursue Serena.

"And put a damn shirt on!" Serena yells when they are no longer in sight.

CHAPTER SEVEN
Hunter

Plopping down in a booth opposite Brady, I let out an audible sigh. Only having woken up thirty minutes ago, I'd rushed out the door to meet him for lunch Saturday morning. My shift at Stirred Up concluded at two in the morning, leaving me groggy and run down.

Business is booming these days, so Drake has asked me to increase my hours. I am making good money but unable to enjoy any of my mounting savings. Every dime I accrue is being saved for moving out of my house as soon as possible. Once I turn eighteen in April, nothing stops me from getting a place of my own except being able to afford rent.

"I thought Elijah was coming," I comment, picking up on Brady's unusual demeanor immediately. Brady is using his index finger to push around a sugar packet, his head drooping low.

"Oh, he's here," Brady responds, looking up with a smirk.

"Yeah?"

"He's in the back with Leina."

"Who's Leina?"

"Our waitress."

"Great," I reply sarcastically. "Guess the pizza is going to have to wait."

The three of us agreed to meet at Sal's, the best pizza joint in our city, through text the night before. Though the inside is worn and unkempt, the delicious food more than makes up for the atmosphere.

The Tucker Girls

Brady's head falls once more as he continues pushing the sugar packet. His usual carefree, jovial demeanor is missing in action today.

"What's with you?"

"She called dibs on herself," Brady mumbles.

I let out a boisterous laugh realizing he is speaking of Serena. I guess they had the talk.

"I'm glad you find this so funny! I mean … who calls dibs on themselves?"

"Serena Tucker. That's who."

"I really messed up. Any other Ulla Meyer girl would have been ecstatic to know I'm interested in them, but not Serena. Now she's avoiding me like the plague. Won't even respond to my texts."

"You are going to see her tonight. Just put on some of that famous Brady charm. She can't freeze you out forever."

Brady slowly nods his head, mulling over what I told him. I'd never seen him get this worked up over a girl. His longest relationship lasted only a week. Serena has changed his mind, though. I think he is ready to leave all that behind and abandon *The Untouchables* label for her.

"Gentlemen," Elijah greets us, sliding in next to Brady with a big grin.

"Thanks for finally showing up, Elijah," I say with annoyance.

"Says the guy who was twenty minutes late. I had to find something to kill time, and I didn't want to sit here with this joy kill," Elijah jerks his thumb at Brady.

Our waitress awkwardly strolls up, looking particularly disheveled, to our table to take our order, locking eyes with Elijah the entire time. She slides Elijah her number before she walks away with our drink orders. I'm witnessing the type of behavior I used to partake in, but it feels so foreign now to observe. I guess a few months really can feel like an eternity sometimes.

"Did you ever find out if Simon's story checked out?" I ask, referring to Simon insisting he didn't slip anything to Serena the night she got sick.

"Dude swears he didn't tamper with her drink. I asked around, and he's not the most upstanding guy, but no one has heard of him doing anything like that before," Elijah responds earnestly.

"What are you thinking?" Brady inquires.

The events of that night have been bothering me for a while. Serena may have been at the party for two hours total. Even if she was severely dehydrated, it feels suspicious. She got sick too quickly.

"We send a message."

"But you aren't sure he even did anything," Elijah counters.

"Right. The punishment needs to be proportional to the crime."

"Which is what exactly?" Brady asks.

"Handing our girls open drinks."

Looking between the two to see if either disagrees with my assessment, I simply see them nod in agreement. Jocelyn was right about one thing. The school needs to know that Serena is off-limits.

"I'm free tomorrow night. Can you guys make that work?"

"I'm in."

"Same."

The three of us fall into a less serious conversation for a while when Leina returns with our sodas. It's nice to hang out with just the guys. This is the first time since school started that it's simply the three of us.

The Tucker Girls

The door chimes as a group walks in, and I immediately spy Hannah and Lindsey accompanied by two boys I don't recognize. When I wave in Hannah's direction, she smiles and returns the gesture. Both Brady and Elijah turn to see who I'm greeting.

"Who's the blonde?"

"Hannah. She's the girl I'm taking to Homecoming."

Brady's head snaps to attention with a bewildered look.

"You are joking, right? Are you taking on charity cases these days? Or are your standards just that low now?"

"Shut up. I don't have to explain myself to you."

"I can always just go ask her myself," Elijah suggests with a smirk, and before I can protest, he leaps up from the booth.

I am on his heels but can't cut him off before he stops in front of their booth. Lindsey slumps in her seat when she notices our arrival.

"Wassup lil Tucker?" Elijah greets Serena's sister.

"Hi," she reluctantly replies.

"Who are your friends?"

"This is Hannah, Rich and Stephen."

Rich is a slender, dirty blonde-haired boy with glasses. I figure since I'm over here, I might as well play into my role. I glare at Rich as if he's the competition. I'm giving an Oscar-worthy performance, causing him to do a double take when he realizes I'm glaring at him.

Recalling the Trigonometry discussion where Lindsey said some guy named Stephen asked her to the dance, I glance his way next. Stephen has curly blonde hair similar to Brady but slender like Rich. I'm less than impressed by the type of guy she's attracted to. Maybe he makes up for it with a great personality.

"Hunter was just saying he was taking a Hannah to Homecoming. You wouldn't be that Hannah, would you?"

Hannah blushes, but before she can respond, I jump in.

"Technically, she hasn't agreed yet. She's still holding out for another offer."

"So you're her backup plan?" Elijah chokes back a laugh.

"The best damn backup plan a girl can have," I respond, shooting daggers at Elijah with my eyes.

Despite the standoff with my obnoxious friend, I can't help but notice Rich shifting uncomfortably in his seat. One can only hope that the poor boy is getting the message.

"I'll get an answer to you soon," Hannah declares, still beet red.

"Sounds good. Sorry for the interruption," I offer up, throwing my arm around Elijah's neck and dragging him away. "Let's go. I want to eat pizza this century."

"Who are you, Hunter? I don't even recognize you anymore. Junior Hunter would have kicked your ass for asking out a girl like that. She's bottom tier."

"I didn't ask for your opinion."

"I mean, Lindsey at least has potential. She's got that whole mysterious thing going for her too. Why not ask her instead?"

I come to a complete halt.

"What's that supposed to mean? What *whole mysterious thing* are you talking about?" I challenge, feeling suddenly defensive.

"Jeez, calm down, son. I'm just talking about her baggy clothes. It's hard to tell whether she has a body like Serena's or not. My guess is she does with them being sisters and all."

Elijah stares at me for a moment, attempting to answer some unspoken question in his mind.

"What did you think I meant?"

"Nothing. Let's go eat," I respond, shoving him towards our booth. "I don't want to be here all day."

The Tucker Girls

CHAPTER EIGHT
Lindsey

Hunter Bowden has this presence about him. When he enters a room, it's like he silently commands everyone's attention. It's another reason I cannot stand the boy on a list too long to count.

To make matters worse, Serena is obsessed with Hunter. I have spent hours listening to her talk about him as she paces in my room late at night. Sure, he's crazy attractive, but I don't understand the appeal. I love Serena to death and try my best not to object to her ridiculous notion about him being *the one*. She's way out of his league, but I can't get her to believe that fact

Yes, Serena's a little boy crazy. There hasn't been a time since seventh grade that she's not been dating or talking to someone, and the boys have always been falling over themselves to gain her attention. There's a good reason why too. My sister is the real deal. She's authentic, fun, graceful, beautiful, adventurous, and outgoing. Everything boys want in a girl all wrapped up in a single person. The fact that Hunter hasn't fallen madly in love with Serena is another reason I loathe him. She deserves someone who will appreciate everything she has to offer.

Tonight is dinner with Serena's new friends, which means Mom has been on a torrent making sure the house is immaculate before their arrival. The fact that Mom is Serena's biggest advocate and knows how important Hunter is to Serena makes this event feel way more significant than it really should. Mom has asked me to change into *something more ideal* twice now, which I have obliged with minimal complaints. I eventually chose a sleeveless lavender blouse and gray skirt on my final attempt, hoping this will appease the woman.

Mom doesn't get another chance to pass judgment because the doorbell rings, and I can feel Hunter's presence before he steps through the door. *Ugh.* Someone please save me from this dinner. It would have been more bearable had I invited my friends tonight, but asking Hannah and Meredith to join this crew seemed like a bad idea. Hunter has to flirt with Hannah every second he's around her to torture me. Inviting Meredith felt like too much for our budding friendship. We've only hung out once, and this dinner is likely to be all kinds of awkward tonight. Instead, I'm going to have to suffer through this experience alone.

Meredith and Hannah are the extent of my friends at Ulla Meyer. I'm not like Serena, who makes instantaneous connections with strangers and becomes immediate best friends with them. I don't have that gene. Considering I'm the reason we moved to Texas, I guess my penance is to watch my sister show me how ordinary people interact in the world while I stumble through it.

My mother is the same as Serena, but my father is wired more like me. He has friends but mostly keeps to himself when he doesn't know people well. That may be why I'm unapologetically a daddy's girl. We seem to get each other in a way that Mom and Serena don't understand.

Do you need further proof that I'm socially inadequate? As everyone enters the kitchen, I hesitate in the adjoining living room while I wring my hands in anticipation of this dinner. It's not that I care what Hunter thinks of me. I absolutely do not. I just don't want to be here. I want to be lying in bed engrossed in the new novel that was delivered this morning.

I wonder how long I can go unnoticed. Hopefully, until dinner is served, then I can eat as quickly as humanly possible and ask to be excused. That's going to be my plan. Dad won't fight me on it, but Mom absolutely will. I plan to sneak away while she's mid-conversation because I know she won't cause a scene by dragging me back to the table in front of guests. Once I escape, I will be home free.

While I listen to my family and Hunter make small talk, I watch Hunter meander through the kitchen, stopping when he gets to the wall with our family pictures. He's studying each photo while Serena lingers just out of arm's reach. It's like he has her in his orbit, unknowingly pulling her along with him everywhere he goes.

"You have a beautiful home, Mrs. Tucker."

"Please call me Elise."

Gag. My mother is trying too hard. I want to pull her aside and tell her that Hunter's not worth the effort. I've told Dad several times about Hunter's less-than-stellar reputation, but Mom refuses to hear it.

"I love these photos you have on the wall. You've captured some great memories."

"Mom is a picture fiend. We don't actually get to enjoy a moment of our vacations because we are too busy posing the whole time. Our plans are scheduled around making the best picture memories," Serena interjects.

I smile at my sister's assessment because it is wholeheartedly true. Mom grumbles at Serena as she opens the oven to check on the lasagna.

"Your mother just wants to remember all the special moments with her family," Dad counters while pulling out plates.

"Thank you, Doug. At least someone in this house appreciates what I do."

"It looks like you all travel a lot," Hunter deduces from the memories. He's focused on one of Mom's montages with pictures from when we visited Barbados two years ago.

"Does your family vacation anywhere special?" Mom inquires.

"Not really."

"We are going to Europe to celebrate graduating high school," Serena beams with excitement, to which Hunter responds with a smile.

"That sounds incredible. Mrs. Tucker, you have great taste in art as well. I love this painting."

My stomach flips when I realize that Hunter is referring to the piece I painted during some of my therapy sessions. For a split second, I feel the warmth of his compliment flood through me, but I squash it away with the thought that he is just being polite.

"Oh, that thing? Lindsey painted that last winter. Doug liked it so much we hung it up."

Notice how Mom says *Dad* liked it. I'm sure she enjoys it being on the wall because of who created it, but she doesn't appreciate the painting itself. It's a textured piece that depicts stormy seas. Serena and Mom don't embrace anything that isn't sunshine and rainbows.

"Lindsey did this?" Hunter points to the painting, his gaze sweeping the room until he locks eyes with mine. What was the point of his question? Does he not think I am talented enough to paint something like that? It's really not anything special. Or was he honestly impressed and expected it was created by a professional? I can't decipher, from his gaze, his true intentions.

Tearing my eyes away from Hunter, I notice Dad has spotted me hiding away as well. With my cover blown, I slip into the kitchen, pulling glasses down and filling them with ice.

"Did you have to use a special paint to get this texture?" Hunter inquires, apparently aware that I've entered the room.

Heat trickles up my neck at the possibility of him admiring my work. It's not that I care what he thinks, but rather that his interest catches me entirely off guard. At least, that's the story I'm telling myself.

"I used acrylic paint. It's a special technique to get it textured like that," I inform him.

"Do you have any other work hanging up?"

"Nope," I reply as I carry some glasses over to the table. Serena smiles at me, obviously happy about something - maybe pride in her sister creating something that this boy finds impressive. Who knows when it comes to her?

"You know what?" Serena chimes in cheerfully. "I have an amazing idea! Why don't we double date with Lindsey and Stephen? We can do one of those paint nights advertised at Stellar Coffeehouse."

"That sounds like a lovely idea," Mom chimes in cheerfully as she bends over to check on the lasagna again.

"Maybe," Hunter replies, his voice sounding suddenly distant.

When I look up from setting down a glass, I notice he's transfixed on my bare forearm. It takes a moment to comprehend that he's staring at my scars. At the realization, my arms quickly fold into my chest, and I hastily retreat from the kitchen.

Shoot. Double shoot. I intended to wear a sweater to conceal my scars, and I completely forgot. I'm self-conscious about them and make my best effort to conceal my arms. No one at Ulla Meyer has ever seen them. I've done a good job hiding them for weeks, but of course, I would slip up this one night. No one bothered pulling me aside to subtly point out my mistake - not even Dad.

Tears brim at the corner of my eyes as I try to wrangle in my breathing. Logically, this isn't a big deal. I know how I should respond to someone discovering insight into my past that I've done everything to move on from, but emotionally I'm in complete upheaval. I feel like I've been sucker punched.

The Tucker Girls

Why have I gone to such great lengths to hide my scars only to let Hunter Bowden in on my secret? The one person who'd likely jump at the chance to use it against me. I'm furious with myself.

Once I'm confident I'm not going to cry, I descend the stairs - this time wearing my sweater - as I hear the doorbell ring. My timing is perfect, as Lexi's arrival is the ideal distraction to slip into the kitchen undetected. I wait awkwardly by the kitchen table as she's greeted by everyone with hugs. I say awkwardly because I'm not really sure how to welcome Lexi. We've only spoken once; the night Serena needed to sleep off her drunkenness. Since then, we haven't talked. What type of greeting does that require? I'm terrible at knowing these types of things, so I typically wait for the other person to make their move first.

Serena just naturally knows how to interact with people. Or maybe it's not all entirely natural, but more that she exudes confidence which makes the other person roll with whatever she's doing. Either way, I lack that gene too.

Lexi makes the decision for the both of us when she wraps her arms around me in a warm hug. Leaning back, I think she picks up on a vibe that I'm giving off.

"Sorry, I'm a hugger."

"Uh. Yeah. It's fine," I reply with a wave of my hand.

Lexi lingers near as if she wants to say more.

"I like your tattoo," I say to break the ice.

There's a tattoo of three small birds flying on her wrist, and Lexi beams when I draw attention to it.

"Thank you! I got it over the summer. I wanted to see how painful it would be, but now I'm itching to get my next one."

"I've already designed what I want," I confess, having wanted a tattoo for years.

"Let's go together!"

87

The Tucker Girls

"Not going to happen," Dad chimes in from across the room, killing the idea quickly.

Lexi turns so that her back is to my parents and gives me a wink.

"Hunter has a friend that can hook us up," she whispers.

I'm thrilled with the prospect, but I would have to get it somewhere subtle to avoid Dad's fury. He refuses to budge, insisting he will do everything possible to prevent me from getting inked up. What he doesn't know won't kill him, right?

"I'd love to meet your parents sometime," Mom says to Hunter as she tosses ingredients into a large salad bowl.

Lexi's body goes rigid, her head turning towards Hunter. I feel the whiplash of how quickly her demeanor changes, and I begin studying her odd expression.

"Sure," Hunter agrees flippantly.

The look shared between the Hunter and Lexi is loaded as if there's some private, unspoken conversation they are engaged in. I can't avoid taking in the entire scene despite the uncomfortable feeling that I'm eavesdropping on an intimate moment.

"Are they available next weekend?"

"My mother may be free," Lexi interjects, walking across the room to stand by Hunter. Well, not really standing next to him, but rather inserting herself between Mom and Hunter. I'm even more bewildered now by what is unfolding in front of me.

Surely someone else in the room notices this, but when I look at the rest of my family, they seem oblivious to this odd dynamic. Based on her glare, Serena noticed Lexi relocating to Hunter's side, but I only see jealousy brewing in her eyes; definitely not the confusion and curiosity I'm feeling.

"Oh, that would be great! I'd love to host her for coffee or tea."

"I'll talk to her tomorrow," Lexi replies with a smile.

"Hunter, will your mother be at the PTA meeting this month? Maybe I can meet her then," Mom continues.

"No, ma'am," Hunter replies with a scoff.

"I'm sure she's swamped. I know the feeling myself. I'm lucky if I can make it to half the meetings."

Mom's not picking up on the vibe Hunter and Lexi are putting off, and it's like I'm watching a train wreck happening in slow motion. The tension in the air is thickening with every additional question offered, but Mom is still oblivious. I don't know why, but I want to scream at her to stop.

"What do your mothers do for a living?" Mom presses on.

"Both my parents work for a large pharmaceutical company. Mom is the COO, while Dad oversees sales," Lexi responds immediately. "It's a lot of traveling, especially for Dad, but they love what they do."

My mother smiles in response then looks at Hunter expectantly. Hunter's looking to Lexi, though. She's shaking her head as if she's giving him permission to not respond.

"I wouldn't know," Hunter mumbles. "I haven't seen her in almost a decade."

There's the unspoken secret that was weighing so heavily between them. It must be a topic that Hunter doesn't like to discuss. Now, when the train has wrecked, everyone finally realizes the gravity of what we were dancing around for several minutes. The pain is visible on Hunter's face, and I can't help but feel sorry for his situation despite my apprehension toward him.

"Mom!" Serena snaps, suddenly irritated at the inquisition that led to Hunter's revelation.

"I had no idea," Mom protests. "I'm so sorry, Hunter."

The doorbell rings, interrupting the tense moment. Dad takes the opportunity to flee the awkwardness of the moment and greet the new arrivals.

89

Hunter's eyes sweep the room and finally meet mine. I should say something comforting, right? I may not understand his situation, but I know pain. When nothing comes out of my mouth, I hope he can at least read the look on my face. I see his vulnerability slip away, replaced with an apathetic look that likely fools most people - just not me. This time, Hunter is the one that abandons our connection when he turns to look out the large window just beyond the dinner table.

"What's with the somber mood?" Elijah booms as he struts into the kitchen. Mom drops the dish towel she was holding and greets Brady and him with a hug.

"We were just discussing my mother," Hunter informs him flatly.

"Oh …. Oooohhh," Elijah's mood immediately turns serious. He takes a moment to read the room before turning to me and smiling. "Hey, beautiful."

Despite observing Elijah compliment anyone in a skirt, I still can't help but smile back. He has too much charm for his own good.

"If anything, you should feel good about yourself. You didn't have your mother around, and you still turned out alright," Brady interjects after hugging Mom. "The pride of Indy Park."

"Shut up," Hunter chastises him.

"Industrial Park?" Dad chimes in curiously.

"Yeah, it's where I grew up," Hunter informs him.

"I work about a mile from there. It's an interesting place."

"A shit hole, you mean," Hunter responds with a scowl.

Lexi reaches for his hand, but Hunter manages to avoid her touch. All the walls are up now, and Hunter is edgy and on the defensive. Mom and Dad tense up when they hear him curse. They are anal about our choice of vocabulary, so I know they are fighting back the urge to correct him.

The Tucker Girls

It dawns on me that this is likely the real Hunter Bowden. The boy standing in the middle of the kitchen looks ready to fight if pushed. The fake persona of a rich kid with no cares in the world has been stripped away. From what Dad has told us in passing, Indy Park is a rough area. When we first moved here, he added an alarm to his car because his co-workers warned him about frequent break-ins. Is that why Hunter is familiar with patching himself up? Did he grow up fighting?

All the pieces begin to fall into place in my mind, and it just leaves me angry. Sure, I feel bad about him growing up without a mother, but my sympathy can't compete with the fire burning in me. He's phony even with Serena. By the look on her face, she's entirely stunned.

I've learned the hard way that avoiding your pain is a one-way ticket to self-implosion. It blew up in my face too, but at least I never pretended that everything was fine. I was brave enough to admit it to the world. Hunter is a coward.

As if I needed more confirmation, Brady greets Hunter with a slap on the shoulder, causing Hunter to let out a painful groan. It's the exact spot where he got cut while shielding me from the fight at school. When Brady asks if he's okay, Hunter lies about it being an injury lifting weights earlier in the day. I'm picking up quickly how Hunter ticks. I see right through his lies, and nothing infuriates me more.

CHAPTER NINE
Serena

I've never been so relieved at the sight of food. We all dish up and start eating, providing the much-needed distraction we'd all been looking for. The air is thick since Hunter dropped the bomb about his mother, and we can't seem to shake the tense cloud hovering over us. Brady mentioned that Hunter lives in Indy Park, and since then, Hunter has been guarded and withdrawn. His body is with us, but emotionally and mentally, he is thoroughly checked out.

To make matters worse, Brady attempted to give me a hug when he arrived, which I expertly dodged, and is still making eyes at me. *Sorry, no.* Brady threw himself between Hunter and me, earning him a well-deserved cold shoulder.

Yes, I'm still hung up on Hunter in the worst way. As much as I had planned to slow play this, I'm beginning to get frustrated with my progress. Hunter's taking some random girl to Homecoming. At the very least, I was expecting him to show up single.

Why can't this boy see what's right in front of him? I wouldn't have pressed him for anything more than a few dances had he just lowered his walls and given me the chance to go with him.

Lindsey insists that I'm infatuated with him. I can always trust her to tell me like it is, which I love about her. Well, most of the time I like that about her. Sometimes I want her to keep her facts to herself. Infatuation may be the appropriate term, though, because I got jealous of Lexi for simply standing close to Hunter. It was a momentary lapse of judgment because I love Lexi, and I know nothing is going on between them.

Speaking of Lindsey, she's busy brooding herself. Last year, I formed a habit of studying her eating habits when things got really bad, and I still examine her meals too closely. Things are much better now, so I should trust she's eating properly, except tonight, where her only fork movements are pushing food around on her plate. Is she regressing, and I didn't even notice? I can't recall her not eating a recent meal, so this must be a new development.

My attention is diverted when I catch Hunter gazing my way. I give him the warmest smile I can possibly manage because I want him to know that I don't care about any of what was said tonight; his mother, where he lives, or how much money his family has. None of that matters.

"Serena?" Brady interrupts my thoughts.

"Huh?"

"We were talking about the ski trip over winter break."

"Yeah! Sounds like you all are going to have a lot of fun."

Elijah makes big eyes at me, jerking his head slightly in my mother's direction. *Right!* I was supposed to ask permission tonight when the topic got brought up. I was so caught up in my head that I entirely forgot the plan we worked out through texts earlier in the day.

"Oh yeah! Mom, do you think I can tag along with them to Telluride?"

Mom gives me a look of annoyance, not appreciating being put on the spot like this. I know for a fact that it would be a solid 'No' if I asked her any other time. I don't bother asking Dad because he won't agree to anything unless Lindsey asks.

"Telluride? That's in Colorado, right?" Dad clarifies.

"Yes, sir," Brady responds cheerfully. "My parents rent a penthouse up there for two weeks every year. Between the flight and drive, it's only about a four-hour trip altogether. We only stay a week, though."

"As long as Brady's parents are there, I think that would be okay," Mom shocks the table with her approval. Even Lindsey looks up with surprise. I don't know if it's guilt over berating Hunter with questions, but I will take it. Lexi releases a squeal of excitement, likely matching my own.

I don't have the heart to inform Mom that Brady's parents won't be staying in the penthouse while we are there. It's not big enough to sleep all of us at one time. My guilt flickers and subsides quickly. I'm a responsible individual, and Lexi will make sure the boys behave - her words, not mine. They aren't just empty words, either. Lexi has a special place in each of their lives, so when she demands something, they fall in line.

"I'd like to meet all of your parents before you leave," Mom interjects.

"No problem. My mother will be eager to meet you as well," Brady responds, putting Mom's concern at ease.

"When would you leave?" Dad asks.

"December 27th. I will be back on January 2nd."

"You'll miss the school art exhibit," Lindsey states with a wounded face.

Shoot! I forgot that I'd promised Lindsey I would attend the exhibit with her. Lindsey's eyes retreat to her uneaten food, attempting to conceal the disappointment that was revealed briefly.

"Are you planning on participating?" Lexi inquires.

"Yeah, I'm working on two pieces."

"The exhibit will stay up through the first week of January. We will still be able to see your work on display."

"It's fine. It's not a big deal," Lindsey mutters dejectedly, but I know she's hurt that I won't be there for the first night.

The Tucker Girls

"Lindsey painted that," Hunter finally speaks up, pointing to Lindsey's piece on the wall and breaking his prolonged silence. It's really sweet that he calls out her work, though Lindsey doesn't bother looking up from her plate to acknowledge his gesture.

"That's sick," Brady interjects.

"Yeah, I love the texture," Lexi chimes in.

"That's what I said," Hunter responds, nodding in agreement.

"So you sing *and* paint?" Lexi asks in admiration. "What can't you do?"

"Be a phony ass person," Lindsey responds with bitterness that surprises the entire table.

What the hell is wrong with her? She was fine just a few moments ago, but now she's staring at Hunter like she wants to rip his head off. My head is spinning as I try to make sense of her sudden mood shift. Sure, Lindsey can be capricious sometimes, but she is never rude. Something is eating away at her composure, though.

"Lindsey Tucker!" Mom shouts, her voice carrying a mix of shock and displeasure.

Lindsey drops her fork, which clangs against her still full plate, and walks away from the table. Too stunned to even know how to respond, I look at my parents hoping they have an answer.

"What was that all about?" Lexi asks, her gaze directed at Hunter as if he has some insight. He simply shrugs his shoulders while staring intently at where Lindsey exited the room.

"I'm very sorry about that," Dad speaks up, his face conveying his confusion. "I don't know where that came from. I'll go talk to her."

Of course, Dad's going to chase after his favorite daughter. Consider me not shocked.

"Doug, let her be," Mom commands, her voice dripping with frustration.

Placing my head in my hands, I cringe at how terrible this evening has gone. It's my worst nightmare come true. My dysfunctional family is on full display, and my new friends have gotten front-row seats to the show.

"So, what's for dessert?" Elijah chimes in, smiling in a ridiculously eager way, forcing my lips to turn up ever so slightly. He's entirely unphased by our family drama.

"I made some tiramisu," Mom replies, hopping up to grab it from the fridge.

"Sounds perfect," Lexi responds, glancing over with a sympathetic look.

No. Nothing about tonight is perfect. It's an entire mess of a night that I hope doesn't sour the one good thing I have going here in Texas.

"Can I walk you to your car?" I ask after Hunter has thanked my parents for dinner with one foot out the front door.

The evening is wrapping up, and I want to try to salvage it in any way I can. Not only do I want a private moment with him, but I also want to avoid Brady, who is lingering on the front porch. I know what Brady wants, and he can forget it. I'm not going to Homecoming with him. His persistence may require me to pull the Lexi card. She's the only one that can likely talk some sense into him.

"Sure," Hunter concedes, holding his hand out for me to lead the way. I purposely avoid eye contact with Brady as I brush past him.

Once I make it to Hunter's jeep, I lean my back against the driver's side door and turn to face him. The person I'm looking at now doesn't resemble the boy that I've come to know since August. All that's left is a shell of a person with clouded eyes that are impenetrable.

"I don't know what to even say."

Hunter nods silently while looking at the keys he's flipping in his hands. I was hoping he would tell me it wasn't a big deal, but I can see that's just not true. What I wouldn't give to be able to tap into his thoughts that are locked away and closely guarded. I fight back the urge to reach out and touch him.

I'm not sure if it's this conversation or the chill of the night, but I feel cold down to my core. A shiver runs through my body, and Hunter must notice because he pulls me into an embrace. With his arms wrapped tightly around me, I lean into him and enjoy the warmth that ripples through me.

Suddenly, everything is right in my world. I've never been this close to him - except if you count the time I was drunk beyond belief - and it's more than I ever wanted. I inhale his scent and commit it to my memory. Turning my head, I allow the tip of my nose to brush along his neckline, causing Hunter to tighten his hold on me.

Hunter tenses as Brady's Land Rover peels away in anger. I know their bro code requires Hunter to back off, but I refuse to accept the two guys' decision without my consent. Brady can be pissed off all he wants. I will not apologize for being in Hunter's arms right now.

"I am so sorry for how tonight turned out. This was just a terrible idea. My mom doesn't know when to mind her own business. Honestly, she's so nosy sometimes. I promise you she will be more chill next time."

"Serena."

I look up and meet his gaze, which has softened. A thrill runs through me as I witness his walls start coming down. My heart hammers uncontrollably, threatening to jump out of my chest as I take in this beautiful boy. Only one thought prevails in this moment; I want his lips on mine. Every other bad thing that has happened tonight fades into the depths of my mind.

"It's fine. You have nothing to be sorry about. My mother abandoned me. Your mother is a saint in comparison to mine. I'm the one who ruined the evening by bringing up my family issues. I could have easily told your mother that I didn't want to talk about my drama, and that would have been the end of it."

I nod as I listen to him explain his perspective, but I can't say that I agree with his assessment. He's not why tonight turned into a series of horrible events.

"Then there was my sister …."

"Again, not a big deal. Lindsey's justified in being pissed off at me. I don't know what I did tonight, but it's likely my fault," Hunter admits as he brushes a strand of hair behind my ear. "Let's look at the positive. Your mother gave you permission to go skiing with us in Colorado."

"Highlight of the night for sure."

"So tonight wasn't a total wash."

"Mmmhmmm," is all that slips out of my mouth. My mind is consumed with his lips. "Kiss me."

"What?" Hunter chokes out, caught off guard by my comment. To be honest, so am I. I've never been this forward with a boy, but I've never had to ask for a kiss, either. My plea just slipped out. I guess my lips have a mind of their own when it comes to him.

After an inquisitive look passes across his face, Hunter leans closer and my breath hitches. The slow-developing moment requires my full restraint to not guide him to me. Just when I think he's going to close the remaining distance, he lifts his chin and kisses my forehead, much to my exasperation.

I let out an audible groan. Allowing my head to lean back against his car door, I close my eyes and murmur curses in my head. I've never wanted something so bad in my entire life, and Hunter chooses to tease me instead of granting my wish.

"Next time, be more specific," Hunter whispers against my ear. "You only asked for a kiss. I got to choose where."

Hunter chuckles as he steps back and gives me some space. A chill immediately rushes over me once more, and all I want is for him to wrap his arms around me again. We part ways while I still have some dignity intact, and thankfully the cold air helps restore some of my senses. I completely lose my wits around Hunter.

As I walk up the driveway, I notice the curtain shift abruptly in my sister's room. Was Lindsey spying on Hunter and me? Balling up my fists, I march towards the front door with more zeal. Lindsey and I are about to have an unpleasant discussion about how she's been acting lately.

CHAPTER TEN
Hunter

Ulla Meyer wins our Homecoming football game in epic fashion. Elijah slips through a tackle and finds the end zone as time expires, sending the crowd into a frenzy. It's only our second win of the season, but that will not dampen our mood. Having a host of friends that graduated last year attending the game elevated its importance to a must-win. I can't spot Elijah or Brady in the dogpile that forms on the field, but I can only imagine they are ecstatic at the outcome.

This feels like a reward for the last two weeks. Tension has been thick since dinner at the Tuckers' house. Brady has been distant, still fuming about me hugging Serena before leaving that evening, and I am entirely fed up with his angst. Thankfully, I've poured myself into a research paper and science project, which has occupied the little free time I typically have. I don't want to dwell on our strained relationship at the moment, especially with him acting like a petulant child. Between school and work, days are flying by.

Serena and I have continued this awkward dance that's become our norm. We are both attracted to one another, but I'm keeping my distance until Brady relinquishes his claim; although if he keeps up his pissy mood, I may change that decision. Serena continues to punish Brady with a chilly attitude, which has thrown my circle into a tailspin. Lexi has felt the need to take Brady's side because no one else seems willing. This whole dibs fiasco is threatening my family, and that's certainly put me in a poor mood as well.

The Tucker Girls

Hannah: Just arrived. You're still picking me up here, right?

Hannah's text comes in just as I pull up to my house. She's driving me crazy, needing multiple confirmations at every step of the process. We'd already agreed this morning that I would pick her up from Serena's house before heading to the dance. Elise wants pictures before we leave. Despite our talk, it seems Hannah needs to double-check - *again*.

Rich never manned up and asked her to the dance, and Hannah couldn't conjure up the courage to just ask him. It was only a minor nuisance that I had to follow through on my promise, seeing as I was planning on going stag anyways. Still, it quickly became a major inconvenience when Hannah and I started working through the details.

What am I wearing? What time am I picking her up? When will I have her back home? Are we eating before the event? Is she expected to dance? Is she allowed to dance with Rich if he asks? All of these questions were practical. I'd provide answers, but twenty-four hours later, she'd want to check to see if the plan had changed. Then more questions would pop into her mind, leaving me with a second part-time job answering all of her concerns. The process would start all over again the next day. By Wednesday, it was taking everything in me to not snap back. Lindsey seemed to find it humorous but wasn't willing to pull her friend aside and tell her to stop being overbearing. In fact, I'm suspicious of whether Lindsey is encouraging the behavior just to torture me.

Hunter: I will be there shortly. Getting changed real quick. No more questions. You know the plan.

Hannah: Sorry! I will stop.

The Tucker Girls

No, she won't. The questions never stop. I am writing it off as extreme nerves, as Hannah has never attended a school dance.

My attention is ripped away from Hannah as I step through my front door. An awful, stomach-turning smell assaults me before I cross the threshold. Had I been a normal kid, living a typical teenage life, I would have no idea what to make of this odor. Unfortunately, I'd grown accustomed to finding scenes like this over the years.

The small den is littered with crushed beer cans strewn all around and a pizza box spilling onto the floor. Pete, who likely knocked the box over when collapsing, is passed out drunk on the sofa. I don't need to examine him to know that he's pissed himself - and the couch. I'm guessing he likely did other involuntary things as I detect traces of fecal matter lingering in the air.

What kind of person gets so drunk that he loses control of his bowels? The answer is my pathetic excuse for a father. To be honest, I prefer him unconscious. If I didn't rely on him to pay essential bills, I'd opt for this to be his permanent state of being.

For a split second, I consider dragging him to his room to contain the smell, but I don't have time to deal with this situation. Pete's an angry drunk too, so waking him from his stupor would lead to a confrontation that wouldn't turn out well for him. He'd get in my face, and I'd have to deck him. Once I start hitting him, it's difficult to stop. I tap into a deep well of anger that lingers from days when I wasn't big enough to fight back. Don't let anyone tell you miracles don't happen because it's truly unbelievable I haven't ended up in jail for homicide.

Pulling out my keys, I unlock the multiple deadlocks on my bedroom door and slip inside. Contrary to the remainder of the house, my room is neat and organized. This is my sanctuary. The one place I can hide from the chaos of life is on the other side of my bedroom door. I'm obsessive about keeping the small room safe and tidy.

Once dressed, I unlock my phone and skim my social media app to discover my friends posting photos with their dates before the dance. Elijah shared a photo with his parents, himself and his date. His mother is the mayor, so they must keep up appearances of a happy family for the town. No one would ever guess that he despises these types of photoshoots by the brilliant smile he's flashing at the camera.

Lexi shares a photo with her mother on their front porch. Brady is even in a photo with his parents underneath their gazebo, which catches me entirely off guard. His parents are never in town. Scrolling through picture after picture, I see couples and families smiling in anticipation of the big event this evening. I try to remind myself that social media isn't real, but damn it hurts to know that I don't have parents available to even pose for a phony photo.

My stomach pulses with pain, and I feel a tremble ripple through my chest. I wander over to Pete until I'm looking down at my father, unable to even process the horrific smell emanating from his body. All I feel is an unbearable ache that threatens to devour me whole.

"Hey, *Dad*," my voice quakes with raw emotion. "You ready to take our photo? I know pictures aren't really your thing, but we need to try and fit in. At least give the appearance that we are one big, happy family like everyone else at my school does. They have to wonder why I never post anything with you in it, so here's our chance to change that."

The trembling is getting worse as I stare at his motionless body. I am clenching and unclenching my fists, unsure of what I'm doing, monologuing with his lifeless form. I can't tell you the last time we even had a conversation with one another.

The Tucker Girls

"Why can't I have a minute of normal from you? I'm not asking for much," I continue, a tear escaping down my cheek. "Why can't you love me? Why? Am I that unlovable? That big of a disappointment to you that you don't have an ounce of anything to give me? And why did you make her leave? I *needed* her. I needed Mom, and you ran her off, you sick bastard."

A choked sob flies out of my mouth, and I feel a surge of anger flood me at the realization that I'm crying over this man again. I swore I'd never shed another tear because of him. A fierce scream rages out as I flip the coffee table over, sending its contents scattering to the floor. Grabbing the table by its leg, I sling it into the nearby wall. Destruction ensues, with both the table and the drywall in complete disarray. Staring at the damage I caused, my chest heaves as I try to catch my breath.

"I. Hate. *You*," I grunt out, furious with Pete.

Sucking in erratic breaths, I storm out the door before I wreck the entire house. Lost in my thoughts, I don't recall anything about the drive to the Tucker house. Gripping the steering wheel tight, I allow myself a few moments to calm down before I knock on the front door. My head isn't in the right place for a celebration, but I gave my word to Hannah, and I have to honor it. I have to be a person people can rely on, unlike Pete.

I'm in no condition for a dance, and I can't even muster a smile as Elise greets me warmly.

"Hunter! Great to see you again! Please come in."

"Thank you, ma'am."

"You clean up nicely," she states as I step into the Tucker house. "The girls were just getting ready to leave, so you arrived just in time. I want to get a picture of you and Serena before they head out."

Serena is planning on riding to the dance with Lexi. I nod in acknowledgment of Elise's comment, and she proceeds to retreat to the kitchen while I wait in the foyer. I'm sure I'm putting off a vibe that I'm not interested in small talk. I'm shaken to the core from my breakdown at home. I desperately need to numb away the aching pain in my chest. My first instinct is to get blackout drunk, but the mental picture of my father lying prostrate on the couch lingers in my head. Even if I had a drink in my hand, I don't think I'd be able to consume it. The thought makes my stomach twist into knots. The man has ruined everything for me, and I can't escape his legacy.

"Hunter!" Lexi calls out in a concerned voice, snapping my attention back to reality. Standing directly in front of me, I get the feeling Lexi had been trying to talk to me, and I'd been entirely oblivious.

"Hey. Sorry, I have a lot on my mind. You look beautiful," I state as I take her in. She's stunning in a midnight blue dress.

Lexi doesn't bother acknowledging my compliment, her concerned eyes busy assessing me. She once told me that I have a particular look following an encounter with Pete. I don't doubt it is written all over my face now.

"Are you okay?"

"Hey, Hunter!" Serena interrupts as she walks into the foyer. "Are you ready for some pictures?"

I wordlessly nod. The truth is that I'm not okay, and Lexi can sense it, but I want her to enjoy the dance uninhibited by my family drama. Taking a deep breath, I turn back towards Lexi and flash the best smile I can manage at the moment. She deserves to have fun tonight.

"Serena, you look unbelievable as always," I state, blown away by how amazing she looks in her copper-colored dress that stops right above her knees.

"You don't look so bad yourself," she reciprocates, twiddling my white tie between her fingers with a gleam in her eye. I'm wearing a black collared shirt, with sleeves rolled up my forearms and dark gray slacks, all compliments of Brady. He allows me to raid his closet a couple of times a year for clothes he loses interest in.

Small talk ensues, and I find myself quickly zoning out once more. Elise puts us through the obligatory photoshoot, and I hope I put on a convincing smile. Each camera click rubs salt into my emotional wounds from earlier in the evening. Lexi and Serena leave at some point, but I can't tell you when. I'm standing on the porch, scanning through social media once more because I'm a glutton for punishment.

When I see Serena post our most recent photos, I am surprised at how happy I managed to appear. I guess the deception of the platform finally settles in. Who knows what's genuine from the slew of posts that flood my screen? Maybe none of it is authentic. Perhaps it's just one giant experiment where we bluff as best we can, attempting to fool everyone into believing that you possess the ideal. It's the great deception of our generation.

An ice-cold object slips into my grip, stealing my attention back to the present moment. I discover I'm now holding a water bottle, but I don't recall asking for a drink. Honestly, I can't remember anything significant since Serena and Lexi drove off. The fog is lifting, though, and I find Lindsey glaring up at me. I assume she's the one who handed me the water, but I have no idea why she would bother.

"What's the water for?"

"In case you're thirsty," she grumbles, her voice combative as usual.

"Here," I say as I attempt to return it. "I'm good."

"No, actually, you're not. Just hold onto it."

"Lindsey, do you mind if I grab one from your fridge," Hannah chimes in, catching me by surprise. I wasn't aware she had arrived.

The Tucker Girls

"No, not at all," Lindsey replies, the edge entirely gone when she speaks to her friend.

With my entire focus shifting to my surroundings, I notice the white frilly dress Hannah is wearing. Her curly hair and makeup look professionally done.

"You look great, Hannah!" I call out as she walks through the open door into the kitchen. Hannah blushes as she turns to accept my compliment with a wordless smile.

"You already told her that," Lindsey gripes, shaking her head in frustration.

"You can never say that enough to a lady," I counter.

"Except you had no idea what you were saying before."

"Did I tell you how beautiful you look?"

Lindsey halts digging through her purse to look up at me. I realize that she's wearing makeup. Miss plain Jane typically does everything possible to look unnoticeable, but tonight's different. She didn't do anything fancy with her hair; she just pulled some of it away from her face in a braid. Her bluish-gray floral dress completes a look that is entirely unfamiliar to me. Lindsey is as breathtaking as her sister when she isn't trying to hide her beauty.

"No, you didn't."

"Good."

Lindsey scoffs at my response. Her expectant face falls when I fail to give her the compliment she was hoping for. Her focus returns to her purse, but this time she digs with vigor closer to thrashing. I begin to feel sorry for the jab. Although her less-than-sunny disposition grates me, my comment was a low blow.

"Lindsey, you look stunning," I concede, halting her search again.

Lindsey steals a glance at me out of the corner of her eye, then pulls out a lip gloss tube and turns toward the front door. She won't even acknowledge what I said despite wanting to hear it. Her odd behavior has me entirely perplexed. It's like she hates herself for needing it.

Before she can sneak away, I catch her by the arm. The impulsive move was unplanned, and I also caught Lindsey by surprise. Her body stiffens and her breath hitches when my hand comes into contact with her. It's the first time I've touched her since the brawl at school.

"You know you would be just as attractive without the sleeves," I state, unsure where this comment is coming from. It's bothered me for weeks that Lindsey chose to run away the minute I laid eyes on her scars during our dinner weeks ago.

Lindsey's eyes widen as she remains planted in place. Her lips part as if she is going to make a remark, but nothing comes out. I break contact with her and slowly lift my hand away. The world seems to stand still as I wait for her to react. With this girl, you can never tell what's coming next; it could be a smile or a fist.

We stay frozen in place for what feels like an eternity with our eyes locked. Finally, she forcefully swallows and tears her gaze away from mine.

"Don't touch me," Lindsey mutters weakly.

"Sure thing, princess."

Once again, I'm standing on the porch alone staring off into the affluent neighborhood. The cookie-cutter homes have their porches lit tonight, contrasting the dark alley where I grew up.

Lindsey doesn't reappear until Stephen arrives, and she proceeds to ignore me entirely. It's clear that mentioning her scars triggers her, so I willingly take every opportunity to give her space. I have no idea what made me bring them up right before the dance. It was poor timing on my part. I'm emotionally spent and ready for the night to be over before it has even begun.

The Tucker Girls

Stephen stumbles over his feet as he spies Lindsey for the first time tonight. The poor guy, accustomed to seeing the same Lindsey I do at school every day, quickly realizes he's out of his league and is entirely inept around her. Stephen is making a valiant attempt to say something, but all that comes out is a broken, stuttered greeting. The cringe-worthy scene provides some comedic relief that I desperately needed.

Despite his blunder, Lindsey appears to find Stephen's struggles charming. I have to do a double take as I watch her offer a shy smile. Choking back laughter, I catch glares from the two bashful lovers.

"Hannah, what are your responsibilities as Hunter's date if he is crowned Homecoming King?" Lindsey asks.

I'm not going to be Homecoming King; Elijah will take that crown. My foreknowledge is one of the many benefits of having Janna on the Homecoming Court Committee. She tipped us off after votes were tallied earlier in the week.

The uncertainty that crosses Hannah's face preempts a million questions ready to burst forth from her mouth. I have to get ahead of this before the onslaught begins.

"No," I state firmly at Hannah. Her head tilts as if I am saying no to only a single question, and she's moving on to the next one. "No. I mean it. No more questions. You are driving me insane."

Hannah's face falls in disappointment. She reluctantly withholds her inquisition for now, but I know it's only a temporary reprieve. Based on Lindsey's smirk, she was purposefully instigating an interrogation to punish me.

"Now might be a good time to share the *other* thing," Lindsey says with a gleam in her eye.

Whatever the other thing is, I know I will not like the revelation. Hannah wipes her palms against her dress before looking up at me doe-eyed.

"I don't dance."

"Come again," I grunt out.

"Well, I don't really like to dance."

Lindsey is enjoying eavesdropping on our conversation far too much. From the corner of my eye, I see her body jiggle trying to hold back laughter. It's like she wants Hannah to push me to the breaking point. Why? Is she still trying to get me to back out of the deal?

"You do realize you are going to a dance?" I ask, baffled at the news. "What are you planning on doing at *the dance*?"

"I don't know. Everyone else is going, so I wanted to go too."

An audible exhale leaks out of me. Why did I ever agree to this?

Lindsey's on the verge of tears at my dismay. I suddenly realize that she's no longer ignoring my antics; she's hitting back. A smirk crosses my face when it registers that I got what I wanted for the past few weeks. She's stepping out of the bleachers and engaging in my game which has been very one-sided at school.

Seeing her smiling in satisfaction is a relief in a lot of ways. I guess being ignored was bothering me more than I realized, and the back-and-forth jabs feel more familiar to me. Hell, Elijah, Brady and I live to pester one another. This adversarial relationship feels entirely foreign to her, though. The more I watch her, the more I realize that I'm the only person she shows any animosity toward, and that intrigues me more than it should.

CHAPTER ELEVEN
Lindsey

"Everyone is staring at me," Hannah complains as she finds me sitting at one of the tables on the outskirts of the room.

My feet are killing me from dancing the last two hours away. I'm having a fantastic time with Stephen - even better than I could have imagined. We've had a blast dancing and hanging out with some of our classmates. Stephen's grown up here, so he knows almost all the juniors in attendance. This loud, overcrowded scene is what I have typically avoided most of my high school years. I find the chaos to be a bit disorienting, but tonight has been surprisingly fun.

Unfortunately, I don't think Hannah has had as good of a time as I have. The minute she walked in, she became a target for all the envious girls in school who are constantly pining over Hunter. They likely have no clue who Hannah is because she has this unbelievable ability to go unnoticed, but that didn't stop them from throwing ugly looks her way. She's flown under the radar at this school, but tonight that all changed. She's been thrust into the spotlight and clearly not thrilled about it.

The jealousy meter is ridiculously high, but it's slowly calming down now that Hunter abandoned Hannah to dance with Serena. Who saw Hunter ditching Hannah midway through the night? This girl right here. He'll do the same to Serena. I get the sense that commitment is low on his priority list, especially when it threatens his enjoyment.

"Just ignore them. They're just jealous," I reply, shrugging my shoulders in an attempt to downplay it. The negative attention would also bother me, but I don't want to add to Hannah's anxiety by admitting that fact. "Just own it. They'd kill for a chance to be you tonight."

"Everybody but you."

"Got that right. I would have rather shown up naked than with Hunter. He's the bane of my existence."

"Ouch. That's a little harsh, don't you think?"

Her comment gives me pause. Looking down at the floor, I waver on whether she may have a point. I've been over-eager to trash Hunter every chance I get. He's arrogant, phony and altogether obnoxious.

My last school introduced me to guys like him, and they were part of the reason I needed a fresh start. His constant pestering in Trig is beyond childish, but that doesn't mean I have to stoop to his level and disparage him. I can be better than that. I need to swallow down my resentment and attempt to write off his sheer existence. It's easier said than done when everywhere I turn, he's there. I can't escape Hunter, and it's clearly affecting me.

The sick part is that a piece of me doesn't want to escape him, which terrifies me the most. Don't get me wrong. The guy Serena adores - the confident, carefree, life-of-the-party boy - is barely a blip on my radar. It's the broken boy, who is silently suffering, that inexplicably calls to me. The term that comes to mind when I see through his charade is a beautiful disaster.

This is why I broke down and saved him tonight. He was suffering and trapped in his own head, and I know how that feels. The look I used to see in the mirror every day was plastered all over his face. So instead of walking away, I used a technique I learned in therapy and forced him to hold an ice-cold water bottle. The sensation grounded him and pulled him out of his abyss.

I should have left Hunter alone, but I was weak and gave in to my impulses. Reaching down and touching my forearm, I can still feel where he grabbed me. It's not that he was forceful that my skin still tingles. His touch was surprisingly tender. It's because of the pleasant chills that raced up and down my arm that has me unable to forget the encounter. My body betrayed me by enjoying our brief connection, and I don't want to think about what it means.

Don't go there, Lindsey. Stay where it's safe.

I look across the floor and see Stephen laughing with Carlos, and a smile lifts my face. Stephen is the type of boy I need. He's kind, caring, funny and intelligent. Serena's boy is poison, and maybe I should keep being harsh so that he continues to believe I hate him because I'd rather him think that than for him to suspect there's a tiny sliver of me that is conflicted. A *very*, very small fraction of a sliver.

Who knows what he would do if Hunter knew how much he scares me? When the fight broke out in the hallway weeks ago, I started falling into depths of darkness, and it was Hunter who I clung to for dear life. He brought me back with his whispers of encouragement and a feather-light touch, and nothing infuriates me more. I was a pathetic puddle of emotions in front of him. *Ugh*! Why did it have to be him who saved me?

"Maybe," is all I can respond to Hannah's assessment. I don't want her to think I'm a terrible person, but I decide to not stop the outward cruelty towards Hunter. He will eventually get the hint and leave me alone for good. It's what's best for both of us.

"Oh no!" Hannah groans, leaning her forehead into my shoulder.

Looking up, I notice Hunter walking over, and I feel the rollercoaster of emotions slam into me again. Thankfully, my contempt overpowers the other emotions that bubble up. What I don't understand is why is Hannah anxious about Hunter coming toward us? It doesn't make sense until I see that he's accompanied by Rich.

"Hey Hannah," Rich says meekly, barely audible over the drumming beat of the music.

"Hi."

"I was wondering …. well …. I was wondering if you wanted to dance? With me, that is. Will you dance with me?"

Rich is so unbelievably nervous that his hands are trembling uncontrollably. Hannah obviously doesn't like to dance, but she has to make an exception because the boy she's crushing for finally broke down and made a move. She hesitates for a long, cringeworthy minute that has me convinced she will turn him down.

Come on, Hannah. Go for it.

"Yes," Hannah finally replies, standing up and giving me a nervous glance.

I slap her rear as she starts to walk away, giving her the biggest grin ever. I couldn't be more excited for Hannah. I know she's dreamt of this for over a year.

"Get it, girl!" I call out, only to see her flash me an annoyed glance over her shoulder. I give her a cheesy grin and two thumbs up until she turns back to Rich and follows him into the crowd of students.

Forget the fun that Stephen and I had tonight. This is peak happiness; watching my friend have her moment that only happens in the movies. I am over-the-top giddy for Hannah until I look up and see Hunter's massive grin. Sure enough, he's watching Rich and Hannah dance as if he made it happen.

"Take that stupid grin off your face," I demand, anger immediately boiling in my stomach. My momentary joy is ripped away, and mean Lindsey is back with a vengeance. I have no idea why, but it bothers me that he feels like he accomplished this feat. If anything, he made things more difficult for Hannah. Rich backed off when Hannah mentioned that she had another offer to take her to Homecoming.

"You've got to be kidding me! You're a real piece of work, you know that? You can't even accept that I got Hannah and Rich together."

"It was going to happen eventually. All you did was muddy the water."

"Bull!" he barks out the challenge. "I was the catalyst. I gave Rich the push he needed."

"*Okay,*" I reply with heavy sarcasm.

As I push out of my chair and try to escape to another part of the gymnasium, he reaches out and grabs my wrist.

Not again! Why does he keep touching me?

I feel the warm, addictive sensation ripple up my arm, making me weak. I'd never experienced anything like this, and my stupid body aches for more contact.

My breath catches again, which infuriates me to no end. A war rises within me when I realize I could easily break free from his grasp, but I'm allowing it for some inexplicable reason. I take hold of some of my inwardly directed anger - at my reluctance to remove his hand - to motivate me to action, and I rip my wrist out of his grasp. It was a delayed reaction, and I suspect he noticed.

"Stop. Touching. Me."

"Woah," Hunter draws back, giving me desperately needed space. "I'm sorry. I shouldn't have done that."

"You're right. You shouldn't have."

"I just …. I just don't get it sometimes. I thought we had a breakthrough earlier."

"A breakthrough?" I ask, puzzled.

"You were pissed at me, so I apologized. You were still pissed and ignored me, so I pestered you until you couldn't ignore me any longer. I thought we got past all that tonight, though. You weren't taking my shit and hit back - thoroughly enjoying yourself while you were at it too - so I assumed we were good now."

"You assumed wrong."

"What is it, Sweats? What about me is so impossible for you to tolerate?"

"Hmmm …. pretty much everything, especially that nickname."

Hunter takes a step forward, invading my space once more. His hazel eyes dig for answers as he intently stares down at me. My heart rate begins skipping, and I nervously peer over his shoulder in hopes that Stephen is coming to save me.

"I helped your friend bag her crush. That has to be worth something, right?"

"It would if you actually accomplished what you claim."

"I'm trying here, Lindsey. Let's put all of this drama behind us and start over fresh - for Serena. She doesn't want us at each other's throats."

For Serena. Out of everything he just said, those were the words that hit me like a kick straight to my stomach. That's why he has been going out of his way to interact with me. It's also why he sacrificially protected me in the chaos of the fight. My mouth is suddenly dry, and I feel lightheaded. Once again, I lean into my anger because now it's all that I have right now.

"*No.* I know it's difficult to wrap your head around, but there are actually people in this world that don't bow down to you. I have *zero* interest in being friends or even acquaintances. You should just stop trying. It's better if we just forget that we ever met."

The hardening of his face tells me my words stung. Good, maybe now he will back off. The fact that he did every decent thing for Serena makes me want to punch this attractive boy right in the jaw. When Hunter stares me down, I feel the need to speak up again to avoid this uncomfortable silence.

"Here's what we're going to do. You will tell Serena that you accomplished your mission: we are best buds. I will back up your story, and you won't have to waste another minute of your life on me."

"*Fine.*"

His meager answer catches me entirely off guard. I'm thrown by his poker face, which gives me no indication of what is going on in his head. A flood of emotions sweeps over me again. It's a mix of regret, fear and relief swelled into a single thread, making my head swirl with confusion. Is he agreeing to leave me alone for good? What if that's not what I really want?

No, this *is* what I want and need. I haven't felt this kind of emotional turmoil in a long time, and I hate every second of it. I'm afraid I will spiral into my own abyss again, and I can't let that happen. I won't force my family to sacrifice everything to give me a clean slate again.

"Fine," I echo somberly.

"I'm sorry I touched you. I won't do that again."

His eyes slide down from my face, spying me rubbing my scars. It's a nervous habit of mine that I need to kick. I'm suddenly terribly self-conscious and need to escape.

"I'm going to dance," I state, brushing past Hunter.

"Oh, Stephen just went to the bathroom," he points out.

"I'll go find someone else," I mutter, scanning the room and finding the nearest boy. I march towards the guy with shaggy, brunette hair walking towards the refreshments table. I've never seen him before, but he will have to do. Anything to allow me to flee Hunter.

"Lindsey, stop," I hear Hunter call out, but it's too late. I've already made up my mind. This is so unlike me, but I don't care. I'm desperate to get away from the boy that wrecks me.

"Hey!" I call out, grabbing the boy by the arm. "Let's dance."

The stranger leers over my body before agreeing with a silent nod. Wow, this guy is a complete pig. It feels disgusting to allow him to stare at my chest, but I'm desperate for a dance partner. Beggars can't be choosers. As soon as this song ends, I will ditch this stranger and never have to interact with him again.

CHAPTER TWELVE
Serena

As we all exit the gymnasium following the dance, I spy Hunter walking several feet ahead with his keys in hand. It's the first time I've seen him since we'd danced about an hour ago. Before I can catch him, Brady slides up next to me and falls in stride. I've successfully avoided him most of the night, but my luck just ran out.

"There you are," Brady greets me with a smile.

"Here I am."

My face must indicate my lack of enthusiasm because Brady's smile dissipates quickly. He really does have an attractive face, but it's not Hunter's face. Lexi keeps encouraging me to give Brady a shot, but I have an unparalleled intensity to my focus, and I don't let distractions get in the way of what I want. It's what allows me to excel in academics, but I've also decided to apply it to my love life.

"I was really hoping I'd get the chance to dance with you, but it almost felt like you were avoiding me."

"*Huh.*"

I mean, what else am I supposed to say? That was precisely what I was doing. Guilty as charged. Part of me wants to soften the blow, but another part wants to tell him to get a clue. So instead, I don't do either. I simply grunt out my one-word reply.

If I wanted to go easy on him, I would tell him I thought about dancing with him for a solid minute. A selfish and fleeting thought crept in to use Brady to make Hunter jealous, but I squashed it quickly. I don't want to pour gasoline on their boy drama. Things have already been tense the last few weeks after I called dibs on myself.

"Well, there's always the Winter Gala."

"Yeah? When's that taking place?"

"This year, it will be the third week in January. The format of that dance is different, though."

"How so?" I ask as I keep my eyes trained on Hunter. He's still up ahead, but we are gaining on him. It's nearly impossible catching up with anyone while wearing these heels. I want to ask Hunter if he will drive me home. Brady is only getting a fraction of my attention, though I am intrigued about this other dance he's talking about.

"Well, for starters, it's more formal attire. The event is an important fundraiser for the school, so they go all out and have us purchase tickets. They have a live band and usually some epic theme. Also, the girls invite the guys. Speaking of which, I'm available if you want to go ahead and lock me in now," Brady flashes his gorgeous smile again.

"Brady, I hate to break it to you, but I'm not going to be inviting you. I'm taking Hunter," I reply flatly.

"Wait. So you've already asked him?" Brady inquires in a shocked tone, his shoulders tensing at the sound of his friend's name.

"Nope, but I'm going to right now. See you around!"

Scurrying away before Brady can take another pass, I catch up to Hunter without breaking an ankle. I slide my arm in his, catching him by surprise.

"Hey there," I greet him. "You weren't trying to sneak off without saying goodbye, were you?"

"No. Never," he replies with a grin.

I love the sound of his raspy voice. No seventeen-year-old should have a voice like that. I practically swoon every time I hear it.

"Where's Lex?"

"She is hanging around to help Janna clean up. Did she not tell you? Do you need me to drop you off?"

"Yes, please. That would be great. Is Hannah meeting you at your car?"

"Nope. Hannah is riding home with Rich."

"*Wow*. When did that happen?" I ask, leaning my head against Hunter's shoulder. He doesn't seem to mind the gesture, and it feels natural.

"Rich finally broke down and invited her to dance. Hell froze over."

"Ha! Good for him. It's about time he stepped up to the plate. You know, maybe he could give you a few pointers."

"Oh, is that right?"

"Yes. You never know. There might be some poor, hapless girl out there waiting for you to get the courage to ask her out."

My comment is successful in getting a deep laugh out of Hunter.

"You're hardly hapless."

"Please tell me more."

"Well, you're clearly desperate for a compliment," Hunter retorts, earning him a sharp elbow to the ribs.

I sneak a glance at him and notice that he's smiling just like me. We come to the end of the sidewalk that leads to the parking lot, and I tug on Hunter's arm to signal us to stop.

"Hey, before we head out, I'm going to check in with Lindsey."

Pulling my phone out, I shoot her a text.

Serena: You ok? Are you riding home with Stephen?

Lindsey: Yep! I think so. He's going to drop me off on the way to hang out with the guys.

The Tucker Girls

Before I can put my phone back in my clutch, it buzzes again with a new text.

Lindsey: Actually, can I ride with you? Or is it too late? If you've already left, don't worry about it.

Serena: No, it's fine. We're out in front of the school by the flagpole.

"Lindsey needs a ride. Do you mind her coming too?"

"If I say I do mind …." Hunter starts before I frown disapprovingly at him. "I'm kidding. It's fine."

We wait about five minutes, discussing the events of the night. Elijah was crowned Homecoming King as we all expected. Claire Lamanory is the Homecoming Queen, which garnered mixed reactions. I don't know her well enough to have an opinion on the matter. Hunter emphasizes how much time she spent lobbying for the crown, insinuating she earned it through hard work. I guess that resonates with me on some level.

Stephen and Lindsey catch sight of me waving them down, and I can't help but gawk as the two say goodnight to one another. Stephen sweetly takes hold of her hand as they talk. I'm out of earshot and can't hear what they say, but I get a good feeling about their general vibe. Lindsey needs a win in a bad way. She's never been on a date before, and after a rough sophomore year, it would be great for her to have a chance at love.

"They make a cute couple," I state, motioning towards Lindsey and Stephen.

"Hmmm. Stephen's a stiff, but Lindsey seems really into him."

Ironically, I was looking at the stars in Stephen's eyes. The boy is clearly smitten with my sister. I'm just unsure how she feels about him, but Hunter seems to have some insider information. Lindsey will sit and listen to me talk about boys for hours, but she's very tight-lipped when it comes to her crushes. Hours of begging get me little to nothing from her as she plays it all close to her chest.

When they finally part ways, Lindsey halts in her tracks as she spies Hunter standing beside me with keys in hand.

"You aren't riding home with Lexi?" she asks, sounding perplexed.

"Lexi is hanging around to help clean up. Hunter offered to drive us home."

"No. Nope. Uh-uh," Lindsey states while shaking her head side-to-side. "I will find another way home."

"Suit yourself. Walk home for all I care," Hunter grumbles, surprising me with his abrasive response. Where did that come from?

I slap his arm in disapproval. If she was unwilling to ride home with him before, that comment only solidified her decision.

"Lindsey, it's one in the morning. Please don't make a scene. We're supposed to be home right now. Do you really want me getting home and telling Dad that you decided to 'find another way home'?"

Lindsey rubs her left forearm, which is one of her nervous habits. Seeing the conflict in her eyes, my protective nature rises within me. I'm not going to force the issue with her. If Lindsey doesn't want to get in the jeep with Hunter, we will find another way home. I pull my phone out of my purse.

"It's fine. We can Uber home."

"What!?" Hunter cries out incredulously. "Serena, this is absurd. I can drive you both home."

"He's right. It's fine. Sorry, I wigged out a little," Lindsey concedes, still rubbing her arm.

"Are you sure? I don't mind requesting a car."

The Tucker Girls

"Yeah," she responds assuredly. "I promise."

Warily eyeing my sister, I decide it's best to ride in the backseat with her rather than in the passenger seat next to Hunter. Lindsey's behavior during the dinner a few weeks back seemed peculiar, and I am getting the same vibe again. Her rude demeanor seems entirely out of character for her.

Once we are driving, I carefully study my sister, who is actively staring out the jeep window. Recalling her pushing her food around on her plate the night we ate dinner with my friends, worry creeps in that she's slipping into a dark place again. Should I say something to my parents? If I'm wrong, Lindsey will go ballistic because Mom will start scrutinizing her every move.

Remembering Lindsey smiling and holding Stephen's hand while she said goodnight makes me second-guess my assumption. She could just be tired and cranky. I know Hunter isn't her favorite person in the world, so I decide I'm overreacting and try to let it go. Reaching over, I brush a lock of hair behind her ear, which awards me a smile.

"Hunter and I were talking about how you and Stephen make a cute couple," I say in an attempt to keep her smiling. But, of course, that was the wrong thing to say, as she proceeds to roll her eyes. For whatever reason, I'm not cool enough to discuss her love life with her. I know I'm a year older, but she acts like I'm Mom regarding these types of things.

"He seems really sweet," I continue, unable to stop talking. I don't like sitting in uncomfortable silence.

"He is," she replies as she stares out the window.

"Just be prepared. I'm sure Mom will want him to come over for dinner soon, and I owe you some payback. I seem to remember someone making a scene a couple weeks ago."

"You wouldn't!" Lindsey protests as she tries to read into my playful smile.

The Tucker Girls

I shrug my shoulders, unwilling to reassure her that I won't mess with Stephen. I most assuredly won't, but she must be having doubts from the way she is assessing me right now. Lindsey proceeds to jab me in the side with her finger, exactly where I'm ticklish, and we both break out in laughter as I try to fend off follow-up pokes. I hold my hands up in surrender after she lands several other successful jabs.

"Okay, I surrender. I'll be on my best behavior."

"Thank you."

My heart swells as we share authentic smiles with one another. Lindsey's not just my sister but also my best friend. It feels good to share this experience with her, especially considering this is my last Homecoming dance in high school. The thought hits me hard, and I feel the tears creeping into the corner of my eyes. I'm not ready to leave all of this behind me.

Hunter's jeep turns into our neighborhood, distracting me from my sentimental moment. I know that time is running out for me to ask Hunter to the Winter Gala before we part ways. Hopping out, I tap on the passenger window, signaling for Hunter to roll it down.

A wave of nerves rolls over me as I prepare to pop the question, which I combat by reminding myself how at ease Hunter was with me cozying up to him leaving the dance. I'm wearing him down. I can feel the walls falling, and I am so close to sealing the deal, but I don't want to push too hard and cause Hunter to retreat. We are doing a delicate dance, so my anxiety may be warranted.

"Thanks for the ride," I say as I lean into the open window.

"Anytime. I had fun with you tonight."

There's the opening I was looking for, I think to myself, fighting back an overeager smile. I need to play this cool.

"I was thinking ...." I pause, hoping Hunter will bite.

"Yeah?"

"No, never mind. Have a goodnight."

I turn to walk away, hoping he will stop me with every part of my being.

Come on, Hunter, say something.

I barely take one step towards my driveway before he calls after me.

"Serena!"

I force away the smirk from my face before I turn back. "Yeah?"

"What were you thinking?"

"Just that it would be nice if you were my date to the Winter Gala," I confess, holding my breath as I wait for his response.

"Yes. Let's do it."

"*Really*? Cool. Okay. Goodnight, Hunter."

"See ya, Serena."

I wait patiently for Hunter's jeep to drive away before I let out a squeal that likely wakes our neighbors, making sure to add a dance to boot. There had been moments when I thought the two of us were a possibility, but tonight it never felt more real. I'd won significant ground by playing the long game and felt so close to locking down my guy.

Turning towards the house, I am startled to find Lindsey staring at me from the middle of the driveway. A shadow looms over her face making it difficult to see, but I can tell from her clenched fist she isn't thrilled at what she just overheard.

"I get it. You don't have to say anything," I mutter as I brush past her. "I know you think he's a jerk, but I really like him. I think you would see he's a decent guy if you just give him a chance and stop busting his balls all the time."

Lindsey doesn't even give me the courtesy of replying. I pause to allow her time to catch up and join me on the porch, but she still remains fixed in place. Exhaustion is hitting me hard, so I give up waiting for her to get over what she just overheard and open the front door to our house. I'll try to help her understand after I get a good night's sleep.

CHAPTER THIRTEEN
Hunter

"Bowden, we need to talk."

Simon steps in my way as I head towards Trigonometry, making a very poor decision for someone already skating on thin ice. My glare must communicate that I have very little patience for this fool that handed Serena a drink the night she got sick at Chaz's house.

Several weeks ago, he tried to approach me during the Homecoming dance, but I blew him off. I guess he's getting bolder with time, but I'm growing more protective of Serena, which means his mere presence irks me more every day.

His trespass is even more aggravating seeing as I have stuck with my plan to prove Lindsey wrong - about me being self-absorbed - by continuing to show up early to class. I spend this valuable time conversing with my classmates, taking an interest in their lives.

Though I've purposely avoided talking to Lindsey since the night of the dance, that hasn't stopped me from catching up with Hannah, Patrick and other students I'd never bothered to get to know. I'm determined to drive home my point that Lindsey's assumptions about me are entirely wrong, though I can't help but concede that I'd likely never talk to any of these people had she never slighted me in the first place. Regardless, she's wrong, and I will force her to listen to all of the quality conversations centered around everything but me.

"What do you want?" I snap, making my annoyance apparent in my tone.

"You need to back off."

The Tucker Girls

"Come again?"

"You heard me," Simon grunts, stepping forward until his chest is inches away from mine. This isn't going to end well for him.

"I have no idea what you are talking about, Simon. *You* are the one who needs to back off before something unfortunate happens."

"Don't play dumb with me. I know you messed with my car," Simon replies, jabbing a finger into my chest.

Averting my gaze and taking a deep breath as I attempt to keep my cool, I lock eyes with Lindsey walking down the hallway. She's not the only person staring at the two of us, as Simon's aggressive behavior has several bystanders stopping to take notice.

I need to wrap this conversation up quickly, or I will miss my daily episode of 'Stick it to Lindsey' - at least, that's what I like to refer to it in my head. Today's conversation was going to be especially enjoyable because I'd planned to catch up with Hannah about how she and Rich are doing. Rich is a very sore subject with Lindsey for obvious reasons. Apparently, everyone is allowed to ask Hannah about her relationship besides me.

"I heard what happened to your car; truly tragic. It wasn't me, though."

Okay, it was me, but I'm not stupid enough to admit it to Simon. He huffs in exasperation, knowing I'm lying to his face.

"*But*, if it were me, do you honestly think the best play is to get in my face and get me more pissed off? Especially considering there wasn't any permanent damage to your car."

Simon's nose flares and his face flushes red, which is a bit much. His precious Audi doesn't have a scratch on it. A few weeks ago, we lifted his car up on blocks and rolled the four wheels away in different directions. To top it off, we smeared his windows with petroleum jelly. All completely harmless shit

129

considering I don't have definitive proof that he slipped something nefarious in Serena's drink. He's done some other shady things at this school, so I write this off as karma regardless of the one incident I care about.

"Do you know how long it took to get my car drivable again? *Hours.*"

"*Sounds awful*," I reply sarcastically. "Hand one of my friends another open drink at a party again, and I promise you that your car will be the least of your worries. Understand?"

Simon glares at me, and I stare back until I see a motion catching my attention over his shoulder. Derek White, the creep Lindsey decided to dance with at Homecoming, yanks on Lindsey's backpack hard enough to bring her to a complete stop. Dread fills her expression as she realizes who just interrupted her progression.

Though her baggy hoodie hides her scars, Lindsey's hand instantly starts rubbing her left forearm in reaction to Derek's appearance. I've only known her briefly, but I recognize her nervous tick from a mile away. She's clearly on edge, and I can't tell whether it's the shock of being surprised or Derek that's ratcheted up her anxiety. The interaction between them captivates my full attention away, leaving Simon talking to just himself.

Why did she have to dance with Derek at Homecoming? I swear the girl is the most impossibly difficult person I know. She was desperate to get away from me and ran straight into the arms of this asshat.

From Lindsey's posture, she becomes increasingly uncomfortable as the prick presses into her personal space. He leans close to her face, causing her to take a step back. I can't hear what Derek is saying, but the evil sneer on his face has my suspicions raised. He's up to no good again.

Simon continues to rant, but I haven't caught a single word coming out of his mouth since Derek showed up. Giving

The Tucker Girls

Simon a forceful shove with my forearm and sending him stumbling backward, I angle my head and watch Lindsey break away from Derek's grip and scamper towards our Trigonometry classroom. Derek smiles wickedly as he slowly follows her steps. By the rosy color of Lindsey's neck, it's clear she's bothered by whatever he's said.

I should mind my own business, considering Lindsey isn't shy about telling boys to get lost. She's had no issue putting me in my place numerous times. Despite recalling that fact, I can't leave this be and pretend like I'm not watching Derek instigate trouble with her. As much as I try to convince myself she doesn't need my assistance, I feel an overwhelming urge to protect her.

Derek has a reputation for antisocial behavior, and my few interactions with him didn't give me a great impression. I think he's pure scum, and the fact that Lindsey has his attention is a major red flag.

Simon attempts to get back in my face, but this time I grab him by the shirt and rip him out of my path. He trips over his own feet and collapses to the floor, causing everyone around me to pull out their phones. It's already too late, though. This altercation is already over.

"We're done here," I grumble, storming away before Simon can say another word.

Lindsey manages to escape into the classroom, but Derek hangs out in the doorway and leers after her with a sadistic grin. His disturbing pleasure from pestering Lindsey sends my pulse racing. Rage ripples throughout my body as I try to remind myself that Lindsey has requested that I leave her alone. The last thing I should be doing is getting into her business but screw it. Even if she hates me more for doing it, I'm diving right in.

The proper course of action would be to make Serena aware of the situation and let her check in on her sister, but I'm not in the state of mind to be making good choices. Maybe Simon primed me for a fight, or I just hate watching people get bullied. Either way, this has become my problem. I'm locked in and ready for a confrontation.

Stepping into the doorway, directly in Derek's line of sight, I startle him with my sudden appearance. All he can see is me. It takes an immense amount of self-control to not pummel this twerp.

"Get lost," I growl.

Derek's face quickly morphs into a scowl as he remains planted in place. My words aren't effective in deterring this prick, so I grab him by the shirt and tug him towards me.

"Are you deaf?"

"What's your problem, man?" Derek protests as he attempts to shake free from my hold. I've got five inches and close to sixty pounds on him. He's not getting free from my grasp.

"You don't belong here. Leave!"

With a sharp shove, I give him the momentum he needs to start walking away from my classroom. Derek almost falls but manages to catch hold of a nearby student to keep himself upright. Still scowling my way, Derek flips me off but continues heading in the direction I sent him. It's a smart decision, too, because I don't know what I would do if he tried to approach the classroom again. I'm not even considering what form of punishment would await me if I mauled him right now. I just want him away from Lindsey.

The tardy bell rings and the hallway clears as I wait for him to meander away. Derek turns the corner and is no longer visible, allowing me to finally regain my wits. I'd gotten worked up quickly without even realizing it. I've been careful these last few years to not fight at school. I settle issues when I'm not under the threat of being expelled, especially now that I don't have my fame on the football field to protect me. Derek had me considering throwing all of those well-thought-out plans to the wind, though.

Turning towards the room, I notice most of the class has been eavesdropping on Derek and my less than cordial interaction - including Lindsey. The second I lay eyes on her, she attempts to conceal the fact that she was watching by shifting her eyes and pulling down her hair to hide her face. Rather than immediately taking my seat, I stop in front of Lindsey's desk and stare down in her direction.

"How long has that been going on?" I inquire with a harsher tone than I would have liked to use.

"Mr. Bowden, please find your seat," Mrs. Seldon calls out from behind me, but I ignore her command as I wait for Lindsey to respond. Class can wait. I need her to answer my question.

Though I kept my voice low, I know for a fact she heard me. Lindsey refuses to answer my inquiry, preferring to stare down at her clenched hands resting on the desk, so I cut my gaze to Hannah. She's close with Lindsey, so maybe she knows how long this creep has been pestering her.

"Hannah, how long?"

Hannah's face is bright red as her eyes dart back and forth between Lindsey and me. From the concerned look on her face, I glean that she knows something, but she does not want to incur Lindsey's wrath if she speaks up. Lindsey balls up her fists, likely fuming that I am forcing the issue, but I honestly could care less. I have to know what's going on. Hannah's reaction indicates this is a more significant issue than I initially believed.

"Mr. Bowden," Mrs. Seldon calls again, grating my nerves. Let her write me up for ignoring her. All I care about is knowing the truth, despite my gut indicating that I won't like what I'm about to hear.

"Hannah, tell me," I plead with as much patience as I can muster.

"Since Homecoming," Hannah responds before cutting her eyes to her clasped hands.

Her response is like a punch right to my gut. My head spins as I try to process this revelation.

"Hannah!" Lindsey groans, throwing her hands to her face.

I hesitate before dropping my backpack and taking my seat, allowing myself to comprehend that Derek has been bothering Lindsey for almost three weeks. *Three weeks.* How was I just now noticing that there was an issue? Yes, I'd been preoccupied with throwing Lindsey's words back in her face, but surely there were signs I failed to pick up on. What else had the creep done that I wasn't aware of? More importantly, why do I care?

Leave her alone, Hunter.

Leave. Her. Alone.

That's what she wants. I'm agitated to the point of needing to shift my weight every few minutes. My hand twitches and I make a fist to keep it under control. This situation has me unnerved, and I am forced to remind myself that I can't protect everyone. My priority has always been my family, and Lindsey can handle this situation without me intervening.

Needless to say, I find it impossible to focus on math while these thoughts circulate in my mind. Whether or not Lindsey wants me involved in her life, I've already decided that I'm going to intervene. I'm going to corner Derek and put a good scare in him. Elijah and Chaz will help me deliver my message loud and clear. If that doesn't work, I will sic the whole football team on this guy. I'll break every bone in his body. Derek is going to back off, or I will bury him. *Then*, I will leave Lindsey alone.

CHAPTER FOURTEEN
Lindsey

I'm almost asleep when my cell phone vibrates again with another message from an unknown number, and I don't have to look at the text to know what it says. Derek continues to send gross messages, but this time I see that it's a series of photos of me from throughout today. My stomach sours the instant I see all the shots he was able to snap without me having any clue he was nearby. This creep was following me the entire school day.

With two quick screen taps, I block the unknown number for the eighth time in two weeks. It's only a minor deterrent because he manages to text me from a new phone number within twenty-four hours every time.

At least this will shut him up for the night, so I can sleep undisturbed. Skimming through the photos he sent once more, my body begins trembling as I realize how vulnerable I really am. He's whispered what he would like to do when he finally gets me alone, and I'm freaking out that he's had ample opportunity already.

Last Friday, I went to the Vice Principal to report the bastard. I'm done running from my problems. After half a day of missing classes, Mrs. Alina informed me that she didn't have enough evidence to support any of my claims. Derek proved that the offensive texts weren't from his cell phone, so Mrs. Alina couldn't act on any of the disgusting messages I showed her. After checking the hall cameras, she couldn't catch Derek doing any of the things that I accused him of, either. According to the Vice Principal, the sneaky bastard has a long history of trouble, but she needs more evidence to take action. She wanted to believe me, but I didn't have any eyewitnesses of him doing more than looking ominously in my direction.

At least, that was the case until this morning when Hunter caught Derek harassing me. Of course, Hunter's the one person in the world that I would need to corroborate my story. Go figure. I have to admit I enjoyed watching Hunter confront Derek for a brief moment. I couldn't hear the banter between them, but the whole class watched the showdown that concluded with Hunter shoving Derek away. It wiped that creepy smile off Derek's face that I despise so much.

Shame rippled through me when Hunter decided to step in and save me again. I *hate* needing his help. All it does is inflate his colossal ego. I couldn't even look Hunter in the eye when he quietly demanded to know how long Derek had been harassing me. A part of me wanted to trust him with the truth, but I couldn't help but feel that showing him any vulnerability would come back to haunt me.

My inability to trust anyone is likely a remnant of everyone in my life losing faith in me over a year ago when my life fell apart. It felt like they all betrayed me when I needed them the most. Their pity was the worst feeling in the world. I never want to feel that way again.

As I watched the altercation in math class, the mixture of shame and satisfaction turned my stomach in knots. On top of all that, there was also a feeling of exuberance that Hunter cared enough to intervene, even if he was only doing it for Serena. It was all too much to process. The war within myself to resolve these competing thoughts made it impossible to concentrate the remainder of the school day.

If there was any doubt that Hunter thought I was weak, Hannah confirmed his suspicions when she told him I hadn't been able to handle the Derek situation for weeks. He must think I'm pathetic for not being able to rid myself of this creep. I shouldn't need Hunter's help, especially after he attempted to prevent me from approaching Derek at Homecoming, but here I am unable to deal with a problem I created.

More than anything, I just want to be able to talk about this ordeal with someone other than Hannah. Don't get me wrong, she's been willing to listen, which has helped. As far as advice, Hannah hasn't offered me anything other than getting Mrs. Alina involved, which resolved absolutely nothing. All it did was piss off Derek even more and put him on high alert.

Who else is there to speak with? I can't go to Serena because she will certainly tell Dad, who will lose his mind. He will fight for the school to do something, but without proof, they will be incapable of action. That will mean the only thing he can do is hound me about every decision I make.

As if she has a sixth sense that I was thinking of her, Serena lightly knocks on my bedroom door before peeking her head in.

"Can't sleep?" Serena asks when she sees me sitting up in bed.

"Nope. You?" I respond, patting my bed for her to come in and sit.

Serena flips on the lights to my room and sits down beside me.

"I'm cramming for a Physics test tomorrow and need a break."

Serena's coursework is ridiculous. It's a miracle that she can balance her grades, social life and extracurricular activities. She joined the school dance team a couple of weeks ago and has been participating in the Future Business Leaders club since the start of the year. It's depressing to have an older sister that achieves so much and sets the bar impossibly high. I will never live up to her standard.

"Don't sweat it, Serena. I'm sure you will do great."

Serena sighs as she leans back on the bed.

137

"I hope so. You never know with Mrs. Plythe. Her tests are ridiculously hard, and anything she has taught is fair game, so I just keep pouring over the notes I've taken over the last six weeks. I swear I have been staring at them so long I'm seeing double."

"Well, I'm glad you took a break then," I reply honestly, realizing it's been too long since we've talked. "I needed a distraction."

"Everything alright?" Serena asks, eyeing me carefully.

I pause as I observe her inspection. Does she know about what's going on with Derek? Did Hunter say something to her after what happened earlier in the day?

"Why do you ask?"

"No reason. I'm just concerned about you. I know this move has been tricky for all of us. The other night I noticed you weren't eating dinner, which worried me. I haven't had the chance to really check in with you."

Relief settles in when I realize that Hunter didn't say anything. I shouldn't be surprised because he never said a word about the fight I stumbled into, either. He's surprisingly discreet when it comes to issues at school.

A thought flickers that I should tell Serena about the trouble I'm in, but it's fleeting, and I come to my senses quickly.

"Linds?"

"I'm fine."

"You know you could tell me if you weren't?"

"I know. Thank you," I reply, shifting my weight uncomfortably. "What about you? Do you ever miss Georgia?"

"Well, yeah, I do. I mean …. I miss the girls: Ashley, Maddison and Danielle. I haven't found friends like them here in Texas. Hunter's group is great, but I don't know if I'll ever be accepted as one of them, you know?"

The Tucker Girls

It sure looks like Serena is part of their clique from the outside in. She's always with them, spending what little free time she has hanging out with Lexi or Hunter.

"What about Dain? Do you miss him?"

At the mention of her prior boyfriend, Serena sits upright.

"I know it sounds bad, but I haven't missed him. Maybe it's because I've been distracted with acclimating to Ulla Meyer or chasing after Hunter," Serena pauses as she bites her bottom lip, "but I honestly haven't thought about him much. Dain's having a harder time letting go, though. He's still calling several times a week, so I've had to stop answering his calls to create some space. He needs to let me go."

"I'm sorry to hear that. I liked Dain."

"Yeah, me too. He is a great guy, but it would never work when we are a thousand miles away from one another."

Serena falls silent as she ponders some unspoken thought. Maybe it wasn't such a great idea to bring up Dain, so I try to change the subject to distract her.

"You know what I was thinking the other day? I want to get sundaes with you like we used to do back home. Hannah said this place called Cone Envy has the best ice cream in the area."

"Yes!"

"Yeah? What about this Friday after the game?"

"Ummm …."

Serena's hesitation lets me know that she already has plans. I should have guessed, given the short notice I'm giving her.

"It's fine if you can't. I just thought we hadn't done it since I was a freshman."

"Yes, I will make it work. I *had* plans, but they aren't as important as bonding with my favorite sister."

"Ha! I'm your *only* sister," I counter.

"Technicalities," Serena laughs. "Even if I had another sister, you would definitely be my favorite. I do have one condition, though."

"What's that?"

"You don't call your abomination that you eat a sundae."

"Don't hate it til you try it! Mint chocolate chip and hot fudge is heaven."

Serena's face sours in disgust, so I jab her in the side with my finger. Things escalate quickly; before I know it, she wrestles me to the floor and pins me down, tickling me until I'm on the verge of tears. I plead for mercy between my laughter and Serena finally relents.

Ten minutes with my sister and my mood has been lifted. The sour stomach that was plaguing me is suddenly bearable, and I find myself smiling again. I ache to tell her what's really going on with me. I hate keeping things from her, but as much as I want to share, I know deep down that Serena doesn't handle difficult things well, and I've already put her through more trying circumstances than she should have ever had to deal with. It's why she prepares and pushes herself to be the best at everything. She doesn't know how to deal with failure.

If I drop my burdens on her, Serena will need an outlet, and I cannot risk my parents being a part of this. I remember how they all treated me like a child who couldn't be trusted with any decisions when I was lost in the darkness; it was constant questioning and supervision to the point that I thought I was going to lose my mind.

After Serena leaves my room, I lay in bed pondering what to do about the stalker situation. Tossing and turning, I think about involving Hunter because he'd likely be able to handle Derek. He practically runs the school, so if he can't do anything, then I'm truly hopeless. Despite this fact, I can't bring myself to ask for his help. I have too much pride to allow him to hold it over me. With the debate still raging in my head, I pick up my phone and impulsively send a text.

Lindsey: Any chance you are still awake? Just looking to talk.

I stare at my phone, waiting for a response for several minutes. I'm about to give up when I feel it vibrate from an incoming call.

"Hey," I say as I answer, hoping this isn't a bad decision.

"Hey, Lindsey. What's up?" Lexi asks in a muted voice.

"Sorry! Did I wake you up?"

"No. I'm just walking in the door."

"Oh. Okay, good."

I pause as I begin to second guess reaching out to Lexi. It was a completely impulsive move on my part. She's Serena's friend, not mine. The last thing she likely wants to do is be brought into my mess.

"Lindsey?"

"Yeah …. Sorry …. You know what? I shouldn't have texted you. It's really not a big deal at all."

"Nope. You aren't backing out of this conversation. You texted me for something, and I'm guessing it's important, so let's hear it," Lexi replies sternly.

"Can you at least promise not to tell Serena? She can't know the things I'm about to tell you - ever."

"Sure, I can keep this between us."

"Thank you. Okay. There's this boy …." I start out, then hesitate as I try to find the words to adequately describe my predicament. Should I just come right out and call Derek a stalker? I think that it's a fair assessment of the creep.

"Wait. I thought you and Stephen were a thing?"

"No. I mean, we are talking, but we aren't together. Not yet, at least. Even still, I'm not interested in this other boy

141

romantically, but I can't say the same for him. I danced with him once at Homecoming, and now he's stalking me. It's creepy, and I can't get him to back off. I was hoping you might know what I should do."

"What's his name?"

"Derek White."

Lexi groans on the other end of the call.

"You know him?"

"Unfortunately. He's a senior too. Derek's a lowlife that has always got a kick out of screwing around with people. I am guessing you're his entertainment now. He's pretty messed up in the head. The more you struggle, the more enjoyment he's getting out of stalking you."

"Fantastic," I grumble, dropping my head onto my pillow. "How do I get him to leave me alone?"

"The way I see it, you have two options: report Derek to the school, or we handle it through less scrupulous tactics."

I proceed to fill Lexi in on my less-than-productive conversations with Mrs. Alina, dispelling the possibility that her first option may work.

"So ...." I continue with a defeated tone, "I guess that leaves me with option two. I don't even know what you mean by *less scrupulous tactics*, but I'm desperate."

"I'm so sorry, Lindsey. Want me to beat Derek to a pulp for you?"

"Yes, please," I respond with a laugh. "But seriously, I don't want you to get in trouble because of me. I was just hoping .... I mean, you've been at Ulla Meyer for years, so I thought you might have an idea. He's really starting to creep me out, and I don't know what to do."

"Well, I'm glad you told me. I'm going to text Hunter ...."

"No. Nope. Not him," I interject quickly. "Can't Elijah help? Or what about Brady?"

The Tucker Girls

I hear Lexi sigh on the other end of the phone, and I can only imagine her frustration with me. First, I call begging for help, only to refuse the first tangible solution she offers.

"Elijah's got a full scholarship offer to UCLA. He can't be caught doing anything that would put that opportunity at risk. And Brady .... Brady comes off like the big, bad linebacker, but deep down, he's a softie. This type of thing usually requires a certain .... uh .... how should I say this .... a certain mean streak that Brady just doesn't have."

"But Hunter has it," I state as I begin understanding Lexi's train of thought.

"Yes, Hunter has it. Don't get me wrong, I love him like a brother and would trust him with my life. Hunter's the strongest of all of us. He's always handled any trouble that's come our way.

"When I was in third grade, this boy - Dennis Greenberg - used to pull my ponytail every day at recess. He was awful like Derek and took great pleasure in seeing me cry. Sure enough, a yank on my hair and a few nasty words would bring the waterworks every time. I figured I was tough enough to handle it and never said a word, but Hunter caught Dennis in the act one day. I'm not sure what Hunter did, but that was the last day Dennis bothered me. In fact, whenever I would see Dennis on the playground after that, he would take off running in the opposite direction."

"You never asked him what he did to Dennis?"

"I did, but Hunter always changed the subject. It took me a long time to understand, but one day I realized that whatever dark thing Hunter was required to do was his burden to bear. I was able to sleep soundly at night in my ignorance. Hunter has always carried the weight of things I'm not sure I could handle, and I'm not just talking about school drama."

I'm not sure what she's referring to, but I have to admit that I'm less opposed to the idea of Hunter intervening after hearing Lexi's story. I'd give anything to make my Derek problem go away. Like Lexi, I'd rather not know what it will take to get Derek to back off, though. I prefer the option where I can sleep at night without being burdened by the details.

"Are you still there?" Lexi asks after my silence lingers.

"Yeah. Thank you, Lexi."

"I'll ask Hunter tomorrow. He's working tonight, so I don't want to disturb him right now."

"No, it's okay. I will ask him."

"Are you sure?"

"Yes, I'm sure. Thank you, Lexi. This is my problem, and I need to be the one to try and fix it. You've already done so much just hearing me out tonight. I really appreciate it."

"Any time. Goodnight, girl."

"Night."

Hanging up, my stomach twists with the thought of asking Hunter for help. Despite knowing that I need to be the one to do it - because this is my mess - I dread the forthcoming conversation and its likelihood to inflate his ego. I can only imagine how elated Hunter will be to hear that I need him.

Pulling the bed covers up, I predict another long, sleepless night ahead. At least I'm one step closer to ridding myself of creepy Derek.

CHAPTER FIFTEEN
Lindsey

My palms are sweaty in anticipation of asking for help as I stand outside the rear entrance to Ulla Meyer. This is the entrance that most students, who drive to school, use because of its close proximity to the parking lot. I keep reminding myself that the worst possible outcome of my pending request is Hunter telling me he doesn't want to get involved, which would be highly unlikely considering he's already confronted Derek once before. From what I could see, it was clear that Hunter hates Derek about as much as I do.

When I woke up this morning, I had the brilliant idea of catching Hunter before classes so I could talk to him without Serena being around. I'm still convinced keeping her out of the equation is mandatory. So here I am, standing outside, in the chilly morning air, while the upperclassmen file into the school. Thankfully, I'm nearly invisible to all of my peers. Barely anyone takes notice of my unusual lingering, except for a smiling boy who quickly approaches as soon as he sets eyes on me.

"Hey, Lindsey! What are you hanging around out here for?"

I smile in return, but my head is spinning a mile a minute at the sight of Stephen. I should have expected to run into him, but I was not mentally prepared for it. No matter how I might try to explain it, telling him I'm out here waiting for Hunter would give him the wrong impression, and that's the last thing I want. Our relationship isn't official, but it's certainly heading in that direction, and I don't want to mess up our momentum with a simple misunderstanding.

"Hi," I respond as I wrap my arms around Stephen. "I'm waiting out here to meet up with a classmate. I want to review something with them before class, but they are taking forever to get here."

Before I leave Stephen's embrace, I spy Hunter's green jeep pulling into the gravel parking lot, and my heart is suddenly racing out of control. Stephen can't be here when I speak with Hunter. Like Serena, he can never find out about the baggage I've been concealing. He wouldn't stick around if he knew how weak and incapable I really am.

"Oh, okay. Do you want me to wait with you?"

"No, that's alright. I don't want to keep you waiting."

"I don't mind," he replies with a shrug. One brief glance into his eyes, and I can tell he's hoping I ask him to stick around. "You look cold. Do you want my jacket?"

"No, thank you. That's really sweet of you, though."

Stephen is incredibly thoughtful. Last week, he brought me coffee while I was swapping books from my locker on my way to first bell. Yes, things are moving slowly, but that's not always bad. I've never dated anyone before, so I'm not sure what normal is, but Stephen seems content with our progress. Despite having more dating experience, he seems even more nervous than I am. He hasn't even kissed me yet. I'm trying not to take it personally.

My train of thought is broken when I lock eyes with Hunter as he weaves through a row of cars, and of course, my traitorous body reacts to the connection. I find it difficult to swallow as my pulse rapidly speeds up. Seeing this boy makes me nervous, and I'm relieved when he quickly averts his gaze. He's walking up, and sharing a laugh, with a boy in a football letterman jacket who I don't recognize.

The Tucker Girls

"Why don't I meet you at your locker? I don't want to make you late for your first class," I implore Stephen, nudging him along. Thankfully, he takes the hint and nods before slowly meandering through the doors. The second Stephen is out of sight, I sigh in relief; the crisis has been averted.

Now that Stephen is out of the picture, I stare directly at Hunter, hoping he looks my way one more time. When he's about fifteen feet away and still not glancing back at me, it occurs to me that he may not look at all. He's preoccupied with the conversation with his friend. They both laugh again, but I can't help but notice Hunter's smile doesn't reach his eyes.

Sure enough, my fear comes true when I am passed by without any acknowledgment. I'd prepared for many different possibilities, but this catches me entirely off guard.

He knew I was standing here. Though I've encouraged us to act like strangers, he's *never* ignored me like this before. My stomach twists violently when I finally get what I'd asked for; however, I quickly realize I don't like it nearly as much as I expected. It's ironic that I now need his attention.

Calling out his name as I take steps toward the entrance, Hunter doesn't bother to look in my direction. My initial assumption was that he didn't hear me, but I notice heads turn my way at the sound of my voice. Everyone heard me, including the boy in the letterman jacket, and I'm suddenly the center of attention. A flush of heat floods my cheeks as soon as I feel the weight of all the staring. I hate feeling all of these eyes bearing down on me like this.

My resolve is shaken, but I'm still committed to my plan enough to chase after Hunter until I can practically reach out and touch him.

"Hunter!"

This time I see him visibly flinch at the sound of his name. There's no doubt about it this time; he clearly heard me. The prick doesn't bother to acknowledge me, though. He keeps

147

marching on, and this time I remain stationary as I watch him walk away in disbelief. What the hell? I'm stunned by the cold shoulder I'm receiving. Hunter and I haven't always been friendly, but this treatment feels inexplicably cruel. He knows I'm chasing after him but is too disinterested to concern himself with me.

"Pathetic," a brunette girl states as she walks by with her snickering friends. "Just a bit of advice: homely girls like you aren't Hunter's type. You're a walking wardrobe malfunction."

The hallway breaks out in laughter at her harsh words, and it takes all of two seconds for me to be completely humiliated. My stomach is wrenching even worse from embarrassment. Terrible memories begin flooding back to me from my high school in Georgia at the worst possible time. Tears threaten to burst forth, so I do the only thing I can do to save what dignity I have left, and I scamper away to the bathroom before they see me cry. I won't ever let my peers see me cry again.

My salvation is hiding away in an unoccupied bathroom stall until ten minutes into my first class. This will be my only tardy of the year, but it's worth knowing that the halls will be empty as I walk to class.

When I finally get a handle on my emotions, I head to Chemistry though my walk is less peaceful than I'd hoped. An unsettling feeling that I'm being watched lingers in the empty hallways. I frantically scan my surroundings but find myself alone. Derek has really screwed with my head. I get the unsettling feeling that he could be lurking just out of sight.

Despite collecting myself in the bathroom and holding it together through first bell, the second I step out into the hall, following Chemistry to transition between classes, I feel the intense humiliation return with a vengeance. I keep my head down as I navigate from class to class, purposely avoiding all eye contact. I can't tell if it's all in my head, but the gossip is extra today. I feel like everyone is whispering secrets, and I have to believe some of them are about me chasing after Hunter. I bet they all think I'm some lovesick puppy the way I was pursuing him.

By the time lunch rolls around, I find myself unable to even consider eating. My stomach is still sour, which has killed my appetite. The only saving grace is that Derek has yet to find me - at least that I know of. I plop down at my usual lunch table with dramatic flair.

"Lindsey, are you okay? You look miserable," Hannah states as she opens her Tupperware to eat.

I expected last period to be excruciatingly difficult, with Hunter sitting behind me, but it wasn't too terrible. I kept my head down and put my full attention into the Trig lesson. Luckily, Hunter showed up just as class started, so I didn't have to listen to him make conversation with my classmates. I don't know if I would have been able to stand the sound of his voice today.

"Just peachy," I reply sarcastically as I lay my forehead on the table. "I just want this nightmare of a day to be over."

"Oh no! What happened?" I hear Meredith ask as she joins us at the table.

"I don't want to talk about it."

I decide I will keep my face planted against this table for the remainder of lunch. I'm an idiot for ever thinking I could trust Hunter. Why am I so dense sometimes?

"Can you please talk about something else to distract me?" I plead pathetically.

"Yeah …. sure," Hannah reluctantly agrees. I can't read her face, but I can picture her concerned look in my head.

"I heard that John Morgan cheated on Gabriella with Tanya McNamara," Meredith chimes in, uncharacteristically sharing gossip that sends a gasp from several girls sitting nearby.

Meredith's friend, Lily, begins talking about how foolish John Morgan is, and the conversation takes off from there. Unfortunately, nothing in the conversation is able to distract my mind from dwelling on this morning's events. I keep picturing myself pathetically chasing after Hunter. He was supposed to help with my troubles, not add to them. Lexi convinced me it was the right decision even though I'd originally had reservations. I won't be caught dead making that mistake ever again.

"Oh my! Hunter Bowden is staring at you, Lindsey!" Lily sings out.

"I don't care. I hate him," I grumble out like a petulant child. "He can fall off a cliff for all I care."

"Lily's right. He's not even trying to hide the fact that he's looking in your direction. He's so hot," Meredith chimes in.

If only they knew that his hotness is a mask for his black soul.

"I'm going to wave him over," Lily responds playfully.

"No!" I retort, popping my head up from the table. I turn my head, purposely shielding my face from Hunter's table.

"Lily, please stop. Lindsey hates Hunter," Hannah chimes in with timidity. I can always count on her support.

"Why?" Meredith and Lily ask in unison.

"Hunter's my hall pass. Blair wouldn't even mind," Lily announces, speaking of her on-again, off-again boyfriend. "Hunter's so freaking gorgeous. Will you introduce us?"

"He's a self-absorbed jerk," I state with hostility, simultaneously risking a peak in his direction. I instantly catch Hunter's gaze from across the cafeteria. Yep, he's staring with an intensity that I dare to match. I hope he can feel the venomous thoughts I'm trying to convey through my eyes. If he does, it doesn't show. Our eyes remained locked until I finally give up trying to murder him with my thoughts. I'm too emotionally drained to bother with him anymore.

The Tucker Girls

Laying my forehead against the table once more, I wonder if Lexi mentioned our phone conversation to Hunter. Why else would he suddenly be staring at me?

"Hannah, how'd you get him to ask you to the dance? If Lindsey's not interested, maybe I can shoot my shot," Lily continues obsessing about Hunter, grating my nerves. She's completely ignoring everything I'm saying about how awful of a person he is.

"Hunter was only helping me get Rich's attention," Hannah confesses.

"Okay, I can definitely work with that."

"You *just* got back together with Blair last week," Meredith chides.

"Like I said, Blair would totally understand. It would be bragging rights that he got with the same girl Hunter Bowden did," Lily retorts.

What is wrong with her? Do relationships really work like that?

"You do realize that's not exactly an accomplishment, right? He's supposedly been with half the school," I interject, without bothering to look up. I shouldn't care about this ridiculous conversation, but I feel compelled to participate.

"Rumors aren't always true," Meredith chimes in. "Maybe it's just all talk."

Lily proceeds to share a rumor that ran around about her older sister when she went to Ulla Meyer. I try hard to listen but can't bring myself to focus. All I can think about is Hunter's sudden interest in me. I really hope Lexi didn't say anything. I don't want Hunter involved any longer. I'm certain I want him to forget that I even exist. At least, I'm fairly sure that I do - probably sixty percent sure.

Hannah begins frantically patting my arm, causing me to look at her.

"Hunter's walking this way."

The Tucker Girls

Sure enough, he's crossing the lunchroom with his attention still honed in on me. The three girls around me all sit upright in anticipation of Hunter's arrival. Groaning aloud, my mind races as I try to figure out what to do. I'm not going to allow him to humiliate me in front of the entire cafeteria, so my flight response wins out.

"I wonder what he wants?" Hannah asks quietly.

"I'm not sticking around to find out."

Slinging my backpack over my shoulder, I hurry off towards the main hall without bothering to look back. Although I feel a bit cowardly for running away and not lashing out for how I was treated this morning, I feel satisfied that Hunter is forced to watch me walk away this time. Our roles are reversed, and I hope he feels just as insignificant as I did.

I pause in the hallway, realizing that I have nowhere to go. Lunch is barely halfway over, so I have over twenty minutes to kill before the next period starts. I finally settle on taking a long walk outside, but first I need to drop my backpack off in my locker. The bag is too heavy to carry around comfortably, plus I will need my coat.

Before I can take a step in my intended direction, a hand grasps tightly around my upper arm. I yelp as I feel myself being dragged towards an open classroom door. My heart races out of control as I squirm to break free, but whoever has a hold of me has an impossibly tight grip.

"Don't walk away from me," Hunter growls in my ear as he pulls me into the unoccupied room before shutting the door behind him.

"You scared the hell out of me!" I fire back, stumbling from the momentum of being dragged. *What is wrong with you?* Are you trying to compete with Derek to see who can freak me out more?"

"Keep your voice down," Hunter barks out when my voice fills the empty room.

The Tucker Girls

"No! In fact, if you don't move out of my way, I'm going to scream for help."

Hunter closes the distance between us in a split second, covering my mouth with his hand. I throw a punch at his face but end up hitting his muscular shoulder instead; excruciating pain ripples throughout my hand. A whimper escapes my sealed mouth as I shake my injured hand. My backpack slips off while I write in agony.

"You are absolutely impossible!" he roars with irritation, matching my attempt to retreat step-for-step until he's backed me up against the classroom wall.

With my uninjured hand, I try to pull his hand away from my mouth, but he's impossibly strong.

"Would you cut it out already?" Hunter pleads, his voice taking a calmer tone. "I just want to talk, but you have to make everything difficult. I'm going to remove my hand, and you are not going to scream. Understood?"

I don't bother acknowledging anything coming out of his mouth because my hand is throbbing in agony. I really hope I didn't break it. Hunter uncovers my mouth and eyes me warily, readying himself for whatever I'm about to do. I consider screaming to pay him back for giving me a scare, but I decide against it. I don't feel terrified anymore despite being caged in by Hunter. It defies logic, but I know he won't hurt me. His eyes aren't filled with malice, just frustration.

Hunter's gaze leaves mine to inspect my wounded hand. He slowly takes hold of it, drawing it closer to himself. Surprising even myself, I allow the contact and silently observe his examination of my injury. His thumb begins rubbing circles where it aches, making me wince in pain. You'd think I'd pull back, but I don't.

"This has got to stop."

"Wh …. what?" I stammer.

"This game you're playing. You want me to ignore you, then you're chasing after me in the hallway. It's getting old."

"It's not a game! I want you to ignore me."

"No more lies, Lindsey."

"I'm not lying! You're the liar," I protest, ripping my hand out of his. I attempt to make a move to get away, but he slides over to block my path.

"You're really starting to try my patience," he growls in irritation. "You go weeks without saying a word to me, but today you were chasing after me. Tell me why."

"I don't have to explain myself to you. I thought I needed your help, but that was a huge mistake."

A staring contest breaks out, with both of us standing off against the other and refusing to back down. I can see Hunter trying to tame the anger simmering inside, and I'm antagonizing it with my stubbornness.

"You made me feel insignificant!" I finally shout, shoving a finger into his chest. "You didn't even acknowledge me. Do you know how that feels?"

"You mean like you do to me every day?"

"That's different. You .... you .... you deserve it! You purposely instigate shit with me for the fun of it."

He's looking so intently at me that I feel he may be searching the depths of my soul. It's unsettling because I'm afraid of what he may find there.

"Okay. We are going to stop this charade. You're not going to pretend to ignore me, and I'll stop antagonizing you. Deal?"

"Nope. No deal. I'm permanently erasing you from my brain. As of right now, you're a stranger to me."

"No."

"*No*?" I scoff.

"That's right. You aren't running away anymore."

The Tucker Girls

What does he mean by running away? Stunned by his statement, Hunter takes the opportunity to grab hold of my injured hand once more. Curiosity encourages me to allow whatever is happening, and he proceeds to slide up the sleeve of my hoodie. I bite back a protest, still wanting to know what is going on in that mind of his.

Pleasurable chills race through my entire body when his thumb trails up my forearm. I suck in a deep breath as I ride the wave of emotions bubbling up within me. His thumb stops when it reaches the scars razed in the bend of my elbow, and Hunter slowly traces each one while maintaining eye contact with me. My body is buzzing. His touch is short-circuiting my brain. My knees feel weak, causing me to lean my forehead into Hunter's chest. I'm not sure what is happening between us, but it feels euphoric. It takes my full restraint not to submit to the overwhelming feelings that have overtaken me.

This all feels way too intimate. Hunter's managed to burst through walls I'd never intended to allow him through.

What are you doing, Lindsey? Why are you letting him touch your scars like this?

My head is treading water as fast as possible, trying not to drown in the flood of overwhelming sensations that make me feel so incredibly good. I can't recall a time that I've ever felt so alive.

The problem is that Hunter Bowden's not someone you share your secrets with. He's not allowed to see me this vulnerable. Hunter - Serena's Hunter - is a wrecking ball that will destroy me if I let him. *Serena's Hunter.* That final thought snaps me out of the trance that'd held me captive.

"*What are you doing?*" I demand, shoving him back a step.

My cheeks must be flushed because they feel like they are on fire. I dare to meet his eyes, and I'm surprised to see a mix of confusion and concern dancing around in them. I don't think he has any idea what was transpiring between us either.

"You really need to learn how to throw a proper punch," Hunter eventually states, breaking the awkward silence between us.

"Do I get to practice on you? If so, can we start the training now?"

"*Very funny*," Hunter replies sarcastically, but I can't help but notice a slight smirk form on his face. "Thankfully, I don't think you broke anything. You need to ice it, or you won't be able to write a thing tomorrow."

His statement sinks in, and I'm taken aback by the fact that he knows I'm left-handed. Maybe it's not that big of a deal considering he's been sitting behind me for months, but I am shocked that he'd notice such a minor detail. He can barely pass our Trigonometry quizzes, so I never expected him to be a guy that would notice something like that. Yes, I snoop into his business, for reasons that defy logic, when I pass his tests back to him in class.

Hunter is still holding my gaze, and I am honestly floored by the tenderness in his eyes. The contrast between this version of Hunter and the cruel boy, with a mean streak, as Lexi refers to it, throws me for a loop. His split personality leaves me wondering which one is the real Hunter.

"Will you *please* move?" I ask in a shaky voice. My throat is still tight from the unexpected intimate moment we shared.

"No. Like I said, I just want to talk."

"Like I said, I'm erasing you from my brain. Who are you again?"

Hunter's brows furrow as he looks away. I must have hit a nerve. *Good.*

"Lindsey, that's not going to work anymore. We tried it your way, but that didn't go so well. You didn't eat lunch and laid your head on the cafeteria table after I ignored you once."

"Oh, get over yourself!" I scoff. "It must really bother you that I don't fall on my knees and worship the ground you walk on like all the other girls at this school. A real blow to your ego."

I've lost all patience with this conversation. I manage to slip past him and start walking away. I need as much distance between us as possible before I injure my other hand on his face.

"I don't know why I ever bothered listening to Lexi. Talking to you is a waste of breath. I have more important things I should be spending my time on," I mutter.

My escape is short-lived as Hunter wraps an arm around my waist and draws me towards him until my back is pressed against his chest.

"Lexi? What does Lexi have to do with this?" he asks with irritation. "What did Lexi say to you?"

His question goes unanswered because it's impossibly distracting being pressed up against his chest like this. I try to squirm away, but he won't let me go. The more I try to wiggle free, the tighter his hold gets.

"Lindsey! What did Lexi say to you?"

"That I needed to talk to you, but that was clearly a mistake. *Let. Me. Go.*"

"Why would Lexi tell you to talk to me? Wait. You said you needed something. That's why you were trying to get my attention."

His question forces me to stop attempting to escape. I'd assumed that he chased after me today because Lexi had told him about our conversation last night. If Lexi didn't say anything to Hunter, then why was he here with me now?

"What were you ... I mean ... Why did you follow me at lunch if you didn't talk to Lexi?"

The Tucker Girls

I feel the rhythm of his chest rising and falling rapidly, though he remains silent. Apparently, he's unwilling to answer my question. I need the answer, though. My heart races with his as I patiently wait for him to give me something. He said he tried to ignore me, but something made him reverse course.

I'm pressed up against his chest, and the connection sends familiar, spectacular sensations running through me once more. Every point at which our two bodies touch seems to reverberate with pleasure and yearning. My traitorous body aches to press into him more, and I am doing mental gymnastics trying to remind myself that I hate this boy even if I'm enjoying being held by him.

"Hunter?" I ask in a cracked whisper. My stupid throat is so dry that I can barely speak.

"I guess we are at an impasse."

"What are you talking about?"

"You won't answer my question, so I'm not going to answer yours."

I let out an audible exhale, and Hunter releases me from his grasp unexpectedly. I immediately miss his embrace the second he steps back.

I can't let him get that close to me again. Every time he touches me, I begin to want things that defy reason.

I hold his gaze for a brief moment before picking up my backpack and turning towards the door. I need to get out of here before I do something foolish.

"It had to do with Derek White, didn't it?" he asks as soon as I reach the door.

With my hand on the knob, I hesitate to open it. This is my chance to tell Hunter what has been going on. I saw the concerned look in his eyes when inspecting my injured hand; he'd protect me. I don't know why he bothers to care, but I guess the answer is Serena.

"Did he …. Has he hurt you?"

The Tucker Girls

"It's nothing I can't handle," I reply bitterly. It's a bluff, but I will find another way to solve my problem before I'm ever caught begging Hunter for help again.

"Can you do me just one favor? Stop walking around school by yourself. *Please.*"

I don't bother agreeing to his request before I exit the classroom and return to the hallway. I'm too emotionally spent to know if I just made the only move that would preserve the last shred of dignity I have or if I made a terrible mistake.

CHAPTER SIXTEEN
Hunter

Why did you follow me at lunch if you didn't talk to Lexi?

Lindsey's question has been churning through my head for weeks now. Why *did* I bother chasing after her? Replaying that day in my head, I remember waking up with the resolution that I would stay out of Lindsey Tucker's business. Although the day before, I had dragged Derek into the locker room and threatened him if he didn't leave her alone. If me slamming him against the locker doesn't deter him, I don't know what will.

Dealing with Derek gave me closure. It tied up the final loose end I had with Lindsey.

Why did I still feel the need to chase after her when I saw how miserable she was in the cafeteria? It's because Lindsey is living in my head rent-free. She's captivating my thoughts, and it's driving me insane. She makes me do irrational things, which is why I need to stay clear of her.

I wasn't her only lifeline at Ulla Meyer. There were other people Lindsey could reach out to if Derek didn't heed my warning and continued pestering her, which is why I should mind my own business. She clearly doesn't want my help. She's made that clear a thousand times over.

On the day in question, my plan of leaving Lindsey alone was set, and I passed my first test that morning when she attempted to talk to me as I entered the school. It was surprisingly difficult to resist the urge to engage with her, but I pushed through it. I refused to cave even when she chased me down the hall.

The Tucker Girls

Then Trigonometry rolled around, and once again, I refused the impulse to reach out to her. I even showed up late to class to avoid the temptation. Thankfully, Lindsey didn't make another effort to talk to me, or I might have broken down and caved.

It was when I stole a glance in her direction at lunch - seeing how utterly defeated she looked - that my resolution finally fell apart. I found it impossible to focus on anything but her misery. My inexplicable soft spot for Lindsey flared up again, and I completely ditched my well-thought-out plan. Despite the death glare she shot my way, I got up in the middle of lunch to check on her.

Of course, that's when this perplexing girl took off running, and I chased after her. I've never met anyone like Lindsey, and whenever I think I know what to expect from her, I am surprised by another curveball she'll throw my way.

This leads me back to the critical question that I have been wrestling with yet unable to fully answer. Why can't I just leave her alone? There's a multitude of troubled youth packed into this high school. What makes Lindsey different? Was it that she's Serena's sister? Or the fact that she shared some of the same mannerisms as her sister? Did the resemblance make me feel more connected with her than I actually was?

Question after question assaults my head in a maddening fashion. All Lindsey has shown me is indifference and ill will. It defies reason that I feel any responsibility to her, but I do. When I finally caught her, I dragged her into the classroom intending to get answers. Lindsey would tell me what was going on, and I would fix the issue so I could exorcize her from my thoughts entirely.

Leave it to Lindsey to flip the table on me once again. Her fiery temper flared, and she injured her hand trying to punch me. That wasn't what threw me for a loop, though. I don't really know how to explain what happened next. Since the first time

161

The Tucker Girls

I'd seen her scars, they'd called to me like a beacon of pain. I wanted to connect with the darkness that she keeps bottled up, and when I did, something happened between us. A connection started forming that I didn't fully understand. I'd never wanted a girl like I did Lindsey at that moment. Thankfully, she came to her senses because I'm not sure what would have happened otherwise.

The entire situation was a complete disaster. Not only did I not get answers from her, but I felt more entangled with her than before. Sure, it was satisfying as hell to know that Lindsey didn't hate me; not entirely, at least. She was lying to herself, and I finally proved it. It was a small victory in a series of defeats.

Lindsey threatens everything that I'm trying to accomplish in my life. The margin of error is slim, so I can't be risking my standing with the school, graduation, work or leaving Amberly for someone who seems to find trouble around every turn. I have a feeling that if I don't disentangle from her soon, my goals will go up in flames.

Even knowing how important it is to avoid her, I have been watching Lindsey closely, monitoring her every move. I have been making sure I do so from a distance, but there's a nagging feeling that Derek is still causing her issues. I just need confirmation before I truly ruin the boy.

When Lindsey exits a classroom, I ensure she arrives safely at her next period. The only time I don't have eyes on her is when she's in the restroom. I've tried to be subtle about my surveillance.

Derek has taken notice, and I am making it clear she's under my protection and there's no window of opportunity for him to continue his torture. I think he's getting the idea. It's hard to tell for sure with twisted people like him. Every time he skulks around a corner, when Lindsey is near, all he has found is me ready to greet him.

The Tucker Girls

Constantly on guard, I have been waiting for him to simply breathe in Lindsey's direction. I just need one wrong move, and I will take action, but he's been on his best behavior. He hasn't given me any reason to believe he's bothering her anymore. Derek must have realized that she isn't worth the trouble and likely found a new victim to torment. I refuse to let my mind think about the poor soul he may have chosen to give his unwanted attention to instead. I can't save everyone.

Of course, Lindsey figured out pretty quickly what I was up to despite my attempts to keep my surveillance low-key. It couldn't have been difficult to figure out when she noticed me showing up in halls I had no business being in. Everywhere she turned, I was somewhere in the vicinity.

At first, Lindsey would roll her eyes or glare at me as she exited her classes. Her reaction wasn't a deterrent, considering I knew her secret; her gestures were just as much a part of her disguise as her baggy clothes. She conceals what she doesn't want the world to see. Lindsey may not appreciate my overbearing concern, but I surmise she isn't as irritated as she's pretending to be.

By the second week, Lindsey changed tactics and began confronting me with various demands such as getting a life, jumping off a cliff and ceasing to exist. You know, the typical repertoire of cutting comments that she's used in the past. By the end of that week, she continued repeating her demands even though her words were beginning to lack the same conviction. She likely realized that they didn't have the desired effect; that or she remembered she was supposed to erase me from her memory. Who can possibly decipher her unpredictable actions? Trying to solve the puzzle that is Lindsey Tucker requires a doctorate in psychology.

By the time Thanksgiving break rolled around, I felt oddly uncomfortable trading my newly established routine with staring at my bedroom walls. The holiday dragged on forever. I

163

practically was bouncing off the walls, impatiently waiting for school, and my mission, to start again. Anything to give me a purpose beyond this hellish home.

It certainly didn't help that any holiday with Pete sucks. Most kids my age spend quality time with loved ones filling up on turkey, mashed potatoes and stuffing. Not me, though. There's no meal or traditions to look forward to. Our only holiday routine is fighting, so I try to avoid drunk Pete as much as possible while locked away in my room. Thankfully Drake threw me a couple extra shifts at Stirred Up to keep me from going insane.

After managing to make myself scarce and avoiding any unnecessary interactions with the world's worst parent once again, I feel a sense of relief stepping back through the rear doors of Ulla Meyer this morning. The familiar sights and smells bring me more comfort than my house ever will. These halls hold most of the best memories of my teenage years.

With every step, I can feel my mood lifting. By the time I spy Chaz and Devon talking in the cafeteria, I've flushed all my bad memories from recent days out of my mind. I squeeze between my two friends, swinging an arm around each of their shoulders.

"Boys, we need a party," I state to raucous agreement.

"Hell yeah," Chaz rumbles, slapping me on my back. "I'd throw one at my place, but my parents don't have any upcoming travel plans."

"Let's do it at my place," Devon offers.

"You sure?" I ask sincerely. Devon's never hosted a party since I've known him.

"Yeah. I got a big backyard. I'm thinking we do a booze and bonfire this Friday."

"Let's get lit," Chaz chimes in with a big grin. "I'm going to need a whole lot of beer to wash down all the turkey I ate the last few days."

"Same," I reply, slapping my abs and pretending like I actually know what Chaz's talking about. I did eat some turkey breast deli meat. So technically that counts, right?

"Are you and Brady still good?" Chaz asks, eyeing me carefully.

"Yeah, we're alright."

Brady and I have been at odds over Serena. The fact that I didn't entirely back off has strained our relationship. If he's that bent out of shape about it, he needs to just confront me and stop pouting around like a baby. We need a good fight and then agree to move on. Needless to say, I did not get an invitation to come to his house for Thanksgiving this year.

"Good cause we need him to bring the alcohol," Chaz states in a relieved tone.

Brady has traditionally been the one to hook us up. He has the expendable income and connections that most of the school lacks.

"I'll let him know we need him," I confirm.

"Alright, let's get the word out then. Start with all the finest ladies," Devon continues. "Speaking of fine women, look at Serena's sister. Did she turn hot overnight or what?"

I turn to see that Serena and Lindsey have just passed through the school's rear entrance. I'm forced to do a double take when I spy the younger Tucker sister. She's ditched the hoodie for a form-fitting navy sweater. Throw in that she's actually wearing make-up, and I hardly recognize her. Based on the gawking of guys nearby, Devon's not the only one taking notice too.

As was evident the night of Homecoming, Lindsey's every bit as attractive as her sister when she's not trying to conceal it. Most of the school is probably wondering who this girl is, likely unable to recognize her.

While I'm trying to process how Lindsey has caught me off guard once more, I take note that she pauses a few steps in to look towards the vending machines. Her face falls when she realizes that the space is unoccupied. I've been waiting there every morning for the past few weeks, but today I changed up the routine when I spotted Devon and Chaz. The fact that she's disappointed to not find me lingering in my usual spot makes my chest swell with an odd sense of satisfaction.

"Woah," Chaz mumbles under his breath. "How have I not noticed this before? She's almost as hot as Serena."

Wrong.

"We're definitely inviting her too," Devon chimes in.

"Both of you are going to leave her alone," I grumble. "Now stop talking about Lindsey before Serena overhears you. She won't appreciate you discussing how hot you think her sister is."

Serena, right on cue, walks up to the three of us. I cannot help but notice Devon and Chaz stand a little taller as she approaches.

"Morning, boys," Serena calls out.

"What's new with my favorite girl?" Devon asks, doing his best Elijah imitation. No one can adequately mirror his smoothness and charisma, though.

Serena flashes her heart-melting smile as she gives Devon a side hug. I don't miss the loaded look she gives me when our eyes meet, subtly conveying her displeasure for going dark over break. She texted me twice, and both messages went unanswered. Yes, I'm a complete jerk, but she would not have wanted to witness the terrible mood I carried with me throughout the weekend.

"Chaz, did you get a haircut?"

Serena is good at noticing small details like that.

"Yeah, I did," Chaz responds as he runs a hand through his thick blonde hair. His cheeks flare up at the unexpected attention. I honestly can't recall a time I've ever seen him blush, but I guess Serena has that effect on people.

"I like it. It looks good on you."

"And what about me?" Devon inquires.

Serena inspects him intently.

"Did you get a haircut too?"

"No. That still doesn't mean my hair doesn't look good on me, too, though. I just wanted to hear you say it," Devon states with a smirk.

"You don't need to hear anything else that will inflate your ego," Serena replies, playfully slapping him on the arm.

Silence settles in with our group, giving Serena another chance to cut her eyes at me.

"Well, it was good seeing you guys again," she says, inching away from our group.

"Serena," I blurt out, grabbing hold of her hip before she can escape. She levels with me with an expectant look, her brows raised as if she's ready for an explanation as to why I ghosted her.

"Yeah?"

"It's good to see you."

She scoffs in response.

"Uh-huh. Glad to see you're still alive and well. I guess your phone must have died? Cause that would be the only reason I can think that you couldn't have bothered to respond to my messages."

"Burrrnnnnn," Devon says with glee, stifling back a laugh.

"I messed up."

"Yeah, you did. Don't worry, though. I will let you make it up to me soon," Serena replies with a wink. Then, with a quick wave, she slips away, leaving me wondering what she has in mind.

"Bro, if you aren't going to take care of your girl, then I'm going to have to step in."

The Tucker Girls

"Shut your mouth, Devon. You aren't going to do shit," I retort with more irritation than I intended.

Unlike her sister, Serena's been good for me to be around. I hate that I have hurt her, even if I did it to protect her. Holidays are the worst time to be near me.

"Pssshh. You obviously haven't locked that down. The way she's lookin' right now, she's going to have boys drooling all day. Seems to me that you've lost a step or two."

The intense glare I shoot Devon is enough to communicate that I'm not fooling around. He may be just stating the facts, but he needs to understand how serious I am about him staying away from Serena.

"I'm just sayin'," Devon mumbles after our stare off, averting his eyes to the floor.

"Just worry about the party this Friday, and I'll worry about Serena."

Without waiting for a response, I march off as I still mull over how I don't want to lose what I have with Serena. She's a shining star in my bleak world right now. Devon's words seemed to unintentionally trigger feelings I wasn't even aware of. Or was it possible I felt guilty over not responding to Serena over the break? Either way, Devon isn't moving in on her.

I don't have time to untangle my emotional web since I am already slacking on my job to watch over Lindsey. Thankfully, she is still loading up her backpack when I arrive at her locker. The door is opened so that she doesn't see me slide up against the nearby locker, but by the way Lindsey's whole body tenses, it's clear she senses my arrival.

I swear the girl possesses a talent for detecting my presence, like a Hunter radar. Waiting patiently for her to shuffle books around, I can't help but be amazed by the amount of weight she carries around each day. Her bag must weigh fifty pounds.

The Tucker Girls

"Hello, stalker," Lindsey says, shutting her locker door and surprising me with a smirk.

This is new. She's been annoyed before. Most recently, Lindsey's been aggravated and confrontational. I'm completely thrown off by the levity of her mood today. It's like the weight of Derek has been lifted off her shoulders.

"Why in the world would you think that is funny? You had a real-life stalker."

Lindsey shrugs her shoulders, unwilling to help me understand the humor. It irks me that she would even joke about it. Something has clearly changed to cause this dramatic shift, and I need to know what it is.

She tries to stroll right by me, but I slide in her way. A flicker of annoyance, that I have grown accustomed to seeing, crosses her face at my obstruction.

"Derek has stopped bothering you, hasn't he?"

"If I say yes, does that mean you will stop following me around?"

Just like that, she has me simmering with irritation. Of course, she will be difficult and respond to my question with a question of her own.

I exhale loudly and look up at the ceiling in frustration. Lindsey uses my momentary lapse in focus to escape, giving me a mischievous smile as she speedily walks away. My legs are twice as long as hers, so I can catch up in just a few strides.

"Don't force me to make a scene. Please just answer the question," I plead when I fall in stride with Lindsey.

"What are you going to do? Drag me into another empty classroom again?" she asks, a playfulness still lingering in her voice.

My head spins, trying to reconcile this version of Lindsey with the angsty one I've grown accustomed to encountering. It's almost like she's daring me to repeat our last encounter, which doesn't make any sense. Is it possible she

169

thinks she's untouchable because so many witnesses are passing by in the hallway?

Whatever her reasoning, I'm not about to fall into her trap. I swing my arm around her shoulder and pull her close. Lindsey attempts to squirm away, but I keep a firm hold on her.

"Let go of me, stalker! People will get the wrong idea if they see us together like this."

"Nope. Not letting go until you answer my question."

"I'm serious, Hunter! If Stephen sees your arm around me, he'll think I'm cheating on him."

"Guess you better start talking then."

I narrowly avoid her stomping on my foot, which clearly indicates she's not planning on talking. Swinging her body towards the nearest wall, I trap her, so she has nowhere to go. Now face-to-face with Lindsey, she's no longer sporting her playful smile. I expect her to keep fighting, but she's incredibly still as her eyes lock in on mine.

"Lindsey."

"Uh-huh," she responds breathlessly in a raspy whisper that sends my heart racing. This moment ended up way more intimate than I ever intended.

"I can make more of a scene if you want to keep playing hardball."

"Okay."

Her response blindsides me. She's daring me with her eyes to follow through with my threat. I lean in until my face is inches from hers before I pause. I hadn't actually given much thought to what I was going to do next. The last thing I expected was for her to call my bluff.

My breathing picks up as my gaze falls down to her lips. Despite countless conversations with myself about keeping my distance from her, I can only think about what her lips would feel like on mine. When my eyes lock with hers again, I notice they are daring me to follow through on my threat, and for the briefest second, I want to give in to their demand. It takes monumental restraint to not close the small gap between us.

Despite knowing she's playing head games with me, and that's the only thing holding me back. After a split-second hesitation on my end, Lindsey blinks a couple times and shakes her head before slipping out from underneath my arm. Thankfully she called a halt to her little game before I did something we'd both regret.

"Tell me why you are bothering to care, and *maybe* I will share the latest Derek update with you."

"Because I'm a masochist," I respond sarcastically. "*Obviously.*"

Lindsey eyes me with scrutiny, then proceeds to leave me without another word. This girl is going to drive me to insanity. I fall back into step with her, giving up the pursuit of answers for now. Eventually, the truth will come out. My sneaking suspicion that Derek has given up must be accurate. It's the only logical explanation.

The fact that she's referring to me as a stalker really sinks in as I walk beside her. I'm nothing like Derek. It sickens me that she would ever group us together in the same category.

"If you honestly want me to back off, I will do that. Just say the word. I'm not stalking you. I simply want to make sure you're alright."

Lindsey doesn't respond to my offer at all. She silently marches on as if I hadn't said a word. It's infuriating when she ignores me. I'm ready to give up on our conversation when she finally speaks.

"Serena is pissed at you, by the way," Lindsey offers up, breaking her prolonged silence.

"I noticed."

"You should make it right."

"You should mind your own business."

The Tucker Girls

Lindsey's fists tighten around her backpack straps at my testy response.

"If you hurt my sister, I will maim you."

"I'd never intentionally hurt Serena."

"Oh, I'm sure you wouldn't. I bet you never intentionally hurt anyone. You just use them and drop them whenever they become inconvenient."

Coming to a complete stop, I am fuming at her harsh assessment. Lindsey stops as well when she notices that I've fallen behind. She faces my glare with equal intensity, neither of us backing down.

I took a knife cut to the shoulder to protect her. Can she really think so little of me? There may have been a time when I would use people for my own satisfaction, but those days are in my past. She's never known that version of me.

Rather than argue with her over all the times I've demonstrated that I'm a decent human being, I decide to concede the point. I may have stopped using people, but I'm certainly no saint. I'm not worthy of Serena's affection either. After all, I am Pete's child. I have a darkness coded in my DNA that should frighten any normal person away. I simply do an excellent job of disguising the truth, much like my brunette adversary standing in front of me.

"You're right," I finally confess as I continue towards her. "I'm not a good person. Not at all."

My admission gives Lindsey pause, almost like she didn't expect me to agree with her. It feels good to pull the rug out from under her for once.

"Lexi seems to think you have redeeming qualities, though."

"Remind me again when you and Lexi became so close," I demand, seeing as this is the second time in recent conversations that she's name dropped my best friend.

The Tucker Girls

Of course, Lindsey refuses to answer the question, simply offering a shrug in response. Go figure. I should have learned by now that she doesn't ever bother to answer anything I ask.

"I have *some* redeeming qualities; for instance, I'm a fantastic human shield during a knife fight."

Slowly, and ever so slightly, Lindsey's lips curve up into a smile. It may just be the most authentic smile I've ever earned from her, and damn if it doesn't make my heart skip a beat. She doesn't offer anything real freely - not for me, at least. I feel as satisfied as if I was just awarded an Olympic gold medal. It's impossible not to respond with a smile of my own.

"There may be a few other qualities that are tolerable as well," Lindsey confesses.

"Oh yeah? Like what?"

Lindsey shrugs as she backs into her first-period classroom, still smirking before she finally turns her back on me.

Despite not getting a straight answer from her, I decide that my job is done here. Lindsey's definitely not being bothered by Derek any longer. Either she has learned to deal with him, or he finally gave up. A twinge of disappointment hits me at the realization that I no longer have a reason to hang around Lindsey. I guess she started to grow on me even though she is a complete pain in the ass.

CHAPTER SEVENTEEN
Hunter

Two days later, I decide to use my recently acquired free time to make amends with Serena. Her face lights up when she sees me waiting outside her third-period classroom, leaning against a nearby locker. Her reaction lets me know this was a good idea.

"To what do I owe the pleasure?"

"I was hoping you may want some company walking to next period," I respond, eyeing her carefully. I'm still trying to gauge if she's still holding a grudge for me going dark over the break. Serena can be difficult to read sometimes. Unlike Lindsey, she doesn't wear her emotions on her sleeve. We talked quite a bit yesterday at lunch, but I'm still unsure where I stand with her.

"Well, I don't know. Seems a little risky if you ask me. People may get the wrong idea," Serena teases, slipping her arm in mine. "I wouldn't want to start any rumors."

"Let them talk," I state, mirroring her smile. There will undoubtedly be gossip circulating by lunch, but I've never allowed rumors to stop me before. People are still talking about that stupid bet of when I will break my vow of celibacy. It's all pointless chatter of individuals with too much time on their hands.

Serena and I are slowly walking through the hallway together, and it reminds me of how effortless everything is with her. I sense that if I'd just stop fighting the natural pull of gravity, we would already be a couple. The only problem is she still hasn't figured out that I'm not a prize to be won. I'm dead weight. She's much better off finding someone that's worth her time.

"I'm sorry about last weekend. I should have responded to your texts," I confess.

"Are you ever going to tell me why you did that?"

My throat tightens as I try to swallow. I don't want to drag Serena into my drama. I've never allowed anyone a glimpse into what I deal with at home besides Lexi, Elijah and Brady. Who knows what Serena would think if she knew the whole truth. I'm not ready to start sharing it now, so I quickly think of a way to brush away the topic.

"Was it another girl?" Serena asks in a meek voice when I fail to respond quickly enough.

"No! Not at all."

"Okay, that makes me feel a little better."

"It's just … And I know this may come as a complete surprise to you … But I'm not always the most pleasant person to be around. The holidays tend to be pretty awful, so I thought it best to keep you out of my mess. Does that make sense?"

"Kinda. Does it have to do with your mother not being around?"

"That's part of it."

Serena intently eyes me, but I can't meet her gaze. This is not how I wanted this conversation to go. The uncomfortable feeling bubbling up in my chest makes me want to ditch Serena in the middle of this hallway. I fight back the urge to run from this conversation, not wanting to abandon her again.

"Next time, can you at least let me decide if I can handle it rather than making that decision for me?"

"I'll try to do better."

Serena sighs in response. She's clearly frustrated that I'm not ready to make her any promises. She wants access to parts of my life that I'm not sure I will ever be able to share with her.

"Are you planning on going to the bonfire Friday night at Devon's house?" I inquire, attempting to divert the conversation.

"Yes. Want to ride together?"

"Yeah, that would be great. I will pick you up around nine."

"Perfect," Serena replies, tugging me towards the hallway my fourth-period class is on. "Come on, I need to stop by my locker before class."

"Works for me. So tell me about your break. Did you do anything fun?"

"Besides eating way too much food? I drug Lindsey out at midnight for some late-night shopping. Usually, Mom comes too, but she was feeling under the weather. Lindsey tried to cancel on me, but I wouldn't let her."

"I bet she was a joy to shop with," I reply sarcastically.

"Be nice," Serena replies, nudging me with her elbow. "That being said, she was a little grumpy about the whole experience. Her mood improved when she found a purse she really liked."

"Is your mom feeling better?"

"Yeah, it was just a minor cold. She was really disappointed not to go with us, though."

Serena sighs, her face falling as she talks about missing out on time with her mother. Jealousy stirs within me at the fact that they have such a great relationship. It's the one thing that my other friends have in common with me; we all have terrible parents. Serena's wholesome family serves as another reminder of how mine is irreparably broken.

I wonder what type of relationship I would have had with my mother if she had bothered to stick around. My stomach twists as I ponder the thought. It's a waste of time to consider such things considering she abandoned me. She wouldn't have disappeared if she had wanted a relationship with me.

"I will swing into Trig since we are already here."

"Oh. Okay. Well, before we part ways," Serena states, turning towards me as we stand just outside my classroom. "I just wanted to make sure we are still going to the gala together."

"Yeah. Of course, we are. Why wouldn't we be going together?"

Serena averts her eyes briefly, then shrugs her shoulders in a defeated manner.

"I don't know, Hunter. To be completely honest, I never know where we stand. You've been distant the last couple of weeks, so I thought you may have changed your mind."

After getting that off her chest, she looks up at me with vulnerable eyes. I finally realize that giving my full attention to thwarting creepy Derek had sent Serena the wrong message. I reach up and brush away a lock of hair that's fallen across her face.

"Serena, I've had to deal with some things that have distracted me. I'm sorry if I came across as distant towards you."

"You have a …. a history with these types of things."

It's odd to see Serena, who's usually overflowing with confidence, fret like this.

"Serena, I wouldn't do that to you. I promise that I will always be straight with you. I will never blindside by hooking up with some random girl. You're too important to me."

Serena's smile returns as she nods in understanding. I think I've managed to make amends for more than just my Thanksgiving break mistake.

We part ways, with Serena heading to her locker and me heading to class. My mind is still replaying our conversation when I'm interrupted by Mrs. Seldon's nasally voice calling out my name.

The Tucker Girls

"See me after class," Mrs. Seldon directs sternly, catching me entirely by surprise. By her scathing look, it doesn't appear that this will be a pleasant discussion. I have no idea what I have done that would cause her to be upset. It's been several weeks since I failed to submit an assignment on time.

Lindsey and Hannah give me perplexed looks as I take my seat, to which I can only respond with a shrug. I spend the remainder of class distracted by the pending lousy news. The additional time does nothing to help me recall what she wants to discuss.

After the bell rings, I patiently wait for the classroom to clear before heading up to Mrs. Seldon's desk.

"Mr. Bowden, it should be no surprise that your midterm assessment will show you failing this course."

"Are you sure, ma'am? I feel as though I've been performing better on my tests."

Mrs. Seldon scoffs at my assessment.

"Yes, I'm quite sure. Your results have been more encouraging, but it's still not enough to bring your overall grade above a seventy. If you do not start taking Trigonometry seriously, you will fail it again. You *must* turn in all assignments and prepare harder for your quizzes and tests if you have any hope of turning things around."

"Yes, ma'am. I can do better."

"Good. I'm glad to hear that."

I feel as though I've been hit by a truck. This isn't the only class in which I'm flirting with failure. I have a difficult time applying myself to things that seem meaningless in the grand scheme of things. I have no intention of going to college, so what's the point in learning Trigonometry? I can't think of a single practical purpose for learning this math.

On top of my lack of motivation, I've been working my tail off at Drake's restaurant. Unfortunately, the late nights make it really difficult to find time to study.

The Tucker Girls

Regardless of its importance, I cannot fail this course. *I have to graduate.* There's no alternative that I can live with.

"Before you even ask, there will not be any make-up tests or extra credit assignments. You get one shot, so I suggest you start taking this class seriously. Find a tutor. Join a study group. I honestly don't care what you do, but do *something*. If you can't turn it around, this will reflect poorly on *me*."

There's the real reason for this pep talk. Mrs. Seldon doesn't want to go down with my sinking ship. And to think I actually thought she cared for a brief moment.

I thank her for her advice and promptly leave class. Though I'm pretty sour about Mrs. Seldon's motives, she did give me one piece of advice that I plan to utilize: find a tutor. It's time to take Serena up on her offer from the beginning of the school year.

I wonder how disappointed she will be when she finds out I can't pass the required courses for graduation?

At most public schools, I would have been good to go with a much lower level of math. Ulla Meyer has to keep up their standards as a school of excellence by setting the bar higher. I don't have the option of holding onto my dignity right now. I will beg Serena for help.

I'm going to need additional time to study, so I will have to ask Drake to cut back on my hours. This will delay my goal of saving enough money to move out in June. If I only drop one shift a week, it should only delay me a month or two. At least, that's what some quick math comes to in my head, but I'm clearly not very proficient when it comes to the subject. I'll have to double-check it tonight after work.

I'm walking in a daze, trying to wrap my head around this latest development when I hear commotion brewing in one of the hallways that run perpendicular to the main hall. Great, another fight. Marcel's crew is up to their same antics once again. Hopefully, none of my friends are caught up in it this time.

After closer inspection, I realize that the situation isn't a fight. People congregate around a locker with intense interest, conversation buzzing amongst them with excitement. I turn towards the scene, pushing through some of the crowd until I see the word *WHORE* spray painted in bright red letters that cover an entire locker door.

A couple teachers are attempting to disperse the crowd, but everyone is too busy capturing the moment with their cell phones to bother listening to their orders. I've seen people carve disparaging things into lockers before, but never attempt anything this brazen. Whoever sprayed this message did it during school hours. This graffiti wasn't here earlier this morning.

Half my brain is still wrestling with my failing grade, which is why it takes me a few seconds longer than it should to comprehend that the locker belongs to Lindsey. My pulse quickens at the realization. I immediately scan the crowd looking for her without luck. A hundred students must be crowding this area, all trying to get a look at the offensive message.

Finally, I spy the teary-eyed brunette burst out of the crowd with cheeks so red, I swear she looks feverish. Based on her trajectory, she's headed straight for Derek, who is observing his handiwork from a distance.

She's going to kill him. Though her tears mask it, I can still make out the murderous look in her gray eyes. If she lays a hand on Derek without proof that he authored this disturbing message, she will be suspended. I can't allow that to happen.

"Move!" I bark out to the bystanders surrounding me.

Forcefully pushing through the crowd that separates us, I bolt toward Lindsey with reckless abandon. Several individuals yell out as I slam into them, but I don't have time to apologize for the bruises left in my wake. Lindsey has a head start that seems insurmountable. As she reels back to hit Derek, I scoop her up into my arms and spin. My momentum carries me straight into the wall, my back taking the brunt of the painful impact. It may be the adrenaline pumping through my veins, but the collision doesn't hurt nearly as bad as I expected.

I feel Lindsey swing all four limbs in protest, displaying uncanny strength for someone almost half my size. It takes every bit of my strength to keep her from wrestling free of my hold.

"Let me go!" she screams in a fit of rage.

Lindsey's anger has overtaken her ability to reason. I'm hanging on for dear life as she bucks and kicks, realizing I need to try and talk some sense into her. My shin gets kicked, sending pain running up my leg, and I groan in pain.

"If you hit him, you will get suspended," I yell, still smarting from her kick.

"I don't care!"

Lindsey breaks free for a split second, but I quickly manage to regain control of her once more. This time, I spin her around so she's forced to look me in the face.

"I did it! I wrote that message!" I scream, shocking her enough that she halts her fight. Her murderous gaze locks in on me, and I brace myself for the punch that I expect is coming any second. Rather than attack, she pauses to study my face.

"Liar," she declares, but in a more muted tone. "You're lying."

It didn't take her long to reason that she's been with me for the last hour and that I couldn't have messed with her locker. I successfully managed to jump-start the logical part of her brain, though. Based on the way her eyes remain locked on mine, she's confused as to why I would throw out a false confession. From my perspective, it doesn't matter what she believes at this

181

moment as long as she's not attacking Derek. I will have plenty of time to explain it to her after dealing with this situation.

"If you are going to hit someone, hit me," I plead. "Please, just hit me."

Even if she gets caught slugging me, I can claim it was just self-defense. I can concoct a story where I'm the villain. No one will question whether it's true. My reputation would work in her favor. My high school career is already tanking, so adding more fuel to the fire at this point won't matter. For Lindsey, it could mean everything. I'm sure she has plans to go to college. Having a fight and suspension on her record would make her a less attractive candidate. I refuse to allow her to throw away her future on Derek White. He's clearly baiting her into this type of response.

Lindsey is still in shock, but I can see the wheels turning in her head.

"Why are you lying," she asks, tears still streaming down her face. It's breaking me to see her in this state.

"You're right. I didn't do it," I agree in a calm voice. "I just needed to distract you from ruining your future. If you need to hit someone, hit me. I can take it."

"No, I won't hit you."

My thumb swipes away a tear before it leaks down her cheek, and Lindsey closes her eyes in response to my touch. It was a stupid gesture because more tears pour from her eyes.

Anger, that I've been suppressing this entire time, begins to boil within me. Derek waited until Lindsey had dropped her guard and then sucker punched her with this unexpected message. I'd swallowed down my own rage, because Lindsey needed me to be a calming presence, but now there's going to be retribution. I'm going to destroy Derek.

As Lindsey's breathing slows, I spy Brady pushing through the crowd toward us. Despite our recent disagreements, I know I can trust him in this chaotic situation. We are always there for each other when it matters - like family should be. Making eye contact with my friend, I jerk my head towards Lindsey and wordlessly ask for assistance.

"You can let me go now," Lindsey says calmly, though I'm not sure I can trust her to not pummel Derek the second I let go.

"Take Lindsey, and don't let her go," I direct Brady, maneuvering Lindsey into his arms. Although she attempts to break free once more, Brady manages to keep her under control.

"Hunter!" Lindsey screams out in frustration, likely not appreciating being passed off. I need my hands free for what's coming next. I give her an apologetic look but then turn my back on her.

The second I face Derek, all I see is red. No one else exists but him and me now. The rage I'd stuffed down wants to come out and play, and I'm not going to deny it. Derek was warned what would happen if he continued messing with Lindsey, and I will deliver on all the promises I made weeks ago. I'm about to introduce creepy Derek to the terrifying monster Pete Bowden molded through years of abuse.

I start marching towards the psychopath who is still gleefully admiring the chaos he's instigated. His expression changes when he spies me coming for him, though. Fear spills over his face, wiping away every trace of smugness.

"I didn't do it!" he protests, raising his hands up as if he's innocent.

Rather than argue with the creep, I save my breath. I reel back and punch him in the jaw, sending his eyes rolling back from the impact. The crack of my fist connecting with his face echoes louder than the mumbling of students surrounding us.

Derek stumbles against the nearby wall, caught entirely off guard by my attack. He wasn't expecting me to come at him on school grounds in front of a crowd of witnesses. It's typically not my style, and Derek's been around long enough to know that, but I'm making an exception today. Let my world burn to the ground as long as he goes with me.

Derek reels back, ready to throw a punch, but I grab him by the hair and slam his head into the wall. He throws an elbow blindly, managing to catch the side of my head. I'm numb to the pain, though. Grabbing hold of his upper body, I drive him into the floor. The sound of his head smacking against the tile draws a reaction from the crowd hovering around us. Derek howls in agony, and I'm eating up every second of his torture like the demented person I am.

Derek frantically attempts to defend himself, throwing aimless punches that do little to deter me. He gives up that strategy after I land a couple of punishing punches to his face. He starts cradling his face to protect himself when I straddle his abdomen. He has nowhere to run now, and I keep pounding on him with both fists.

"I warned you!"

Punch.

"You don't look at her."

Punch.

"You don't talk to her."

Punch.

"You don't touch her stuff."

Punch.

"You don't even breathe near her."

Punch.

Derek's blood is trickling onto the floor, and it's likely splashed on my clothing too. Some brave soul tries to intervene, grabbing hold of me from behind. I quickly shake them off and return to my work.

"She's mine! Don't you ever forget that."

Breathless, I return to my feet as I look down on his trembling body. Then, with a swift kick to his chin, Derek's body goes entirely limp. His wailing is finally muted. I give a couple more kicks to his abdomen for good measure before relenting.

I hear people screaming my name, but they are trying to speak to a boy who doesn't exist. At this moment, I'm the monster that my father created. Pete's blood runs in my veins, and it's never been more evident than at this moment.

Derek will *never* mess with Lindsey again.

Looking over at Brady, I mouth the words *Bury Him*. Based on his facial expressions, he's taken aback by the brutality of what he just witnessed, but eventually he nods in understanding. I am going to need his help to finish Derek. This beating was just the first phase of my retribution.

Although I try not to look her way, I cave and take in Lindsey's reaction. She's frozen in Brady's arms, her complexion looking especially pale. I can only imagine how horrified she is from watching me beat Derek to a bloody pulp. Though my scars aren't visible on my body like hers, they are ugly as well, and she's getting an up-close-and-personal view of them for the first time.

Two teachers grab hold of me, dragging me away from Derek and escorting me to the principal's office. It's not until I plop down in a chair and wait to be called in that I begin to assess myself. I have several scratch marks on my arms and Derek's blood on my shirt.

Placing my head in my hands, I cringe at the consequences that are about to be dished out. I'm not ignorant. I know the conversation with the principal is going to be grim. I will likely be expelled from school because this isn't the first fight I've participated in at Ulla Meyer. My ticket out of Amberly just burned to ash.

I sigh heavily when I see the bleak look on Mr. Grayson's face as he waves me into his office. It's time to atone for my sins.

CHAPTER EIGHTEEN
Lindsey

Night has set in while we wait for Hunter to emerge from the school's office with a verdict. The blanket of darkness beyond the windows clouds all visibility to the outside world. It feels appropriate for the night to captivate my attention because it mirrors the gloomy mood that looms around me.

Our group, consisting of Lexi, Serena, Elijah, Brady and myself, are all dealing with our anxiety in our own way. While I stare off into nothingness, Serena keeps attempting small talk, which no one is entertaining. Elijah is pacing the hallway, unable to sit for longer than a minute before hopping back to his feet. Lexi's head is buried in her hands while she sits on the bench next to Serena.

Finally, there's Brady, who hasn't left my side since Hunter ordered him to manhandle me. Rather than join in on the gloomy mood, he's texting non-stop on his stupid phone. When I hear him chuckle to himself, I turn to give him a death glare. How can he sit here and laugh at meaningless texts while Hunter may be getting expelled? Could he possibly be that heartless?

Hunter has been in there for hours. I already had my turn being interrogated by Mrs. Alina. Once again, I had no proof that Derek was the culprit, so she released me with nothing more than sympathetic words. It makes me ill that Derek is going to escape unscathed again, other than being pummeled by Hunter.

Brady catches the malicious look I throw his way when he fires off another text and shoves his phone back into his pocket.

"How are you holding up?" he asks in a hushed voice that only I can hear.

"Just peachy," I reply sarcastically. "You don't have to hover around any longer. You did your job. Good boy. Hunter will be so proud."

I wave my hand in the air, indicating for him to go away.

"Sorry, no can do. Hunter ordered me to look after you, and that's what I'm going to do."

"You're kidding, right? He told you to 'take her,' which you did. Mission accomplished. Now run along and give me some space."

Brady sighs as he leans his head back against the wall. He's not budging from his seat. I would get up and move, but I know he'd follow me wherever I went.

The sound of a door opening cues us all to attention, but it's not the office door. Instead, Stephen walks through the school entrance with two grease-stained takeout bags from the local burger joint. The smell of hot fries races ahead of him and has me salivating instantly.

"Hey, Lindsey. How are you doing?" he asks with a loaded look.

Stephen has no idea why I'm waiting around considering I'd already been questioned, and I know he's dying to ask a million questions, but he's withholding them for now. If I thought that giving him the answers he wants would help, I'd undoubtedly offer them, but I know that none of what transpired today would make any sense to him. Heck, it doesn't even make sense to me.

Our brief conversation was strained at best when he left school hours ago. I'm not sure what he heard about the incident, but he did confirm that he saw my locker. I felt so sick just thinking about the awful message; my brain shut down. Since then, part of me has been worried that I'd somehow caused permanent damage to our budding relationship, which is why I'm so relieved to see Stephen return.

"I've been better," I confess with a shrug.

"Here, I brought some burgers and fries for everyone. I figured you all might be getting hungry, and I wasn't sure how much longer you would have to stick around."

"That's so thoughtful!" I respond with a warm smile.

"Thanks, Stanley!" Elijah chimes, snatching a bag from Stephen and opening it up.

"*It's Stephen*," I shoot back.

"Yeah. That's what I said," Elijah replies as he walks away, opening the bag and offering its contents to Lexi, but she waves it off.

Stephen opens the other bag and angles it towards me, and I don't hesitate to grab a container of fries. Hopping from the bench, I close the distance between us.

"Walk with me?"

Stephen nods his head in agreement. We slowly meander away from the others to get some privacy. When we stop and turn towards one another, I discover Brady leaning against the wall nearby. He followed me once again.

"You've got to be kidding me," I grumble in frustration. "Do you mind?"

"Nope. Don't mind at all," Brady replies nonchalantly.

"*Get. Lost*," I snarl.

"I would *but* I just don't know Stanley all that well. I'm not very comfortable with you hanging around him."

"His name is Stephen," I respond through gritted teeth. "And you don't have to know him very well. I know him. He's my boyfriend."

Brady gives me a skeptical look as if he doesn't believe that fact but finally relents with a shrug, choosing to provide us with a little more space.

The Tucker Girls

"I feel like I'm in the Twilight Zone," Stephen states once we finally have some privacy. "Are you going to tell me what's going on? Why did your locker get defaced? And why did Hunter Bowden brutally attack another kid?"

"The kid's name is Derek. He's been tormenting me for a couple weeks, and I was too embarrassed to tell you. I thought he'd stopped his antics, but today he decided to spray that message on my locker."

"Lindsey, you should have said something."

"I know. I know. I wanted to think that I could deal with it on my own. Anyways, that's why Hunter attacked him. He knew that Derek was the one who spray painted that message."

"Why did Hunter bother to care?"

He did it *for Serena*. I shake my head to dismiss that nagging thought.

"Cause he and my sister are talking," I reply. "I guess he was trying to score points with Serena."

"Hmmm."

As I stuff another fry in my face, I can see that there's more he wants to ask, but he seems to hesitate with this next question.

"Some people were talking …. saying that you and Hunter are together, and that's why he went ballistic," Stephen finally states reluctantly.

She's mine.

I can still hear echoes of Hunter screaming at Derek's, and I can't comprehend what his words mean. My head is numb from wrestling with everything that transpired today. The only conclusion I came to was that his anger had him yelling things that didn't make sense.

"*What*! No. No. That's ridiculous, Stephen. I'm with you. Nothing is going on with Hunter and me. They got the wrong Tucker girl."

189

"Yeah. That's what I thought," he replies with a nod, though I'm not one hundred percent sure that he believes me.

She's mine.

As I recall Hunter's words once more, I picture him throwing punch after punch at Derek, and a shiver runs through me. Everyone had warned my sister and me about this version of Hunter since we'd arrived in Amberly. As often as he's had me pinned in a confined area, you'd think I would have been terrified of what he may do, but I'd never felt unsafe around him. It was Derek who truly terrified me.

Stephen lets out a sigh of relief after he's taken a minute to digest my answer.

"I just needed to hear you say that. Sorry, I knew it was all complete nonsense."

"You're fine. And thank you again for the food. You're the best," I say as I lean forward and kiss his cheek.

Stephen's smile lights up his face.

"Don't you have a massive Calculus test tomorrow?" I inquire, remembering our conversation this morning.

"Yeah. I have my backpack in my car. I can grab my stuff and study here until you're ready to leave."

"No, please go home and study. I will never forgive myself if you bomb the exam."

"Are you sure?"

"Yes. Please. That would be one less thing I need to worry about right now."

"You know I could just drive you home. You don't need to wait around for Serena."

"That's kind of you, Stephen, but I feel responsible for what Hunter did. I need to know what happens to him."

"Okay," Stephen remarks, clearly not understanding my reasoning.

After a brief embrace, we say goodnight to one another. Serena flashes me a measured smile, likely having watched

Stephen and me interact from afar. She's halfway through a burger that I'm sure she won't be able to finish. Her stomach can't handle it right now.

Returning to my bench, I lean against the wall and rub my eyes. It's been an emotionally charged afternoon, and I'm on the verge of collapse. I want a redo on the entire day.

Elijah offers Lexi food once more, and this time she lifts her head up from her hands.

"How can you possibly eat right now?" Lexi chastises him.

Elijah pulls the bag back towards himself.

"I can always eat."

"Must be nice."

"Don't start this nonsense again," he replies, shaking his head.

"What nonsense?"

"You always do *this*. You act like you are the only one that cares about him," Elijah retorts.

"That's cause *I'm the one* who will have to pick up the pieces," Lexi responds, her voice rising as she gets to her feet.

"Fine! I'll take responsibility for Hunter this time."

"By taking responsibility, you better not mean getting Hunter wasted. That's the last thing he needs right now."

"Would you two calm down?" Brady chimes in.

"Stay out of this, Brady!" Elijah and Lexi shout out in unison.

"Fine," Brady mumbles to himself, then leans in close to me. "I hate it when mom and dad fight."

I shake my head at his ridiculous comment but can't stop my lips from turning up.

"Have you ever considered why they've kept Hunter so long?" Lexi asks pointedly, still glaring at Elijah.

"I'm sure you're going to tell me," Elijah grumbles.

"They need a parent to show up."

"Shit," Elijah responds, suddenly realizing a significant detail I don't completely understand. I remember Hunter saying that his father worked a lot. Is it possible that he's unavailable? How long would they keep Hunter if his dad can't show up?

"Yeah," Lexi responds, throwing her hands in the air. "Just a minor detail that you overlooked."

"I don't understand. Why isn't Hunter's father here yet? It's after six o'clock." Serena asks, but no one bothers to respond to her question.

"I don't know how Hunter walks away from this without getting expelled," Lexi continues, dread crossing her face.

"He's not getting expelled," Brady chimes in.

"What makes you so sure?"

"After what Mr. Grayson just learned about Derek, he'll be giving Hunter a freaking award."

Everyone throws inquisitive looks at Brady. He sighs, obviously reluctant to share the information he's been withholding.

"While you were in the office," Brady begins, jabbing a thumb in my direction, "and you all were still in class, the police showed up. They searched Derek's locker and discovered enough meth to get the entire school high. While digging through the rest of his things, they also found a can of spray paint that was used on Lindsey's locker. Needless to say, Derek will no longer be attending Ulla Meyer. He will need an excellent lawyer, or he will end up in juvie."

The possibility of never seeing Derek again feels too good to be true. I try to tamper the hope rising within me, since it would devastate me if Derek showed up to school tomorrow morning.

"You buried him," Lexi states aimlessly as if she's processing the fact externally to herself.

"That's what Hunter told me to do," Brady replies matter-of-factly.

The Tucker Girls

Bury him.

I recall seeing Hunter mouth those words to Brady before teachers dragged him to the office. A chill runs down my back as I realize what Brady just admitted to; he planted drugs in Derek's locker.

"How did you get in his locker?" I ask, my voice barely a whisper. I'm stunned at what transpired without me being aware.

"Me? I didn't do anything," Brady answers with a smirk, turning to look directly at me. "You should know, though, that we run this school. Gaining access to lockers isn't as difficult as it sounds."

"How'd you find the spray paint?" Lexi inquires.

"Sanchez found it in his car," Brady chimes, his pride on full display as he beams with delight. "Can you believe that? The idiot didn't have the sense to toss it."

"Wait. So you had someone break into his car?" I interject.

"Keep your voice down!" Brady chastises me, scanning the hallways nearby. "And yes. I got someone to go through his car in case there was something we could use, and we stumbled upon the spray paint. So we really lucked out."

Our group silently processes the revelation for a few minutes before anyone is able to say anything. Derek will be hard-pressed to avoid punishment with the amount of evidence that the police discovered. As much as I hate the guy, I have difficulty swallowing this news. He deserved the beating he received, but the drugs feel excessive. Where did they even get that much meth on short notice? The guilt is already weighing heavy on my conscience.

"Regardless of what you just said, Hunter could still get expelled," Elijah says, finally breaking the silence.

"Maybe," Brady replies with a shrug. "At least he can claim he was defending Lindsey."

Was Hunter defending me? Brady's statement immediately stirs up a complex set of emotions that are difficult to process. Satisfaction, irritation, gratitude, anger, curiosity and fascination all swirl around inside me, leaving me unable to process it all. My brain can't handle all of this right now.

It shouldn't have come as a shock that he would defend me. Hunter's protected me before. I suspect that he inexplicably cares about my well-being.

Looking across the hallway to my sister, I remember that she's the explanation for Hunter's behavior, and this revelation grounds me from believing that I'm anything special to Hunter.

"What did he mean when he said I was his?" I ask Brady, barely above a whisper. I don't want to invite the others into this discussion.

He turns his head so he can meet my gaze. I feel silly even asking the question and immediately regret the decision. I must come off sounding hopeful, as if I want reassurance that he cares about me.

"Now that's a great question, isn't it?" Brady whispers back. "Knowing Hunter, he wasn't just sending a message to Derek, but to the entire school that you aren't to be messed with."

I stare down at my feet, letting Brady's statement sink in. Word will spread quickly throughout the school. I cringe at what people will make of Hunter's declaration. Stephen's already heard rumblings, so I assume it will be public knowledge by tomorrow morning.

Brady nudges me with his shoulder.

"Good news is you're one of us now."

"What is that supposed to mean?"

"You're one of *The Untouchables*. No one's going to mess with you now. Hunter has put the entire school on notice."

"One, I don't want in your stupid club. Two, I'm dating Stephen, which I thought was against your rules."

"Does Hunter know you are dating the stiff?"

The Tucker Girls

"It's none of his business!" I declare, my voice drawing the attention of everyone around.

"Okay," Brady replies with a shrug. "I'd tell him if I were you."

"Nope. I have no plans to tell him."

"Anyways, *The Untouchables* label was never really about who we were dating," Brady continued in a hushed voice. "I guess it sort of went that way after Lexi …. Well, that's not important right now. My point is that Hunter, Lexi, Elijah and I are all misfits in our own way. We've always marched to our drums since we were in elementary school. We recognized the outcast in each other, and it sort of drew us together.

"I don't know you very well, but I get the sense that you will fit in really well. You're a natural misfit. You don't seem to want to play by the rules either."

Brady's assumption catches me off guard. I would have never labeled myself a misfit. The last few years certainly changed me, and I'm no longer the girl that wants to conform. That said, I still don't recognize the version of myself that was prepared to destroy Derek after I found the graffiti. I was possessed; ready to be suspended if it meant exacting revenge. I would have never done something like this before the catastrophe that occurred last year.

"So …. Hunter says the word, and I'm instantly in your gang?" I ask bitterly.

"Pretty much."

"What about Janna?"

"What do you mean?"

"She sits at lunch with you guys every day. She's in your club, too, right?"

Brady scoffs at my question.

"No, she's definitely not. Hunter decides who's in our group, not Lexi. Janna sits with us because Hunter allows it. I think Lexi struck a deal after Hunter played around with her."

"That's stupid. Just to be clear, I'm not sitting with you all at lunch."

"Okay," Brady responds with a smirk. He finds something humorous about my statement, but I am being entirely serious.

"What about Chaz? Or Devon? Or Serena? Serena has to be in, right? But she's not a misfit. She's the antithesis of an outcast."

Brady's gaze diverts to my sister, and I see his face change slightly as he takes her in. He's got it bad for Serena. A pained look crosses his face as he stares at Serena. He cares too much for her, yet she's all in on Hunter.

"No one else is in our circle, but that doesn't mean we aren't friends with people. And you're right. Serena is perfect. She's not like us, but Hunter said she's in, so that's the end of it."

"And nobody objects to his orders?"

"Only you," Brady replies, chuckling to himself. "Speaking of which, I admire your spirit. You got spunk."

"Whatever."

I don't stand up to Hunter for Brady's entertainment; I do it because he triggers my anger so effortlessly. When I'm furious, I find it easier to be brave and stare down the bully.

Suddenly the door to the office busts open, and Hunter marches out, pausing to take in all of us waiting around for him. I expect him to say something, but instead, he stomps off towards the exit. He doesn't even offer a simple acknowledgment to his friends who have anxiously awaited the verdict.

Serena hops up the second Hunter appears, and I notice her face fall as he marches past without even a glance in her direction.

What a self-absorbed prick! My blood is boiling as everyone begins collecting their belongings, accepting Hunter's behavior as if it was normal.

The Tucker Girls

No! I refuse to allow him to dismiss us like this.

I bolt from the bench and burst through the door, goosebumps forming all over as the cool night air collides with every inch of exposed skin on my body. It doesn't take me long before I'm able to catch up to the brooding boy.

"Hunter! Hey! I'm talking to you, you big dummy!"

My words simply bounce off him like they have no power. The fury burning inside leads me to slam my fist into his back, and I hear Hunter groan in response. The blow hurt me more than him, I figure. Even still, the stubborn idiot doesn't bother to turn and face me. Instead, he plants his feet and remains fixed in place.

"All those people back there ... all of *your* friends ... you owe them a thank you! You can't just blow them off like that. It's rude!"

Hunter whips around with fervor, an intensity being communicated with his eyes that has me backpedaling.

"That's ironic coming from you," he yells, matching my fury. "Have you ever shown an ounce of gratitude towards me?"

"I never asked you to throw away your life for me! I didn't tell you to beat Derek to a bloody pulp! You did that all on your own. It was over-the-top and completely unnecessary."

"No! *You don't understand.* There are people in this world that will keep coming at you until you're willing to hit them back. They get enjoyment out of hurting others, and until you give them a reason to stop, they will keep coming and coming and coming ... they won't stop ... not until you make them bleed."

I get the sense that he's not just talking about Derek anymore. He's speaking from personal experience. Growing up in Indy Park must have done a number on him.

As we stare each other down, I notice his eyes soften slightly.

The Tucker Girls

"Lindsey, you need to stay away from me. What you witnessed today .... that monster .... that's me. I'm not someone you should be around. I'm not safe."

Something about his statement irks me, fanning my flames further. I scoff, looking away momentarily only to meet his eyes once more.

"*You* follow me around. Maybe *you* should give *yourself* that speech."

"You're right. I'm going to stay away from you. I will do what I should have done long ago and leave you alone."

My mind is racing a million miles per hour as I try to digest what is happening. Why does it feel like we are breaking up? It's like I'm losing him when I actually never had Hunter to begin with. I never wanted him, yet he is telling me we're done. My stomach is stabbing with pain to the point that I feel sick.

"We're done here. Go home."

After delivering those orders, Hunter turns his back on me again and begins to walk away.

"I don't take orders from you," I retort. "Oh, by the way. For your information, I'm not yours. You don't own me, and you never will own me. I will never be one of your girls. Don't let me catch you saying those ridiculous words ever again."

I witness his shoulders tense as I get in that last parting shot. With a slam of his jeep's door, he revs the engine and peels out of the parking lot, leaving me still reeling from the intense conversation. It takes me a minute or so to regain my bearings.

Meandering my way toward the school, I meet Serena on the sidewalk. Without me having to ask, she wraps her arms around me. I'm guessing she was too far away to hear our conversation, but she clearly heard me screaming at Hunter.

"He doesn't get to treat you like that," I grumble into her shoulder, trying to explain why I was yelling at her guy.

The Tucker Girls

"Hunter's had a rough day …." she begins to counter before I cut her off.

"Don't you dare make excuses for him!"

"Okay," she relents, releasing me from our embrace. "Let's go home. I'm tired."

CHAPTER NINETEEN
Serena

Ten days have passed since anyone has heard from Hunter. I've spent this weekend attempting to catch up on schoolwork since the dance team had several performances this week, but I'm finding it almost impossible to concentrate. Basketball season is in full swing, and we had three home games in six days. Gia, our coach, wanted us to learn a different routine for each game which meant I fell behind on school work trying to memorize choreography.

The week's bustle helped distract me from obsessing over Hunter's absence. Rumor is that he was suspended, and not expelled, but since he's not responding to texts, no one knows for sure. I've personally texted him fifteen times in ten days. It's Thanksgiving break all over again. I feel pathetic that I didn't stop after the first message. I'm coming off desperate, and I cannot help it. My heart is tied up in Hunter, even if my brain is screaming for me to pump the brakes.

I jump out of my chair at the sound of my phone vibrating across my room. My stupid heart is thumping wildly as I hope to see Hunter's name on the screen. Dashing over to my nightstand, I lift up the phone only to find Dain's name on the screen.

I growl loudly in frustration, throwing the device into the pile of pillows on my bed. I'm losing my mind over this boy. Staring up at my ceiling, I try to collect myself. *This isn't you, Serena.* Why can't I get a hold of myself?

"Everything okay in here?"

The Tucker Girls

Lindsey pokes her head into my room, likely inquiring as to why I just freaked out. Her face is covered in specs of paint. She must be working on a new art project, which is typically an outlet she uses when feeling overwhelmed.

Despite Derek getting expelled, it was a tough week for her as well. Rumors are flying around fast regarding her locker and Hunter's fight that followed, and suddenly she's been thrust into the spotlight. Lindsey despises all of the attention she's been receiving.

"Yeah, sorry. I'm just having a moment," I reply.

Since the day of the fight, Lindsey's been withholding important details from me, and it's caused a rift between us. I've brought up the topic multiple times, but Lindsey continually changes the subject. I just don't understand how Hunter knew Derek was the one that spray-painted her locker. To beat Derek to the point of being taken to a hospital, he had to have known beyond a reasonable doubt, right? Or did he simply make an educated guess?

"Want to come paint with me? It's really helped me in the past. Plus, you'd get some quality time with your favorite sister," Lindsey says with a cheesy grin.

As much as I want to hold onto my frustration, I love Lindsey too much to stay mad at her. She will tell me what happened in time. I have to trust that there's a good reason she's keeping the details of the fight to herself. I can almost guarantee they don't paint Hunter in a good light, which may be why she's refusing to tell me.

"Are you even sure you want my help? I'm not artistic like you. I'll probably make a big mess."

"Yes!" Lindsey's eyes light up. "It's going to be so much fun. As you can see, I paint myself just as much as I do the canvas."

I laugh as she points to several blotches of color that are scattered over her attire. She's wearing some of Dad's old clothes that should have been retired years ago, but they are perfect for her task.

"I guess I'd better change then."

"Yes. Wouldn't want your nice jeans looking like this."

Just as Lindsey finishes speaking, our doorbell rings, and my heart begins racing once more. The possibility sparks impractical hope in me. I'm so foolish, but I can't help it.

Dashing over to the window, I spy Elijah's Lexus parked along our curb. It's not the green jeep I was hoping for, but that doesn't mean Hunter isn't here. I almost barrel Lindsey over as I sprint out of my room, racing down the stairs and catching the tail end of Mom greeting Elijah and Brady in the foyer.

I usher both boys into the living room where we can talk privately, quickly giving them hugs before looking at them expectantly. I'm hoping they have some update on Hunter, though neither appears to be in good spirits, which is concerning.

"Anything?" I ask when neither speaks up.

"Not yet, gorgeous," Elijah replies in a downtrodden tone. "He does this sometimes; goes off grid for a bit, but he always reappears when he's ready."

"Why doesn't he at least answer our texts?"

"Hunter needs to unplug from time to time. I'm sure getting suspended threw him for a loop," Brady chimes in. "He's probably been drowning his sorrows and isn't sober enough to check his phone."

"Where's Lexi?"

"She's coming. She wanted to drive by Hunter's house on the way here," Elijah responds.

"What happened to you?" Brady inquires with surprise, looking past me.

I spin around to find Lindsey standing just past the living room threshold.

"I've been destressing from the past week," Lindsey responds with a shrug.

"Doing what exactly? You look like you played paintball and lost terribly," Brady inquires, stepping around me to get a better look at Lindsey.

"Har har har. I'm doing art, doofus."

"Must be one helluva project. By the way, how's Stanley?"

"*Stephen.*"

"Right, *Stephen.* How's Stephen doing these days," Brady asks with a playful smile.

"He's fine. I'll be sure to let him know you were concerned about his welfare."

Brady slides up next to Lindsey, and alarms start going off in my head. He was practically attached to her hip after the graffiti incident, and now he's taking an immediate interest again the second he lays eyes on her.

"Stop flirting with Serena's sister," Elijah grumbles, picking up on the same vibe I am. "We have business to take care of."

"I wouldn't dare flirt with her. She already belongs to someone else," Brady replies with a smirk.

My eyes dance between Lindsey and Brady, getting the sense that I'm missing the significance of his last comment. She and Stephen have been dating for weeks. This isn't groundbreaking news, but Brady is acting its top secret intel with his smug smile.

"Alright, lover boy. Leave my sister alone unless you want to get castrated," I threaten, tugging him away from Lindsey.

"Relax," Brady responds nonchalantly. "I only have eyes for one Tucker, and that's you."

"Uh-huh. Either way, stay on that side of the room," I direct, pointing to a couch. Brady complies, plopping down and kicking his feet up.

The Tucker Girls

The doorbell rings again, and I race to the door once more. Despite knowing who to expect on the other side, I'm still disappointed to only find Lexi standing there. Her eyes look weighed down from the last ten days. I know she loves Hunter, and him going dark has her worried. She quickly hugs me before joining the others in the living room.

"I'm guessing he wasn't at his house?" I ask while Lexi is still busy greeting the others.

Elijah holds up a hand as if to stop me, nodding in Lindsey's direction. I'd forgotten my sister was still lingering on the fringe of the room. We'd agreed to meet at my house to talk, but Lindsey isn't supposed to be a part of this conversation.

"She's good," Brady calls out, waving his hand dismissively. "Hunter said she's in."

My head swivels between Lindsey and Brady, trying to piece together this new revelation. When did Hunter decide that Lindsey was included in this tight-knit circle? I thought they were a very exclusive clique, but now everyone seems to be getting let in. I thought it meant something to Hunter to be a part of his 'family,' but apparently, the rules have changed, including inviting individuals that have no desire to participate.

There's no way Lindsey wants any part of this group, but I did. From the moment I first met *The Untouchables*, I knew they had something special and wanted to be a part of it. I'm not sure why I wanted it as badly as I did. Was it the exclusivity of their group? Or was it how they looked after one another as if it was them against the world?

I'm honestly not sure what the draw was, but it felt like a significant victory when they started letting me into their inner circle. The fact that I was even invited into this private discussion today shocked me. They were trusting me more and more, and I was proud of my accomplishment, but now Lindsey was allowed to participate as well. I couldn't help but feel incredibly frustrated by this unexpected shift. I wasn't the only one, either. Lexi and Elijah both appear floored by the news.

"It's true," Brady continues as if he can sense the doubt lingering between Elijah, Lexi and me.

"Why would he do that?" I ask, immediately feeling ashamed that the question slipped out. I can only imagine that Lindsey can sense the envy leaking through my voice.

"It doesn't matter," Lindsey interjects angrily. "I don't want to be in this club. No offense. I already told you that, Brady."

It irks me even more that Lindsey rejects the offer so flippantly. She has absolutely no appreciation for what is being freely given to her, likely because she did nothing to earn it.

"Lindsey, please just stick around," Lexi pleads. "We need your help."

"We do?" Elijah asks incredulously.

"Yes, we do."

"How can I help?" Lindsey inquires, looking equally perplexed.

"Hunter has, in the past, disappeared for several days at a time. He always withdraws when the pressure gets to be too much. Hunter will stop responding to calls or texts during those periods, and then suddenly he shows up again like nothing ever happened," Lexi starts.

"Exactly! So why are we having this emergency meeting?" Brady irritably interrupts, only to have Lexi cut him off with a wave of her hand.

"Let me finish. This may just be another case of Hunter retreating or laying low after his recent suspension, but I wanted to piece together what happened in case I'm missing something important. I feel like each of us has a piece of this puzzle, and maybe if we assemble the pieces together, we will have the full picture. Does that make sense?"

The Tucker Girls

I nod with the others, but I don't think I have anything to share in this conversation. Hunter has been distant from me for weeks. His change in demeanor started a couple of weeks after Homecoming, but that didn't have anything to do with the fight.

"Alright. Now that we have that settled, I'd like to start with the night that you called me," Lexi states, looking directly at my sister. "You were supposed to tell Hunter about Derek."

"Wait!" I exclaim. "What phone call? And what do you mean 'tell Hunter about Derek'?"

My eyes are darting back and forth between Lexi and Lindsey. The realization hits me that I've been missing some critical facts surrounding Hunter's fight, and it rocks me.

"Derek had been bullying me for a while," Lindsey reluctantly explains. "I *was* going to tell Hunter, but he was a prick and blew me off. When I tried to catch him before school, he walked right past me as if I was invisible."

"So how'd he know Derek messed with your locker? Hunter didn't seem to have any question in his mind that he was guilty," Brady inquires.

"Hunter knew Derek was messing with Lindsey weeks ago," Elijah shares. "A bunch of us dragged him into the boys' locker room and threatened him if he didn't leave her alone."

"How'd I miss that?" Brady whines. "I love when we get to instill some fear into cocky kids. Did you drag him under a cold shower? Or give him a swirlie?"

My hands go to my head, and I start rubbing my temples. Each new disclosure is like an earthquake in my mind as I try to reconcile these revelations. I was entirely oblivious to the fact that Lindsey had been bullied for weeks. What kind of sister am I to not notice that she's being tormented right in front of me?

"How'd Hunter know if you never told him?" Lexi asks, pointing the conversation back to Lindsey.

The Tucker Girls

"Did you tell Mom and Dad?" I blurt out, unable to hold it in any longer. Lindsey cuts her eyes at me briefly, shooting over a searing look.

"No! You're not going to tell them either," Lindsey responds before turning back to Lexi. "I don't think Hunter knew exactly what was happening, but he picked up on things here and there. He caught Derek messing with me in the hallways on my way to Trig, and Hannah decided to tell him it wasn't a one-time event. Eventually, I believe Hunter put two-and-two together, but I honestly don't know. It's not like we ever sat down and talked about it. We can barely get two words out before our conversations break down into arguments."

The guilt that blankets me, when I hear that Hunter intuitively knew Lindsey was being harassed, yet I didn't, feels impossibly heavy. I could make a million excuses about how busy my schedule has been, but that doesn't matter when the truth is I failed my sister - *again*. She needed me, and I couldn't see it.

"And then the graffiti happened?" Lexi questions as she's still trying to connect all the dots.

"No. Hunter started following me every second I was at school like he was my bodyguard or something. So Derek got spooked and backed off for a couple of weeks, and then the locker situation happened."

Everyone stares at Lindsey as we process that last key detail she glazed over so quickly. Hunter was protecting Lindsey. That's why it felt like he'd been so distant; he was busy spending time with her. Jealousy bubbles up out of nowhere as I glare at Lindsey, her eyes unable to meet mine.

"Why would he do that for you? I don't understand." I ask, though I don't recognize my own voice.

"I have no idea! I honestly don't know why he did what he did. Like I said before, we never spoke about it. In fact, we've hardly talked, and when we do, we fight. So the only logical conclusion I came to was that he was doing it for you, Serena. Why else would he care?"

"Thank you for filling in all the missing pieces," Lexi continues, ignoring Lindsey's and my side conversation. She might be ready to move on, but I'm not. Nothing makes sense anymore. "So …. Hunter beats the hell out of Derek, gets suspended and disappears. Am I missing any other details? Has anyone heard from him at all?"

I wordlessly shake my head in response to her question.

"No," Elijah replies, still appearing agitated. "Devon said none of the guys have heard from him."

"Nothing here either," Brady chimes in. "I called him this morning, but he didn't pick up. I'm just going to throw this out there, but has anyone asked Tess?"

"Who's Tess?" I ask.

"Don't start stirring up trouble, Brady," Lexi snaps before giving me a weary look.

"I'm not stirring up anything! You already said Hunter has a pattern, so I'm just pointing out that maybe one of us should check in with Tess. He may have been …. uh …. hanging out with her while laying low."

A sickening ache forms in my stomach at what I think Brady is implying.

"Does she attend Ulla Meyer? Cause I talked to a girl named Tess this week," Lindsey chimes in, catching us all off guard.

"What'd she look like?" Elijah questions.

"Black hair, green eyes, and a permanent pissed-off look etched into her face."

"That's Tess," Elijah replies with a smirk. He obviously finds Lindsey's description somewhat humorous.

"What'd she say?" Lexi asks.

"She confronted me in the hallway and wanted to let me know that I should stay away from Hunter.'

"Hmmm. Marking her territory," Brady remarks, nodding his head to himself.

"Shut up, Brady. If you're not going to contribute anything of value, keep quiet," Lexi snaps. "Did Tess say anything else?"

"No. I told her I wanted nothing to do with Hunter, and that was the extent of the conversation. She threw a couple threats in there for good measure and then walked away."

"Don't worry, Lindsey. I'll deal with Tess, so she doesn't bother you anymore," Elijah replies soothingly.

"I'll deal with it," Lexi retorts. "You *dealing with Tess* is exactly what we don't need right now."

"I'm not going to sleep with her, Lex. I am actually taking this issue seriously. She needs to step off of Lindsey," Elijah quips back. "So what's your plan to stop her? You goin' to throw down with her again? That's your solution?

"No. I'm not fighting anyone. I know how to get her to back off - at least until Hunter decides to show up. Then he needs to be the one that deals with her."

"Just let it be," Brady interjects. "Tess already feels threatened by Lindsey. Any response from us will likely feed into her insecurities."

"Why would she feel threatened by me?"

"Cause the only other girl Hunter has fought for was Tess," Brady states matter-of-factly.

"Will someone please fill me in on who this Tess is?" I blurt out in frustration.

Nervous glances pass between Brady, Lexi and Elijah while they wordlessly decide who will answer my question. Finally, Elijah speaks up.

"Hunter is a one-and-done kind of guy," Elijah starts, before Lexi interjects.

"*Was.*"

"Fine. Hunter *was* a one-and-done kind of guy. He'd hook up with a girl, and then he was done with her; there were never any repeat sessions. Tess was the exception to the rule. She's the only one he's ever returned to for a repeat, which went to her head. Tess is from Indy Park too, so she's rough around the edges like Hunter, and he's always treated her differently than the other girls."

Yep, I wish I'd never asked. I can feel the blood drain from my face.

"Whatever was happening between them has been over for a while," Lexi encourages me, placing a hand on my shoulder. "Hunter's been done with her. Tess, on the other hand, still feels like she owns him. I really doubt that Hunter has any interest in Tess any longer."

Silence lingers in the room as I stare down at my feet. Finally, I'm forced to take a seat. I feel ill.

"Thank you for bringing up Tess, Brady. That was really helpful," Lexi remarks sarcastically.

"Hey, had I not mentioned Tess, we would have never known she approached Lindsey. *You're welcome.*"

"I think we should leave the Tess issue alone," Elijah chimes in. "Confronting her will only instigate more trouble. Once Hunter returns to school, she'll realize that Lindsey's not a threat to her. Although, I think you should be prepared, Serena. She's likely to confront you once she learns Hunter was fighting for you, not Lindsey."

"I'll be fine. I can handle her."

"I'm sure you can," Elijah replies with a wink. "Until then, let's all agree that we will let each other know as soon as we hear from Hunter. We will all feel better once we know he's alright."

"I think he texted me yesterday," Lindsey confesses, shocking our entire group again.

The Tucker Girls

Everyone snaps to attention at her announcement. By the time Lindsey has her phone pulled out, Lexi is at her side. After a quick inspection, Lexi is jiggling with laughter. Her entire mood is elevated in a single glance.

"Was it him?" Brady inquires.

"Oh, it definitely was Hunter. That's his number. He texted he was sorry," Lexi replies, still smiling to herself.

"Why's that funny?" Elijah chimes in.

"Lindsey replied with the middle finger emoji."

Elijah and Brady join in with Lexi's laughing, finding humor in the update as well. Unfortunately, I'm unable to find anything funny about the news. All I can think of is that Lindsey was the only person Hunter bothered reaching out to in the last ten days, and my jealousy flares up once more. He'd ignored all of our calls and texts, only to reach out to her.

"That was all he texted you?" Elijah asks.

"Yep."

"Well, at least we know he's not dead on the side road somewhere," Brady states.

Lexi shoots him a death glare, but I have a feeling that Brady was simply giving words to the unspoken fear that's been lingering inside of her. Lexi's mood improves dramatically after seeing Hunter's text, and everyone sticks around to eat and watch a movie. Everyone except Lindsey, who retreats back to her room.

Although I enjoy the company, I can't shake the irritating feeling that lingers over me. Lindsey's been keeping secrets again. She even had a text from Hunter that she failed to mention. I was wrong when I thought there was a rift between us. No, a canyon-sized gap divides the two of us, and its name is Hunter Bowden.

CHAPTER TWENTY
Serena

Hunter's back. I'm trying my best not to be excited. I'd given myself a pep talk before walking into school today in preparation for his return. I'd let my guard down too quickly when he pulled his disappearing act over the holidays. I was crushed when Hunter disappeared again, and I can't take this constant assault on my heart. I'm not going to be his personal yo-yo that he can push and pull whenever it suits him.

At least that was my resolution when Lexi texted that he was back, though my commitment wavered the second I saw him in the hallways before first period. Oh, did it waver. One glance at Hunter lingering in the halls and my willpower is tested more than I could have ever imagined. I want to run to meet him; ask him how he's doing, and confess how much I missed him.

Instead, I press on towards my classroom without stopping to talk, keeping my dignity intact. Hunter is hugging Lexi, and I can't help but stare at their embrace. I should be thinking about how relieved Lexi must feel to know that he's alright, but instead, I'm consumed with petty, jealous thoughts. I can see how much he loves her. My head knows it's more of a sibling type of love, but my heart rejects any and all reason right now. My feelings getting all twisted up remind me how important my new resolution is for my own good. I can't take any more of his drama.

Do not stop, Serena.

A battle rages inside me, but I snap my head forward and keep moving. Today's an important day. We have a pep rally in the afternoon, and the dance team is performing. If I allow

Hunter to occupy my thoughts, I will botch the dance routine we have been working on for weeks.

"Serena!" Hunter calls out from across the hallway.

Stay focused, Serena.

"Serena, wait up."

Hunter falls into step with me, having raced across the hall to catch up to me.

"Hey, Hunter," I reply nonchalantly, refusing to stop for him or even look at him. I don't want any ounce of excitement to seep into my voice. "How have you been?"

"So it's going to be like that, huh?"

"I have no idea what you're talking about," I state, feigning ignorance.

"Serena," Hunter protests, stepping out ahead and forcing me to come to a complete stop. "Talk to me."

"I don't know what else I need to say. You disappeared *again*. The last time you ghosted me, I asked for you to let me make the choice. Let me decide whether I can handle you when you are upset. I'm sure the last week has been hard on you, but I could have been there for you through it all. Instead, you broke my trust. My texts went unanswered *again*."

I'm trembling from all the emotion that is inconveniently bubbling up, and it's shocking how honest I'm being. Glaring up at Hunter, I decide to continue when he doesn't interrupt me.

"What's the saying? Fool me once, shame on you. Fool me twice, shame on me. I'm the fool, Hunter. I thought I meant enough to you not to be tossed aside when it's inconvenient."

"You do," Hunter interjects quickly. "You definitely do."

"*Right*," I snap bitterly, averting my eyes. "Well, it sure doesn't feel that way. I'm just done with all of this."

I instantly regret saying it after those words fly out of my mouth. Am I really done with him? My heart protests, aching for me to give him one more chance.

The Tucker Girls

Silence descends on us as I wait for Hunter to acknowledge my confession. I watch him shift uncomfortably from foot to foot.

"Is the dance team performing today?" Hunter dares to ask, reaching out to touch the curls in my ponytail. I'd spent all morning curling my hair for the ceremony. He can't see my uniform because I'm still wearing my coat, but my makeup and the stars painted on my face should be dead giveaways.

"Yeah. There's a pep rally this afternoon."

"Gotcha."

I scan my eyes around the hallways trying to find something to captivate my attention. I refuse to look him in the eyes. I'm afraid I will tear up if I don't distract my mind and reel in my emotions.

"Serena, I'm not good with relationships. It's not my strong suit, but that doesn't mean I can't get there. I need more time. You are …. really good for me. There are things about me that …."

"We don't need to rehash this all over again," I interrupt. "You are still making the important decisions without me, and that's just how it will be. Here's the thing, Hunter. I need more."

"You need more, huh?"

"Yeah. I do."

Hunter nods, a slight smile forming on his lips. Why is he smiling?

"Alright then, I will give you more."

"Hunter, I don't want …."

"What? You're really done with me? I must admit that I didn't think you were the type of girl that'd divorce your future husband so quickly."

A smile escapes my lips despite my best attempt to conceal it. Hunter's correct; I'm not entirely ready to move on despite being terribly mad at him. I just want him to let me in.

The Tucker Girls

I'm confident that I can handle whatever he's trying to shield me from.

"Let's just say the divorce papers haven't been signed yet," I tease.

"Good! You had me worried there for a second."

Hunter leans in and kisses me on the forehead.

"See you at the pep rally," he whispers before retreating. His eyes twinkle mischievously, and I sense he's up to something. I will see him at lunch before the pep rally, so I'm left trying to decipher the meaning behind his statement as he walks away.

Our senior class president, Andres Helter, taps the microphone before asking everyone to quiet down. The gymnasium is standing-room only as the entire student body is in attendance for today's pep rally. Conversation dwindles down, but Andres is required to give a few more calls to silence before everyone finally complies.

The dance team is lined up facing the packed stands, patiently waiting for our routine to start. The format of today's ceremony has us performing after Andres and Mr. Grayson both give brief speeches. After our dance, the basketball teams will be introduced individually, followed by the cheerleaders doing a routine. The whole event will last about thirty minutes.

Remembering Hunter's promise, I scan the bleachers for him. I think I might have success when I spy Elijah, Lexi and Brady, but Hunter is not sitting with them. My search quickly consumes my thoughts, distracting me from where my mind should be right now, which is mentally walking through my moves in preparation for the routine.

As much as I fight to regain focus, I can't help but keep scouring the gymnasium for him. Lindsey and Hannah come

into focus near the top of the far bleachers. I'm not shocked to
see both of them inconspicuously hiding away up there.

"Welcome, everyone, to our winter pep rally!" Andres
says as he kicks off the pep rally.

One of the gymnasium doors slams shut, disrupting
Andres' flow. He pauses longer than he should, collecting
himself following the distraction. He fumbles with his following
few words as his eyes, along with everyone else's attention, zero
in on Hunter as he struts into the gym. Of course, he'd make a
late entrance and show no remorse for it.

I'm still holding my pose, facing the stands with my
arms behind my back and my feet shoulder-width apart, but I'm
tempted to turn my head when Hunter walks along the far wall
rather than take a seat.

What is he doing? Only teachers are standing in that
part of the gymnasium, so he's clearly out of place. Is he waiting
for our routine to finish to congratulate me? If so, that would
almost make up for the stunt he pulled over the last week.

Distracted by my thoughts, I am pulled back to attention
when I hear Andres stumble once more. Not only that, but a
murmur breaks out throughout the student body.

"Serena," Celicia, one of my teammates, whispers
urgently while still holding her pose. "Hunter's coming."

"What?" I whisper back, fighting even harder to resist
the urge to turn my head.

"*He's coming.*"

What does she mean by 'Hunter is coming'? Is he
planning on interrupting the pep rally?

The next thing I know, Hunter is blocking my view of
the rest of the room. I swear I stop breathing, unsure of what's
about to happen. The entire ceremony has been paused as
everyone else is anxiously anticipating his next move.

"Hey," Hunter greets me as if everyone isn't watching
the two of us.

The Tucker Girls

"Hi."

"You once asked me to kiss you. Do you still want that?"

I swallow, but my throat is so dry it fights going down. Is this really happening? As I stare back in disbelief, I realize that he's actually serious.

Scanning the room, I realize that we have everyone's attention zeroed in on us. The moment feels surreal; had it been weeks prior, I would have tackled the boy and kissed him. Now, everything is complicated. I want him to kiss me, but I'm also scared he will break my heart. Eventually, I give in to what I have always wanted. I nod in consent, unable to speak the words.

"Good," Hunter whispers, his lips turning up at my answer.

He slowly places the palm of his hand on the small of my back and draws me to him, cupping my chin with his free hand. Leaning down, his lips lightly brush against mine as if he's inviting me to participate. The simple gesture causes a wave of excitement to race through my body, and I'm completely entranced. I'm suddenly able to tune out everyone and everything around me. All that exists in my world right now is Hunter and me.

I break free from my rigid posture and throw both hands around his neck, ensuring that he's not ending this kiss before it even gets started. I press into him, intensifying the kiss. This is it. I've been dreaming of kissing this boy since I met him, and now I'm going to enjoy this moment for as long as possible.

Hunter shows no indication that he's going anywhere, either. He tugs me closer so that our bodies are pressed tightly together. Only the sound of the school's raucous cheers breaks through our intimate moment, and I finally come back to my senses. I remember that the entire school is watching us make out.

The Tucker Girls

"That's enough, kids," Mr. Grayson interrupts with an annoyed tone. His comment cues us to end the best kiss of my entire life.

I can't help but smile as Hunter finally leans back, his eyes still locked in on mine. Stealing a glance at the student body behind us, there's a large contingent of kids on their feet whooping and hollering. Spying Lexi, she is sporting a smile that almost rivals mine. The only person I don't see in the crowd is my sister. There's an empty spot next to Hannah.

Hunter slowly backs away, eyeing me intently. I told him I needed more, and he managed to deliver on his promise. Hunter helped erase all the bad memories from the last week and write an incredible moment that I will cherish for a long time.

I don't even care that, amongst the crowd, evil glares are being thrown in my direction from some petty girls. They had their chance with Hunter, but this is my time. I've finally broken through and accomplished what seemed impossible for the last few months.

Eat your heart out, Ulla Meyer. Your golden boy is mine.

CHAPTER TWENTY-ONE
Lindsey

Two school days are all that stand in the way of me and the holiday break. It's getting progressively more challenging to focus on my schoolwork, as all I can think about is laying in bed, vegging out, watching cheesy Christmas movies on Netflix and drinking hot chocolate. It's going to be a glorious, and uneventful, reprieve from Ulla Meyer.

Knowing that I'd be distracted during this final week, I channeled my inner Serena and completed all outstanding assignments ahead of schedule. I have one last hurdle - an exam in US History - tomorrow afternoon, but I'm beyond ready for it. The note cards in my backpack, which are covered with important dates, people and battles, are a testament to my readiness. I've spent hours pouring over those index cards, memorizing every boring fact in painful detail. I'm going to crush this test.

I'm determined that nothing is going to ruin my favorite holiday. Last weekend Mom and I made gingerbread cookies, which was the first time we'd spent quality time together since the move. I credit the holidays for giving us a reason to be together. It felt good to just hang out and talk. She didn't press me to discuss my relationship with Stephen as I expected. She and Serena are similar when it comes to that regard; they love trying to read the tea leaves when it comes to my barely existent love life. I guess having Stephen over for dinner last weekend gave her enough insight to satisfy her curiosity.

Speaking of Serena, thankfully, she didn't ruin the approaching holidays by sharing the details she'd recently learned about the Derek situation with our parents. That would have been disastrous, but she surprisingly kept quiet about it. Maybe I was wrong to not trust her during the whole ordeal.

We'd likely be on better terms if I had confided in her with even a few details. Serena has given me the cold shoulder since the impromptu meeting with Elijah, Brady and Lexi at our house. It was a noticeable and immediate shift the following day, and since then, she's stopped offering me rides to school.

I know she's frustrated that I withheld so much information, and I honestly can't blame her. My brain was in a fog during the Derek catastrophe, and the muddled feeling lingered in the following weeks.

I have every intention of apologizing, but finding the right opportunity has been difficult. When Serena has been home, which is less frequent these days, she's floating around on cloud nine; or rather cloud Hunter, now that they are official. At least I think they are a couple considering they sucked face in front of the entire school.

Since the pep rally last week, nothing has been able to wipe the stupid smile off her face. It's impossible to have a serious conversation with another individual who's not currently residing in reality. I barely register on her radar now.

In my mind, there's no need to rush to apologize. I will have plenty of time to beg for forgiveness over the break, even if Serena is spending half of it skiing in Colorado, which I'm still envious of. Mom and Dad would never allow me to go out of town unsupervised if the roles were reversed.

I'm pondering my parents' clear bias in favor of my sister as I spy Hannah and Rich kissing in the hallway outside our Trigonometry classroom. Good grief. Everywhere I turn these days, people are making out. There must be something in the air.

"Get a room," I mumble, teasing them as I pass.

The Tucker Girls

Hannah responds by playfully swinging her hand at me while still maintaining the kiss. It's an impressive feat considering she would have smacked me had I not scampered away quickly.

Looking back at Rich and Hannah, I'm laughing when I feel Hunter's presence. He's early to class for the first time since brawling with Derek, and the smile slides off my face instantly. I hate that I have this uncanny ability to detect Hunter's presence. It's incredibly annoying.

Hunter's head down and scribbling away on a sheet of paper in his three-ring binder, likely finishing his homework at the last minute. At least, that's what I'm assuming. Why else would he be here early? More importantly, why do I care? He should be able to do whatever he wants - and *kiss* whoever he wants - without me giving a flying flip.

He doesn't bother looking up when I slide into my chair, which isn't surprising. Neither one of us is talking to the other. He told me I should leave him alone, which was a ridiculous demand since I have no interest in engaging with him, and now I'm in an impossible situation. If I say anything to Hunter, it proves his theory that I can't stay away from him. On the contrary, by not talking to him, it appears as though I'm bending to his demands. Either way, he's winning, and it irritates the hell out of me.

I have finally concluded that there's nothing I want to say to him, so I will mind my own business. It's still my choice regardless of whatever he told me to do. I can't let him occupy my head more than he already does, so I try my hardest to pretend that Hunter's not sitting directly behind me.

"Hey, Lindsey!"

Caught off guard by the unexpected greeting, I look up to see Hugo standing beside my desk, smiling down at me. Hugo's eyes radiate warmth, and I can't help but return his smile. He's an attractive boy, with caramel-colored hair and high cheekbones, who's never bothered to say much to me before. So I'm curious why he crossed the room to talk today.

"Hi."

"I heard you submitted a piece for the art exhibit?"

That's interesting. How'd he hear about that?

"Uh .... yeah, I did, two, actually."

"That's so cool. I'm entering something as well."

I'm suddenly way more interested in this conversation, shifting in my seat to face him directly.

"Really!? Are they paintings too?"

"No. I'm into metalworking. This may sound lame, but I spend my weekends scrounging the local scrap yard for metal that I can weld into sculptures."

"That's not lame at all. It sounds incredible! I can't wait to see what you will present at the exhibit."

"Go sit down, Hugo," Hunter grumbles without looking up from his binder, catching Hugo by surprise. "Class is about to start."

Hugo's incredible smile falters as his eyes dance between Hunter and me. I'm sure Hugo has heard of Hunter's claim on me. That gossip is going around school like wildfire, and it's impossible to ignore. When I walk through the hallways, students scramble out of my way like they are in awe of me. Between that and the staring, it's all absolutely ridiculous. If only they understood how little I mean to Hunter.

I roll my eyes in response to Hunter's comment, never understanding why he always has to be a jerk. Hugo isn't bothering Hunter, yet he still feels the need to grunt orders at him.

Thankfully, Hugo continues on as if he never heard Hunter's rude remarks.

"Anyways, I have this one piece that's too big for the art show. I'd need to rent a trailer just to haul it here, so I don't know how I'd even get it into the school. I'd love to show you some time - that is, if you would want to see it?"

I hear a snapping noise behind me as if an object was just broken in two. It may have been a pencil.

"She has a boyfriend, dipshit. *Get. Lost.*"

Hunter's voice is dripping with contempt, and, with two simple sentences, he manages to trigger my anger. He does it so effortlessly, like flipping a light switch.

"Since when do you care about committed relationships?" I snap, whipping my head in his direction.

"Never said I did," Hunter shoots back. "But you do."

"Don't pretend like you know me. You don't have a clue what I care about, and you certainly don't speak for me. Now take your own advice and leave me alone."

By the time I turn back towards Hugo, his eyes are nervously bouncing between the two of us. He's realized he has stepped into a minefield. I'm sure my sudden contempt for Hunter makes me look a little unhinged. He effortlessly stirs up raw emotions with just a simple prod.

"I'd love to come by your house to see your art," I reply, managing to strike a friendlier tone despite the anger still raging within me. "Do you think Stephen and I could swing by over break?"

"Oh," Hugo replies, pausing to carefully think through his next words. "Yeah, I guess that would be fine."

"Cool! Well, we can plan something for the night of the exhibit. I'm sure we will have plenty of free time before everyone arrives."

"Sounds good. See ya around, Lindsey," Hugo waves as he crosses the room, finding his seat in the far corner.

I'd been on the verge of making a new friend, with an interesting hobby, and Hunter had to swoop in and ruin it. The bastard never knows when to stop.

The Tucker Girls

My blood is boiling, and when Mrs. Seldon calls Hunter to the blackboard to solve a problem, my mind is consumed with thoughts of jabbing my pencil into his back.

I swear I've never been a violent person, but Hunter brings out this nasty side of me. He beckons to my darkness, daring it to come out and play with every word that comes out of his mouth.

Shockingly, Hunter flawlessly solves the problem correctly, which is entirely unexpected. I was waiting for him to fail so I could greet him with a triumphant smirk when he returned to his seat, but now my plot is foiled.

"Great job, Hunter!" Mrs. Seldon enthuses, rewarding Hunter with a rare smile.

"The blind squirrel found a nut. *Whoopee*," I mutter while I doodle in my binder. I am putting the finishing touches on my 'Hunter is a Loser' banner I've been designing in my spare time. It's actually looking pretty legit if I do say so myself. Maybe I should convert it to digital format, print copies and post them all over the school. That would be epic but would also stoop to Hunter's level.

Snickers break out around me, causing my head to snap to attention. I spy Hannah scowling at me disapprovingly, and she's not the only one; Mrs. Seldon is irate. My voice must have carried farther than I'd expected.

"Lindsey Tucker! I would have never expected a comment like that to come out of your mouth. That was rude and completely unacceptable," Mrs. Seldon chastises me, and I feel my face flush with color.

"I'm so sorry, Mrs. Seldon!"

I am mortified that I allowed that remark to slip out of my mouth. It's one thing to ponder terrible thoughts, but verbalizing them shows how much I've allowed Hunter to affect me. I've never gotten in trouble at school before; never tardy, written up or reprimanded. My record has been squeaky clean until this very moment. Mrs. Seldon's disapproving glare makes me want to run away and hide in my locker. Is she going to write me up?

"Don't say sorry to me. Hunter is the one you need to apologize to."

"No, no, no," Hunter quickly interjects, waving both hands. "Lindsey doesn't need to apologize. I'm as surprised as she is that I got the right answer. It is amazing how much more I understand when I don't fall asleep in class."

The classroom erupts with laughter, but I can't join in. I'm in awe of Hunter deflecting the unwanted attention away from me. He simply shrugs in response to becoming the new object of Mrs. Seldon's irritation. When the class quiets down, my rude comment seems like an afterthought.

Hunter purposely avoids eye contact with me as he returns to his seat. The frown on his face communicates something, but I'm not exactly sure what. Is he mad about what I said? Or is it that he felt he needed to step in and save me from Mrs. Seldon's wrath? Either way, I feel responsible for that scowl.

When the bell rings at the end of class, Hunter darts for the door before I can say anything to him. I hustle to collect my things and bolt after him, waving off Hannah when she calls out to me. I manage to catch Hunter just before he reaches the main hall.

"Hey!" I shout out, causing Hunter to stop. "What was that back there?"

"No idea what you're talking about," he mutters, looking anywhere but my eyes. He's suddenly putting off a very peculiar vibe, at least compared to what I'm familiar with. Typically he's more than willing to banter, but I get the opposite feeling now. It's almost like Hunter's half preoccupied and doesn't have time to fully engage in our conversation.

"You did not have to draw attention away from me in class. I am perfectly capable of taking responsibility for my actions."

"Okay."

"*Okay?*"

"Yeah. Okay. Whatever you want."

I cock my head in confusion. What is happening right now? *Whatever you want.* It's the least Hunter-like thing I'd ever heard come out of his mouth.

"Are we done here?" he asks, appearing bored when I don't immediately respond.

"You can't possibly be serious."

He rolls his eyes at me, causing my body to tense in irritation. I'd like nothing more than to knock that look off of his face, but I decide against it after recalling nearly breaking my hand the last time I attempted it.

"Oh, I'm being completely serious," Hunter responds coolly. "I need to get going. I've got places to be."

I eye Hunter carefully, examining him for some clue as to why he's suddenly acting so strangely. This version of him looks familiar, and I finally remember where I'd seen him behave this way before - the day he ignored me when I tried to tell him about Derek. So he's trying to avoid me again like he'd promised he would do. Where was this side of him when Hugo was being friendly?

"Fine. Run away," I mutter, waving my hand flippantly.

I will not be caught dead chasing after this boy again. I'd intended to offer an apology for my harsh words, but I'm not in the mood to provide him with anything now. If he wants to avoid me, so be it. I'm certainly not going to argue.

Hearing my comment, a scowl flickers across Hunter's face. I can't help but feel slightly pleased with myself that I managed to break through his apathetic mask and affect him. Considering he affects me so easily, it only seems fair. His reaction is not as satisfying as getting the intensity I'm longing for, but it will have to do.

When I step back to leave, Hunter reaches out and takes hold of my upper arm, guiding me away from the middle of the hallway. The simple contact spreads warmth throughout my arm, which is the sensation I've unknowingly craved for weeks. It's an addictive feeling I'd love to bottle up because the moment he lets go, it quickly dissipates.

On top of it all, Hunter's aroma surrounds me. It's been too long since I'd been close enough to smell it, and the second I breathe it in, I'm reminded of how badly I missed it. It's oddly comforting, and I inhale it deeply. Unfortunately, his fragrance only manages to add to my confusion. I'm not supposed to want these things, but that doesn't change the fact that I do.

"You are not good for me," Hunter grumbles, interrupting my thoughts and leveling me with his fierce eyes that are all too familiar.

The mask has come off, and his words hit me like a slap in the face. *How am I not good for him?* He'd once told me that he's the monster, but now he's trying to flip the script. In his mind, I am the problem. If I wasn't still reeling from his closeness, I'd punch back with a rebuttal to his insult.

My eyes must communicate the mixture of hurt and confusion swirling within me because his glare softens. I watch his gaze slide down until it fixes on my lips, and a thrill runs through me like I've never experienced. My heart is threatening to burst with excitement, and it takes all of my willpower not to give in to what I sense he's wanting.

Hunter must come to his senses because he releases my arm and jerks away, giving me enough room to gather my bearings. My head stops swimming, allowing me to finally think clearly.

"I am on the verge of losing *everything*, Lindsey, and it's all because of you."

The Tucker Girls

"What do you mean?" I inquire, but it comes out as a whisper.

"First, it was a knife cut to my back that got infected. That was a real bitch, by the way. Then, I almost got expelled for defending you. Now, I'm losing out on the first two days of my ski trip because I have to be Mr. Grayson's lackey for the week to 'take full responsibility for the fight.'

"All of this would have never happened had I just left you alone. I can't keep going down this path. I need to graduate high school and get out of Amberly as soon as possible."

Of course, all of his problems are my fault. He isn't taking any personal responsibility for losing control and beating a kid to the point of being rushed to the emergency room. I may have wanted him to intervene with Derek, but I never wanted him to go berserk. I never asked for the monster he let loose.

"Well, don't worry," I reply, the strength returning to my voice as I put distance between us. "I'll make this easy for you. Consider this our last conversation. Break a leg skiing for me. *Literally*."

Storming away, I'm so mad that I'm trembling. My eyes begin to blur from the tears forming, and I quickly escape into the restroom. Once enclosed in a stall, I take slow, deep breaths to regain my composure.

Hunter proved how easily he can provoke strong emotions out of me as I manage to force back the tears. I hate him, and I hate myself for being so susceptible to it all.

As I splash water on my face, I look up at the mirror and study my face. My cheeks are still flushed with color. Taking a few deep breaths, I try to calm the raging storm within.

Maybe Hunter is right. All we do is incite the worst in each other, and it's downright toxic. We should cut ties and move on, yet as the idea solidifies in my mind, I'm less and less convinced that I will be able to follow through with it.

CHAPTER TWENTY-TWO
Hunter

My phone rattles in my pocket, alerting me to another incoming text, as I carry a tray of food from Ulla Meyer's cafeteria towards the art exhibit hosted in the gymnasium. I'm purposefully ignoring the messages because I'm not in the frame of mind to read the exuberant texts that have kept my phone buzzing all evening.

Elijah, Lexi, Brady and Serena are at Telluride and are likely ready to hit the slopes. There's a pit in my stomach from knowing I'm missing out on one of my most cherished traditions.

Instead, I'm stuck in Texas serving food at a high school event showcasing fellow students' artwork. Mr. Grayson extended this opportunity to me when I was on the verge of getting suspended, and I quickly agreed. It wasn't my only concession. I also agreed to play on the varsity soccer team in the spring. I haven't played soccer since middle school - choosing to focus on football which I thought would be my meal ticket - so I wasn't thrilled to hear his offer. When it came to soccer or expulsion, I would choose soccer every time.

I'm scheduled to hop on a flight early Monday morning, giving me four and a half days with my friends, so all is not lost. Brady, who pays for my airfare every year, has been gracious in rearranging my tickets to accommodate this inconvenience.

Weaving between the crowd of people, I successfully deliver another round of appetizers without incident. I've had several close calls where individuals bumped me along the way, but my experience at Stirred Up helped me avoid a messy accident. I've been carrying food through inebriated crowds for years, so I'm well prepared for this type of situation. Aaron, the other designated food runner, has been less fortunate. He's already dropped three trays tonight.

On my return trip to the cafeteria, Elise Tucker emphatically waves me down from across the room. I'm caught off guard by her unexpected appearance, but I quickly recall that Lindsey's presenting tonight. I've been purposely staying busy to avoid catching sight of the troublesome brunette.

"Hunter! What are you doing here?"

"Hey, Mrs. Tucker."

"How many times do I have to tell you to call me Elise," she corrects, greeting me with a warm hug. "I think of Doug's mother whenever someone calls me 'Mrs. Tucker.'"

Serena inherited Elise's talent for making you feel at ease around them. I'm not a hugger, but I don't object when Elise wraps both arms around me.

"Sorry, Elise, I'll get it right eventually."

"Good! Now explain to me why you are here and not in Colorado."

"Serena didn't tell you?" I ask, to which she shakes her head in response. I can't blame her for leaving out this bit of information. Serena wouldn't have been allowed to travel to Colorado had her parents known why I'm stuck serving at this event tonight.

"I volunteered to serve tonight, and my boss needed me to pick up an extra shift tomorrow, so I'm flying out first thing Monday morning."

"Oh, aren't you being extra responsible! I'm sure Serena is disappointed you won't be there the full week."

"Serena texted earlier that she and Lexi are spending the entire day at a spa, so I'm confident I will be the last thing on her mind."

"You'd be surprised," Elise states with a smirk. "Serena's smitten with you."

"I'm fond of her as well."

The second the words come out of my mouth, I'm second guessing what I said. *I'm fond of her as well?* Did that just come out of my mouth? Elise doesn't appear put off by my comment, but it sounded awkward to my ears.

I change topics rather than continue to talk about Serena's romantic interest in me with Elise.

"How was your Christmas?"

"It was lovely! I tried to savor every moment because Serena will be off at college next year. Who knows if she will even want to come home for Christmas."

"I'm sure she will."

Elise smiles in gratitude for the assurance, yet her eyes still convey sadness. I can't help but wonder what it would be like to have a mother that cared for me as much as Elise loves Serena.

"Have you had a chance to see Lindsey's paintings yet? I'm biased, but I feel like she's been the star of the night."

"No, I haven't had the chance. I've been busy running food all evening. I think the turnout far exceeded what anyone was expecting, so I've been going nonstop."

"Well, come on! Now's the perfect time to go check out her art. The crowd's finally dying down," Elise enthuses, grabbing ahold of my arm and pulling me through the remaining crowd.

"No. No. No. I'm supposed to ...." I attempt to protest, waving my hands.

"It will be fine! You can take a quick break."

Tension coils inside me as I allow Elise to lead me to Lindsey. My plan is about to unravel the second I'm in her presence. She's my own personal quicksand. No matter how hard I try, I can't seem to shake free of Lindsey's orbit - and all the trouble that accompanies it.

The Tucker Girls

My apprehension is justified the second I lay eyes on her. Lindsey's breathtaking in a sleeved, midnight blue dress that stops at her knees. The rich blue color makes her gray eyes pop even more than usual.

I remember how beautiful she looked the night of Homecoming, but she has no equal tonight. My already knotted stomach sours further, begging me to turn and run in the other direction. Elise doesn't allow me the opportunity to slip away, though.

Lindsey's busy answering questions from several individuals admiring her work, and I can't help but notice the pure joy on her face. Having watched her over the past few months, I've seen her grace Hannah, Serena and even her stiff boyfriend with those vibrant eyes and warm smile. Hell, she will even share it with strangers like Hugo, but never me. All I receive are burning glares and bitter words.

I would give anything to have her look at me that way once. It's a good thing that she hasn't. Otherwise, leaving her alone would be an impossibility.

That said, I have figured out what is good for me, and it is not Lindsey Tucker. My emotions always lead the way when I'm around her, which means I end up making terrible decisions. I feel the complete opposite around Serena; clear-headed and in control.

Lindsey's body goes rigid, and it's abundantly clear that she's aware of my presence. She is always on high alert when I'm near, confirming how much she detests me. Despite the distraction of my arrival, Lindsey carries on her conversation without a noticeable misstep.

Elise leads me past her daughter so she can show off the paintings, and I'm shocked to discover three on display attributed to her. I could have sworn Lindsey had mentioned only presenting two. The first piece is textured, like the painting that hangs in the Tucker kitchen, and depicts something abstract that

The Tucker Girls

I don't comprehend. The colors are warm against the white canvas, so it's pleasant on the eyes, even if it's incomprehensible.

"This is my favorite," Elise chimes in over my shoulder, and I nod in artificial agreement.

The second piece is an oil painting depicting a young child's bicycle. Based on the basket and frilly pink strands exploding from each handle, I'm guessing it was her bike growing up - or possibly Serena's.

While both paintings demonstrate talent, neither move me like the one at their house - that is, until I see the final piece. Primarily black and white, it depicts a smiling, shirtless teenage boy illuminated by a hanging light fixture. He casts a long, black shadow that stretches the entire length of the canvas. A deranged hand reaches out of the dark shadow onto the white, tiled floor as if a creature is crawling out of the black pit. Of course, this painting would speak to me. Taped to the bottom corner of the frame, I see its title: The Monster.

It is no coincidence that this painting's title shares the same label I gave myself when I spoke with Lindsey in the Ulla Meyer parking lot after the fight with Derek. Lindsey was truly inspired while creating this piece, and I feel incredibly exposed for having been put on display for the crowd.

Did any of the passersby realize that the boy that inspired this painting is keenly aware of the beast lurking behind him? In fact, he can't escape it. I put up a pleasant front so everyone else feels safe and secure despite my demons. It must be effective because my peers worship the ground I walk on.

The title might as well be 'Hunter Bowden' because this painting depicts me perfectly.

"This painting has drawn the most attention tonight. I begged her not to bring it, but she was so stubborn," Elise continues to talk, but I can barely hear her. "Frankly, she's been watching too many horror movies if you ask me. Every time I look at this one, it gives me the creeps."

The Tucker Girls

Cutting my eyes in Lindsey's direction, I spy her anxiously awaiting my reaction. I meet her stare, beating down the emotions begging to bubble up.

"Hey, Linds!" Elise trills, taking hold of my arm once more. "I brought Hunter over because I figured he would want to see your work too. What do you think, Hunter?"

"Lindsey's crazy talented," I reply flatly, backing away slowly. "I would stick around, but I don't want to be caught slacking on my job. It was great seeing you, Elise!"

Slipping away into the crowd, I don't give Elise the opportunity to protest my quick exit. I lose myself in the hustle of the event once more, successfully managing to avoid the Tuckers for the remainder of the evening. No matter how busy I get, I am unable to shake the image of Lindsey's painting from my mind.

The Railyard sits in the old industrial area of the city close to Indy Park but was renovated into an outdoor space quickly becoming a local favorite. This outdoor concrete paradise has several fire pits packed with kids attempting to stay warm on this chilly evening. Food trucks line the curbs surrounding The Railyard, offering all kinds of overpriced options that, no matter how hungry I am right now, I can't bring myself to waste my money on.

I spot Gabe and Idonis as I walk up, having just seen them at the art exhibit earlier in the evening. They are fellow seniors at Ulla Meyer that I have known since elementary school. They extended an invitation to join them at the event tonight, which was as good an excuse as any to avoid going home for a few more hours. I wouldn't consider either a friend, but neither can be as bad as Pete or the trash he occasionally brings home.

The Tucker Girls

I'm making small talk with the guys when I see Idonis' eyes bulge, triggering me to turn to see what caught his attention. Tess is wandering over wearing a revealing top and pants that leave nothing to the imagination, clearly freezing her ass off to get attention. By the gleam in her eye, I know what she wants before she's even said a single word.

"Let's take a walk," she beckons, motioning her head towards a fire pit that's less occupied.

"Sure," I agree reluctantly. I'm not interested in what she's offering tonight, but we need to talk. It's been weeks since Tess and I last spoke, so I decide to take this opportunity to catch up. "Alright, guys, I'll catch up with you later."

They both adorn ridiculous grins as they wave at my departure, still ogling Tess as she walks away. There was a time when Tess and I were close, but those days are long gone. I've purposely put distance between us, which she adapted to fairly quickly.

That's the one thing I've always admired about Tess; she can roll with the punches. She's also discreet. Most girls I've been with shed tears when I push away, but not Tess. She never expected me to be her prince charming. She's always accepted me for everything I am.

On top of all that, Tess grew up in Indy Park. While growing up here, we've gone through things that my other privileged Ulla Meyer friends would never understand.

"What are you doing on this side of town?" Tess inquires as we walk. "I haven't seen you over here in Indy in forever."

"Killing time. I had nothing better to do tonight."

"Where are your *rich friends*?"

"Really? It's going to be like that?"

I come to a complete stop, forcing her to turn to face me. I let many things slide with Tess, but she will not trash my family.

The Tucker Girls

"*Fine*. Where are your Ulla Meyer friends …. that just happen to be rich?" Tess asks, subtly sliding in the last part of the question causing me to laugh.

Tess nudges me with her shoulder, matching my smile.

"They are skiing in Colorado."

"Oh, that's right. How come you aren't with them?"

I shrug, unwilling to go into any details. The days of me sharing my life with her are long gone.

"Alright, play it close to your chest," Tess continues, not forcing the issue. "Did blondie go with them?"

"Yes, Serena tagged along."

Tess casually slips her arm into mine, and I remove it with my other hand. I know where this conversation is headed, and I'm not having any of it. Our discussion isn't progressing the way she's hoping.

"Tess, don't," I protest, facing her and placing my back to the fire pit behind me. The pavers that line the pit are tall enough to sit on, so I take a seat. Tess steps closer, moving between my legs.

"I've missed you, Hunter," she states, purposely softening her voice to sound more appealing. It's the same tone that coerced me into many things in the past, but I find it doesn't quite have the same effect anymore. "You know I've been thinking."

"About?"

"I've been thinking about the bet going around school - the one about when you will break your abstinence pledge. The pot is over eight thousand dollars. Isn't that crazy? Why don't you and I come to a deal where we share in the winnings?"

As much as I want to, I can't scoff at her idea. I'm not going to lie; four thousand dollars would be a windfall for me. I'm sure it would be for Tess as well. It would allow me to move out on my birthday, which seemed like a pipedream until Tess' proposition.

The Tucker Girls

Two years ago, I would have jumped all over this arrangement, but I'm no longer the guy that's interested in meaningless sex even if Tess agrees to the proposition.

There are decisions that lead me down the same path as Pete, and I'm purposely choosing a better way. No matter how much money is on the line, I know how slippery the slope will be if I allow myself to dip my toe into that lifestyle again.

"Come on, Hunter. Let's get out of here. Go back to my place like we used to do."

As I silently mull over Tess' offer, I spy Lindsey standing by an adjacent fire pit with one of the girls from the exhibit. She's intently staring in our direction, closely monitoring Tess and me from afar. I lock eyes with Lindsey, and she quickly averts her gaze to conceal her blatant staring.

I feel her fingertips graze my thigh, but it does little to distract me from the subject of my ire. Seeing Lindsey again reminds me of how she exposed me at the art exhibit without my permission.

"Really?" Tess huffs out, having followed my gaze. "I don't understand what you see in her?"

"Leave it alone, Tess."

"No, I mean really. Blondie is more popular and attractive. So what is it about *her*? Is it that she doesn't want anything to do with you? Is that what you find appealing? Cause I have been racking my brain trying to understand why you would fight for *her*. Why's she so special?"

"*Enough*," I bark out, having lost my patience with her rant. "I heard you had some words with her. If you mess with Lindsey again, we will have problems."

"Okay! *Shit*. I'm sorry. It's frustrating, that's all," Tess replies meekly, flailing her arms. "None of them - not *her* or blondie or Lexi - understand what it's like to have to scrape and claw to survive. Have any of them ever had to work a day in their life?

The Tucker Girls

"You and I both understand what real life is like; how it sucker punches you every chance it gets. I'm one of the few who understand *you*, so I don't get why they are so important to you."

"Because it has nothing to do with money, Tess! It's about them being there every time I've needed them. Can you say the same?"

"I've been there through a hell of a lot of things too!" Tess snaps back, the pain seeping through their face. It's not a lie, either. Many nights, I crashed at her place to escape the hell waiting for me at home.

"Yeah, you were and would still be in my life, except you've never left room for anyone else. Whenever you're around Lexi, Elijah and Brady, it descends into a territorial fight. I got sick of it. *You* forced me to choose, so I chose them."

"I think you forget how good we were together," Tess replies, softening her voice once more.

I scoff in response. To Tess' detriment, I know all of her moves before she makes them.

Tess lets out a huff when I don't acknowledge her statement.

"They're not like us, Hunter! You know it, too. Deep down, you know it. *They are using you.* Ulla Meyer treats you like their king, and your friends make sure that they are tagging along and reaping all its benefits."

"Hey Hunter," Lindsey interjects, suddenly appearing beside Tess. Her sudden appearance surprises Tess, causing her to stumble back a step.

Lindsey edges around Tess and astonishes me by dropping into my lap. The heated disagreement that Tess and I were engaged in comes to a screeching halt, and it takes me a second to process this unexpected turn of events.

Lindsey leans into me, and I consider dumping her on the ground in retaliation for the art piece but decide against it to see where this is going.

The Tucker Girls

Adapting to this surprising development, I catch Lindsey off guard when I sling my arm around her waist and pull her towards me until her back presses against my chest. Lindsey tenses at our proximity, and I get the feeling that she's affected as much as I am by this moment. I may have initially made the move to mess with Lindsey, but I wasn't prepared for how much I enjoy having her this close. The contact, and her smell, have my heart pounding like a drum.

"Lindsey," I murmur, turning towards her so my nose brushes up against her cheek. I don't miss the shiver that ripples through her from the slight contact.

"Hmmm," she purrs, meeting my gaze.

The second our eyes meet, I realize how peculiar this sudden change really is. This doesn't feel like hate at all.

What are you doing, Hunter?

The girl that's constantly fighting and pushing me at every opportunity is allowing me to hold her. My head is spinning, trying to understand this dangerous game we're both playing. One of us needs to blink before we collide.

"You're cold," I comment, having felt her chilly hand graze mine. "Where's your coat?"

"I forgot it at school. That's why I came over here to steal your warmth."

"Is that so?"

"Yep," Lindsey replies, flashing a smug grin.

"Well, I'm glad you came over. We need to discuss your masterpiece. When were you planning on sharing that you'd painted me?"

"*Please.* Don't tell me it didn't boost your ego to see that I painted you," Lindsey replies. "Besides, everyone loved it. I was receiving compliments the entire night about that one painting."

"Well, it was of me. What'd you expect?"

Lindsey rolls her eyes in reaction to my cocky response.

"I'm sure everyone you spoke with already told you this, but your submissions were amazing. Your mom was beaming with pride."

"Thank you," Lindsey replies, looking down at her hands and blushing from my compliment. "It's just a hobby that helps me to process life. It's a great way to get things out of my system."

"Did it work?"

Lindsey cocks her head inquisitively.

"Did you get me out of your system?"

"If only it were that easy," she answers, leveling me with a heated look that steals my breath. She's playing games again and trying to mess with my head, but I'm not going to call her on it. I'm enjoying her company too much to risk the confrontation.

We proceed to stare into each other's eyes, and for the first time since we met, I am confident that she feels something for me too. It's conflicted, but there's something else in her gaze - intrigue. Either that, or she's a great actress.

Tess, who'd become irrelevant the second Lindsey walked over, huffs out in frustration.

"I'll catch up with you later, Hunter."

"Sounds good," I mumble, not bothering to tear my eyes away from the beautiful puzzle leaning against me.

Lindsey smirks as she watches Tess meander off towards another group, and I become more confident that I am just an unknowing participant in some sort of retaliation.

"Alright, I will see you around," Lindsey states, lurching forward in an attempt to escape, but I pull her back against me.

"Where do you think you are going?"

"I accomplished my mission. Tess warned me to stay away from you, and I don't appreciate being threatened so ...."

"Tess threatened you. So you decided to use me?"

"Pretty much."

Even though I expected this was Lindsey's motivation, I still feel the pang of disappointment.

"That's two times you used me tonight. Is there anything else you'd like to squeeze out of me while you are at it?" I ask bitterly.

"Hey," Lindsey says to steal my attention, attempting to read my eyes. She can feel the shift in my mood.

"You should find someone else the next time you want to exact revenge," I grumble, removing my hand from her waist.

"Hunter."

Lindsey's eyes search mine, and I feel she knows she went too far.

"What's going on?"

"You could have told me about the painting. You have no idea how intrusive that feels to have your worst qualities drawn out into the open like that."

Lindsey stares at me intently as she comprehends my frustration.

"I should have gotten your permission. I'm sorry."

She takes me by surprise when she covers my hand with hers.

"I messed up."

I nod before looking up at the star-scattered sky and audibly exhale. Lindsey can see my hurt, and I don't like it. I take the opportunity to put my indifferent mask back on.

"I told Tess to leave you alone. She won't threaten you again. She's harmless, I promise. She wouldn't dare mess with you, no matter what she says. She feels threatened by you and is acting out of that fear."

"That's what Brady said."

I involuntarily go rigid at her mentioning Brady. Since when do they talk?

"What? I can't have a conversation with one of your friends?" Lindsey responds defensively, sensing my unease.

"No, that's not it. I just didn't realize you two talked to one another."

Lindsey rolls her eyes in response.

"Relax. It was one conversation where he was explaining that Tess is very territorial. He mentioned that Tess is the only other girl you've fought for, so now she thinks I'm a threat," Lindsey pauses, examining my face for a reaction. "The irony of Tess' threats is that you were doing it all for Serena."

Lindsey's last conjecture hits me like a truck. Can she be that willfully ignorant? I've never once given Lindsey the impression I've felt obligated to do anything for her because of Serena. My surprise morphs into irritation the longer I ponder her statement.

Lindsey hesitantly stands but appears reluctant to walk away. As I get to my feet, I notice she's closely watching me, trying to decipher my silence.

"What'd I say this time?"

"Forget it. I need to leave," I grunt out.

The swirling emotions inside are reminders that I shouldn't be near Lindsey. A few words from her lips, and she's triggering strong emotions that I am struggling to keep bottled up.

"*Really*? Hunter, you're all over the place tonight. What's going on? What did I do this time to upset you?"

"I beat the hell out of Derek *for you*. It had *nothing* to do with Serena," I grumble out.

"That doesn't make any sense. Why would you do it for me?"

"Apparently, I'm a damn fool," I remark, frustration dripping from my voice. "Trouble seems to follow you around. You must have the worst luck of anyone I know. As much as I want to leave you to your problems, I keep getting involved because I feel protective of you. No matter how much you didn't appreciate it, I couldn't help myself. I don't know how to turn it off, either. I wish I knew how because it's driving me crazy."

The sounds of the conversations nearby swim around us, preventing us from being swallowed by our silence. I can hardly bear to look in Lindsey's eyes. For some reason, I'm vulnerable tonight. I hate every second of it too. Rather than stopping, I keep the confessions coming.

"When I'm around you, I lose the ability to think clearly. I didn't even plan to jump Derek, but I let my emotions get the best of me at that moment."

"You were able to think clearly enough to stop me from killing him," Lindsey counters.

"Yeah, that was actually easy. I couldn't let you throw away your life on some low life."

"But you had no issue throwing your life to chance?"

Averting my eyes, I shrug in response. I know I need to leave because nothing good will come out of this conversation. My commitment to avoid this girl has already gone to shit, and now I'm bearing my soul to her, which will come back to haunt me. If I stay, I am only going to add to my misery.

"I've gotta go," I say, running my hands over my face.

Lindsey doesn't protest my declaration, but I see her shiver in reaction to the cool breeze blowing through. Her hands begin rubbing her arms in an attempt to conjure up warmth.

Without giving it much thought, I slip off my jacket and drape it around her shoulders while she watches my movements attentively.

When I step away from Lindsey, I expect her to try and return my jacket, but she surprises me by wrapping it tighter around her body.

"Goodnight, Lindsey."

"Hunter ...."

"Yeah?"

"Thank you," she states sincerely.

"For what?"

"For everything. For being there every time I've needed you."

Her unexpected gratitude floods me with unexpected warmth. I thought I'd never hear her say those words, and it makes everything I've suffered entirely worth it. I'd go through hell again to hear her gratitude.

Wanting to leave on a high note, I wordlessly nod. I turn to leave, letting Lindsey's 'Thank you' replay over and over in my head.

For some inexplicable reason, I decide to turn back and spy Lindsey tilting her nose towards my coat, inhaling its scent, and smiling.

Damn.

She's genuinely smiling.

CHAPTER TWENTY-THREE
Hunter

My hopes of a quiet night at work, before leaving for Colorado, are dashed by six o'clock sharp. People poured into Stirred Up in droves, forcing us to standing-room-only occupancy within the first hour. It was July the last time we were this busy, and I feel that the holiday break contributes to the large turnout and enthusiastic crowd; that and the live music Drake has booked through New Year's Eve.

If we were fully staffed, it would be challenging to serve all of these customers; however, Drake could barely pull together a minimal staff tonight. In fact, he's neglecting his typical managerial responsibilities to bartend because we are stretched so thin. So I'm glad I agreed to pick up this shift. Regardless of how chaotic it is, I am deeply indebted to Drake in so many ways that this is the least I can do to repay him.

I refill the ice trays, behind the bar, by emptying the two buckets I'd carried from the kitchen, quickly glancing at the juice bottles and noticing that Drake's running low on pineapple. I make a mental note to pick up more on my next pass through the kitchen, which will be very soon. After I help Carly, one of our servers, turn over a table and clear the dirty dishes, I'll be headed there.

"Can you pick up the pace?" Drake barks out over the band, flashing a smirk to let me know he's teasing. "These people want to eat sometime soon."

One thing that I appreciate the most about Drake is his ability to keep his cool under pressure. In fact, he seems to thrive in the chaos.

"Anytime you want to switch jobs, just let me know," I retort. "I can pour drinks in my sleep. I'd love to see you do the dirty work for once."

"Ha! I paid my dues, Hunter. Now it's your turn."

"If you tell me to appreciate the process one more time, I'm going to gag," I shoot back.

"Hey!" Drake shouts after me, calling for my attention.

I halt, turning around to catch the serious look on his face.

"Thank you," Drake calls out. "I owe you."

"You can pay me in shots," I reply, pointing to the row of liquor sitting in front of him.

"No chance! Now get back to work, you delinquent!"

I fall right back into the hustle, quickly turning over Carly's table and managing to grab dirty dishes off of Logan's table on the way.

Having done this job for years, I've learned to be incredibly efficient with my time. When the restaurant is hopping, you can't afford to waste a second of time.

I'm refilling the pineapple juice when I feel my phone vibrate from a call, which takes me by surprise. My friends strictly text me, so my immediate assumption is that it's some telemarketer or misdial on the other end. Curiosity eats away at me to the point that I pull out my phone, and the name on the screen has me hustling to find a quiet spot in the rear of the restaurant.

"Hello?" I answer once I can get away from the commotion.

"Hey Hunter," Lindsey's cracked voice plays through my speaker, and I can instantly tell something's wrong.

"What's going on?"

There's a pause before I hear her speak again.

"I …. I need a ride. Do you think …." Lindsey starts before I interject.

The Tucker Girls

"Yeah. Send me your location. I'm on my way."

"Ok."

Lindsey's been crying. It's evident in her voice. All kinds of terrible possibilities are running through my mind right now, and it's all I can do to shut down my wandering thoughts and avoid full-blown panic.

Weaving through the packed crowd, I wave down Drake from the other side of the bar.

"Emergency! I need to go!" I shout out at Drake, who throws me a concerned nod before waving me on. I hate leaving him in this predicament, knowing how much it will hurt to lose the extra hands, but I don't have any other option. Lindsey would have never called if the situation wasn't serious.

Lindsey shared her location with me by the time I am in the jeep, and I tear out of the parking lot with reckless abandon. The app tells me it's a ten-minute drive, but I will make it in five.

I'm bending, if not breaking, all the rules of the road. Driving serves as an ample distraction from the possibilities that want to creep into my thoughts. I'm trying hard not to consider that Derek has done something to Lindsey again. If that's the case, I will end him.

The directions lead me to an unfamiliar cul-de-sac in Lexi's neighborhood, and I have strong suspicions about which house I'm looking for before I've even parked - at least, I think it counts as parking when I stop my car in the middle of the street. What can I say? The curbs are lined with vehicles, and I don't have time to waste searching for an opening.

My high beams illuminate the house that's practically vibrating from the music emanating through its walls. My lights reveal an empty front yard, though.

Calling Lindsey's phone, I feel frustration building up when it goes unanswered and sends me to voicemail. Marching up to the front door, I decide to start by searching this party. She may be in one of the neighboring houses, but I'm trusting my gut for now.

The second I step into the house, I recognize several familiar faces from Ulla Meyer, confirming my suspicion that I'm in the right place. Several people call out my name to greet me, but I've got tunnel vision at this moment. Surveying what I can see of the party, I don't spy Lindsey in this crowded foyer or any of the adjoining rooms.

Rather than scour each room, I approach one of my classmates - Rina, Remi, Rian, or some other name that begins with an 'R' - that greeted me when I walked in.

"Have you seen Lindsey Tucker?"

"Who?" she responds with a perplexed look.

"Serena's sister!"

"Serena has a sister?"

An audible growl escapes from my overflowing aggravation, causing the girl to retreat a few steps.

Apparently, Lindsey's still relatively unknown amongst her peers because it takes three other attempts before I finally find someone that recalls seeing Lindsey an hour ago near the rear of this mansion.

Edging my way through the crowd, I start down a hallway that runs deep into the house, but I only get ten feet in when I spy Lindsey halfway down. She's leaning against the wall, looking up at Stephen, who's running his mouth and waving his arms in an animated fashion.

It's clear to me that the stiff is worked up. On the other hand, Lindsey is hugging herself while she quietly watches his dialoguing. Her gaze cuts away from Stephen long enough to see me approaching, and she leaves Stephen mid-sentence.

Lindsey's tear-streaked cheeks shine, reflecting the room's lighting, and I can't put words to the wrenching feeling that grips my stomach. In one glance, I'm wrecked. I don't know if she can sense my concern, but she averts her eyes as she wordlessly slips by me on the way to the front door.

"You called *him*?" I hear Stephen yell while in pursuit, his face beet red. I halt him with a firmly placed hand to his chest, which draws his immediate ire. "Of course, you called *him*! It all makes sense now."

"Enough," I growl, smelling the alcohol emanating from his breath. "You're drunk. Go sober up and leave Lindsey alone the rest of the night."

"Get your hand off of me," Stephen barks back.

"Walk away, Stephen."

Rather than heed my advice, he attempts to slip by me. *Wrong move, jackass.*

With one forceful shove, I throw him against the nearby wall causing partygoers to scatter away quickly. I press my forearm up against his throat.

"Don't test me. I'm not in the mood," I growl. "And if I find out you laid a hand on her, I will come back here and make you pay in blood. You understand?"

"It was a stupid fight," Stephen retorts, attempting to wiggle away. "I would never hurt her."

"You better hope you don't see me again," I threaten before releasing my hold on him.

I storm out of the house before I lose my cool and pummel the guy. I don't care if it was just a fight; whatever he did has Lindsey devastated. For his sake, I really hope what he said is true - that it was only an argument. There's no place he will be able to hide if I find out he is lying.

A shudder ripples through me when I consider what almost happened to Serena at the start of the school year. My school is full of rich, privileged kids that will do despicable things.

Lindsey's standing alone in the front yard, her arms still draped around her body by the time I walk up. Rather than give into my raging curiosity and demand to know what's happening, I surprise myself by remaining calm. I get the sense that we're both wired very similarly. When our emotions run high, we need space, so that's what I'm going to give her. So I decide not to press for answers no matter how badly I want them.

Lindsey momentarily meets my gaze, and I wordlessly jerk my head towards the jeep, beckoning her to follow. We walk in silence together as the drumming party music still fills the air.

Once I sit in the driver's seat, I pause before shifting into drive. I assume she wants to go home, but I don't know for sure. If it were me, I'd be headed to the nearest bottle to drown away the intense emotions.

Looking over at Lindsey, she's staring out the passenger window with fresh tears trickling down her cheek. Each sniffle that I hear rips me apart. I'd give anything to be able to alleviate her pain, but this isn't something I can fight off. I just need to be her ride tonight.

Reaching my hand across her body, I notice her flinch at my sudden movement.

"I'm just putting your seatbelt on," I explain softly, pausing in case she objects to my aid. Her silent nod lets me know she's consenting to my offer, so I proceed to clasp her buckle.

Although I feel better having Lindsey secured, my head is spinning from getting so close to her momentarily. I'm becoming increasingly affected by her presence with every encounter; her fragrance may be my favorite smell.

"Do you want me to take you home?" I ask, attempting to focus on the task at hand. I need something to give my attention to rather than my raging hormones.

"Not like this," Lindsey protests, her voice uneven and broken from her emotional state.

"Fine by me. I'm keeping you then," I remark, hitting the accelerator. I'd rather stay close in case Lindsey decides to talk about what happened anyways.

If Lindsey doesn't like my suggestion, she certainly doesn't make it known. We catch every traffic light on the way, doubling the length of our ten-minute drive. By the third red light, I finally hear Lindsey mumble a few words.

"I just want to be normal."

"What do you mean?" I ask, unsure of what she's talking about.

"I want to be a normal girl that can have a normal relationship," she continues. "Why can't I just be like all the other girls?"

"You're going to have to give me more than that. What do you mean by 'be like the other girls'?"

Lindsey huffs in frustration, clearly upset that I can't miraculously read her mind. She's barely giving me anything to go off of here.

"Is Stephen pressuring you to do stuff you don't want to do?" I ask, gripping the steering wheel tighter.

"No ... I mean ... I just thought we were on the same page. Things were going slow, but I thought we were both okay with that, but tonight ..." Lindsey starts, then stops herself. "Forget it. This is too weird talking about relationship stuff with you."

"Fine by me."

My curiosity is still raging war in my mind. I can't shake off the possibility that Stephen may have hurt her.

"Just tell me this. Do I need to go hunt down Stephen tonight?"

"No!" Lindsey adamantly protests. "We just had an argument, that's all."

I'm relieved to hear her say that, as the knot that had formed in my stomach loosens. Rather than worry about what may have happened to Lindsey, I can now process the fact that she called me for help. I know Serena's out of town, but surely there are others that she could have called for a ride. Instead, *she chose me.*

I steal a glance in her direction only to catch Lindsey staring down at her hands. My chest inflates like a balloon as I realize she trusts me. I have no clue how deep that trust runs, but I'm about to put it to the test. I expect her to be apprehensive about our destination, considering she doesn't like loud, crowded spaces. I imagine that reluctance is dialed up when she's emotional like this. I don't have many other options right now, though.

"Where are you taking me?" she asks when we pull into the Stirred Up parking lot.

"My work. I walked out on my shift to come to get you, and they need my help tonight."

"Hunter! Why didn't you say something? I could have found another ride," Lindsey exclaims.

"Don't worry about it," I reply as I cut off the engine. "Now, just to forewarn you: it's going to be very loud and crowded in there."

The apprehension she's feeling is palpable. She just traded one over-stimulating experience for another. I watch her eyes dance as she considers this unexpected development, and she subconsciously begins rubbing her forearm. I reach over and take hold of her hand, preventing her nervous tic.

"Do you trust me?"

Lindsey's eyes snap to mine, and she answers with a nod. She didn't even need a second to consider my question.

"Good. If you decide you want to leave, I will take you home immediately. Just say the word. Alright?"

"Okay."

"Plus, if you stick around, I'll have a surprise for you."

"What kind of surprise?" she asks, slightly perking up.

The Tucker Girls

"My boss, Drake, makes the best milkshakes in Amberly. He'll hook you up tonight for free."

"Well, what are we waiting for then?" Lindsey inquires, flashing a muted grin as she opens her door.

As we walk up to the bar, I hope I'm not making a bad judgment call. This could go sideways quickly. As hesitant as I feel, I don't have any other good options. I have to give this a try because my co-workers need me.

Midnight arrives all too quickly, and Lindsey and I rush out of the restaurant, desperately attempting to make her curfew. The girl hustling beside me doesn't resemble the one I picked up a couple of hours ago from the party. Gone are the tear-stained cheeks and red eyes. It's difficult to pinpoint the exact moment she snapped out of it because I was running around like a madman trying to catch up on the time I'd missed, but her spirits are clearly lifted now.

"What was the name of that last band?" Lindsey asks as she's buckling in.

"The Forte Forties."

"Really? That's unfortunate. They need a better name because they were incredible. I've never seen anyone play the saxophone like that lady with the purple sweater."

"Her name is Cherinda. They're here almost every night during the summer. If you liked them that much, you should come back and see them again."

"Is that allowed?" Lindsey asks as she looks out the passenger window. I can't read her face to understand what she means by her question. "Logan said you never bring any friends to Stirred Up."

"Logan doesn't know what he's talking about. Lexi and Brady stopped in for dinner back in July."

The Tucker Girls

"But you've never brought a girl here before?"

"Lexi is a girl."

"You know what I mean. None of your hookups?"

"Nope," I respond, realizing that I've never wanted to share anything in my life with the girls that I'd been with before. I've always kept firm boundaries when it comes to allowing people into my personal life. "Why do you want to know?"

"Just curious. That's all."

I spy Lindsey inspecting black writing on her hand.

"What's that?"

"Oh! Logan wrote his number on my hand."

"Of course he did. I love how he had time to hit on you while I was busy with his tables."

"He was very friendly," Lindsey counters with a chuckle. "Drake was pretty amazing too. The milkshake was as good as advertised, and he ended up bringing me a burger that I didn't even come close to finishing."

A smile crosses my face as Lindsey talks about Drake. Unsurprisingly, he went out of his way to make her feel welcome because he does that for everyone. Drake's one of the best people I know, and I am incredibly thankful I have him in my life.

"So are you gonna ditch the stiff and give Logan a call?" I inquire bitterly.

Lindsey smirks in response.

"I mean, Logan is pretty cute," she states matter-of-factly.

My face must contort in response because Lindsey bursts out laughing.

"Jealousy doesn't look good on you."

"Me? Jealous?"

She raises her eyebrows, smiling the brilliant smile that I'd longed to see. Lindsey finally graced me with it, and it's even better than I imagined. The jeep drifts into the other lane while I am mesmerized by her gift, and when my attention snaps back to the road, I'm required to rapidly correct course.

"I mean, I guess I'm slightly jealous," I confess.

"Oh really?" Lindsey asks in surprise, turning in her seat to face me.

"Yes. Although I'm fairly certain Logan would give me his number too if I asked," I tease.

"Very funny. You know that's not what I meant."

A few minutes pass wordlessly, and it gives me the space to wrap my head around what happened tonight. The burning question that has been eating me up the entire night finally comes out.

"Why me?"

"Huh?"

"Why did you call me? You could have gotten Meredith or Hannah to give you a ride .... or called your parents. Why me?"

Lindsey's facing out her window again, so I can't read her expression when she doesn't immediately respond. I do catch sight of her fidgeting with her hands nervously.

Turning into her neighborhood, I purposely slow down to eke out a few more seconds with Lindsey. Despite knowing she's going to miss her curfew, I'm hoping she will give me an answer.

"Hunter," Lindsey blurts out, causing me to look in her direction. "I should have never called you tonight."

A pit forms in my stomach as I suspect I know where she's headed with this confession. If she's feeling guilty about asking me for help because of Serena, I want to snuff it out. Regardless of my complicated feelings for her sister, I know there's room for us to be friends. I'm beginning to realize that I enjoy being around Lindsey, and I don't want that to stop because of whatever Serena and I are.

"No," I quickly interject. "Lindsey, you shouldn't feel guilty about calling me to pick you up. That's not why I asked. I just wanted to know *why* you called me. Did you run out of other options?"

"No. It's just …. I don't know. I guess I knew you'd come. Well, I didn't know you would come because I wasn't sure you were even in Texas, but I knew if you were here, you would help me. It's what you've always done.

"On top of that, I didn't want to get asked a million questions about what happened tonight."

Lindsey pauses to take a deep breath.

"That doesn't change the fact that I shouldn't have called you tonight. It was a stupid argument, but I got all up in my emotions and reacted without thinking. You were the first person I thought to call when things went sideways.

"But the fact is, you showed up for me, and I can't tell you how much that means to me. I …. I really appreciate it. You also helped me avoid going home for a few more hours too. If I showed up early, I would have been interrogated by my parents."

Lindsey's appreciation is something I will need more time adjusting to hearing. It feels out of place from the girl that's always been ready to battle me.

"Do you mind stopping in front of my neighbors?" she asks, pointing to the curb ahead. Her question helps me realize that we're nearly at her house already. I'd been driving on autopilot while caught up in my thoughts.

"Uh, yeah, I guess," I answer, taken aback by this odd request. I wrestle with how comfortable I am with dropping her off where she'd still have a long walk to her house. Even in a neighborhood like this, Lindsey walking around alone after midnight isn't the best idea.

"Don't take this the wrong way, but you've got a reputation."

"Who? Me?" I reply in feigned ignorance.

Lindsey rewards me with a smile again.

"Just a little bit of a bad rep," she responds, showing me a small gap between her thumb and pointer finger. "And the last thing I need is to show up late with you. I'd rather my parents think I was off with Stephen."

"Makes sense. I'll stick around until you text me that you made it inside safe."

Rather than hop out of the jeep like I'm expecting, Lindsey stills as she watches me intently. I wonder what thoughts are hidden behind that scrutinizing stare.

"When are you leaving for Colorado?" Lindsey asks.

"Tomorrow."

"Okay," Lindsey whispers, then slowly nods as she's considering my response. "Can I ask you a question?"

"Sure."

"Why did you shout that I'm yours during the fight with Derek?"

My hand tightens on the steering wheel at her unexpected question. I wasn't prepared to be blindsided by this bomb.

Recalling that fight, I was raging mad and had no idea what I was saying in the moment. Those weren't premeditated words that flew out of my mouth.

"You should get going. You're already twenty minutes late."

"I'm fine. Another five minutes won't kill me."

I shift uncomfortably in my seat. She may trust me, but I don't know if I trust her. All Lindsey's done is give me grief since I've known her. One night doesn't change our history.

"It didn't mean anything."

"*Liar*. You're lying. I can see it all over your face."

Damn.

The Tucker Girls

When did Lindsey become the world's best lie detector? Nothing is ever easy with her. Unfortunately for Lindsey, she's not getting the answer she wants.

"Believe what you want."

Lindsey's eyes narrow as she glares at me.

"Just tell me, Hunter. I need to know."

"Sorry, I've already granted your one wish tonight."

"I deserve to know," Lindsey growls. "Do you realize the rumors running around school about me because of what you said? People practically treat me like a pariah now. Everyone thinks I've earned the title painted on my locker."

"Who cares what they think? You know the truth."

"I do! I care, Hunter! Unlike you, my reputation matters to me."

"You'll survive. At least they know not to mess with you now."

Lindsey's breathing rapidly as she continues to get more worked up. She wants vulnerability, but I don't even know where to start with her. I've built up so many walls over the years, I wouldn't know how to let anyone in even if I wanted to.

"Forget it!" she snaps. "You know, every time I believe you might be a somewhat decent person, you remind me again that you're a complete ass."

Lindsey fumbles around as she attempts to unbuckle her seatbelt. Her agitation makes it difficult for her to unclasp it on her first two attempts.

My hand twitches anxiously, and I fight the desire to share what she wants to know to keep her here for a few more minutes - or for her to leave on a better note.

When she pulls on the door handle, I panic and lunge across the passenger seat to grab hold of the door, preventing her escape.

"Just wait," I plead. "Please."

The Tucker Girls

I wait for her to attempt another escape, but Lindsey surprises me by listening to my plea. I have no idea what my next move is, seeing as I'm improvising on the fly.

I release the door and edge back slowly, pausing when my face is inches from hers. I'd planned to retreat into my seat, but being this close to Lindsey has me reconsidering my options.

The intense attraction for her, that I'd fought off countless times, stirs within me once more when I make eye contact with Lindsey. I wonder if she feels this pull towards me as I feel towards her. It isn't easy to read her expression because she's been a statue since I decided to invade her space.

Time seems to stand still. The only sound in the jeep is our breathing as our faces slowly inch closer.

What are you doing, Hunter?

Lindsey must be asking herself the same question because her expression looks slightly terrified. Other mixed emotions are difficult to discern, but I spy a sliver of desire in her eyes that calls to me.

There's a million reasons why I should ignore what I'm seeing, but I manage to ignore them all.

Screw it.

Shoving away all reason, I close the remaining distance and press my lips to her. I am slow and intentional with each brush of my lips against hers, waiting for some violent reaction to my unexpected move. I wouldn't be surprised if she clocked me for this. Instead, Lindsey's lips hesitantly respond to mine. At first, it's slight movements that mirror my lips, but then something flips; she begins kissing me back.

Our connection only fuels the desire that is raging within me, and I feel the urgency to claim more of her. This kiss between us is too slow and too shallow. I need more.

Deepening the kiss, I slip my hand behind her head. I toss aside the restraint of how this started. My lips begin punishing hers, and she moans in response. A worry bubbles up that I've gotten too rough, but Lindsey responds by fisting my coat with two hands and dragging my body into hers.

My seatbelt strains to keep me from jumping to her side of the car. It's the only thing grounding me in this moment.

You're mine.

Lindsey wanted to know why I'd said those words to her before. I still can't explain it, but I feel it in every fiber of my being now that we are entwined together.

I've never met anyone like her before. Yes, she takes every opportunity to fight me, but maybe it's completely worth it because all I can think about is how I want more. I want more of her banter, darkness, hard-earned smiles, and trust, but most of all, I want more of *her*.

The dizzying desires racing through me are disorienting. It's all terribly confusing, but it also feels incredibly satisfying to finally respond to the tension that's been building between us for weeks. You'd think this kiss would alleviate that tension, but with each moment that passes, my desire only grows. All I can think about is why I waited this long to kiss her.

The flood of sensations - her smell, touch and lips - are almost too much to handle. It's an overwhelming assault on my senses. I force myself to pull back so we can both catch our breath, but I'm nowhere near done with her. I peek through my hooded eyes to see Lindsey as affected as I am.

Suddenly, Lindsey slams her hands into my chest to create more space between us.

"*What. The. Hell. Hunter.*"

"I don't know .... I just ...." is all I can say. The logical part of my brain is malfunctioning at the moment.

Lindsey frantically pulls the door handle and jumps out of the jeep, scurrying away as if her life depended on it. My chest is still bobbing up and down as I watch her run away without looking back once. It's then that I realize I just made a terrible mistake.

The Tucker Girls

This was never supposed to happen. Ever. What did I just do?

I remain parked in the jeep until well after two in the morning attempting to wrap my head around why I thought kissing Lindsey Tucker was a good idea. I never get the text saying she's safe inside, nor do I expect one after the stunt I pulled.

Out of a long list of terrible ideas I've had in my life, this one is in competition to win. I'd made it a priority this year to make better decisions, but tonight I regressed.

Once again, I lost my ability to think clearly around her. One slight, minor misstep and now I'm going to be stuck with a nasty, lingering Lindsey hangover for the remainder of the night.

CHAPTER TWENTY-FOUR
Hunter

Unlocking my bedroom door, I slip out into the hallway and am shocked to overhear conversation coming from the kitchen. Usually, Pete has to leave no later than seven for work, so I purposely set my alarm for one minute afterward.

Walking down the short hallway, I discover a woman, with disheveled hair, drinking coffee at the kitchen table. It looks like Pete had another sleepover last night.

The lady smiles warmly when I come into view, catching me by surprise. It's not the type of friendly welcome I typically receive from the women he brings to our house. It's not that they never smile my way, but it's usually communicating a very different type of message.

A sizzling sound emanates from the kitchen, and it's only then that I realize that Pete is cooking breakfast. The aroma hits my nose, and my belly groans in response. This whole scene strikes me as odd. Pete never cooks anything. I want to pinch myself to double-check if I'm still dreaming.

"You must be Hunter," the lady concludes, causing me to come to a complete stop. "Why don't you join us for breakfast?"

Assessing her intently, I decide whoever this woman is, she's too nice to be caught up with my deadbeat father.

"Thank you, but I will pass."

Stepping up to the table, I look down at the poor woman whose name I'd rather not know. She doesn't appear to be too offended at my rejection; more so intrigued to meet me. I immediately pity her. Pete will ruin every good fiber of her being.

"Look, you seem like a nice lady, so let me give you some free advice. You're too good for him," I say, jabbing my thumb in the air towards Pete. "There will be nothing good left in you once he's done with you."

Her eyes widen in shock. I can't carry her fate on my conscience. If anything happens to her now, at least I gave her the opportunity to run.

"What'd I tell you?" Pete grumbles out from behind me. "I told you he's a lil shit."

"Peter!" the woman exclaims. "Please don't use that language around me."

She looks at me apologetically but doesn't realize that I'm entirely numb to Pete. There's very little he can do to affect me anymore. I've been hardened from years of abuse.

I take the opportunity to escape, walking out into the crisp, cool morning air. The sun is breaking through the horizon, providing me enough light for a safe run. At least as safe as anyone can feel in Indy Park. I've been running in the early morning for years, though, and never had any problems.

Quickly hitting a brisk pace, I need this run after a long, sleepless night. I tossed and turned in bed, wrestling with the conflict building up inside of me.

I've gotten myself into a tangled mess over the last few months. My plan was clear at the start of the school year: avoid drama, focus on graduating and get the hell away from here. Those objectives are sinking in murky waters now, and I feel the pressure to course correct before it's all too late.

Considering I've managed to piss all over the things that matter in my life, I'm using this morning run to clear my head. It's not that I don't realize the core issue. The wrecking ball, that is Lindsey Tucker, is laying waste to my decision-making ability. I'm hoping some fresh air and pain will ground me back in reality.

The conclusion that I've known for a while bubbles up again: I need to stay away from Lindsey. The problem is the more determined I am to avoid her, the more she becomes wedged into my life. Not only have I been unable to leave her alone, but I stupidly kissed her.

Why did you have to do such a boneheaded thing?

Lost in the moment, I was overcome with big emotions that still scare the shit out of me. I didn't even recognize that version of myself. The walls I've built up to protect myself began showing cracks, and I can't explain the discomfort that comes with knowing I'm vulnerable. I can't allow another person close enough to cut me open like my mother did.

Serena is who I need right now. When I'm with her, things stay light-hearted and fun. She's safe. Since I've known her, she hasn't threatened to trudge through areas of myself that I keep locked up securely.

On top of that, Lindsey is a real pain in the ass. She irritates the hell out of me. The dynamic between us was starting to shift, though. I was beginning to get the impression that we weren't destined to be enemies forever. Last night was almost normal until I decided to kiss her; then, everything fell apart.

Now I'm left obsessing over every decision I made. Why do I feel responsible for Lindsey? Why didn't I just drop her off at her house after the party? Why didn't I just let her leave when she was frustrated with me? Who cares if she thinks I'm an ass? Most importantly, why did I kiss her?

Pushing my legs harder with each question, I sprint through the streets as my lungs burn from the punishment. I find the pain a great distraction from my thoughts, but I can't run from this decisive moment looming over me.

My bag is packed and waiting for me in my bedroom. The airline ticket, that will take me away from Amberly, is lying

The Tucker Girls

on my bed waiting to be redeemed. Everything is in order except for me.

What is wrong with you, Hunter?

This trip means everything. It's my chance to pretend to be normal with my friends. It's also one of the few opportunities I get to put some distance between myself and this cursed town.

The only roadblock is Lindsey. My miscue is weighing heavy on my conscience since I watched her scamper away from my jeep. I feel my chest tighten, and it's not just this run pressing in on me. No, a monumental decision hangs over me like a dark cloud that could have severe consequences.

When my body can't take any more punishment, I stop at the corner of an intersection and lean over gasping for air. Six minutes of sprinting, and I can barely stand. Sweat is pouring off of me as I stare down at the pavement. I close my eyes, trying to silence the war raging in my head. It would be much easier to think straight had I gotten more than two hours of sleep.

You leave in a couple of hours. You've been dreaming of Colorado for over a month. Get your shit together.

Regardless of the pep talk I am giving myself, I still feel like I'm being torn in two and I don't understand why. This decision should be a slam dunk.

Times up, Hunter. What's it going to be?

CHAPTER TWENTY-FIVE
Serena

Hunter finally arrives today! That's the thought playing over and over in my head as I lay sprawled out on the couch this afternoon. Despite being sore from a full day of skiing yesterday, I am wearing this stupid grin because Hunter's plane will land any minute.

Don't get me wrong, it's been fun hanging out with his friends to start the week, but I came here specifically to be with him. It's been a major disappointment that he's been delayed getting here, but I understand why. Hunter was required to serve at an event as penance for participating in the fight at school. Despite his late arrival, I keep reminding myself that at least he will be here to celebrate New Year's Eve.

Considering we didn't see each other early on in the holiday break, it feels like an eternity since I've been around him, and it makes my chest flutter with excitement at the thought of him walking through the penthouse door. The anticipation is building with every second. Hunter promised to let me know when he landed through text this morning, so I have my phone in hand and am waiting on his update.

Looking around the room at our crew, I notice Lexi reading something on her phone with an exuberant smile. At first, I surmise she may be texting Hunter, but that's definitely not her Hunter face. No, that look is somewhere on the spectrum of amused to irritated. This is entirely different as she taps out a reply message before tucking away her device. Her eyes meet mine, and she quickly attempts to conceal her smile.

The Tucker Girls

"Who are you talkin' to, Lex?" I ask playfully, dying to know who put that twinkle in her eye.

"Nobody," she states flatly, begging me with her eyes to stop prodding since we have an audience. It's too late, though. Elijah looks up from his phone in intrigue.

"What's going on?"

"Nothing! Nothing is going on," Lexi grumbles adamantly, shooting a death glare my way.

"Then you won't mind sharing who you're texting with," I suggest, and I'm confident I will pay for this later. Lexi will likely cover my face in toothpaste while I sleep tonight.

"It's just a friend. That's all."

"Who?" Elijah inquires, his interest peaking as he leans in.

"Nobody you know."

"What school does he go to?" I inquire.

"Who said it was a 'he'?" Lexi asks, raising her eyebrows in a challenge.

"Fine. What school does she go to?"

"*He* goes to Ulla Meyer," Lexi retorts, getting testy.

"Then it's likely one of us knows him," Brady chimes in, joining the conversation.

"He doesn't run in your circles."

"Come on, Lexi. Just tell us about him. We can be cool about it," Elijah turns on his smooth voice to cajole her.

"No. I know how you boys get, and the last thing I need is for you to hunt him down," Lexi fires back. "I'm done talking about this."

With that final statement, Lexi hops up from the couch and walks back to the bedroom we've been sharing together. I can't help but notice how Elijah's eyes follow her the entire way.

"Watch this," Brady whispers to me with an impish grin.

"Does Hunter know about this guy?" he calls out across the penthouse.

"No!" Lexi hollers back, suddenly appearing at the doorway and pointing her finger menacingly at Brady. "You aren't going to tell him either."

"He doesn't like to be left out of gossip. Maybe I should text him," Brady continues instigating her.

"I swear, Brady Fischer. You do not want to start with me today," Lexi growls.

Brady waits for Lexi to disappear again before he bends over laughing.

"In case you haven't noticed, that question is my go-to. 'Does Hunter know?' It's like magic. Instantly gets people fighting mad."

"Quit causing trouble," Elijah grumbles out. His mood has shifted considerably since Lexi's revelation. He shifts his weight a couple of times before hopping up from the couch and declaring that he needs fresh air.

I consider following him to see if he's alright, but in that second, my phone begins to vibrate. Hunter's face is on the screen, causing me to jump up to my feet.

"Hunter's calling!" I squeal with exuberance. "Hunter's here!"

He's finally in Colorado. The wait is over!

CHAPTER TWENTY-SIX
Lindsey

"Thank you for coming tonight," Meredith declares as she hooks her arm in mine and leans into me. "I'm serious. I know how much you despise school parties, so it means a lot that you'd come anyways."

"Don't thank me yet. I've brought Jane Eyre, and I'm not above sneaking away to read when you're not looking," I tease, but I'm only partially kidding. I do, in fact, have Jane Eyre tucked away in my overstuffed purse.

"No! Lindsey, please do not abandon me in my time of need! It's already embarrassing how few people showed up, so I need you."

"It isn't embarrassing, Mere," I counter quickly. "Maybe people already had plans. It is still the holiday break."

"No, it's embarrassing," Lily chimes in, joining our conversation. "Meredith, I thought you said you invited the entire junior class?"

"I did!" Meredith groans out. "I texted everyone *and* posted it all over social media."

"It's still too early. I bet more people are coming," I offer up, trying my best to give her a little bit of hope.

Lily shoots me an incredulous look, which I do my best to ignore. Regardless of whether I'm sensible or not, I dislike watching Meredith suffer this humiliation. There are barely forty people in this house. I'm confident I'd only be able to get twenty to attend a party if I threw one, so forty still seems like an accomplishment from my perspective. I can tell Meredith was hoping for her house to be packed like many of the school parties that Ulla Meyer is notorious for throwing.

It's a shame that Serena is out of town. If she were in Texas, I know she could triple this turnout with just a few text messages. She's quickly become one of the most popular girls at school and already has the influence to draw a large crowd.

I won't lie that part of me is hoping the meager turnout will cause an early end to this event. Stephen's looming around, and I am in full avoidance mode. I'm not ready to reconcile after he was an obnoxious drunk last night. We haven't spoken since our fight despite his numerous texts and calls. Apparently, he can't take a hint because he's been trying to get my attention tonight.

My reluctance to speak with Stephen isn't just because I'm pissed at him. Hunter kissed me, and I have no clue how I will disclose that secret to Stephen. There's also the fact that I also kissed Hunter back. It wasn't just a peck either. I really went for broke before I came to my senses.

Guilt is weighing heavy on me for that unconscionable mistake, and I know I have to eventually tell Stephen the truth about what happened. My confession will have to wait for another day because I have zero interest in saying a word to my boyfriend tonight.

My stomach twists in a knot the second Hunter kissing me sneaks into my thoughts, which has been happening more than I'd like to admit today. It's infuriating to not be able to stop thinking about him, and I've found myself bordering on obsession. Though I tried to talk myself out of it, I've been checking social media every hour, waiting for Serena to post a photo of her and Hunter at Telluride. I know it will wreck me the second I see them together, but I can't stop from this masochistic habit. I hope it will soften the blow when I see how happy Serena is in the forthcoming photo.

The Tucker Girls

"I need a distraction," Meredith whimpers, looking as tortured as I feel inside.

"Let me make you a drink," Lily offers, testing my patience.

"You know Meredith doesn't drink," I retort, frustrated that Lily would even mention alcohol. While I consider Hannah and Meredith friends, Lily and I have never hit it off. Tonight she's reminding me of why with her insensitive comments.

"Jeez, I was just offering it because it will help her relax," Lily replies with a shrug. "Why don't you help take her mind off this party? Oh, I know! How about you dish on why Hunter Bowden showed up at Dane's house last night and then took off with you?"

Of course, she had to go there. *Ugh.* How about I *don't* dish about that? I'd willingly discuss any topic other than Hunter.

"Yes! Lindsey, like, what the hell? I saw you and Stephen arguing, so I walked away for barely ten minutes, and when I returned, you were gone. Everyone was gossiping about Hunter arguing with Stephen before stealing you away. What happened?"

"There's really not much to the story …." I start before Lily interjects.

"Come on, Lindsey! Don't hold out on us. Did you leave with him or not?"

Both girls are looking eagerly at me as if they know there's some undisclosed detail that they are missing out on.

"Yes, I did," I admit, pausing to figure out what to share. "Alright, I was really upset during the argument with Stephen, so I called Hunter. He drove to the party and picked me up."

"And?" Meredith implores with raised eyebrows.

"And what?" I ask, wishing they would stop prodding. I don't want to lie, but there's also no way I'm disclosing the details they desperately want to know.

The Tucker Girls

"Since when do you have the hottest guy in school chauffeuring you around?" Lily asks in disbelief.

"Not to mention fighting for you," Meredith chimes in. "I heard what he did to Derek."

"Wait! I never asked him to do that!"

Both girls start smirking at me, causing me to feel very uncomfortable. I know what they are inferring from all these signs, and there may have been moments I allowed myself to toy with those same conclusions, but now he's with Serena causing my heart to ache unexpectedly. Allowing that one kiss has shifted my whole world, and now I've become way too attached to Hunter.

"Poor Stephen," Meredith states sadly after I don't offer any additional juicy details.

"What do you mean, *poor Stephen?*" I blurt out furiously.

"Agreed. There's no way he can compete with that. Hot, rich and mysterious. The triple threat," Lily chimes in, wiggling her eyebrows at me.

She's convinced Hunter's competing for me. I would say that could be true if last night was any indication. The way he kissed me felt like he was more than just interested; he kissed me like I was all he ever wanted. It makes my heart beat faster just remembering the kiss, but then again, he's in Colorado now.

We both likely got caught up in the moment. The chemistry between us has led to some close calls before, but this time it went too far. It was definitely a mistake; otherwise, he'd still be here.

Doubt creeps into my mind, and I second guess not trying to talk to Hunter after the kiss. It freaked me out, and my flight response took over. Now, I'm not entirely sure what to think. To add to my confusion, Hunter's also a notorious player, and I'm likely just another checkmark in a long list of girls he's made out with. It probably meant nothing to him.

The Tucker Girls

A nauseating wave sweeps over me as I picture him kissing someone else. It's the kind of jealousy I never imagined myself feeling for any boy, let alone Hunter. But, as I said, our one kiss has changed a lot on my end. Apparently, I'm feeling anxious over Hunter's hypothetical hookups now.

Lily and Meredith are both giggling, stealing away my wandering thoughts. Replaying Lily's last statement in my head, I get hung up on the fact that they both believe Hunter is rich. It shouldn't come as a big surprise considering most of the kids at school share that assumption.

Does anyone at the school know who the boy that they spend their weekdays worshiping really is? Do *I* even know the real Hunter? He does a great job of keeping everyone at arm's length, even his closest friends. Even Lexi, Elijah and Brady have no idea where he goes when he hides from the world. Hunter is a complete mystery.

"Please tell me he's coming to this party?" Meredith pleads. "If people know he's here, everyone will show up!"

"No. He's in Colorado."

"Oh," Meredith's face falls in response. "What's he doing in Colorado?"

This is definitely not the topic I want to discuss now. It still feels too raw. Why did he have to kiss me just to leave? I was foolish enough to allow that moment of weakness, and it's been wreaking havoc on my heart all day.

"Who's in Colorado?" I hear Stephen ask, sliding into our conversation.

I hope, with all my being, I don't visibly cringe at his sudden appearance because internally I tense up into a knot. There goes my plan to avoid him all night. Since I'm cornered in the kitchen, I have no easy exit that allows me to slip away.

"No one," I say coolly before Meredith or Lily can respond, drawing inquisitive looks from both of them. Thankfully neither corrects my dishonest answer. They must

273

catch on that this would be a taboo topic with my current boyfriend.

Stephen silently nods, attempting to hold my gaze but I avert my eyes to the girls. I'm not ready for this pending conversation less than twenty-four hours after our heated argument. Stephen lingers around in awkward silence, still failing to pick up on the fact that I have no desire to talk to him.

"How's it going, Stephen?" Lily finally asks, breaking the lingering quiet.

"Not great," he replies, still locked in on me. "Last night really sucked. Speaking of which, do you both mind if I talk with Lindsey privately? I've got an apology that I need to make."

No! I desperately plead, with my eyes, for them both to refuse his request, but they agree despite my silent appeal. The second Meredith and Lily walk away, Stephen steps into my personal space putting me further on edge.

"Can we not do this right now?" I beg.

"Lindsey, please just hear me out. You won't answer my calls or texts; I just want to talk. You don't have to say anything, but at least let me apologize for being an idiot last night. I need you to know how sorry I am for what I said."

Regret is written all over his face, but I'm unable to find an appropriate response for this occasion. On the one hand, I refuse to dismiss his offense when the hurt still lingers. On the other hand, I took off with another boy and ended the night kissing him, so I'm certainly not an innocent party either.

"Lindsey," Stephen speaks up when I don't immediately respond, cupping my face with his hand.

Stephen's touch feels entirely ordinary; there's no pleasant prickling sensation or warmth emanating from the area of contact, unlike when Hunter touched me last night before. It's impossible not to compare the two moments when Stephen's hand is pressed against the same cheek Hunter's fingers grazed the night before. Hunter's gesture made my heart feel like it was going to explode, but I'm not feeling even a shred of that right now.

Has Stephen ever made me feel even an ounce of what I'd felt last night? There was a time when I was excited about us reaching new relationship milestones - the first time we held hands, danced or kissed - as it was my first time experiencing those landmark moments. I'd never had a boyfriend before. All of it pales in comparison to what I've now experienced.

I retract from his touch, finding it suddenly unwelcome. What is going on with me? Is it possible that Hunter has entirely ruined my perception of Stephen, or was it the argument that tainted my opinion? It is likely a little of both if I am honest with myself.

"I feel like I'm losing you all over a stupid, drunk argument," Stephen states, obviously picking up on my hesitation without me even having to vocalize it. "Please, don't let my one mistake ruin everything that we have. I didn't mean any of what I said."

"I find that hard to believe," I finally interject. "It felt like you'd been feeling those things for a while. It just took you getting drunk to finally say it."

"No, that's not what happened."

"*Oh, sure.* So you want me to believe that last night you had this epiphany that we should be having sex? Because it sure seemed like you've been talking with Rich about it based on your comments. You knew quite a bit about what he and Hannah have been doing - things Hannah has never shared with me."

"I .... uh .... I just ...." Stephen sputters.

"Yeah, that's what I thought," I shoot back, fuming mad. All the anger from last night is rekindled inside me in a flicker of an instant.

"Okay! Rich shared how they are progressing in their relationship, and I wanted the same for us. Is that so wrong?"

"Yes! It is wrong when you bring it up while drunk *and* belligerent. You made it clear last night that you think I'm some sort of prude for not being ready."

Stephen sighs audibly and turns his back to me, walking a few steps away before returning.

"I wish I could take back everything I said," Stephen responds, his voice calmer in an attempt to de-escalate this argument. "If you aren't ready, then neither am I. I'm willing to wait as long as you need, alright? I mean it."

Stephen's saying the right things now, but his words from the night before still echo in my head. My attention falls to my feet as silence descends on our conversation, and I don't have anything else to add. I can't tell if he's being honest or simply saying whatever it takes to put a stop to our argument.

Either way, this emotional day has left me with a limited capacity to deal with this, and I can't fully reconcile with Stephen until I've had more time to process what has transpired within the last twenty-four hours.

Finally, I nod my head in acknowledgment of his promise, which seems to put Stephen more at ease.

"Can we go see what the others are up to? Meredith needs my support tonight, and I don't want her to think I'm abandoning her."

"Yeah! Definitely. Let's go," Stephen agrees, placing a hand on the small of my back as we walk to find the others. Once again, the contact is anything but welcomed. I want to squirm away every time he touches me.

Needing a distraction, I slip my phone out to recheck social media. I can't help myself. I give over to my burning need for confirmation of what's happening in Colorado. Neither Lexi nor Serena have posted anything in the last three days, so I will need to wait a while longer to see the update I've been waiting for. My hand shakes as I slide my cell into the back pocket of my jeans. I'm a complete wreck.

The Tucker Girls

Joining the rest of the party, I find everyone packed into Meredith's living room. All the seats are taken, so I sit on the floor near Hannah, who appears very uncomfortable. It takes a second for me to catch up with what is happening around me, but I realize that Hannah's apprehensive because the group has started a game of Truth or Dare. I'm in complete agreement with her mood. Hopefully, we can both opt out of this ridiculous game.

Stephen plops down next to me, not leaving an inch of space between us, much to my irritation. The more distance I try to create between us, the more clingy he's becoming.

The game cycles through several individuals, and I must admit that some of the ridiculous dares have me laughing until I can't breathe. Rich completes his dare, which forced him to put on Meredith's mother's clothes and strut around the room, and I think maybe this game isn't so terrible when I hear Rich call Stephen's name.

"Dare," Stephen responds confidently.

"I dare you to kiss Lindsey."

Jerk.

I'd love to punch Rich in the face right now.

The room groans in response, likely thinking this is the weakest dare in the history of the game. Little do they know that this is the last thing I want to do right now.

Hannah's leg nudges me, and I look up to see her apologetic expression. She knows her boyfriend is being a butt-monkey too.

Stephen eagerly cups my face and leans in, his lips finding mine. Once again, the intimate contact lacks any weight, and I feel almost numb kissing my boyfriend. It's one more piece of evidence in the mounting case that I'm entirely ruined, and I withdraw from Stephen slowly. I can't help but notice his eyes communicating how meaningful the act was to him, but the scales are entirely tipped in his direction.

The Tucker Girls

The air in the room has changed as we part, and I'm wondering if everyone was able to discern my indifference in a moment intended to be romantic. Was it written all over my face?

No, something else is happening that has nothing to do with Stephen's dare. I follow everyone else's eyes to discover Hunter leaning against the far wall of the room, staring directly at me.

All those feelings I'd been searching for this evening with Stephen suddenly flood over me, and my heart beats wildly at the sight of the boy that should be in Colorado.

What is he doing here at Meredith's party? Based on the intensity of his gaze, I sense that I'm the reason for his unexpected appearance, and it sends my head swirling.

No one, and I mean *no one*, has ever chosen me over Serena besides my father, and even then, I'm pretty sure it's closer to a tie. To be honest, I'd choose Serena as well, yet Hunter showed up for me tonight. That intoxicating fact dances around in my head, defying my comprehension.

"Sorry I'm late to the party," Hunter greets everyone with his raspy voice, and I can't believe how much I enjoy hearing it again. It's only been a day since I last heard it, but it feels like an eternity. But, like I said, our kiss has flipped everything on its head.

"Hey, Hunter!" Meredith pops up from her seat, rushing over to him. "Lindsey said you were in Colorado. What are you doing here? I would have invited you if I knew you were in town."

I can see a glow on her face that was absent before; it conveys hope. If Hunter is here, others will follow.

"Yeah, I was supposed to fly out this morning, but I've got unfinished business that I need to take care of."

Oh boy, I'm in trouble. I guess my new nickname is *Unfinished Business.*

The Tucker Girls

Clingy Stephen slips an arm around my back, trying to desperately lay claim to me. He must sense the gravitational pull Hunter has on me, and I'm sure it only stokes his fear that I'm drifting away - which I very much am.

Hunter's gaze narrows in on Stephen at my side, and I see a flicker of irritation before he quickly conceals it. I must not do a great job of hiding my annoyance because when his eyes return to mine, I swear he picks up on it.

His perplexed look confirms he definitely saw something, and I cut my eyes at Stephen to answer his unspoken question. Hunter slightly smirks, apparently thinking Stephen's desperate attempts are humorous for some reason. Or is he enjoying the fact that my boyfriend is annoying me? Who knows with him.

I'm not quite sure which, but the answer isn't what is captivating my thoughts. I'm stunned by this new development that Hunter and I are now having a conversation without speaking a single word. Am I dreaming, or is this actually happening?

A nudge from Hannah steals my attention away, and I quickly notice that the entire room is watching Hunter and I interact. My cheeks warm from the unexpected attention, and I have a strong desire to go hide in a closet from the embarrassment. I wasn't flirting with him, but I'm sure it looked that way to everyone in the room.

"So .... uh .... Hunter, are you sticking around?" Meredith asks, breaking the awkward silence.

"We'll see," he replies cryptically.

Meredith shoots me a pleading look, and I know exactly what she's asking of me.

"Lindsey, can we talk in the kitchen?" Meredith inquires with big eyes.

"Yes!" I exclaim, wriggling free of Stephen's hold and hopping up to my feet.

The Tucker Girls

Follow me.

Of course, Hunter understands what my eyes are saying as he silently nods in response. This is the new, absurd world I'm living in where he's highly tuned in to my wavelength. I have to bite my lip to not smile like a fool. It feels incredible to be connected to someone like this again, especially since I thought I'd never get a second chance at it. It's the kind of chemistry that you just can't manufacture.

"What's up?" Hunter asks, trailing Meredith and me into the kitchen.

"I need your help getting people to show up to this party," I state on Meredith's behalf. "The entire junior class was invited, but not many people showed. Do you think you could help us out?"

"Yes! *Please!*" Meredith chimes in enthusiastically.

"How many people do you want here?"

Meredith shoots a giddy yet puzzled look my way. I shrug, unable to answer that question for her.

"I don't know .... let's say two hundred. Can you do that?"

"Two hundred, huh? Give me a sec," Hunter responds, pulling out his cell phone and walking into the empty dining room to perform his magic.

Meredith squeals as she shakes me, jumping up and down. After several minutes of suspense, Hunter emerges from the dining room with a smile.

"They are on their way."

"No way!" Meredith exclaims.

"It may not be two hundred, but it will be close. There's a large group hanging out at Jesse Baker's house, so they will shut it down and head this way."

"Thank you! Thank you! Thank you!" Meredith shouts as she dances away in pure glee.

The Tucker Girls

Hunter's gaze follows her until she's out of sight, then he turns to find me smiling at him.

"Thank you," I state more subtly, feeling my heart race wildly now that the two of us are alone.

"It was nothing."

"No! That was definitely something. You just made Meredith's day."

Hunter shrugs, and silence falls between us as we stare at one another. I'm dialed in on him, so I don't miss that he's slowly inching closer to me.

"You're here," I finally manage to say ineloquently, inching backward to try and keep my composure. He's too close, causing my heart to practically leap from my chest.

"Yeah, I'm here."

"I don't understand."

Hunter takes a deep, jagged breath and, for the first time since I've met him, I notice that he's nervous. His confident mask has been shed, and I know whatever is about to come out of his mouth is difficult for him to put to words.

"Honestly, neither do I. All I can say is every time I tried to picture myself getting on that flight to Colorado, I couldn't do it. Any choice that had me leaving you here in Amberly wasn't going to work."

Hunter covers my hand with his, preventing me from rubbing my scars. I'd been unknowingly drawn to them again.

"I've driven myself mad trying to leave you alone."

"That sounds miserable," I respond, not prepared to confess that I understand his misery.

"It is," Hunter agrees as I feel myself back against a set of cabinets. I'm trapped with nowhere else to run. "Especially you, of all people. You piss me off all the time. You play head games with me just for fun."

"Oh, and you're just an innocent angel?"

Hunter smirks at my snippy comeback.

281

The Tucker Girls

"You know I've never claimed to be perfect."

"So what's your point then? We both know that we are toxic for each other. You already knew that, though. You told me I was bad for you."

"See, that's where I'm beginning to think I was wrong," Hunter confesses. "Maybe we've been toxic because we've been fighting what's been happening between us the whole time."

"That's an interesting theory," I reply, my mouth dry from nerves. I swear I'm melting from the intensity of his heated gaze.

Closing my eyes, I try to process his words, but his fragrance envelops me. My slight grip on reality is assaulted the second his familiar aroma fills my nostrils. I'm transported to a place where everyone else in the world fades away, and it's just him and me. I want to stay here forever.

"You and I aren't so different, Lindsey. We're both so guarded, we missed the truth," he continues.

"And what's that?"

"That we both want each other. We understand each other more than we'd like to admit, and something about that connection pulls us together."

"I'm sorry to inform you that I don't feel a thing," I bluff.

Despite wanting Hunter here with every fiber of my being, I'm terrified of him. I still haven't opened my eyes because I'm not sure what I will do if I look into his captivating eyes again. If I lower my walls and allow him in, he will shatter what remains of my heart. I'm not ready to take that risk. It took so much work to piece myself back together last year.

"Cut the shit, Lindsey," Hunter replies sharply.

I feel his hand slip under my sleeve, and I suck in a deep breath knowing where he's headed. I could rip my arm away and stop his slow progression up my forearm, but I'm not going to do that. No, I want this. It takes only a few seconds before his thumb slowly traces the contours of my scars.

"No more hiding behind lies or oversized hoodies," he continues. "I see right through you. You might have fooled me for the past couple of months, but I don't believe your lies anymore, not after you kissed me like you did last night."

Opening my eyes, I desperately suck in several deep breaths trying to steady myself. I'm overwhelmed by the intimacy of Hunter exploring the remnants of the worst experience of my life. As intrusive as it feels, a part of me is reassured by his knowing I'm damaged, yet he still wants me. He's embracing the worst of me.

"What are you *really* thinking?" he asks in a whisper. "Please, Lindsey, be honest because this is torture not knowing how you truly feel."

Hearing the vulnerability in Hunter's voice almost breaks me. I'm hanging on by a thread.

"I'm scared," I reply with shocking honesty that trembles in my voice. "I don't trust you."

"Yes, you do. If you didn't trust me, I wouldn't have been the first person you called last night."

"Not like that," I counter. "I …. I …. don't trust you with my …. my heart."

Hunter's eye twitches at my confession. I struck a nerve with my honesty, but he asked for that. His thumb pauses its exploration of my scars as he stares intently at me.

"So, where do we go from here?" I ask cautiously. I'm not sure if we've hit an impasse or not. I can't read his body language.

"I need you to choose me."

My eyes dart up to his, searching for a clue as to what he's asking me to do.

"Lindsey, I know you're scared. I am too. I've spent my entire life not trusting anyone but myself, but I am laying it all out for you. Part of me still thinks this is a bad decision and that I can't trust you. Prove me wrong."

"I need you to acknowledge your feelings. But, ultimately, nothing I do matters if you keep pushing me away. I need you to choose me. I can't be the one always making all the moves. I bailed on work to show up for you last night. I kissed you. I chose you over Serena and my friends by skipping out on Colorado. I will keep choosing you. At some point, I need you to choose me. I just need you to move in my direction - even if it's just an inch. I'll do the rest. Just give me something - *anything*. Please."

Letting his words sink, I feel my stomach twist in knots. I consider what 'moving an inch in his direction' would mean - what it would cost me. It feels like a huge risk that could easily blow up in my face. This boy is notorious for running through girls like a tornado, and I feel like a wildflower in his warpath. There may be nothing left if I allow what remains of my guard down. My head is screaming for me to run, but my heart is aching at the possibility of whom Hunter will kiss if I reject him. That's not a good enough reason to choose him, though. If anything, being afraid of who he hooks up with if I turn him down is even more reason to stop this from moving forward.

His expectant gaze goes unanswered as I feel torn in half and unable to give him the response he's hoping for. My entire being is short-circuiting while this decision hovers over me. I can sense Hunter's anxiety rising with every passing second, but I'm paralyzed with indecision.

Stephen suddenly walks into the kitchen, breaking my stupor. I clear my throat and yank my arm from Hunter's grasp, attempting to compose myself.

"Hey, Lindsey. Everything okay in here?" Stephen asks, peering around Hunter to get a good look at me.

I slip past Hunter, using this interruption as an excuse to escape.

The Tucker Girls

"Yes! Everything's fine," I reply nervously. "Hunter and I were just talking. I'm going to rejoin the party in a minute."

I try my best to ignore Stephen's scrutinizing look he casts in my direction.

"Why don't we rejoin it now?"

"She said she will be there in a minute, *Stiff*," Hunter bites out in irritation.

"What's your problem, dude?" Stephen snaps back.

I shoot Hunter a threatening look while placing my hand on Stephen's chest. This is the last thing I need right now.

"I'll be right there, Stephen," I reassure him in a calm voice. He reluctantly nods before leaving the kitchen.

"Was that really necessary?" I spin towards Hunter. He turns his face, avoiding my burning gaze. "Did your timer go off or something? It's like you can't go more than ten minutes without being a jerk."

"It's just …. I don't like the way he doesn't listen to you," he responds, taking the edge off his voice. "I don't like how he touches or kisses you either."

"Except none of that is *your* business."

Hunter audibly exhales before meeting my gaze once more. He walks up next to me and stops when our arms are touching.

"About your choice …. take your time," Hunter states reassuringly. "I'll be waiting when you're ready to tell me what you want."

He starts to walk past me, and without thinking, I grab hold of his wrist firmly.

"Where are you going?"

Hunter looks down at where I've taken hold of him, and I feel the warmth of my cheeks blushing. I am clinging to him in desperation, fearful that he will disappear for the remainder of the evening. It's not a good look; I should know because Stephen's been clinging to me all night.

"I'll be around," he replies with a smile. "I just invited over a hundred people to this party. They'd kill me if I bailed before they got here."

Releasing Hunter's wrist, I nod in understanding. He slips away, and so does time, as I try to wrap my head around what just unfolded. I am in shock, but I give my best effort to disguise it as I rejoin the party and meander from group to group throughout the night.

Swarms of people descend on Meredith's house, and it quickly becomes overwhelmingly crowded. For once, the chaos feels comforting, as it mirrors the activity in my head. My thoughts are consumed with possibilities and consequences.

All I wanted since this morning was for Hunter to choose me, but now that he did, I'm paralyzed with fear. Maybe I'd be more open to risk had the world not already shattered me once.

Attempting to table the decision, I try my best to embrace the party for Meredith's sake. I've never been great at making small talk, but tonight I suck at it. My mind is constantly replaying Hunter's words. Even Stephen's attempts to crowd me barely register on my radar. My focus follows Hunter's every move as I pretend to converse with my classmates. I can't help but notice how he comes alive when surrounded by his classmates. Hunter thrives in scenes like this, but I'm left reeling from the loud music and overcrowding. We couldn't be more opposite, which is even more reason why his proposal is ridiculous.

Around eleven, I catch Hunter giving me a meaningful look, and I casually slip away from my current conversation to talk with him. Based on the sheer number of kids crammed into Meredith's house, it takes me several minutes to maneuver through the crowd.

The Tucker Girls

"Do you have a ride home?"

"I drove myself," I respond, suddenly wishing I hadn't. It would have given me a good excuse to be alone with him again.

"Sounds good. Well, I'm headed out. I'll see you around Lindsey."

"You're leaving so soon?"

"Yeah, I have a few things I need to do."

"At eleven at night?"

Hunter smirks in response, apparently enjoying my sudden interest in his comings and goings.

"I promised Chaz I'd drop in on him."

"Oh."

The air between us feels thick enough to slice through, and I'm no closer to knowing what to do than I was two hours ago. The next move is mine, and Hunter is trying to give me space. The fact that he'd bothered offering me a ride home felt like he was wavering on his promise to allow me to choose him, though. It still feels like he is inching in my direction. Maybe I could just wait him out?

"See ya, Lindsey."

Just like that, Hunter slips away, and I'm left standing alone in the swarm of classmates. I count each step that he takes as he walks away, caught up in a daze. Though I am surrounded, I feel entirely alone. The same empty, sinking feeling in my chest, which reared its ugly face this morning, starts flaring up as soon as he is out of sight.

The thought of not knowing when I will see Hunter eats away at me. What if he disappears for the remainder of the holiday break? Am I prepared for him to go dark once more? What if he loses patience with me and decides to move on? Countless girls would jump at the chance to be his distraction for the night.

As my head spins with questions, Hannah catches me by the arm. I startle at the unexpected contact.

"Hey," Hannah says with a remorseful look. "I just want to apologize for Rich earlier. He knew you were still fighting with Stephen, and it was such a thoughtless thing to dare him to kiss you."

I'm having an out-of-body experience, because I hear every word she says, but I'm unable to respond. I'm numb to everything except the sheer panic of Hunter leaving. Being caught between the fear of being too close to Hunter and the fear of losing him is crushing me.

Hannah tilts her head in concern.

"Lindsey, are you okay?"

"No. Not at all."

Slipping past Hannah, I wade through the crowd and out the front door, dashing straight towards the cars lining the sidewalk. Looking both ways down the street, without a clue where I am headed, I spy Hunter approaching his jeep to my left.

"Hunter!"

He freezes, slowly turning to see where the panicked call came from. The confusion on his face lets me know I've caught him off guard. Thank goodness I'm in sneakers because I take off into a sprint and close the distance between him and me in a split second.

"Lindsey, what's wrong?"

"Yes," I blurt out breathlessly.

Hunter stares down at me with a puzzled look. He's wondering what I just agreed to, and so am I. The word just slipped out. Now that I'm standing in front of him, I find my mouth drying again. I know I need to elaborate, but I'm paralyzed.

Dang it, Lindsey! Say something!

Hunter shifts his weight from foot to foot as he attempts to remain patient with me malfunctioning once more.

The Tucker Girls

"What do you mean? Yes to what?"

I can't meet his eyes any longer. This inept display is downright embarrassing, so I decide to stare at my feet instead. Then, taking a deep breath, I inch closer to Hunter until the toes of my sneakers touch his. Reaching over, I gradually grab a handful of his coat and pull him towards me. He wanted me to move an inch - and I don't know what that means - but this gesture feels more like a millimeter. It barely registers on the Richter scale.

"I guess that will have to do," Hunter says, taking hold of my chin and angling it up at him before claiming my lips with his.

I savor the thrill that runs through me the second he kisses me. I've been unknowingly craving this rush since last night. All the confusion that'd gripped me before evaporates away. This feels right. It feels more than right. In fact, I've never felt anything this incredible in my entire life.

Lost in my crippling fear was that I'd missed the way my body buzzes with excitement when I kiss him. I feel alive. My hands desperately tug him closer as I ache for more.

Hunter slips his hands below my waist, takes hold of my thighs, and lifts me off the ground. I respond by wrapping my legs around his waist. Our repositioning allows me to pull him closer. Hunter interprets the intentionality behind my movements, spinning me around, so my back is pinned up against his jeep, giving me the intimate contact I desperately want. There's not even a sliver of air between us.

Hunter matches my fervor as he deepens his kiss. He's holding nothing back. There's an earnestness to his passion that speaks to me. If I had any remaining doubt that he was being disingenuous, it has finally been quashed.

He knows that I'm not whole. I feel it every time Hunter explores my scars, yet he still wants me. I have no idea why. Maybe it's because he's broken too. All I know is that I'm overwhelmed by this realization, and it doesn't take long before a couple of tears break free down my cheeks.

Breaking free from our kiss, I lean my forehead against his while I try to catch my breath. Hunter's thumb swipes across my wet cheek, causing me to meet his concerned stare.

"What's wrong?" he whispers breathlessly.

"Nothing."

"Lindsey, you are crying," Hunter counters. "What did I do wrong?"

The sound of approaching party-goers startles us, and I wiggle free from Hunter's grasp until he sets me back on my feet. I manage to put some distance between the two of us before three classmates walk by. Hunter and I stand wordlessly by his jeep until the group drives off down the street.

"I'm just emotional. That's all," I state when he's still intently staring down at me. His hand slowly wipes my other damp cheek, and I lean into his touch.

"I don't believe you."

"It's true. Look. If you are looking for an easy girl, I'm not it. I'm an emotional, complicated mess."

His eyes sparkle as he smiles in response.

"I can do complicated."

"Are you sure?"

"A hundred percent sure."

He says it with such confidence that I can't help but feel reassured. I want to believe he can be that guy.

"So, are you sure you want to do this?" Hunter clarifies, directing his finger between him and me.

"I think so."

"*Wow*. That's reassuring."

"Hunter," I plead, closing the distance between us. "You wanted honesty. This is me being honest. I want this, but I also have a couple of stipulations."

"Stipulations, huh?"

The Tucker Girls

"Yes."

"What kind of stipulations?"

"I'm not going to be one of your girls," I state firmly. "I mean it. I won't be another one-and-done hookup of yours."

"Okay."

"Okay?"

"*Yes*! Lindsey, that's not what's happening here," Hunter replies earnestly, gently tracing my cheek with his thumb. "I'm down with whatever stipulations you have."

"Really?" I ask in disbelief, considering the possibilities of his offer.

"I'll do my best."

"You are not allowed to disappear when things get hard. And you will not ghost me."

"Wow. All of these rules," Hunter teases.

"Are you in or not?" I banter back, a smile forming on my lips.

"I'm in. I'm all in."

"I'm all in, too, then."

Hunter seals our pledges with a kiss, but this time he trails additional kisses down my neck, sending pleasant chills all over my body.

"Come to Chaz's with me," Hunter implores, meeting my gaze again.

"I can't. I need to have a difficult talk with Stephen and still make it home before curfew."

Hunter nods in understanding, kissing me once more before stepping back. I slip my hand in his, unwilling to allow him to leave just yet.

"I want to see you tomorrow," Hunter confesses.

"I'm free all day."

"Let's do breakfast, then. Text me when you wake up."

I silently agree, giddy inside with the prospect of seeing Hunter again so soon. The only thing able to sober me up is the thought of breaking this news to Stephen. I don't plan on telling him about Hunter, but I need to explain my change of heart. It's time for me to break up with my first boyfriend.

Despite how challenging the conversation with Stephen will be, I have confidence that I am making the right decision as I stare into Hunter's eyes. I only have one big outstanding question left. How will I ever explain this to Serena?

CHAPTER TWENTY-SEVEN
Lindsey

Today is New Year's Eve which should carry some significance in my life, considering tomorrow will be an entirely different year, yet it barely registers when I wake up. Most of my classmates are likely trying to decide which party to attend to ring in the new year this morning, but I hardly give it a passing thought.

My mind should be occupied with the emotional breakup with Stephen last night, which left me entirely drained and depleted by the time I got home; however, I find myself upbeat as I get dressed. None of these important details can distract me from the fact that Hunter is on his way to pick me up for our first date - at least, I think it's a date. I wonder if he's labeling it the same way.

Taking a quick peek in the mirror, evaluating the third outfit that I've tried on, I decide that my black long-sleeve blouse and jeans are good enough. I considered raiding Serena's closet for more stylish clothes, but my guilty conscience has already reared its ugly head enough in the thirty minutes since I've been awake. I cannot borrow her clothes to go on a date with the boy she fell head over heels for; that would be beyond salvage.

My stomach is in knots because Serena has no idea what's happening between Hunter and me. She comes home in two days, and I plan to explain how I've managed to fall for Hunter, too, once we are face-to-face. I'm not expecting it to be a pleasant conversation, but she will have to forgive me eventually. Right?

Serena can have any guy she wants, just not Hunter. Is it really so bad that I get the one thing in the world that is out of her reach?

Shaking my hands and trying to clear my mind, I know Serena isn't the only reason I'm wound up this morning. I'm terribly nervous about being alone with Hunter. It's the kind of restlessness that's intertwined with excitement, and I'm not sure what to do with all of this energy. A smile keeps appearing on the other side of my mirror, and I can't quite seem to bury it away. It's an unusual sight to see me giddy like this.

Bounding down the stairs, I steal a glance out the front window and am relieved to see Hunter hasn't arrived yet. I still have time to check in with my parents before I sneak away for the morning.

"Morning!" I greet Mom and Dad, my voice sounding more cheery and energetic than I intended.

Come on, Lindsey. Play it cool.

I'm not a morning person, so greeting them with enthusiasm is entirely out of character for me. One look across the kitchen, spying my parents both eyeing me inquisitively from the table, and I know I alerted them that something is going on.

"Good morning, dear," Mom answers. "You're already dressed?"

"Yeah," I reply with a shrug. "I have plans."

Dad pauses eating to examine me wordlessly as I walk by, and I lean in and kiss his cheek in passing.

Yep, I'm not acting normal at all, and I can't seem to stop this ridiculous behavior. Recalling Serena floating around the house a few weeks ago, I'm likely resembling her ecstatic behavior right now. It's not lost on me how much that grated my nerves at the time.

"Speaking of plans, don't think your father and I didn't notice you coming in late last night," Mom retorts with a severe look.

"Elise," Dad responds, giving my mother a meaningful glance that I cannot interpret.

"I was fifteen minutes late. Serena does it all the time."

Mom and Dad are having a staring contest, but I know how this ends. Mom always wins these battles.

"I'm just pointing out that she was late. I'm not punishing her."

"Look at her. I haven't seen her this happy since ...." Dad's statement trails off before he can mention Ava's name. Even though he catches himself just in time, I still tense up at the near mention of her.

"*Hello*, I'm right here."

Mom audibly sighs before flashing me a warm smile.

"Are you doing something with Stephen this morning?"

"No, we broke up," I reply matter-of-factly.

Dad chokes on his coffee at the news.

"*What*!?"

"Yeah," I shrug. "It happened. It's not a big deal."

"When did you break up with Stephen? I liked him," Mom protests.

"Last night. That's why I was late."

"Are you okay?" Dad inquires, looking baffled by the disconnect between my demeanor and the breakup.

"I'm better than okay."

Right on cue, my smile bubbles up again. *Ugh.* I'm acting more and more like Serena with every passing minute, making me want to slap myself silly.

"Good! Well, you don't need a boyfriend anyways. You're too young."

"Serena was dating boys in middle school," I interject, and Dad simply gives me a *Yeah, but you're different* look. I hate that look.

The Tucker Girls

"Doug, there's nothing wrong with dating," Mom corrects, turning back towards me. "So are you going off with Hannah then?"

"Nope."

I'm not offering up Hunter's name to my parents. I can only imagine the firestorm that would ensue if they found out I am hanging out with him.

My phone buzzes as I try to avoid my mother's scrutinizing glare.

Hunter: Here.

Lindsey: Okay!! Stay where you are. I'll be right there.

Hunter: You have five minutes.

Lindsey: Til what?

Hunter: I come and get you.

Lindsey: Don't you dare!! I mean it. I'll be out in five.

When I texted Hunter after waking up, I told him to park a few houses down again. I need to talk with Serena before word gets out that Hunter and I are talking - or dating - or whatever we are doing. If she finds out before I tell her, it will make matters exponentially worse. It will be World War III. Chaos and destruction will ensue. I'm already expecting an epic fight when we sit down to talk. I don't want to pour kerosene on that fire.

"Lindsey," Mom's stern voice beckons.

"Yeah?"

"Who are you hanging out with?"

"Just a friend. We're going to get breakfast together."

The Tucker Girls

"Do I know this friend?" Mom inquires, continuing to try and dig up more information despite my evasive answers. There's a rule in our house that Mom meets our friends before she allows us to hang out with them, but she's already met Hunter, so it's not like I'm breaking her rules.

"Do you scrutinize Serena whenever she hangs out with a friend?" I ask in an irritated tone.

"Don't bring Serena into this," Mom retorts, her cheeks flushing red.

"Elise, don't you think we should ease off a bit?" Dad interjects, trying to de-escalate the pending argument.

"I only ask because I care about her. I'm sure plenty of parents never ask what their kids do, but I'm not that type of parent."

"I know you care. Lindsey knows that as well, right?"

Dad hits me with pleading eyes, begging me to just agree with him.

"Yes! I know you love me, Mom."

"I do love you."

"Lindsey, you remembered that your mother and I aren't going to be home tonight, right?" Dad interjects again.

"Yep. I remember."

Hannah is letting me stay the night with her since my parents will be in Fort Worth celebrating the New Year with some of his new co-workers and their spouses.

"Please call us if something falls through and you can't stay with Hannah. We can drive home after the party if we need to."

My parents don't like me being home by myself, which is fine since I don't care to be alone at night anyways.

"You don't need to drive that late with all the drunk people leaving the parties. I will be fine."

Dad levels me with a disapproving look.

"Okay! I will call you if plans change."

"Thank you."

The sound of the doorbell sends me into a panic, as I nearly throw the chair to the floor in a mad dash to the front door. Assuming Hunter is rebelling against my explicit instructions, I can't let my parents see that I'm going off with him.

"Love you! Have fun!" I shout out, despite hearing my mother calling for me to wait.

Sure enough, Hunter is standing on the other side of the door when I open it. Grabbing his arm, I forcefully drag him down the steps toward where his jeep is supposed to be parked.

"Come on!" I urge, knowing full well I don't have the strength to pull him across the lawn, despite how angry I am, when he's twice my size. Thankfully, Hunter cooperates and hustles along.

"You couldn't wait five minutes like I asked?" I huff out in frustration as I climb into the passenger seat. "If one of my parents had opened the door and not me, it would have ruined everything."

"I got impatient," Hunter states with a shrug. "You were taking too long."

I stare at him in disbelief. His carelessness is going to ruin everything. He's not concerned enough about whether Serena finds out about us.

"Forget it," I state angrily, pausing before I even finish buckling my seat belt. "This was a stupid idea. You're obviously not taking this seriously."

I twist around and prepare to hop out of the jeep.

"Lindsey, wait!" Hunter reaches over and takes hold of my arm.

"No! If Serena gets word that we are together before I can talk to her, it will destroy her. This isn't a game."

"You're right. You're right. I'm sorry. That was a stupid move on my part," he confesses, appearing as regretful as his words sound. "I hardly slept last night and didn't think through my actions. I'll be more careful from now on."

My heart rate is starting to slow down, and I take the opportunity to look at him. I'd been so busy trying to get Hunter away from my house that I hadn't inspected him closely. The evidence of his long night shows. Shadows are cast under each of his eyes that were not there the night before.

Regardless of whether he slept, I won't sacrifice my relationship with Serena over his carelessness.

Relenting, I slip back into my seat and buckle in. I don't miss how Hunter eyes me warily before starting the jeep. I threw him for a loop when I almost bolted.

Settling in for the drive, I notice how clean and tidy his jeep is. I'd only ever ridden with him at night, so the darkness had concealed its near-perfect condition. Out of Hunter's many qualities, I never would have pinned him for a neat freak.

Running my hand over the passenger-side console, I wonder how he was able to afford something this nice. From what little I know, his family isn't filthy rich like most of our classmates. I don't even understand how he attends Ulla Meyer. My parents paid a fortune in tuition this year alone.

"Your jeep is nice. When did you get it?"

"Last year."

"Was it new when you bought it?"

Hunter briefly cuts his gaze my way.

"No," he responds sharply. "You wondering how a guy from Indy Park afforded this?"

"Kind of. Yeah."

"Obviously, I stole it," Hunter replies sarcastically.

"That's not what I was insinuating. I was just curious."

Eyeing him as he wordlessly drives, I wonder if he will ever answer my question. Hunter is incredibly guarded. I am butting up against his walls and losing. It's a reminder that he still doesn't trust me - at least not enough to talk about anything meaningful.

"*Forget it.* Let's stick to meaningless topics. *Beautiful weather today, isn't it?*"

"Lindsey."

"*What?*"

"It's a hand-me-down, okay? Like everything else I own," Hunter responds as he furrows his brow. "Brady gave it to me when he bought his Range Rover. I couldn't buy a vehicle like this. Hell, I can't even afford the insurance."

Silence descends over us as I realize I'm digging into an area of his life that he's ashamed of. I can feel how much he hates needing the charity of his friends.

"Thank you," I say in a subdued tone. "I won't tell anyone. You can trust me."

Trust. Everything between Hunter and me hinges on this fragile concept. We have chemistry for miles but are lacking in a critical area of our relationship.

"Do you normally have trouble sleeping at night?" I ask, attempting to change topics.

"Not usually."

Lindsey, meet another wall.

Hunter steals a glance my way, and I'm surprised to see conflict in his eyes.

"What's wrong?"

"It's just …. I didn't sleep well because my father never came home last night."

"What!? Have you tried calling him? Have you called the police?"

"No. Lindsey, he does this sometimes. We don't really …. get along. It's complicated …. but I still need him for things."

"So he disappears sometimes? Like you do?"

"No. Not like me."

"Hunter, I don't understand."

"Forget it. He's fine. He's likely home already. I ....
shouldn't have said anything."

My brain swirls with confusion. If Dad disappeared,
even for a night, without anyone knowing where he went, I think
I would have an emotional meltdown. Hunter's not making any
sense. The way his hand wrings the steering wheel tells me this
topic has Hunter on edge.

"Can we pick another topic?" he asks in a softer tone.

"Sure."

"So you haven't told Serena about us yet?" Hunter asks
as he turns onto the interstate.

"No," I reply, feeling anxiety ripple throughout my body.
"She'll be home tomorrow, and I'm going to have the
conversation then. Face-to-face."

"I'd like to be there when you talk to her."

A sarcastic laugh escapes me when I hear him say that
with a straight face.

"No, you absolutely do not want to be there. It's going
to be a bloodbath. In fact, this may be the last time you see me
breathing because she may go straight for homicide."

"She was upset when I called to tell her I wasn't coming
to Colorado."

"Wait! You called her? Did she ask why you weren't
coming?"

"Yeah, I was vague, though. I told her there were some
things I needed to take care of here in Texas."

"I'm sure she appreciated that," I state.

"It was mostly me talking. She was silent nearly the
entire conversation, but I could feel her frustration through the
phone."

Unlike me, Serena's too proper to lay into Hunter as he
deserved. If he stood me up that way, there would be hell to pay.
Her silence speaks volumes to me, though.

The Tucker Girls

"When Serena's quiet, you know you've pissed her off."

"If you think I should sit this one out, I will," Hunter relents, thinking better of getting involved in our sisterly dispute. Serena and I are best friends now, but that doesn't mean we don't fight with the best of them. We don't stay mad at each other long, though.

Our go-to makeup ritual is driving to get ice cream. I'm convinced all problems in the world can be solved over a sundae. This pending argument may need more than just a sweet treat to resolve.

We pull up to a small, brick building that, I'm guessing, is our destination. Its front door reads 'Gilded Griddle' in gold lettering, and I take a deep breath to slow my racing heart. I'm not sure I will be able to eat anything with the butterflies in my stomach fluttering wildly. I'm not prepared to be seen with Hunter in public.

Hunter opens the passenger door for me, and I slide out next to him. He's eyeing me closely, expecting some sort of reaction from me.

"What?"

"Lindsey, are you sure you're ready for this?"

Great. He's picking up on how nervous I am right now.

"For our first date? Yeah, I think so," I respond honestly because a part of me is unsure about all of this. Based on our conversation on the way here, there's still so much I don't even know about Hunter. "Wait. This is a date, right?"

Hunter laughs at my question.

"It's whatever you want it to be," he answers, brushing away a strand of hair covering my face. The endearing look on his face does all kinds of crazy things to my heart. "Do you want this to be a date?"

"Yes," I say breathlessly as my head still spins from his touch.

"Good. Me too. Come on, let's go get something to eat."

The second we walk into Gilded Griddle, I know it was an excellent choice on Hunter's behalf. I am unable to recognize a single person in the entire restaurant as we navigate to our table. It's comforting to know that no one here cares a lick about Hunter or who the girl is that he showed up with him. It will take me a while to get used to the attention that will come with being close to this boy because I'm certainly not ready for it today.

Sliding into a booth across from Hunter, I don't immediately pick up the laminated menu. Instead, I need to get something off my chest that's been eating away since Meredith's party.

"Last night, you wanted honesty from me. I want that from you too."

Hunter sighs and levels me with a reluctant look.

"Lindsey, there are things you aren't going to want to hear. You need to be sure you want the answers before you ask questions. Some things are better left unsaid."

I avert my eyes to the menu to consider his statement. This relationship won't work if he's constantly hiding all his secrets in a closet. They will eventually spill out, and I'd rather be prepared for them than be caught entirely off guard.

"I'll give you the answers you want, but I want more answers from you too," Hunter offers up, sliding his hand across the table and touching my forearm.

My breath hitches at realizing what he wants to know, and I'm not ready to share those details with him. I haven't talked about it in nearly a year with anyone, including my family.

"Let's start with the easy ones first," Hunter suggests, likely reading the hesitancy written all over my face.

"Okay. How many dates have you been on before?"

The Tucker Girls

"None. This is my first."

"What?" I ask incredulously. "Seriously? You are lying."

"Seriously. Hence the name *The Untouchables,*" he replies with a smirk.

"So does that mean you have to relinquish that title?"

"I don't know. Honestly, I don't care, either. We never wanted to be called that from the start. I'm hoping we will end all the nonsense, but first, you will have to be seen with me in public."

I motion my hand towards all the customers sitting around us, raising my eyebrows at Hunter.

"You know what I mean. Ulla Meyer needs to know you and I are together."

Our waitress arrives in time for me to avoid responding to his statement. Whatever he has in mind, it can't happen until I've spoken with Serena. Even then, I'm unsure how long I need to wait to spare her feelings. The last thing I want is for her to see us together everywhere she turns.

After placing our orders, I fire off my next question to distract Hunter from our previous topic.

"And how many girls have you ...." I start to ask, but realize I'm uncertain I want the answer to this question. I guess this was what Hunter was warning me about. Ignorance is bliss.

"Been with?" Hunter finishes for me. "I haven't exactly kept a count."

"If you were to guess ...."

Stop Lindsey! I'm shouting in my head, yet the words keep pouring out of my mouth.

"If I were to guess, I'd say around twenty-five."

"Oh, *wow.*"

The estimate hits me like a bus, and I feel my head spinning as it tries to comprehend him sleeping with that many girls. Considering the rumors I'd heard, it shouldn't surprise me, but the figure still catches me off guard.

Hunter hooks his foot around my calf under the table, drawing my attention away from my hands.

"I wish I could take it all back. Even before I met you, I'd decided that I wasn't going to continue having meaningless sex. And now that I've met you, I regret my actions even more."

Hunter shifts uncomfortably in his booth as he watches me silently process the news. Taking in the uneasiness in his eyes, he's likely guessing I'm rethinking our agreement, but that's not the case. It's simply a struggle to digest that I expect us to be different. I'm not here for a flippant fling, but that's all he's ever known. Hunter has no experience with a committed relationship which is even more terrifying.

What's so different about me that he will want to stick around?

"Lindsey ...." Hunter pleads with me knowing my thoughts are running wild. There's a tinge of fear laced into his voice.

"Why me? What makes me any different than those other girls?"

"This isn't likely going to help my case, but you wanted full honesty," he states before pausing. "I can't explain what's happening because I've never felt like this before with anyone. I feel like I crossed the point of no return with you when I couldn't leave Texas knowing you were here. My first instinct when I get close to someone is to push away, but you're different. The closer I get to you, the more I want.

"I never made any promises to those girls, but I'm telling you that I want so much more with you. Like I said last night, I'm all in. I'm offering you honesty, no matter how difficult that may be for me. You have no idea how difficult it is to give you answers that will not paint me in the best light. Each one has the potential to send you running away, and it's frightening."

Each truth could send me running away like his mother. Hunter may not even realize it, but the fear in his eyes communicates a more profound pain that I'm tapping into when I press him to share his secrets. This realization plows over me, wreaking havoc on my heart. He's just as shattered as I am, and my heart breaks for him.

Reaching across the table for his hand, I interlace our fingers together.

"I'm not running anywhere, Hunter."

My reassuring words don't squelch his anxiety, but they are true. His confession was the type of vulnerability that I've longed to hear, and now that I have seen this side of him, I find myself falling even harder for him. This is more than physical attraction. I have the sense that he understands the brokenness in me like no one else can.

The rest of our breakfast passes with simple, casual conversation, which I find flows effortlessly between us. Walls are starting to come down, even if we avoid difficult topics. I don't have the burning desire to have all my questions answered since I've seen him open up a little. I know it's only a matter of time before I need to answer his questions, but thankfully he doesn't press me on the issue. It may take a while, but I know he's someone I can be vulnerable with as well; he'll understand my pain. He may not have scars on his arms like me, but he has them all over his heart.

"This is Chaz's house, right?" I ask hesitantly as Hunter pulls in front of a familiar mansion.

"Yes. Do you trust me?"

"That depends. Want to tell me why we are here?"

I'd agreed to Hunter's undisclosed plan while we were leaving brunch, but now he is pushing my boundaries. We'd

The Tucker Girls

decided that we were going to keep things low-key until I'd spoken with Serena, but here we were sitting out in front of his friend's house. I might as well be wearing a shirt that reads *I'm with Him* considering how flippant we are with our discretion.

Hunter laughs at my question.

"Lindsey, please just trust me."

I exhale in frustration, really hoping this isn't a bad idea. I nod my head in agreement while I scan the street for cars I may recognize. I'm not above making a run for it if there are a lot of people here.

I slide out of the jeep and cautiously follow Hunter up the driveway to the front door. He doesn't miss the sharp look I throw his way, but it doesn't throw him off. Hunter just responds with a smirk.

Chaz answers the door shortly after Hunter knocks, looking like he just rolled out of bed.

"Hey, dude," Chaz sleepily greets Hunter, glancing over in my direction as he hands Hunter some small object. "Have fun."

"Thanks, man. Not a word about this, okay?"

"My lips are sealed," Chaz responds, casting a puzzled expression my way before shutting the front door.

"What just happened?" I inquire, perplexed by what I just observed.

"Follow me," Hunter jerks his head towards the side of the house with a grin on his face, refusing to answer my question. I swear he's enjoying keeping me in the dark, which drives me crazy.

When he notices me hesitating to follow him, Hunter throws me a pleading look while slipping his hand in mine. I reluctantly walk with him hand-in-hand around the house and through the acres of backyard until we step foot on the dock. It's only then that I realize the small thing Chaz had slipped Hunter was a key. Everything begins to make sense when I see Chaz's family boat docked, and my excitement level surges. Hunter spies my smile, which only causes his smile to brighten.

Hunter is taking me on a private ride on this boat; just him and me. I'm in complete shock by this thoughtful gesture. Every time I think I understand Hunter, he does something entirely unexpected. I never took him for a guy who would set up a surprise like this on the first date.

To top it all off, it's a sunny, pleasant day for December. They occasionally get these warmer winter days in Texas, providing a nice reprieve from winter. We used to have them in Georgia as well. The breeze is chilly, but I'm willing to bear it if it means getting to ride out on the lake.

The boat looks expensive, with a canopy covering half its thirty-foot length. Hunter hops in, appearing to be very comfortable with this vessel by the ease with which he navigates it. Based on what I'm observing, I have to assume that he and Chaz must take this boat out often.

"Are you going to join me, or are you going to watch me from the dock?" Hunter teases as he holds out his hand to offer assistance boarding the boat.

"I'm just still in shock. I wasn't expecting this at all," I declare as I take hold of his hand and step down into the vessel.

As soon as I step onto the vessel, Hunter draws me toward him, his affectionate gaze staring down at me. Heat trickles down my neck as I meet his eyes, and my heart begins racing uncontrollably right on cue.

He leans down and lightly kisses my lips, stirring up desire within me. His gesture is a tease, and before I can deepen the kiss, he backs away and continues untying the boat from the dock.

"Hey! Get back here," I plead.

"There'll be plenty of time for that once we get out on the lake. Unless you want to make out in full view of Chaz's neighbors."

The Tucker Girls

"Oh yeah."

Duh. Embarrassment washes over me when I realize how easily I lost my wits when he gave me that heated look.

Before we depart, Hunter hands me a blanket which I quickly wrap around my shoulders. Sure enough, the cold breeze turns frigid the second we are skimming across the water. Feeling cozy draped in the blanket, I find it incredibly peaceful watching the scenery pass by as we navigate the lake.

A spark of inspiration hits me. I try to commit every detail of this scene to memory so that I can paint it later.

Watching Hunter's back as he navigates us towards the middle of the lake, I shake my head in disbelief at this surreal moment. Is this real life? For the last four months, I've hated this boy, but everything is changing so quickly that I find it hard to keep up. Hunter now has my heart fluttering every time I get close to him.

None of this makes sense, but does falling in love necessarily have to? What if the two of us were inevitably intertwined, and it just took us a while to figure it out?

All too soon, Hunter cuts the engine and allows the boat to coast slowly to a halt. The tranquility of our surroundings greets me as the vessel slowly rocks back and forth, and there's not another soul in sight. I close my eyes and embrace the stillness of my surroundings.

The absurdity of this situation would have bothered me before, but it's beginning to feel more natural - as if this is how my world was always supposed to be.

"Amazing, isn't it?" Hunter inquires as he sits on the bench beside me.

I nod my head in agreement. Everything about this moment is perfect.

"This is crazy, right?" I ask, searching his face for agreement.

"Honestly? It's unexpected, but nowhere near the craziest thing I've ever done," he responds with an earnest look. His hand reaches up and affectionately brushes my cheek, inviting my heart to race wildly once again. "None of this made any sense to me until we kissed, and then everything became crystal clear to me."

My head nods unintentionally, but not because I don't understand; I absolutely do in an inexplicable way. I'm simply caught up in his gaze. Hunter leans in, his breath warming my face. I wrap both hands around his neck and draw him the remainder of the distance to me. Once we are kissing, nothing else matters. All my concerns and confusion melt away.

As Hunter said, things make more sense when I stop overanalyzing the situation; I'm trying my best to embrace letting go. I lean into it and quickly lose myself in Hunter, finding it hard to decipher where I end and where he begins.

Hunter's the first to interrupt our kiss despite my groans of protest. I try to guide his lips back to mine, where they belong, but he keeps them out of reach by leaning his forehead against mine.

"I swear I didn't bring you out here just to make out."

"Sure you didn't," I tease, angling to find his lips again. I'm an addict and cannot help myself. I'm not ready to move on to whatever he has planned, and Hunter doesn't pull away this time. Eventually, my curiosity overcomes me.

"What else did you have planned for today?" I ask, breaking free from our kiss.

Hunter's satisfied smile greets me, and he knows he's piqued my interest.

"Do you happen to have a book with you?"

"No," I reply, slightly embarrassed by my book nerd self, who carries novels everywhere I go. I guess I have a reputation as well.

"You don't have a book?" Hunter asks skeptically.

"No," I lie, which Hunter sees right through. "Okay! I have my Kindle with me. It's not technically a book."

"Was that so hard to admit?"

"Maybe. What do you need a book for anyways? Bored of me already?"

"Definitely not. No, I need it for the next part of our date."

"Okay .... Out of curiosity, what was your backup plan if I didn't bring one?"

"I had a backup plan," Hunter answers, tapping a compartment next to him.

"You brought a book!? Which one did you bring?"

My curiosity is raging, as I am dying to know what type of book he reads.

"It doesn't matter because you brought a book."

"Hunter! I want to see what you brought," I demand, reaching for the compartment only to have Hunter swat away my hand. If he thinks a simple swat will deter me, he's dead wrong. I'm on a mission now.

"Not going to happen," Hunter replies with a smile.

I lunge across his body for the compartment, but Hunter reacts too quickly and wraps his arms around my waist. Despite my limbs flinging in a desperate attempt to reach the enclosure, Hunter effortlessly holds me at bay. He pulls me into his lap, and I huff out in exasperation.

"Please let me see it."

Hunter responds by trailing kisses down my neck, and my focus wavers.

"You can't distract me."

"Are you sure?" Hunter inquires, continuing his progression. On cue, my head gets foggy.

"What was I looking for again?"

"My reading selection. This will be one secret I will hold onto for a while. I can't let word get out that I read. It'd be bad for my rep."

"Fine!" I concede, flapping my arms in frustration. In the back of my mind, I decide to wait until he's driving the boat again to search for his mysterious novel.

Pulling out my Kindle, I nuzzle my back against Hunter's chest and stretch my feet out across the remainder of the bench. Hunter tosses the blanket over my body, successfully covering both of us.

"So what am I doing with this?" I ask, holding up the device.

"Read to me."

"You want me to read to you? Out loud?" I ask in disbelief.

"Yeah. Is that weird?"

"No. It's just …. unexpected."

That seems to be the word of the day.

"I'm halfway through The Notebook. Do you want me to start from the beginning?"

"No, keep going where you left off. I've read it before."

Interesting. I mentally lock away this additional tidbit for later.

I start reading, pausing every couple of pages to check in on Hunter. I'm not convinced this is something he wants to do, but he gives me a reassuring nod every time. After a chapter of interruptions, I hit a groove and get lost in the story. Three chapters fly by without me having to stop.

"This is why I love this book so much. Noah and Ally fight like a real couple. There's something about their relationship that feels so authentic."

Pausing for Hunter to reply, I'm met with silence. Based on his chest's slow rise and fall, I realize he's fast asleep.

The Tucker Girls

Slowly leaning away from his chest, I scoot across the bench, so I can turn to face him. Staring into his perfect face, I'm taken aback by how peaceful he seems as he leans against the boat. There's an innocence to his expression that catches me off guard.

Considering he had a restless night's sleep, I decide against leaning against him again so as not to risk waking him. I pull the blanket up to his chest, stopping when my face is inches from his. Closely inspecting his peaceful state, my heart begins doing funny things.

I could get used to this. I start picturing more days like today, filled with Hunter and me hanging out, and it makes me smile.

I lean in and place a light kiss on his forehead.

"Please - whatever you do - don't break my heart," I whisper to him, taking the opportunity to verbalize my greatest fear to his unconscious state. The longer this day goes on, the more I'm surprised at how comfortable I feel just being with the boy I used to hate. My heart is bending towards Hunter in ways that excite and terrify me all at the same time.

CHAPTER TWENTY-EIGHT
Hunter

Lindsey is glowing, and it has nothing to do with the fluorescent paint streaked in her hair or the three glow sticks hanging around her neck. Her eyes are beaming with life in an unfamiliar way since we stepped off Chaz's boat. There had been a certain sadness she'd been carrying around since I'd met her that I'd grown accustomed to seeing.

A switch has been flipped inside her, though. She's happy, and damn does that realization have me in a euphoric state. I want to think I had something to do with her cheery mood.

We're attending a house party blanketed in darkness except for the blacklights illuminating each room. Despite the limited visibility, I see Lindsey's inquisitive eyes dance around the room as she studies the scene surrounding us. She's chewing on her bottom lip, something I've noticed her doing several times today. I know a question is stewing in her mind, and I'm curious to hear it.

Lindsey hasn't noticed yet, but I've been studying her while she's watching the crowd around us. I'm trying to read every fraction of an expression on her face to gauge her response.

Why did I bring her here?

I don't know what's wrong with me - maybe it's the fact that I'm trying to sabotage a good thing before it goes sour or my trust issues are flaring up again - but I invited her to a friend's party after we'd spent the day together knowing how much she despises these types of events.

The Tucker Girls

To her credit, Lindsey hasn't bolted for the door, and we've been here almost an hour. Deep down, I know it's better for her to run now. Hell, I can't have anything tying me down to Amberly. I'm leaving in five months and never looking back. I feel the itch to rip the bandaid off and get it over with, but I doubt I'd be able to leave her alone even if she started having second thoughts. She's my obsession, and spending time with Lindsey today only fuels my insatiable desire for her.

That still doesn't stop me from potentially ruining it because I am an ass. It's in my DNA.

I draw her back towards me until her body is pressed against my chest, allowing my burning desire to rage further. Lindsey must read what I feel from the look in my eyes because I swear she blushes and quickly looks away. If she minds where my thoughts are wandering, she certainly doesn't show it as she shifts further into me and rests the back of her head on my shoulder.

"This is where you hide when you disappear for days?" Lindsey asks inquisitively, motioning towards the party surrounding us.

"One of the places," I admit with a shrug. "SACS' social scene doesn't intersect with Ulla Meyer, so I don't have to carry any school drama with me when I come here."

SACS stands for Saint Agnes Catholic School. It's a private school on the other side of town. Don't let the school's name fool you; they throw some wild parties. Tonight's event is fairly tame since Liv is hosting, and she is selective in who she invites into her home. It's the only reason I even considered asking Lindsey. Even if I'm testing her, I don't want to push her too far.

Lindsey's shaking her head in disbelief, leaving me to wonder what she was expecting me to drag her into tonight. I've spent most of the day unsuccessfully reading into her expressions, hoping to understand her mind.

The Tucker Girls

"So you just hop from school party to school party?"

"Pretty much. I like to stay busy."

The alternative is to be home, which is incredibly unappealing. I'd rather gouge my eyes out than spend an additional unnecessary minute with Pete.

"Do Brady and Elijah ever come with you?"

"Not here. Brady will join me if I go to a Montepe party. That's his school of choice when it comes to girls."

"Is Montepe another private school?"

"Yeah. It's on your side of town, though. Only five miles from Ulla Meyer."

"I see." Lindsey nods to herself, and I can see her wheels spinning. She's unraveling a puzzle in her mind with each answer I provide. "And this is where I'll find you if you disappear again?"

"Are you planning on hunting me down next time?" I whisper in her ear, causing a shiver to run through her body.

"Yes."

When Lindsey looks up at me, I see the determination in her eyes. *Damn.* I believe her, and it resonates in a specific chasm in my heart that's taken residence over the last decade.

I trace a line down her neck with my lips, causing Lindsey to shudder again. I love how she reacts to the slightest whisper or kiss; excitement ripples throughout her entire body every time. Before I can reach her shoulder, Lindsey turns into me, slides both hands around my neck, and meets my lips with hers.

Though a crowd surrounds us, I tune them all out even when a few shouts rise around us. I swear people must live boring lives that two strangers kissing gets this much attention. Lindsey must have had a more difficult time ignoring the shouts because she withdraws and leans her forehead into my chest to hide from the onlookers.

The Tucker Girls

"I wouldn't have believed it if I didn't see it," Liv's voice rings out as she walks into the kitchen with two large tote bags.

"Hey, Liv!" I greet her, slipping away from Lindsey and pulling Liv into a hug. Though she's painted like Lindsey and me, it's her white tank top that practically illuminates the entire room.

"I didn't know you were coming tonight. Who's this?" Liv asks cheerily, overly excited to meet the mystery girl I showed up with.

"Yeah …. sorry about that. It was a last-minute decision. This is Lindsey. She's my …." I start but hesitate before slapping a label on her. I give Lindsey a curious look, hoping she will help fill in the blank.

"I'm his girlfriend," Lindsey declares confidently, reaching her hand out to Liv. "It's nice to meet you."

"Hi, I'm Olivia," Liv responds with a warm smile, shaking Lindsey's hand. "Girlfriend, huh? You know Hunter has never shown up to a party with a girl before, much less a *girlfriend*. This is different."

"Why am I not surprised?" Lindsey answers, shooting me a weary look.

"You're awfully late to your own party," I redirect the conversation back to Liv.

"I made a run to the store to restock on food. People were getting hungry and cranky," Liv answers pointing to the tote bag she just set down on the floor. "How long have you been here?"

"Not too long," I answer.

"Are you staying until midnight? We have some fireworks that are going to light up the sky."

You're call.

317

Lindsey reads my expression effortlessly. I'm not sure what time she will want to leave. If it were up to me, I would stay until Liv sent everyone home.

"I hope you don't mind, but I may steal Hunter away before midnight."

"No, I completely understand," Liv replies with a smirk. "Talking about stealing people away, I need you to share some of your secrets with me. I need all the details. Leave nothing to the imagination."

Lindsey tries to interject, but Liv quickly hooks her by the elbow and draws her away with a mischievous smile. They are walking towards the kitchen when Lindsey looks over her shoulder, pleading with me to rescue her from whatever Liv has in mind, but I shake my head in laughter, indicating I'm not intervening.

Lindsey scowls at my response, and I know I will pay for this later. She's in good hands with Liv, though, and has nothing to fear. Liv is good people. I've known her since her brother, Josh, and I played Pop Warner football starting at the age of seven. Speaking of Josh, I spy him strutting into the den with a big smile.

"Bowden! What's up, my man?"

"Shipley!" I yell, rushing over to embrace my old friend. "It's been too long! How's UNT going?"

Josh graduated from Ulla Meyer last year.

"It's alright. I'm redshirting this season which is hard. I want to get out on the field and play. You know? Go hit someone who's not my teammate for once," Josh replies while surveying the scenery. "Hunter, you need to come to a college party with me this semester. You haven't partied til you've experienced one of our Mean Green parties."

I nod my head in acknowledgment, but tagging along with Josh doesn't have the same appeal that it would have even a week ago. My world has been thrown into chaos by a certain beautiful, gray-eyed brunette.

Watching Lindsey from across the house, I see her huddled together with Liv and Faith conversing. Lindsey looks my way as if she can sense me locked in on her. Her attention is fleeting, though, as a boy steps up to shoot his shot with my girlfriend.

Guys have been checking her out all night, but no one had bothered to approach her with me close by. I'm about ready to walk over there and drag the boy away when Lindsey shoots me a look, telling me to chill out. My irritation must be evident all over my face.

"Who's the girl you're making eyes with?" Josh inquires, distracting me from all the terrible things I'm considering doing to the boy trying to make moves on Lindsey.

"That's Lindsey. My girlfriend."

"Girlfriend?" Josh chokes out, almost spewing his beer. "I never thought I'd hear those words come out of your mouth."

"Things change," I say with a shrug.

"Obviously. She's hot. Where'd you two meet?"

"At school."

I know I'm being short with Josh, but it's taking a ton of restraint not to walk across the two rooms right now.

Lindsey's more beautiful every time I look at her. When we first met, she went out of her way to be invisible. The problem is that the world is starting to notice how breathtaking she is ever since she stopped drowning herself in hoodies two sizes too big.

"What does your pops think about you having a girlfriend? My dad tells stories all the time about how your father was a living legend in high school. No girl could lock him down. I can't imagine him supporting this."

My shoulders tighten the second Josh references Pete. *Damn.* Why'd he have to go and mention the devil himself? My father hadn't crossed my mind for nearly twelve hours which was approaching an all-time record.

"I haven't told him yet," I reply coolly.

"Ah, gotcha. He'll probably tell you to keep your options open. I'm telling you, the girls at UNT are the most beautiful in the world," Josh states as he slaps my rigid back. "How's your old man doing these days anyways?"

"Fine."

"Well, tell him I said 'Hi.' You're lucky as hell to have him as a parent. I used to be so envious growing up when he coached our football teams. The guy was my hero when we played Pop Warner. I will never forget him running practices with a beer in each hand. He was funny as shit too."

My stomach sours at Josh's ignorant comments. It's not his fault that he has a high opinion of my father because he used to be incredibly charming when he wasn't entirely plastered; that was before Mom left us, though.

Things dramatically turned darker after she bailed, and the few redeeming qualities my father had left dissipated. All that remains is a raging shell of a man. I assume he can still be charming when he wants to, considering he has women rotating through our house periodically.

Josh's father is a quiet, reserved man who barely says a word to anyone unless they speak to him first. It's funny how envy works because I would kill for one day of normalcy with a boring father I could count on - someone who'd care about how I was doing or if I had a good day.

My chest aches as I wish for things that will never happen. The feeling lingers with me long after Josh leaves, and I can't remember what he said before walking away. I'm triggered and reeling, leaving me wanting to drown my thoughts in a liquor bottle.

"Hey," Lindsey states, standing in front of me though I don't recall her walking back over to me. "Where'd you go?"

The Tucker Girls

Her eyes closely inspect my face, looking for some clue to my brooding mood.

"I need a strong drink," I grumble.

I turn to walk towards the liquor when Lindsey catches hold of my hand.

"Why don't we get out of here instead?"

Lindsey can sense I'm spiraling. She tightens her hold on me when I attempt to pull away, pleading with her eyes. There's something about her gaze that anchors me.

Though the storm is still raging inside of me, I agree to her request with a silent nod. Interlocking our fingers, she draws my hand towards her and kisses it before leading me out of the house.

"Are you sure your parents are okay with me being here when they aren't in town?" I ask as I follow Lindsey into the Tucker house.

"Since when do you care about things like that?" Lindsey teases with a nudge of her shoulder.

"Since it could mean preventing me from seeing you. The last thing I need is you getting grounded. What if the neighbors let it slip that you had a house guest? Or even worse, they see me here. I have a reputation, you know?"

Lindsey shakes her head at me while smiling.

"Oh, I'm fully aware of your reputation."

I draw Lindsey in close, gazing into her eyes and enjoying the smile she shares freely with me now. I will always cherish it, knowing how difficult it was to earn.

Lindsey leans up to kiss me, but at the last second, she slips out of my arms and scurries away with a playful grin.

"I invited you in, but there's not going to be any funny business tonight. Understood?"

"Define *funny business*," I demand, chasing her into the kitchen as she squeals in laughter.

I finally corner her, with both of us laughing.

It's hard to believe that I was a complete wreck before we arrived at the Tucker house. Lindsey has managed to lift my spirits in record time.

"Hunter, I mean it," Lindsey declares, pointing her finger at me though she's still smiling.

"I promise. No funny business."

"Good," she plants a kiss on my cheek before pulling me into the living room. "Because we need to talk."

"This doesn't sound good. What's up?" I ask, plopping down on the couch facing the television. I'm keeping a cushion distance between Lindsey and me to avoid any *funny business* from happening.

"What happened at the party tonight?"

I shift my weight uncomfortably on the couch.

"I'm not sure what you mean."

"Yes, you do. Hunter, I've seen that look on your face before - the night of Homecoming. You were physically there, but mentally you were somewhere entirely different."

I suck in a deep breath, taking in my surroundings before responding to Lindsey's question.

"Liv's brother and I were reminiscing on old memories that triggered some unpleasant thoughts," I pause, unsure of the proper phrasing to satiate her curiosity without diving into too much detail. This is the last thing I want to discuss this evening. We've had an incredible day. I don't want it to end with us discussing how terrible my father is. "I guess I'm just …. It's not really a big deal. I'm fine now."

Lindsey keeps her gaze lowered as she traces a pattern on the cushion with her finger, listening to me fumble with my words. The silence lingers, and I can sense she wants more details.

The Tucker Girls

The problem is she'll regret it the second I tell her my sob story about my childhood. It will make her sad, but there's nothing she can do to fix it. I just have terrible luck when it comes to my parents. There's no reason for her to carry the burden of knowing how awful my life has been.

"I'll make you a deal," Lindsey offers, still watching her finger move about the couch.

"And what's that?"

"You tell me what triggered you, and I will answer any question you ask."

"Any question?" I verify in disbelief, and I can't help but notice her face tighten as she nods in agreement.

Honesty and openness are incredibly important to her, and she's offering me the one detail that's been eating away at me since I started to get to know her; the story behind the scars.

"Deal."

I suck in another ragged breath and prepare to tell my story. Where do I even start?

"Liv's brother, Josh, was asking what my dad thinks of you, and that set me off. I've got a lot of painful memories when it comes to Pete, so when he comes up in conversation, like he is right now, I can't help but feel animosity and resentment boil up inside of me. My inclination is to drown those memories out in alcohol when they pop up, but tonight you gave me a better option. Speaking of which, thank you for that."

Lindsey's gaze is fixed on my face now as she takes in my words.

"You're welcome. Have you ever thought about going to therapy?"

I scoff at her suggestion.

"What?"

"The last thing I need is a stranger charging me hundreds of dollars to listen to my problems that they cannot fix."

"Hunter, sometimes talking about your pain can start the healing process. I can't explain to you how much it helped me cope."

"I'm glad it worked for you, but I'm fine."

Lindsey sighs in frustration, disappointment on full display on her face.

"Okay," she concedes.

Silence descends on us, confirming exactly why these topics should remain taboo. It makes everything awkward.

"When do I get to meet your father?"

"I just told you about how much pain he's caused me, and you want to know when you get to meet him?" I ask in disbelief.

"He's still a part of you even if he disappointed you. I want to know everything about you."

"Pete is *never* getting anywhere near you," I state bitterly.

Lindsey's eyes widen at my abrasive statement.

"Pete Bowden has a nasty streak. There was a time when he had some redeeming qualities, but after my mother left, those all seemed to fade away. Either he's bitter and angry, or he's passed out drunk. It's a miracle he's able to hold a steady job.

"Even if he could manage to be sober enough to meet you, I'd never allow him to be in the same room as you. You see, Pete likes to get violent when angry, and if he ever laid a hand on you, I would kill him. I mean it. What I did to Derek would be child's play compared to what I would do to my father if he were to hurt you."

Lindsey strains to swallow as she intently stares at me.

"Did he … has he ever … hit you?" Lindsey asks in a broken voice, barely even able to ask the question.

"Yes. I used to be his human punching bag until I got big enough to give it worse than he could ever dish it out."

The Tucker Girls

My answer forces Lindsey to shut her eyes as she takes several deep breaths. When her eyes open, I see a pitying look. "Don't," I declare, shaking my head. "Don't you dare pity me. I'm a survivor. I'm stronger now because of what I went through. I didn't need a mother, and I sure as hell don't need a father."

My voice sounds so convincing, I almost believe the words coming out of my mouth.

"Hunter …." Lindsey mutters, searching for words. "You once told me that some people won't back down until you hit them back. You were talking about your Dad, weren't you? And that's also why you have experience stitching yourself up?"

Lindsey's asking questions, but they feel rhetorical. She already knows the answers. She's putting the puzzle pieces together, finally making sense of everything she's observed. The conclusion I'm anxiously waiting for her to come to is that Pete is a part of who I am, and because of that, I carry the monster with me. This fact alone should terrify her.

I don't see fear on her face, though. She's stunned by my unexpected revelation. I patiently wait for her to process everything, hoping with all my being that she doesn't get cold feet.

"And …. and …. your mother left you with him?"

"To her defense, Pete didn't start beating me until after she left. She sure as hell never looked back, though. Not once did she ever check in to make sure I was okay."

"Hunter …." Lindsey whispers, struggling to swallow. "I'm so sorry."

"For what? You didn't choose my parents for me."

If the topic wasn't terrible enough, I see sadness creep back into Lindsey's eyes. The sight brings an indescribable ache to my chest.

"I didn't mean to press you to talk about things you weren't ready to discuss," Lindsey replies.

The Tucker Girls

I look away as I shrug. There's never a good time to tell someone you have an abusive father. I hadn't intended to tell Lindsey as much as I did, but once we started talking, the words seemed to just come out.

"Who else knows?"

"I've never told anyone. Lexi, Brady and Elijah figured it out as we grew up. It wasn't difficult to deduce when they constantly saw me with bruises all over my body. We just never talk about it."

"They never tried to help you?"

"They did! I can't tell you how many nights I've crashed at one of their houses because I was too scared to sleep in my own home. They were kids, too, though. They respected me enough to know that I'd ask if I ever needed any help."

Lindsey looks up at the ceiling and draws in several deep breaths. I can see this news eating away at her, and I regret telling her. This shouldn't be her burden to carry.

"It's your turn," Lindsey finally states after she composes herself. "Go ahead and ask the question you're dying to ask."

"Okay. What happened to all the baggy clothes? Why did your wardrobe change out of nowhere?"

Lindsey lets out a sarcastic laugh.

"That's not what you want to ask."

"It'll do for now until you're ready to tell me about the scars."

Lindsey examines me for a moment, searching for some undisclosed detail and takes another deep breath before turning to face the blank television.

"When my family moved to Savannah, I was eight years old. My very first memory was of a freckled-faced, loud-mouthed girl with auburn hair hopping into the moving truck and helping us unload. I remember wondering who in the world this stranger was carrying our stuff around without asking if we

326

needed help. Her name was Ava, and she talked the entire time we worked, going on and on about our school and the neighborhood and television shows she enjoyed."

A slight smile tipped up at her lips as she recalled her story, though I couldn't understand what this had to do with explaining her wardrobe change.

"I was introverted and shy, so this boisterous girl baffled me. We were complete opposites. She wouldn't stop talking even to catch her breath. Ava put Serena to shame when it came to being social. All I wanted was for this strange girl to leave me alone, but she tagged along with me the remainder of the afternoon, and my parents invited her family over for dinner that night.

"Lo and behold, Ava continued to show up day after day. She'd knock on our door and ask if I could come out and play. I begged my parents to lie and tell her I wasn't home, but they never did. They encouraged me to get to know Ava, and after a couple of weeks, we became friends.

"At some point, I started to look forward to her ramblings, and she appreciated my listening ear. It turns out we both enjoyed being outdoors and painting.

"The summer passed by quickly, and every waking second we spent together. By the time school started, we were inseparable. We even had the same third-grade teacher, which made showing up at a new school almost seamless.

"I'd never had a friend where we clicked like that. As the years went by, we only got closer. We'd have conversations without having to say a word, and we knew each other so well that we'd finish each other's sentences. It would always freak people out, but I knew secretly they were all jealous.

"Who wouldn't want a friend like that?"

Lindsey sucked in a jagged breath while a single tear slid down her cheek.

The Tucker Girls

"Navigating our first year of high school was tricky, but Ava was bold and didn't let anyone push her around. She was my shield, and her self-assuredness made it easy to hide behind her. Serena and I weren't very close then, so she didn't bother looking after me."

A small smile forms on Lindsey's face.

"Ava and I used to make fun of how boy-crazy Serena was. I've always been in Serena's shadow, and it's impossible to live up to her. I wasn't talking to boys like Serena, which made me feel inadequate in so many ways, but Ava made me feel less abnormal. We both had other interests. Ava would always say, 'Boys our age are boring and aren't worth our time.'

"Anyways .... over Labor Day weekend of our sophomore year, Ava's family took a trip to Jacksonville to see her grandparents. I'll never forget that it was a surprise trip and ruined our plans to see a movie that starred some heartthrob that Ava was drooling over. We'd agreed to see it the following weekend when she returned.

"Monday night, at dinner time, I remember coming downstairs to eat dinner with my family when the phone rang. That was the night my whole world fell apart. Ava and her mother died in a car accident on the way home from Jacksonville. Ava's father had called from the hospital to let my parents know."

Tears pour down her face now as she struggles to continue. This story is tearing her apart, and I want to give her permission to stop.

"Lindsey ...."

"No," she interjected with a wave of her hand. "Please, let me finish."

"You know how they say there are stages to grief? I was never able to get past depression. I'd rotate between denial, anger and suffocating sadness. One day she was here, and the next, she was gone.

The Tucker Girls

"It seemed impossible to wrap my mind around it, but that wasn't the hardest part for me to overcome. It was this tremendous guilt. Ava had this spirit about her that let everyone around her know that she was going to conquer the world. I just couldn't understand why it had to have been her to die. If anyone wasn't worthy of living, it was me. The world would have been better off had we been switched. I should have been the one to go, not her. She had so many plans ahead of her, while I was content to live as her sidekick. The guilt was too much to bear, and I felt genuinely lost without her.

"My parents knew I was struggling, but they had no idea I was cutting until it was too late. One night I had this terrible thought that if there were a heaven, then I'd rather be with Ava than to stay here on Earth without her."

Rolling up her sleeve, Lindsey points to the longest scar on her arm. It also stands out because it's raised higher than the others.

"That's the night I did this to myself, and Serena found me knocking on death's door. I feel terrible for what she walked in on. I can only imagine the trauma she carries with her from that night, but she saved my life. After spending days in the hospital, my parents got me into therapy, and I worked through my pain.

"High school is a ruthless environment, though. The second I showed weakness, the kids latched onto it, and I didn't have Ava to cling to any longer. Serena tried her best to protect me, but she couldn't be everywhere at once.

The bullying and harassment sent me spiraling further. Finally, my parents decided a fresh start was in order, and Dad found an opportunity here in Texas. My family uprooted their entire lives to help me run from bullies because I couldn't handle my grief, and I'm not sure I will ever forgive myself.

The Tucker Girls

"I don't cut anymore, but it doesn't mean I still don't struggle with it. It all still hurts so bad. I still miss her. I still wish it had been me to die and not her."

Lindsey's tears turn into sobbing, and I can't take it any longer, closing the distance between us and pulling her into my chest as her body shakes.

"I want my best friend back," she cries into my chest.

"I'm so sorry," I whisper as I kiss the top of her head. I don't know what else to say. Every encounter I'd had with Lindsey now makes more sense in light of her revelation. I feel like an idiot having not been more gentle with Lindsey when I first met her. Instead, I antagonized her just like the kids at her prior school.

Her sobs intensify, and I'm heartbroken for her. I've never had anyone I care about die, but it doesn't take much empathy to understand how unbearable it must be when it's someone you love.

"I've got you," I whisper to her, wishing there was a way I could alleviate the burden she carries with her.

I know all too well that some things in life can't be fixed. You have to learn to cope with them remaining broken and hope that they won't one day break you.

Lindsey and I are both shattered pieces of something that used to be whole. I'm wondering if that's what drew us together from the beginning: our shared pain. We understand each other in a way that others never could.

"Why did it have to be you?" she asks between sobs, desperately trying to wipe away tears.

"What do you mean?"

"I didn't want it to be you."

"I know," I reply softly, finally understanding what she means. I don't take her question personally. I'm the asshole that pushed her every chance I could get since we met. I don't deserve to be the person going to help her through this nightmare, but that's precisely what I'm going to do. I will put her back together piece by piece until she's whole again. I swear it to myself. I don't care if she lives in Amberly. I will find a way to overcome my demons if it means helping her.

Fireworks explode in the distance, ringing in the New Year and sealing my resolution.

"I've got you," I repeat again. "I'm not going anywhere."

Slowly leaning back into the sofa, I draw Lindsey down with me, keeping her head pressed against my damp chest. I hold her until her tear ducts run dry. Eventually, I feel her breathing steady, and when I steal a glance at her, I notice that she's fallen asleep. I pull a blanket, that's draped over the couch, down to cover the two of us.

I should grab a pillow for her and slip away before it gets too late. I'm too selfish, though. I hold out for a little more time with her, not wanting this day to end.

The additional minutes turn into hours. I'm not sure exactly how much time passes before my eyes get too heavy, and I accidentally drift off to sleep.

CHAPTER TWENTY-NINE
Hunter

Rain pelting the windows stirs me awake, and I can feel Lindsey's rhythmic breathing matching my own. Craning my neck and spying on her peaceful face, I am struck once more by her perfection. Even with her face stained from where her mascara ran free, she's breathtakingly beautiful. Seeing Lindsey this serene is a relief, considering the state she was in last night.

I've lost feeling in the shoulder she's leaning on, and it's painful when she shifts her weight and groans. Lindsey's gray eyes pop open seconds later, darting between me and the surrounding room as she tries to sort through her disorientation.

"Good morning," I greet her, my voice cracking as it adjusts to the new day.

Lindsey scrambles to an upright position in a panic, then quickly proceeds to jump to her feet.

"No. No. No," she frets. "You can't be here! Oh my gosh! I fell asleep. You let me fall asleep! Why didn't you wake me up?"

I already miss the spark that I'd seen in Lindsey's eyes the night before. The fright spread across her face hits my gut almost as hard as the devastation I'd seen when she told me about Ava.

Standing up, I attempt to pull her towards my chest, but she slips away.

"Hunter! I'm serious!"

"Okay. I'm leaving," I concede, waving my hands in defeat.

"What time is it?"

The Tucker Girls

"Nine," I reply after checking my watch.

"*Frick*! My parents could be back any second. They will kill me if they catch you here, especially considering I'm supposed to be at Hannah's house."

"Frick? Really? How old are you? Five?"

"Shut up!" Lindsey snaps, but she can't stop the corners of her mouth from turning up in a slight smile.

"I'm sorry I didn't leave, Lindsey. Our conversation was so heavy last night, I didn't want to wake you up. I had every intention of leaving, but I accidentally fell asleep."

Placing a kiss on the top of her head, I expect her to scold me again, but she reaches out, grabs a fistful of my shirt, and pulls me closer. I hear her inhale deeply, reminding me of her smelling my jacket the night we were both at The Railyard.

It hits me how much I'm not ready to leave Lindsey. Even though we've spent the last twenty-four hours together, I don't feel the urgency to put distance between us as I have with every other girl I've ever been with. Usually, I'm itching to get away. This time is entirely different, though. I'm anxious about the uncertainty of when I will see her again.

I take in a deep breath as I hold Lindsey tight. Amberly's chokehold doesn't feel as suffocating any longer. Lindsey has stirred up something inside me I haven't felt in a long time: hope. I have the space to breathe and don't have to jump off a rooftop to experience this relief. Every fiber of my being wants to cling to Lindsey, so I don't lose this solace.

"You promised me no funny business last night," Lindsey mumbles into my chest.

"I swear I didn't do it on purpose."

She pulls back but pauses to give me an indecipherable look.

"What's that look for?"

"I like you," Lindsey confesses, blushing a little. "I *really* like you."

"I *really* like you too."

Tracing her neck with my fingers, I feel Lindsey shiver in response. I kiss along the line I traced and hear Lindsey's breath catch. I briefly consider all the other places I'd like to kiss her but find the restraint to stop.

Lindsey silently beckons me to follow her towards the front door. Grabbing my coat off the couch, I'm thankful I brought it inside last night. The rain has picked up and is falling in sheets now.

"I want to see you tonight," Lindsey admits as she walks beside me. "Are you free?"

"I can't. I have a shift at work tonight," I reluctantly inform her. A part of me wants to call in sick, but I can't do that to Drake - not when I bailed on him during my last shift.

"Can I drop in and see you?"

"Yes. That would be amazing. Text me when you are on your way, and I'll make sure Drake has a milkshake waiting for you."

"Perfect!" Lindsey says, her infectious smile returning. "I should probably warn you that I'm mostly in this relationship for the free milkshakes."

"Ouch."

Lindsey nudges me playfully with her shoulder.

"I'm only kidding. I'll see you tonight," she promises, kissing me on the cheek as she slips her hand into my arm. "Now get out of here before I get in trouble."

I awkwardly pause before opening the door, not feeling ready to leave just yet. The ten or so hours I will have to wait to see her again feels like an eternity.

"Oh! I'm going to need that," Lindsey states, pointing to my shirt.

"What? My Shirt? Nope. I don't think so," I reply, tugging the fabric toward my nose and enjoying Lindsey's perfume. "It smells like you. It's staying with me."

The Tucker Girls

Lindsey levels me with a feisty gaze, placing both hands on her hips.

"It's either your shirt or your coat. You decide. One of your garments is staying with me."

"It's raining out there. Besides, you have one of my coats already. Do you really need two?"

"It doesn't smell like you anymore. You can have the other back when I see you tonight."

I reluctantly hand over my coat, much to her delight. Lindsey squeezes it tight to her chest like it's a precious prize.

"You're so demanding. Out of curiosity, how long have you been smelling the first coat I gave you?

"That's an interesting question. I'd love for you to stay and chat, but times up!" she states, purposefully avoiding my question. I can't help but notice her blushing cheeks, indicating she was likely enjoying it well before I ever kissed her.

Lindsey turns and opens the door, and I slide up behind her and wrap an arm around her waist. I kiss her lightly on her neck once more, but she doesn't shiver with pleasure this time.

Lifting my gaze, I spot the reason Lindsey has gone entirely rigid. Serena is standing on the porch, surrounded by suitcases, staring at the two of us in disbelief. Lindsey's worst nightmare has come true.

The Tucker Girls

This story will continue in the sequel: The Wrong Tucker Girl.

Did you enjoy reading this book? Be sure to follow me on the Instagram handle **@thetuckergirlsbook** for updates regarding the sequel!

The Tucker Girls

A Note from the Author

Thank you for taking the time to read The Tucker Girls! Eleven months ago, I started this project with the intention of publishing my first book. Although I don't consider myself a writer, I had a story that I wanted to share about a broken boy and two sisters that fall in love with him.

This project would have never been possible if not for the support of my family and friends. They were willing to read *rough* drafts and give me invaluable feedback. They were also the ones that encouraged me when I struggled to reach each milestone. Thank you, Tori, Lauren and Kevin, for being willing to read my first draft despite its many flaws.

Once again, thank you to my readers! It means the world to me that you would take the time to read my book. I don't think I will ever be satisfied that The Tucker Girls fully captures the story I wanted to tell. But at some point, I had to call it a finished product despite it not being all that I hoped it to be.

This story is intentionally incomplete because it will have a sequel, but there were still so many details that did not make it in the final edition. I ended up choosing the ones that moved the plot forward, but also opened the possibility of spin-offs. It's my hope that this story drew you in as it did me.

My plan is to begin writing the sequel shortly after publishing. There are plenty of twists coming in the sequel, including plot points you have likely assumed are resolved. If you are interested in following my progress, please follow my Instagram account **@thetuckergirlsbook**. I will post updates regarding my progress with The Wrong Tucker Girl. I'm also interested in your feedback. Please let me know where you think this story should go.

Finally, if you find yourself in a dark place, please seek help. Don't wait until things get worse before you take action. The US National Suicide Hotline (https://988lifeline.org/) provides 24/7, free and confidential support for people in distress. You have value and worth, even if your circumstances attempt to tell you otherwise.

Romans 8:38-39